THE HANGING TREE

THE HANGING
TREE

BEN AARONOVITCH

First published in Great Britain in 2016
by Gollancz
an imprint of the Orion Publishing Group Ltd
Carmelite House, 50 Victoria Embankment
London EC4Y 0DZ

An Hachette UK Company

3 5 7 9 10 8 6 4 2

A CIP catalogue record for this book
is available from the British Library.

ISBN 978 0 575 13257 3

Typeset by Input Data Services Ltd, Somerset

Printed in Great Britain by Clays Ltd, St Ives plc

MIX
Paper from
responsible sources
FSC® C104740

www.orionbooks.co.uk
www.gollancz.co.uk

*This book is dedicated to all librarians everywhere —
for they are the true keepers of the secret flame
and not to be trifled with*

Through the streets our wheels slowly move;
The toll of the death bell dismays us.
With nosegays and gloves we are deck'd,
So trim and so gay they array us.
The passage all crowded we see
With maidens that move us with pity;
Our air all, admiring agree
Such lads are not left in the city.
Oh! Then to the tree I must go;
The judge he has ordered the sentence.
And then comes a gownsman you know,
And tells a dull tale of repentance.
By the gullet we're ty'd very tight;
We beg all spectators, pray for us.
Our peepers are hid from the light,
The tumbril shoves off, and we morrice.

Tyburn ballad as transcribed by Francis Place

1

One of Sir Roger's Lesser Works

I dreamt that I heard Mr Punch laughing gleefully by my ear, but when I woke I realised it was my phone. I recognised the number on the screen and so wasn't surprised by the cool, posh voice that spoke when I answered.

'Peter,' said Lady Ty, 'do you remember when we spoke at Oxford Circus?'

I remembered her finding me after I'd managed to get myself buried under the platform. I remembered her leaning over me once they'd dug me out, her breath smelling of nutmeg and saffron.

'One day I will ask you for a favour. And do you know what your response will be?'

'Yes ma'am,' I said, remembering what I'd said then. 'No ma'am – three bags full, ma'am.'

It was five in the morning – still dark – and rain was smattering against the French windows at the far end of Beverley's bedroom. The only serious light came from the screen of my phone. The other half of the big bed was empty – I was alone.

'One of my daughter's friends has had an accident,' said Lady Ty. 'I want you to ensure my daughter is not implicated in the subsequent investigation.'

Oh shit, I thought. That kind of favour.

She gave me the address and what she knew of the circumstances.

'You want me to prove your daughter wasn't involved?' I said.

'You misunderstand,' said Lady Ty. 'I don't care what her involvement is – I want her kept out of the case.'

She really had no idea what she was asking for, but I knew better than to try and explain.

'Understood,' I said.

'And Peter,' said Lady Ty, 'Nightingale is not to know about this – is that clear?'

'Crystal,' I said.

As soon as she hung up, I called the Folly.

'I rather think I'd have to have taken an interest in any case,' said Nightingale once I'd briefed him. 'Still, I shall endeavour to adopt a façade of ignorance until such time as you need me.' He paused and then said: 'And you will let me know when that moment arrives.' It was not a question.

'Yes, sir,' I said, and hung up wondering why everyone felt the need to be so emphatic at this time of the morning.

Beverley owns both halves of a 1920's semi-detached house on Beverley Avenue in SW20. It's a strange place, half-furnished and underused. Beverley told me when I first visited that she 'sort of inherited it' and hasn't really decided what to do with the property yet. She sleeps in a ground floor room with easy access to the back garden. There's just the Ikea bed with an incomprehensible name, two mismatched wardrobes, an antique mahogany chest of drawers and a Persian carpet that covers half the bare floorboards.

I reached out and felt the empty side of the bed – there was just a trace of warmth and a hint of oil on the pillow – Beverley had slipped away hours ago. I sighed, got out from under the warm duvet and shivered. The French windows were half open, letting in a cool breeze and the smell of rain. The bathroom upstairs didn't have a shower so I had a quick bucket bath in the huge oval tub, which I knew from happy experience easily accommodated two people at once, and got dressed.

Everything related to operational matters in the Met is monitored. Which means you can't just open your AWARE terminal and go fishing for information without having a damn good excuse.

So while I was buffing up my shoes I called DC Guleed, who I knew was doing the night shift in the Homicide Assessment car that week.

'Hi Peter,' she said. Behind her I could hear a hushed indoor ambience and people being professional.

I asked whether she'd heard of a shout in Knightsbridge, a suspicious drug-related death.

'Why do you want to know?' asked Guleed, which I suspected meant she was on the scene.

In the background I heard a vast and familiar Mancunian voice demanding to know who Guleed was talking to – DCI Alexander Seawoll. Who, as SIO, shouldn't even be out of bed until the Homicide Assessment Team had finished their work.

'It's Peter,' she called back. 'He wants to know about our suspicious death.'

'Tell him if it's not one of his he can fuck off,' said Seawoll.

'Do you have an interest in this?' asked Guleed.

'There may be some related issues,' I said, which was sort of true given that Tyburn's daughter was involved. I heard Guleed pass this on and some grumbled swearing from Seawoll.

'Tell him to get his arse down here pronto,' he said.

'He wants you to come in,' said Guleed and gave me the address.

Before I left I switched off my phone and stepped out the back into the garden. The rain had eased to a misty drizzle that quickly beaded my hair and the leather of my jacket. Beverley's garden is vast by London standards, running fifty metres down to the bank of the river, and twice as wide as her neighbours'. Despite the light pollution sullenly reflected off the low cloud, I decided not to risk tripping over the random bits of garden furniture I knew littered the overgrown lawn and conjured a *werelight* to show me the way.

Beverley Brook rises in Worcester Park in southeast London and flows through a ridiculous number of other parks, recreation grounds and golf courses before joining her mother at Barn Elms. She says that while she averages half a cubic metre of water per second, she's had it up to six cubic metres per second a couple of times. And unless she gets some more care, attention and the occasional bottle of Junipero Gin, she's not

4

going to be responsible for where that surplus water's going to end up.

Not a threat, you understand. But it's wise not to take a river for granted – trust me on this.

At the end of Beverley's garden is a bank fringed with young alder and ash striplings that drops down to the river. For most of its length Beverley Brook is shallow enough that you can clearly see the stones at the bottom, but here there was a deep pool overshadowed by a weeping willow. The surface was dark and coldly reflected my milky blue *werelight* as it bobbed around me in a slow orbit.

'Hey, Bev,' I called. 'You in there?'

For all I knew she was kilometres away visiting her mum's place in Wapping. Or patrolling the Thames for waifs and suicides, or whatever else it was she and her sisters spend their time searching for.

But she's been known to surface when I've called her name, and once she leapt like a salmon, naked and glistening, into my arms – so it's always worth a try.

This time there was no response. Just the drizzle and the grumble of the Kingston Bypass on the other side of the river. I waited about a minute, just so I could claim I'd waited five, and then headed back-up the garden.

I walked out via the side gate, past Beverley's Kia Picanto to where the Orange Asbo was parked. Once inside I checked my evidence bag was in the back and that the Airwave charger was plugged in, started her up and headed for Knightsbridge.

*

One Hyde Park squatted next to the Mandarin Oriental Hotel like a stack of office furniture, and with all the elegance and charm of the inside of a photocopier. Albeit a brand new photocopier that doubled as a fax and a document scanner. Now, I have – as Beverley says – *views* about architecture. But there's modern stuff I like. The Gherkin, the Lloyd's building, even the Shard – despite the nagging feeling I get that Nazgûl should be roosting at the top. But the truth is that in the case of One Hyde Park my boy Sir Roger was definitely just putting in the hours for the pay check. It's not ugly as such ... it's just not anything in particular. It is famously the most expensive block of flats in Britain, which just goes to show that property really is all about location, location, location.

The actual building is comprised of four towers that the brochures call 'pavilions' running between the Oriental Mandarin Hotel on the east side and the Edinburgh Gate into Hyde Park on the west. The north and south aspects are wedge-shaped to maximise natural daylight. As a result, if you look at a floor plan it looks like two Star Destroyers have backed into each other during manoeuvres. As I approached up the A4 I saw that all the lights were out on every floor, except for one flat half-way up the second tower from the end – so no trouble finding the crime scene, then.

Parking was a different matter, but the secret to avoiding a ticket when you're police is to snuggle your reasonably priced unmarked motor in amongst the Battenberg checked IRVs and sprinter vans that accumulate at any crime scene. These I found crowded under the strange concrete canopy that stretches over the Edinburgh Gate. I noticed they also blocked the driveway to where the car lifts waited to whisk the money-mobiles of the rich down to the underground car park.

I'd read that the facilities below ground included a private gym, swimming pool, squash court and wine cellars – I really hoped that I didn't have to go down there. It's not that I'm claustrophobic, only that I've had practical experience of just how much the sodding earth can weigh and the taste despair can leave in your mouth.

Guleed was waiting by the cylindrical glass entrance to the lobby. Having worked with me on numerous occasions, she fell on me with cries of glee.

'I don't suppose you'd just consider fucking off?' she said.

I was shocked.

'Language,' I said.

'Don't you start,' she said.

I noticed she was wearing a rather fine purple silk hijab with a fringe design picked out in silver thread, a matching jacket and an elegant long black skirt. I did not think she'd planned to be out policing tonight.

'Did you have a date?' I asked.

'No,' she said. 'Birthday party.'

'I thought you were in the HAT car this week.'

'I swapped,' she said. 'So I could go to the birthday party.'

'Oh,' I said. 'Sorry.'

'Is this going to be like the thing with the BMWs?' she asked.

'I don't know,' I said. 'I've only just got here.'

Guleed nodded to the PCSO guarding the entrance.

'Put him on the list,' she said and then to me: 'You're going to love this place.'

She led me through the transparent cylindrical airlock style door onto a mezzanine balcony and down a set of stairs into a double height reception area with leather chairs and the sort of meaningless sculpture that's bought by the ton by particularly greedy banks. Through transparent walls, rumoured to be bulletproof, I could see a small faux garden and – through another layer of security glass – the dim and dangerous streets of downtown Knightsbridge.

Beside the reception desk stood a fit looking man with brown skin, black hair and a good quality off-the-peg suit. Possibly Indonesian, I thought. He also managed the trick of looking both alert and bored out of his skull at the same time – ex-Job, ex-military, ex-intelligence – something like that.

The level of security struck me as a bit paranoid but, as my dad says, the more they have the more they worry about it being taken away.

The security man gave me and Guleed a sour look as we passed and I responded with a friendly smile and a cheery 'Good morning'. Because I am an officer of the law and, providing I'm not nobbled by political considerations and/or influence peddling, my arm doth reach into all places, yea even unto the citadels of the mighty.

This particular citadel of the mighty was reached by a glass-sided lift which ran up a completely transparent service core that allowed one – and one assumes that here one refers to one as one – to appreciate the view over Hyde Park which, after all, is what one has paid upwards of ten million to enjoy.

The glass elevator led out into a cross passage where we did the dance of the noddy suit whereby the grave dignity of the law is mitigated by the need to hop on one foot while you try and get the stupid paper leg over the other. Guleed, it turned out, was wearing leggings under her skirt – which she left, along with her scarf, in the clear plastic bag provided. Once we were safely zipped up in our hygienic forensically-neutral paper suits Guleed led me to the left, where a pair of mahogany doors had been propped open with a portable light stand. Beyond was a short hallway with a curved far wall and a lot of abstract art on the walls.

In home furnishing terms, past a certain point, more money doesn't get you anything except an increase in insurance premiums. An elegantly proportioned room can have whitewashed walls and a bare wooden floor. But if it's an awkward shape, then all the piano-finish rosewood occasional tables riches can provide aren't going to do anything more than annoy the cleaners. One Hyde Park, I saw, had all the basic architectural charm of a brutalist council flat – except on a larger scale. The rooms were much wider, of course. But pressure to maximise the number of flats meant that the ceilings were disproportionately low.

We found Seawoll just around the corner in what the plans listed as a 'study'. The architects had laid out each wing to maximise the light, with a long central corridor and side rooms branching off like the veins in a leaf. This meant they all had walls on the diagonal, severely restricting the decorator's choice about where furniture could be placed. If you didn't want to block the doors, the access or blot out the windows then the beds, cupboards, shelves and all the other stuff that turns a concrete box into a home had to go where the architect thought they should go. In the study, this meant a desk that could neither face the window for the view nor face away to take advantage of the light. Instead, the black mirror-finish desk with the stainless steel legs stood in front of matching glass fronted bookcases that, as far as I could tell, contained a number of lumpy glass and chrome objects and a couple of soft porn albums cunningly disguised as cutting edge nude photography. Still in their shrink wrap, I noticed.

Seawoll sat in the executive leather operator's chair behind the desk wearing a dangerously stretched noddy suit that made him look like the Michelin Man's slightly deflated older brother.

'You'll notice that you can't swivel all the way round,' he said. 'What fucking use is a swivel chair if you can't fucking swivel on it?' He spotted me trying to read the titles on the books.

'Don't bother, they're just window dressing,' he said. 'As far as we can tell nobody lives here.'

I looked at a framed photograph of a young white woman with a dog.

'Who owns the place, then?' I asked.

'Some tax dodging shell company out of Jersey,' said Seawoll, running his fingers along the bottom of the desk top – looking for secret drawers, I guessed. 'We won't be able to trace that until the lads at Proactive Money Laundering can drag one of their experts out of bed.' He gave up on the idea of secret drawer and jabbed a finger at Guleed.

'Sahra,' he said. 'Get on the phone and give them a kicking.'

'Gladly,' said Guleed, and left.

'Her brother's an accountant,' said Seawoll, watching her go. 'So. What the fuck are you doing here?'

I considered lying for all of about two nanoseconds, but I don't have a death wish – not even a figurative one. Of course, philosophically speaking, truth is a slippery concept and one should always be alive to nuance.

'I got a tip off from a source that there might be some tangential Falcon involvement,' I said. And because I saw Seawoll begin to draw himself up, 'Lady Cecelia Tyburn-Thames believes her daughter may have been here when the incident occurred.'

'And she wants you to put the fix in?'

'Yes.'

'Do you know what the "incident" is?'

'Accidental drug overdose,' I said.

Seawoll nodded.

'So I bet you're wondering what the fuck I'm doing here?' he asked.

I felt a trickle of sweat work its way down my back.

'You wanted a peek into the lifestyles of the rich and shameless?' I said.

'Because nobody was supposed to have access to this flat,' he said. 'Did you see the DPG cars downstairs?'

The Diplomatic Protection Group do bodyguard work for Royals and those people HM Government would rather were not done-in while resident in the UK. They're routinely armed and drive around in red liveried vehicles – red to indicate that they are not there to break up fights, find your toddler or tell you the bloody time.

'No, sir,' I said.

'Really?' said Seawoll. 'The lazy buggers must have sloped off for refs.'

He explained that, what with the screened entrance, bulletproof quality glass on the lower levels and the kind of semi-professional security that would gladden the heart of a putative generalissimo, this was the sort of place that the DPG knew they could park their high value targets.

'Qatari Royal Family amongst them,' said Seawoll.

And then not have to worry about them until they ventured forth to shop at Harvey Nicks or go to the opera or impoverish a small nation – or whatever else it was the very, very rich did when they had time on their hands.

'So when a bunch of fucking kids waltz into the building, the DPG wants to know how. And I get woken up in the middle of the fucking night,' said Seawoll. 'And told to find out on pain of getting a bollocking. Me?' he said in outrage. 'Getting a bollocking? And just when I thought things couldn't descend further into the brown stuff – here you are.'

With a grunt he levered himself to his feet, causing the chair to bang against the bookcase behind him and set the various objet d'bollocks rattling.

'See,' he said, once he was up. 'Not even room enough to lean back and get yourself a bit of light relief. Mind you, there's a media room next door that would do very nicely for a private viewing room.' He must have seen that I'd lost the thread of his conversation.

'Like they used to have in porn shops when there were proper porn shops?' he said slowly, and then shook his head. 'I suppose you lot get your mucky pictures uploaded to your phones.'

I wondered if he talked like this to Guleed. I doubted it, somehow.

He led me through to the media room, which was a cool grey-green and lined with sound absorbing material. There was a vast television, wider than some of the screens I've seen in retrofitted multiplexes, and an elegant curving sofa that actually suited the room it was in. It had also, if I'm any judge, been shagged upon in the last few hours. There was a V-shaped stain in the middle and the throw cushions, in amethyst and teal covers, had been pushed onto the floor. There was an island of wine bottles in the centre of the coffee table and a pair of wine glasses on the shelf by the Blu-ray player – both were white with fingerprint dust.

'Behold,' said Seawoll. 'The wank palace itself.'

'I don't think they were wanking, sir,' I said, and Seawoll sighed.

'You've always got to push it, haven't you Peter?' he said, and outlined the details of the case.

At twelve thirty a 999 call had been made by a young man from a mobile phone asking for an ambulance and claiming that his friend 'Chrissy' was having an overdose and needed help. He was . . .

'. . . hysterical, desperate and,' said Seawoll, 'obviously out of his box.'

But when the ambulance arrived, security wouldn't let them into the building, claiming that the flat was unoccupied. The ambulance crew reported it to CCC who sent an instant response vehicle around, which ran straight into a pair of DPG officers responding because the building alarm was set up to inform them directly. Everyone piled up in the lifts, security opened the flat door and, *voila*, they found Christina Chorley, aged seventeen, lying in the entrance hall in the midst of a seizure.

She'd been dragged there by her boyfriend James Murray, also seventeen. James told the paramedics and everybody else in the immediate vicinity that 'It was just E's, it was just E's.' Had he taken them? Yes, he had. Who else was in the flat? It was just them. Oh god, it was just E's.

Off in the ambulance went the pair of them while both sets of police kicked their problem upstairs until it bounced off DCI Seawoll's bedroom window.

'Metaphorically speaking,' said Seawoll.

The 'entrance hall' was the wide, wedge-shaped, low ceilinged room with an unparalleled view over Hyde Park. I was getting used to the sheer amount of money wasted on the furniture, which was spread out like something designed for *The Sims*. In amongst the money there were signs that people had been having a good time — more bottles, wine glasses, empty cellophane packets, a flat pool of oatmeal coloured vomit on the carefully chosen hand-woven cream wool rug. Definitely more than two people. At least six or seven, I thought. Maybe more, if they were particularly tidy teens.

Not so tidy that they didn't leave their pills behind when they scrambled to get out.

'We think they left as soon as James Murray made his 999 call,' said Seawoll. Both the police and the paramedics entered a description of the pills into the TICTAC database and got a name – *Magic Babars* – and the worrying information that this particular brand tended to be heavy on the PMA, otherwise known as paramethoxyamphetamine, or Dr Death. Not MDMA, otherwise known as Ecstasy, otherwise known as the drug that allows you to listen to really dull music without your brain imploding from boredom. Seriously. PMA is a lot more toxic than MDMA and kicks in slower, so users have been known to swallow another couple of pills thinking the first were duds, and then suffer what Dr Walid would describe as 'deleterious effects'.

Given that Christina Chorley had died on the way to hospital, it was important to find out who else had taken the Magic Babars in case they needed treatment – and to find out quickly. Before James Murray keeled over himself.

At first James had tried to claim that he and Christina had been alone in the flat, but five minutes with DI Stephanopoulos, who, having been pulled untimely from her wife's embrace, was particularly pissed off that morning, saw him coughing names as fast as they could be written down.

'Amongst them was the name Olivia Jane McAllister-Thames,' said Seawoll. 'Now, I've got a few questions that need answering. Like, how did they get in? Where did the drugs comes from? And can I get a result before this case turns into a great big fucking media shit storm?'

I joined him at the window. It was getting light and a thick mist was washing out the trees and pastures of Hyde Park and the city beyond. Seawoll pointed down to a pair of statues in the faux garden at the back of the estate – two bronze heads that looked like they'd been flattened in a Corby trouser press and then had their brains scooped out.

'It's called *Waiting For Enlightenment*,' said Seawoll, looking at the statues. 'But if you ask me it's a fucking rip-off of *The Foothills of the Headlands* from *Yellow Submarine*.' Which meant nothing to me. 'God, money is so wasted on the rich.'

'Do you want me to statement Olivia McAllister-Thames?' I asked.

'No,' he said. 'I want Sahra to do that.' He waved airily back at the flat. 'Have you had a chance to check for any tingles?'

I said, with some dignity, that I had done an initial Falcon assessment and found nothing that indicated that a supernatural event had taken place on the premises.

'Thank Christ for that,' said Seawoll. 'In that case you can go with Guleed and make sure nothing weird happens to her.'

Seawoll, like most of the senior officers who were aware of the Folly, might not like me using the M-word.

But they weren't about to ignore anything that might have an impact at an operational level. It's understandable. You may not want to dwell on the fact that eighty percent of infant homicides are committed by the parents, but you're still going to make the grieving mum and dad your prime suspects until proved otherwise.

'In fact,' he said, 'I'm making you personally fucking responsible for making sure nothing weird happens to her. If you can't guarantee that, I want your boss down here to do the job instead – understand?'

'Yes, guv,' I said.

Guleed always claimed that she'd joined the police on a dare. 'My sister bet me I wouldn't send off the application,' she'd told me when we'd been doing the thing with the haunted BMWs, 'but I didn't think I'd be accepted.' When I'd asked about the mandatory interview, she said she'd had nothing better to do that day. 'What did your parents think?' I'd said.

'They thought the starting salary was a bit on the low side.'

'What about your friends?' I'd asked, and Guleed had changed the subject.

Guleed was one of Seawoll's favoured few, one of his Valkyries. And he was determined to push her up the fast track. Sending her off to handle a tricky interview like the one with Olivia McAllister-Thames was part test, part toughening exercise, and part vote of confidence.

Tyburn lived a kilometre east of One Hyde Park, just

off the Shepherd's Market, in a five storey Georgian terrace whose elegant proportions would have caused the most hardened Canadian property developer's soul to weep to see such beauty – just prior to having the place gutted and filled with the latest in personality-free interior design. I couldn't see Tyburn doing that – she wanted the connection with the past, with the old institutions and traditions of the city. She saw it as her birthright.

I rang the doorbell and as we waited me and Guleed intoned the Londoner's lament.

'Look at this place,' said Guleed.

'I know.'

'How much do you reckon?'

'Eight million,' I said. 'Last time I looked.'

'Alright for some,' said Guleed, to which my ritual response would have been 'isn't it just?' But right then the front door opened and Lady Ty stood there looking at us if we'd turned up with some colourful pamphlets and an evangelical zeal to get her to change her energy supplier.

I let Guleed do all the talking – I'm good that way with my colleagues.

When Lady Ty led us into the kitchen, Olivia wrinkled her nose and shot an inquiring look at her mother, who cut her off with a glare.

Olivia McAllister-Thames was pale, much lighter than me, with brown hair that fell into the sort of natural ringlets that my mum would have sacrificed her first born to possess. She'd retained her mother's eyes though, a deep brown colour and pinked up at the corners like a cat's. She wore an oversized amber rugby jersey that fell almost to her knees, jeans and purple flip-flops. Sitting next to Olivia was a white middle-aged man who Lady Ty introduced as her solicitor. He got up politely as we entered and shook our hands – Olivia did not. We all sat down at the kitchen table.

Outside London, modern policing leans towards table-free interviews on the basis that it's easier to read someone's body language, and record it on CCTV, if there isn't a cigarette scarred stretch of laminated chipboard in the way. I wondered if Lady Ty knew that, which was why we weren't doing this in the living room – or if she just didn't want me rifling through her Blu-ray collection.

Guleed passed me the statement form, so I had to hunt around in my pockets for a decent pen. Most statements are taken by hand, and it pays to picky about your writing implements and cultivate an easy flowing style – I use a Mitsubishi uni-ball, in case you were wondering.

We started with caution plus two, which involves us scaring the interviewee to death with the normal caution – 'You do not have to say anything, etcetera, etcetera . . .' – and then right when they're sure we're going to march them off to the cells we throw in 'but you are not under arrest at this time and are free to leave if you want to' at the end. The solicitor nodded sagely as Guleed reeled it off, Olivia stared at the table and Lady Ty gave me a sour smile at 'free to leave'.

Guleed warmed up by asking where Olivia went to school. St Paul's, which was a hideously expensive private school in Hammersmith, although because she was a day student it probably only cost the equivalent of a police constable's starting salary. She was hoping to go to Cambridge, but first there was the gap year – Olivia pronounced it 'gap yar' – when she planned to do good somewhere in the third world.

'Teaching English,' she said. 'Or building orphanages – I haven't decided which.'

'Somalia perhaps,' said Lady Ty. And then, to me, 'or Sierra Leone.'

'Mrs Thames,' said Guleed, 'I'd be grateful if you could allow your daughter to answer the questions on her own.'

I saw a flash of anger on Lady Ty's face followed by a hint of amusement and respect.

Guleed asked where Olivia lived, whether this was her only address and other questions she already knew the answers to but which allowed her to circle around to where Olivia had been last night. I clocked the brief – he looked a bit complacent to me, but there was a sheen of sweat on his lip. Family solicitor, I decided, more used to conveyancing and moving Lady Ty's wealth around than to police interviews.

'Was your mum here last night?' asked Guleed.

Olivia hesitated and her eyes flicked towards her mum, who stared fixedly at Guleed.

'Yes,' said Olivia, 'as far as I know.'

'Was your father at home too?' asked Guleed.

'He's out of the country,' said Lady Ty.

Guleed asked where he might be.

'Is this relevant?' asked the lawyer.

'Just establishing a timeline,' said Guleed.

'He's in Dubai,' said Lady Ty. 'On a contract.'

'Really,' said Guleed. 'What kind of contract?'

'He's a civil engineer,' said Lady Ty and then, staring directly at me, said, 'He specialises in hydrology, water management systems, that sort of thing.' She looked back to Guleed. 'He's the top man in his field.'

Me and Guleed knew all this, of course, because not only had we asked for an IIP check before we'd arrived, and not only do I, as a matter of routine, keep dossiers on all the Rivers these days, but also because Beverley had got pissed a couple of weeks previously and spent all night bending my ear about Lady Ty and her 'perfect bloody husband'. According to Bev there were only two things that could improve George McAllister-Thames in her mum's eyes, one was a medical degree and the other was a bit more of a suntan.

'And what do you do?' asked Guleed.

'Detective,' said the lawyer, staring at her. 'Really?'

'I'm curious,' said Guleed.

'Hasn't the starling told you?' asked Lady Ty.

'The starling?'

Lady Ty tilted her head in my direction.

'Your colleague,' she said.

'She sits on a bunch of quangos,' said Olivia, staring at a point on the table midway between us. 'And is a director on like a gazillion boards.'

'Five,' said Lady Ty. 'I'm a non-executive director for five firms.'

'So not the Goddess of the River Tyburn then?' asked Guleed.

I winced and Olivia rolled her eyes, but fortunately Lady Ty was in a whimsical mood.

'That's not precisely a job, now is it?' she asked. 'And rather beside the point.'

The lawyer opened his mouth to speak, but Guleed quickly turned to Olivia and asked how many people had been in the flat.

'Don't know,' said Olivia.

'I see,' said Guleed. 'Why don't we start with the people you *do* know were there.'

Olivia squirmed in her seat like a five year old – this is why your brief tells you to keep your mouth shut during an interview. She made Guleed work for it, but in the end she confirmed that she along with several others had been in the flat. She hadn't known the dead girl, Christina Chorley, and she didn't know how the party had gained access to One Hyde Park.

'We went through the hotel next door,' she said. The Mandarin Oriental Hotel provided a complete package of services for the denizens of One Hyde Park, ranging from cleaning and catering to dog walking and aromatherapy, and there was an underground tunnel from the hotel to the estate. From there, the kids travelled up the segregated service core and into the flat.

'I was just following everyone else,' she said and claimed to have been a bit squiffy. One of the guys might have known the codes to the security doors – she thought his name was James, but she didn't know his surname. So it could have been James Murray, the unfortunate Christina's boyfriend, but you can't afford to make assumptions like that. She did know the names of Albertina Pryce, a fellow student at St Paul's, and *her* boyfriend Alasdair somebody or other who was at Westminster, Maureen who was someone's older sister and Rod, whatever that was short for, Crawfish or something like that – definitely Scottish.

'He had one of those posh Scottish accents,' said Olivia.

Guleed circled around the names and the timeline for twenty minutes, twenty minutes being about the amount of time it takes your average suspect – sorry, I mean witness – to forget the details of the lies they've just told you, before asking about the drugs.

'What drugs?' asked Olivia, her eyes flicking towards the walnut reproduction French farmhouse cupboard with, I was pleased to note, one shelf that displayed a 1977 Jubilee commemoration plate along with two more plates with photographs custom printed on them – one each for Olivia and her brother from at least three years ago. Judging by the pained expressions, formal pose and school uniforms they'd been reproduced from school photographs. My mum has a shelf like that in the living room with, amongst others, a Lady Diana commemorative plate set and my Hendon graduation photo.

'These,' said Guleed and showed Olivia a picture on her tablet – a spray of small pink pills lay across a sheet of white paper. Each one was marked with a smiling elephant's head – Magic Babars.

Olivia glanced at the picture, then sideways at her mother, and I saw her make the wrong decision. But, before I could say anything, she opened her mouth and stuck her future in it.

'Yeah, I bought those,' she said. 'What about it?'

2

Teenage Kicks

Guleed had to arrest her; she had no choice. The brief knew it, too, but before he could get his mouth open Guleed was on her feet and doing the caution. Lady Ty, who'd been staring disbelievingly at her daughter, snapped her head around to look at Guleed — and there was an expression I never thought to see on her face. Abject fear. It was gone in an instant, replaced by a look of calm determination which is the signal for any sensible son of West Africa that it is way past time to be vacating the area. She stood up, and as she did I felt a sudden drag, as if I'd been caught in an icy undertow. I swear the mugs on the drying rack by the sink started to rattle.

I followed her up and said her name as loudly and as forcefully as I dared.

'Tyburn.'

She glared at me and then down at her daughter, who was looking up at all the grown-ups with a shocked expression that showed that only now, at the end, did she understand the sheer depth of the shit she'd just dropped herself in. Looking back, I reckon the only reason it didn't all go pear-shaped right there in the kitchen was because Lady Ty couldn't figure out which one of us she was more pissed off with.

'Why don't we all sit down,' said Guleed, 'while I arrange some transportation?'

Me and Tyburn took our seats but I noticed Guleed fade out the kitchen door, the better to demand shitloads of back-up. We were going to need transportation back to Belgravia, a search team for the house plus, please god, some Falcon back-up for me and a senior officer to throw the warm comforting blanket of rank over the whole proceedings.

'Am I really under arrest?' asked Olivia.

The brief cleared his throat.

'You,' said Lady Ty to her daughter. 'Not one more word. You,' she said to the solicitor. 'I want the best criminal solicitor you know waiting for us at the police station when we get there.'

The solicitor gulped, bobbed his head, and opened his mouth to speak before thinking better of it. Pausing only to gather up his briefcase and papers he made a speedy exit from the kitchen.

'I—' said Olivia.

'Shut up, you stupid little girl,' said Tyburn.

And so we sat in silence for the ten minutes it took Guleed to rustle up some official transport, whereupon she returned to the kitchen and told Olivia that she would have to accompany her to the station. We all stood up again, but this time Lady Ty had herself under control and she watched her daughter being led away without any major property damage.

Although I did make a mental note to check with Thames Water that afternoon – just in case.

'Is this your idea of three bags full?' she said once we were alone. 'I should have left you under the ground.'

And it was while I'd been underground that I'd had what I thought at the time was hallucination. A waking dream that I'd stood on the Oxford Road when it was a ribbon of dust through the countryside and talked to a young man with a sword at his hip and a gleam in his eye. The locals called him Sir William and he wanted me to stay to have a chat but I had business in the land of the living. When I was done with that I enlisted the help of the Folly's official archivist, Dr Harold Postmartin, to see what the histories said. We tracked down a reference to him in the *Rotuli Parliamentorum* which as any fule kno is all in Latin – he was listed as Sir William of Tyburn, although the translation could have been read as 'of the Tyburn'.

I'd have liked to ask Lady Ty whether our young Sir William had been an earlier incarnation of the Tyburn and did she have any memory of him or sense of continuity or was there a total break when he 'died' in the mid-nineteenth century.

But it's a wise man who knows when to keep his gob shut, and so we spent what felt like a really long time in silence until finally Lady Ty's head jerked round to face the front of the house.

'Well, that's you off the hook,' she said. 'Your Lord and Master has arrived.' A couple of moments later Nightingale opened the kitchen door and stepped in. He gave Lady Ty a formal little nod.

'Cecelia,' he said. 'How are you holding up?'

'Oh, I'm just gratified to be getting the personal touch,' she said.

'Why don't you come with me,' said Nightingale, 'and we'll see if we can sort this out.'

It's what you say, even to people standing over the bleeding body of their significant other with a claw hammer in their hand. And the weird thing is that most people, even the ones that have got to know that whatever happens it isn't going to end well for them, come along quietly and let themselves be sorted out.

I didn't think that Lady Ty was going to stay quiet indefinitely but, sometimes, that's the joy of being a lowly constable. You get to foist your problems onto your elders and betters.

Before he left the kitchen Nightingale caught my eye and gestured upwards – he wanted me to check Olivia's bedroom before the main search team got there.

The problem with forensics is that the better it gets, the more inconvenient it is to work around. In the old days the police could get away with clomping around in their size twelves and poking things with a pencil. Now they can pull a viable DNA result off a sample the size of ladybird's eyeball and you've got to be wearing gloves at the very least. I used to walk around with a spare pair of gloves in my pocket, but now I've got a set of booties in there as well – just to be on the safe side. You've got to watch those booties when walking on polished wood though, so I left them off until I'd located Olivia's room on the second floor.

It was a big room, expensively wallpapered in a subtle blue and lavender pattern with reconditioned sash windows that looked out over the street. The high ceiling had its original plaster mouldings and it was, if you threw in the en-suite bathroom, about two thirds the size of my parents' flat. Her walk-in wardrobe was easily the size of my old bedroom and totally wasted because, as far as I could tell, the bulk of Olivia's clothes were spread out in a nice even layer across the floor.

I stooped to check some of the labels – mostly high-end high street with a couple of designer bits. In contrast, her shoes were neatly ranked on a set of purpose-built shelves at the foot of the bed. Some of the heels were a bit outrageous, especially a pair of blue Manolo Blahnik pumps that looked like an invitation to ankle damage to me.

There was no way Lady Ty didn't have a cleaner, and judging from the absence of dust in the gaps between the bannisters, he or she was coming in at least four days a week. Still, I doubted that our hypothetical cleaner had been in early enough that morning to change the linen on the neatly made bed. I looked closer – there was a dent in the coverlet and the pillows had been scrunched up. My guess was that Olivia had come back and slept on top of her bed, briefly, before me and Guleed had arrived to brighten up her day. She'd been casually dressed and freshly laundered when we'd interviewed her, which meant she must have showered and changed.

I checked the en-suite bathroom and there, on the

floor, was last night's party gear and her bath towel. I kept my distance and made a note to inform the follow-up search team so they could bag them up. I stepped back into the bedroom and tried to get a feel for Olivia.

There was a poster of Joan Armatrading facing the bed. It was a blow up of her 1976 album cover, custom framed and hung with care. It seemed a bit retro for Olivia. I mean, I only knew about Joan because she was one of the few non-jazz LPs that my dad had allowed in his collection, alongside *Sgt. Pepper's Lonely Hearts Club Band* and a few very early Jethro Tull's. I'd played the shit out of it when my dad wasn't home until I'd got old enough to bootleg my own taste in music.

Next to Joan was a photo-montage sprawled across the metre or so of wall between the poster and the wardrobe door. Most of the pictures were inkjet hardcopies on standard gauge printing paper and pasted to the wall with Evo-Stik but some had obviously been cut from magazines. Fashion magazines, judging by the glossy quality of the paper – I recognised Alek Wek, Azealia Banks and a smattering of white pop stars and actors. The other photos were phone snaps – mostly selfies – Olivia at parties, clubs and school. Olivia out and about in London.

I got out my phone and took reference pictures of all the people featured in the snaps and made a rough note of how many times they appeared. One white girl was the out and out favourite – wide set blue eyes, a mass of curly black hair that either flopped untidily over her face or was pulled back into a variety of pigtails, bunches and, in one instance, elaborately piled up on her head. The latter saw her and Olivia posing in formal dresses outside somewhere gilt-edged and posh looking – they had their arms comfortably wrapped around each other's waists and were grinning mischievously at the camera. Best Friends Forever, I decided. None of the other boys and girls turned up with anything like the same frequency and all, with the exception of one snap of her brother and another of her mother, were white.

On top of her sturdy work desk, textbooks and folders were arranged with obsessive neatness. English, Geography and French. I flicked through them looking for hidden notes, but all I found was Post-it notes and a lot of colour coded highlighter pen. One thing was for certain, Olivia had no intention of failing her A-levels. With what her mum was like I didn't blame her. Her bookshelves were interesting, pre-teen at the bottom mixed in with a couple of board games, older books above them – Roald Dahl, *Diary of a Wimpy Kid* and Harry Potter graduating up to *Twilight*, *The Girls' Book of Excellence*, Malorie Blackman and, surprisingly, Zola's *Le Ventre de Paris* in the original French. Because it stuck out, I opened it up and found it was full of pencilled notes in the margin – mostly English translations of difficult words. My French is actually worse than my Latin, but even I could tell that this was advanced stuff for an A-level student.

I went back to the collage and looked again – judging by the design of the frontage they were posing before, the picture of Olivia and her BFF in formal dress could well have been taken in a French city. A couple of the others definitely had Beaux-Arts architecture in the background – possibly France again. If I'd been standing in anything but a multi-million Mayfair terrace I might have been thinking of possible importation routes. But rich kids don't need to hoof drugs over the border themselves. The rich have people for that sort of thing, and disposable people at that.

There were two mains sockets in the room, both with their own tangle of chargers and extension cords and I spent a couple of minutes matching them to her laptop, printer, her high end playbar, one spare for an iPhone that I suspected even now was being placed in front of the custody sergeant at Belgravia nick, and another spare that might have been for a different brand of phone. I made a note to check what Olivia carried, and whether it or a second phone had been handed in. A black lacquered wooden tray on the desk held paper-clips, a Post-it pad and scatter of USB sticks – those I decided to leave for the technical forensics guys from Newlands Park.

I sat on the bed, took a deep breath and closed my eyes.

I hadn't found any controlled substances, or drug paraphernalia. It might have been hidden away, but if it was the follow-up POLSA team would find it. I couldn't feel any *vestigia* in the room either. I'd always felt something with the various gods and goddesses of the rivers – even when they were reining it back on purpose – but there was nothing here apart from the usual background.

What did the child of a river and a mortal inherit, and from whom? Fleet was married to a Fae but Beverley said all her children were adopted. Oxley had Isis who had obviously caught longevity from somewhere and Effra had Oberon who Nightingale called an Old Soldier – note the capital letters.

And if I had kids with Beverley, not that kids were on the table, what would they be like – apart from staggeringly good looking of course? Would they be riverlets, streams, storm drains or just ordinary?

Which reminded me to phone Beverley.

'Hi babes,' she said. In the background I could hear water slapping against a vertical surface, the hull of a boat or more likely a piling of some sort. I asked her where she was.

'Up at Eel Pie Island,' she said. 'Sorting out a dispute – these people are cheeky, you know. They think buying a house on an island is just another investment opportunity.'

'Isn't it?' I asked. That end of Richmond/Twickenham had become hipster central since the big money had started pushing all the TV producers and literary editors out of Hampstead and Primrose Hill.

'Nah,' she said. 'Live on an island in the middle of a river, especially this river, you've got to put out some signs and favours if you want to prosper. You still at my house?'

'I'm on a shout,' I said – obviously Beverley hadn't heard about her niece yet.

'Pity,' she said. 'I was hoping you'd be keeping the bed warm for me.'

'Sorry,' I said. 'Listen, the job I'm on, I can't say anything right now, but you need to contact your mum.'

'Is this like a job job?' asked Beverley, 'or a magic job job?'

'I don't know and I'm not supposed to tell you anyway,' I said.

'You might be able to tell her yourself later,' said Beverley. 'She said she might be turning up for your dad's gig.'

Which I'd forgotten about.

'Just call your mum,' I said. 'It's important.'

Beverley promised she would just as soon as she'd sorted out some recalcitrant islanders.

And our kids would be . . . ? I thought after we'd hung up. Good at swimming?

I wasn't going to learn anything more in this room – it was time to hit the factory floor.

What with the jazz thing, the underground thing, the business with the haunted car, the Russians and let's not forget the mould – however hard we try to – Belgravia MIT had bowed to the inevitable and given me my own desk in the Outside Inquiry Office. I say my own desk, but actually I shared it with Guleed and a white DC called David Carey. Neither of them were that happy with the arrangement, not least because it was a two person desk.

'Oh, it's going to be one of those jobs,' said Carey when I settled in beside him. 'Is it too late to put in for a holiday?'

I told him it was, but if he was lucky Guleed would do all the heavy lifting.

'So long as I don't have to deal with any more weird cars,' he said.

The job had acquired an operational name, MARIGOLD, and a quick call to the case manager in the Inside Inquiry Office got me access to HOLMES. I entered the results of my preliminary search of Olivia's bedroom and downloaded the pictures I'd taken of the collage on the wall. Then I went hunting to see if anyone had developed a definitive list of the kids who'd been at the party, to see if I could match them up. I did that until Carey pointed out that the current list was on the whiteboard – along with photos. I matched up Albertina Pryce to one of the pictures in Olivia's collage but none of the others. I asked Carey whether this was the confirmed party list, but he said they were still waiting on statements.

Down the corridor in an interview room Olivia, now sitting next to a solicitor with a properly expensive suit and a suitably belligerent Scouse accent, had sensibly decided to keep her mouth shut. Guleed was pissed off, because not only had the preliminary search of the Tyburns' house not turned up anything useful, but of the six separate sets of prints lifted from the pill packets none had matched Olivia's. Nor, in fact, had any of the prints recovered from the flat at One Hyde Park. Guleed wanted to know if Tyburn could magic away fingerprints, but I said probably not without wiping everything else. She asked me to check with Nightingale, and I said I was sure because I'd made a point of coming up with a list of modern forensic techniques and then going through them one by one to see if Nightingale could counter them.

'Did anything work?' asked Guleed.

'So far nothing,' I said. 'You can burn the top surfaces off a scene, but it's pretty obvious that you've done it.'

'I can imagine,' said Guleed, who'd once seen me roast a duck by accident.

Since Olivia was seventeen she was allowed an adult to remain with her as well as her solicitor. Naturally she chose her mum, which meant that for safety's sake Nightingale had to be in the interview room, too. Given the circumstances, DI Stephanopoulos had decided she'd better sit in too – although whether that was to maintain status for the MIT or out of sheer curiosity, no one knew or dared to ask. Stephanopoulos was a short white woman with a brown flat top haircut that had never been fashionable, even in the 1980s, and a face that relaxed into a scowl. It was rumoured that out in the suburbs there was a big house, a wife, and a garden full of chickens and tulips and rainbows and the novels of Terry Pratchett. But if there was, none of that ever made it south of the North Circular. And certainly never as far as Belgravia nick.

In the normal course of events inspectors never conduct interviews, yet Olivia merited two – I wondered if she felt special. Though she didn't say anything useful over the course of three hours, demonstrating exactly why inspectors have better things to do than interviews. It was also why Nightingale was still in the interview room when Dr Walid called and said that he had something to show us at the mortuary.

When I told Guleed where I was going, she asked to tag along.

I asked her if she was sure.

'It's going to be Falcon stuff,' I said.

'Since I can't seem to escape it,' she said, 'I figure I might as well learn a bit about it.'

'Can't argue with that.'

In the far off days of last year, Nightingale would have expected me to discourage her from coming, but our policy framework had changed. Earlier in the year we'd had what would have been called a 'Multi-Agency Forward Strategy Planning Session' if it wasn't for the fact that it was me, Nightingale, Dr Walid and Dr Postmartin sitting down for tea in the atrium and hashing out how on earth we were going to cope with the increase in magic. The reason for the meeting was mainly that Dr Walid wanted to train up an assistant, someone with a background in your actual pathology.

'Someone who knows more about brains than the lower intestine,' said Dr Walid, world famous gastroenterologist.

He had his eye on a promising doctor at UCH. His problem was that he would have to come up with a budget in order to cover the salary because, strangely, after six years of continuous study, freshly minted doctors like to get paid.

'Golf clubs not being cheap,' I'd said.

'Never mind golf,' said Dr Walid. 'Think of the overdraft.'

The result was Dr Jennifer Vaughan, a ferociously clever white woman from Newport who had entered medical school with high hopes of becoming a healer only to find that the puzzle was more interesting than the person, and she found herself gravitating downwards towards the morgue and a career in pathology. I knew way more about her life than she would have been comfortable with, including the time she'd nearly been cautioned for breaching the peace at the Supakart Centre in Newport, because I was the one who'd had to carry out the vetting process. It was your basic Baseline Personal Security Standard (BPSS) vetting that all civil servants had to undergo, plus a few extra bits we'd tacked on to cover what coppers like Seawoll liked to call 'weird bollocks'.

I didn't actually ask whether she herself or any member of her family had ever been a fairy, but I skated pretty close. It didn't help that she had the kind of Welsh accent that made her sound like she was being sarcastic even when she wasn't.

'Are my swimming habits really a concern to the Metropolitan Police?' she'd asked during one of the three interviews I'd conducted. I told her she'd be surprised.

'I certainly hope so,' she'd said. 'Otherwise this will all have been a bit of a waste of time, won't it?'

If you want to get the full force of her actual sarcasm, for comparative purposes, get her started on the mischaracterisation of hyperthaumaturgical degradation as a cerebrovascular disorder, strokes, aneurysms and the like, when it was quite obviously caused by direct physical trauma to the brain.

'Admittedly, many of the signs do mirror those we see in stroke victims,' she'd said. 'But that's no reason to be making assumptions, see. Especially when you have such nicely prepared brain sections to examine.'

Luckily me and Guleed weren't subjected to your actual slices of Christina Chorley's brain, because Dr Vaughan had already prepared a series of images which she showed us on her tablet. Even better, we were at the Ian West Memorial Forensic Suite at Westminster Mortuary which had a glassed-off observation room which meant that we didn't have to smell the bodies either. Trust me, this is a bonus even with a nice fresh corpse like Ms Chorley.

I introduced Guleed to the doctors Vaughan and Walid. They shook hands and then Dr Walid leant casually against a work surface with his arms folded and watched while Dr Vaughan took us through her findings.

'This was the cause of death,' she said pointing to a smudge.

I caught Dr Walid's eye and asked if it was a cerebral aneurysm.

'No,' said Dr Vaughan slowly. 'It is not an aneurysm because an aneurysm is caused by a weakening in a blood vessel which distends over time and then, if one is unlucky, ruptures causing an intracranial bleed. Which as we know is not very good for the brain, is it?'

'But that's intracranial bleeding,' I said. 'I've seen slides like this before.'

'That may be so, but it is not caused by an aneurysm,' she said and Guleed gave me a pitying look.

Guleed always knew how to keep her mouth shut, and had this mad way of just fading into the background whenever she wanted to. Well, we all have our ways of dealing with difficulties – mine is to ask stupid questions.

'It's not natural causes, though,' I said. 'Is it?'

'Well,' said Dr Vaughan, 'here's the thing. If you look at this close-up here – see where the brain looks spongy? These are indications of tiny points of tissue damage to the brain.'

'Caused by what?' I asked.

Dr Walid chuckled and Dr Vaughan sighed.

'To be honest, my guess would be that somebody sliced open her brain, pricked it with narrow bore needles and then reassembled the brain – seamlessly mind you – and then popped it back in her head with her none the wiser.'

'That seems an unlikely scenario,' I said.

'It does, doesn't it,' said Dr Vaughan. 'In any case, one of these pinpricks also jabbed a blood vessel, which led to the intracranial bleeding, which was the ultimate cause of death.'

I asked what caused the pinpricks, if not narrow bore needles, and Dr Vaughan gave me a sunny smile.

'As you know, I've been reviewing Dr Walid's case-work,' she said. 'And reviewing the "literature" he's supplied on related subjects. Now, to be fair to the colleagues that came before us, these gentlemen didn't have access to modern imaging techniques, but even so they can be remarkably vague as to the distinction be-tween cerebrovascular and physical trauma. However, they did leave some excellent specimens behind.'

A room full of them, I knew, some of them dating back to the eighteenth century. Apparently it was good form in the old days for a wizard to leave his body to the Folly along with his notebooks, unreturned library books and any spare valuables he had lying around – cash, antiques, good quality arable land in the Mid-lands or home counties. It was the land bequests that underpinned the charitable fund that was paying Dr Vaughan's salary.

'You'd better not tell the Hunterian you've got these,' Dr Vaughan had said when she was introduced to the Folly's collection. 'Or they'd be down here backing up a lorry to your front door and no mistake.'

Now she studied her tablet. 'Many of them show the same pattern of pinprick injury,' she said. 'It's too early to reach a firm conclusion, but this pattern of organic brain damage matches the early stages of hyperthauma-turgical degradation.'

'She was a practitioner?' I asked.

'Or the victim of sequestration,' said Dr Walid.

Sequestration . . . There were some terrible things that could get inside your head and make you do stuff both physically and magically. Such things had no com-punction about using you up and letting you die, as the overuse of magic turns your brain into Swiss cheese.

Mr Punch was one such thing.

Still they appeared to be quite rare, so Christina being a practitioner was more likely. There's no such thing as magical talent – anyone can learn magic the way anyone can learn to play the guitar. It's just that trying to tackle the opening to 'Stairway to Heaven' isn't going to kill you. Well, not directly anyway. You also don't learn it spontaneously. Somebody's got to teach you the basics, even if that's just three chords and a vigorous strumming action.

Dr Vaughan concurred that sequestration was unlikely.

'Self-taught?' I asked.

'The pathology can't really tell us how,' he said. 'But according to the pre-war literature, fully trained practitioners rarely injured themselves to this degree.'

After all, not killing yourself was the point of quite a lot of the training.

'So,' said Guleed. 'Does this mean she was doing magic when she died?'

'You said the M-word,' I said, but Guleed ignored me.

'Not necessarily,' said Dr Vaughan. 'The PMA she took could have raised her blood pressure to the point where a blood vessel, weakened by the organic damage, gave way. The seizures and other symptoms would have been incidental to the cause of death.'

A pre-existing medical condition wasn't going to help Olivia McAllister-Thames, because supplying the drugs was in and of itself an unlawful act. So it wouldn't serve as defence in law. Still manslaughter. Still a maximum sentence of life imprisonment for Olivia, and a lifetime in the shit for me.

'If Christina was a trainee witch . . .' said Guleed.

'Wizard,' said Dr Walid – just as I said, 'Practitioner.'

Guleed exchanged a look with Dr Vaughan.

'Whatever,' she said. 'If she was. And if she wasn't self-taught, who taught her?'

'Good question.' I said. 'Perhaps we should go ask her father.'

3

Driving While Cheerful

Contrary to what you see on the TV, you don't just waltz up to a grieving relative and start asking them difficult questions – well not unless you think they did it, and even then you're expected to have some evidence to back you up. First you have to clear the interview with the SIO or the DI in tactical charge – which in this case was Stephanopoulos. And she wanted to know why.

'There's some evidence that Christina Chorley might have been a practitioner,' I said and explained Dr Walid and Vaughan's findings, which led to Stephanopoulos asking the same questions I had. So I shared the same lack of answers that Dr Walid and Vaughan had given me – this is known in the police as intelligence focusing. First you identify what you don't know. The next step is to go and find some likely sod and question them until they give you some answers. In the old days we weren't that bothered whether the answers had anything to do with the facts, but these days we're much more picky.

Stephanopoulos sent us over to Seawoll's office.

'Yeah, okay,' he said. 'But this had better be done with some fucking tact and diplomacy.'

*

Martin Chorley didn't actually live in London, but out beyond the M25 in a two million quid eighteenth century rectory near High Wycombe. Fortunately me and Guleed were saved a schlepp up the M40 because Mr Chorley, having formally identified his daughter that morning, had moved on to his place of work in the City. He'd outright refused a Family Liaison Officer – plenty do – but had already been statemented as soon as he'd made the identification. Because, for police officers, 'close relative' frequently rhymes with 'prime suspect', Mr Chorley had already accumulated quite a large section in HOLMES. From that me and Guleed got all the salient details — birth, school, degree, work history, the big family home and the complimentary chairman's flat above the office in Little Britain.

'What, no villa in Tuscany?' I asked.

'He prefers America,' said Guleed, who was going through twenty years' worth of travel documentation. 'Washington, New York, Miami, couple of trips to Atlanta – most of these are going to be work related.'

As were the trips to Berlin, Paris and Geneva – in his capacity as chairman of something called the Public Policy Foundation. There'd been a helpful note from whoever had run the initial check – *Influential think tank, watch it*. I checked the address and me and Guleed headed off to put our sensitivity training to the test.

The wind had picked up by the afternoon and on Ludgate Hill the tea-break smokers were huddled under the inadequate awnings – designed that way on modern buildings to discourage rough sleepers – trying to get their nicotine fix before hypothermia set in.

City traffic is always grumpy in the rain, and so was Guleed when my shortcut to avoid St Paul's put us behind an Ocado delivery van for twenty minutes. Fortunately it peeled off before we hit the Rotunda and we did a quick spin around the Museum of London and into the bit of Little Britain that runs beside Postman's Park.

The trees in the park still had most of their leaves, and the street was narrow and shaded and smelt of wet grass rather than the busy cement smell you get in the rest of the City. The office was based in a Mid-Victorian pile whose Florentine flourishes were not fooling anyone but itself. There was a brass plaque by the door engraved with 'Public Policy Foundation' and beyond the doors a cool blue marble foyer and a young and strangely elongated white woman behind a reception desk. Because it's not good policy to, we hadn't called ahead to make an appointment. Which gave Guleed a chance to tease the receptionist by not showing her warrant card when she identified herself.

The receptionist's expression did a classic three point turn from alarm to suspicion and finally settling on professional friendliness as she picked up the phone and informed someone at the other end that the 'police' had arrived to talk to Mr Chorley. We agreed later that while she'd lost points for the hesitant way she'd identified us as police, it was good effort overall.

'Definitely in the top half of the leaderboard,' said Guleed while we were waiting for someone to show us upstairs.

Martin Chorley's office was carefully designed to be

46

unpretentious with varnished floorboards, mismatched throw rugs, a John Lewis leather sofa set and a glass-topped desk which I happened to know came from Ikea because I'd considered getting it for the tech cave.

Chorley himself was my height, generally slender but with a spare tyre that was going to see him spending much more time in the gym in future. His hair was dark brown and conservatively cut, his eyes a pale grey and closely set. Judging from the rumples he was wearing yesterday's suit trousers – no time to change – but a fresh pale blue shirt with packing creases. Mint in its wrapper, I guessed, and kept in the office for emergencies.

He offered us coffee and we declined. Generally you only accept a beverage if the subject is going to make it themselves – creating a sense of normality – or if you're going to make it, giving you a good chance to snoop around their kitchen. He himself scooped up a bottle of Highland Spring from his desk and waved us onto the black leather sofa while he lowered himself carefully into the matching armchair. His face, I saw, was grey and there were smudges under his eyes so I started gently enough – explaining that this was a routine follow-up interview, blah blah blah, and got about half a sentence in before he cut me off.

'I heard you made an arrest,' he said. He spoke with that deliberately toned down posh accent that, before they allowed regional dialects on the radio, used to be known as BBC standard.

The law of the police interview is inviolable – information is only supposed to flow in one direction. But you've got to handle grieving parents carefully, otherwise they might write to the *Telegraph*. Or, in the case of someone like Martin Chorley, call the editor at home.

'An arrest has been made,' I said. 'How it relates to your daughter's death remains unclear.'

He nodded glumly at this and took a sip of water.

I waited to see if he'd ask who, exactly, had been arrested. When he didn't, I went back to asking the routine questions that disguised the real reason I was there.

Nightingale's definition of a rogue practitioner was essentially 'one that is practising magic without the sanction of the Folly'. Since the only currently sanctioned practitioners were me and him, I'd pointed out that this was not a very useful definition. Besides, there were still a number of wizards of the old school who, despite having 'rusticated' themselves, could still practise if they had to. Not to mention all the Rivers, Russian night-witches, fae, demi-fae – and who knew what other kinds of fae – running around doing stuff that looked suspiciously like magic to me.

So we refined our definition down to 'someone who practised magic in breach of the Queen's Peace', and started developing a series of sophisticated tools for determining whether someone's nearest and dearest might have been dabbling in the metaphysical equivalent of sticking their head in a microwave for fun and profit.

'Had you noticed any recent changes in Christina's behaviour?' I asked. 'Any sudden new interests?'

'She's seventeen,' he said. 'So yes, lots of sudden interests.'

He turned his head to look out the window and took a deep breath.

'Any of them particularly noteworthy?' I asked.

'Any of what?' He turned back to face us.

'Any of the new interests,' said Guleed with a note of respectful curiosity – it was her party trick. According to legend she'd once got a confession out of a rapist just by looking sympathetic and nodding occasionally.

'Me personally,' Stephanopoulos had said, 'I'd have nailed his testicles to the chair.'

Ah, the good old days, I'd thought.

Martin Chorley succumbed.

'History,' he said. 'She started reading a great deal of history. I did find it a little bit odd because she wasn't taking history at A-level.' He was hazy about exactly when and where her interest had been focused, and I could see that pressing him was just going to make him angry. So I let it go. Tact and fucking diplomacy and all that.

A specialist POLSA team had already turned over Christina Chorley's room at St Paul's – I made a note to go over their report and see what she'd had on her shelves.

Martin Chorley said that most of his daughter's interests had seemed to centre around her phone.

'I never thought to ask,' he said. 'I was just glad—' He stopped and his lips turned up in a humourless smile. 'I just never thought to ask.'

'Was it unusual for Christina to stay in town over the weekend?' asked Guleed.

'I believe I've already been asked these questions,' said Mr Chorley.

'I'm sorry, sir,' said Guleed. 'Narrowing down the timeline is crucial and we find that people sometimes remember more once they get further away from an incident – every little detail helps.'

We also find that people tend to forget exactly what lies they told the last set of coppers they talked to. But either Mr Chorley had an exceptional memory or his earlier statement – that he thought his daughter had been staying with her friend Albertina Pryce – was true.

'She generally stayed with Albertina when she spent the weekend in town,' he said.

'Did she ever stay with anyone else?' asked Guleed.

'Not that I know of,' said Mr Chorley. 'There were sleepovers, you know. Girls' stuff. I did consider tracking her phone, but one doesn't want to hover – do you? Since her mother died I found it quite difficult to find the right balance to be father and mother at the same time.'

Guleed nodded understandingly.

Christina's mother had died three years previously in an RTC on the A355 just short of the junction with the M40, having lost control of her Mercedes C-Class and drifted into oncoming traffic. According to the accident report, she'd been four times over the legal alcohol limit at the time but since she'd hadn't killed anyone else the coroner went easy on her and ruled it as death by misadventure.

'Do you think I should have?' said Mr Chorley. 'Been more of a helicopter parent?'

Guleed gave a 'what can you do' sigh and looked sympathetic.

'Did she ever have any trouble with her phones?' I asked.

This got a frown.

'What sort of trouble?' he asked.

'Did she seem to lose or claim to have broken her phone?' I asked. 'More often than you'd expect?'

'You think she was selling them?' asked Martin Chorley. 'For drug money?'

Actually, I thought she might be destroying them through the power of her magic, but I felt that saying this might violate Seawoll's rules about tact and diplomacy. Also, I was looking to see how Mr Chorley reacted – for some indication he might know why damaged phones were significant. But what he mostly was, was bewildered and sad.

There's being thorough and there's being cruel, so I zipped through the rest of my questions. Guleed followed my cue and didn't ask any additional questions of her own.

'Did you get anything useful?' she asked as we stepped back into the rain.

'Not really,' I said.

'Didn't think so.'

Useful or not, it still had to be written up because a) empirically speaking a negative result is still a result, b) someone cleverer than you might make a connection you missed and c) in the event of a case review it's sensible to at least look like you're being competent. So back we went to our desk share at Belgravia and did just that.

'Do you think it's odd he only had the one?' asked Guleed.

'One what?'

'One kid,' she said. 'These rich people usually have three or four.'

'I don't think it's compulsory,' I said and then thought of something. 'Have we talked to the nannies yet?'

According to the whiteboard the MIT had identified five of the kids at the party, leaving two unidentified – assuming we had the count right. One of them – 'Rod Crawfish or something' – DC Carey had tentatively pegged as Roderick Crawford, also at Westminster and in the same year as James Murray. He was heading off to Primrose Hill to TIE him with a brand new DC called Fergus Ryan.

'Fergus Ryan,' I said. 'Really? Where's he from?'

'Redbridge, I think.'

Three of those kids, unlike Christina, had two or more younger siblings and, consequently, the families had live-in nannies.

'Told you,' said Guleed. 'Big families.'

All the nannies were already actioned to be statemented, but I was thinking that Christina Chorley probably had a nanny when she was young and that 'the slave always knows more about the master than the master knows of the slave' – even if I couldn't remember who'd said that. Tracking them down without alerting Mr Chorley was going to be a bit of a bastard, so I suggested it as a further action in my report in the hope that Stephanopoulos would palm it off on someone else. Once I'd dropped the report in the Inside Inquiry Office

I went looking for Nightingale. I found him downstairs in Stephanopoulos' office reading a hardcopy that some kind soul must have printed out for him.

'Any luck?' he asked, looking up.

'Not really,' I said and briefed him on the interview, my ideas about former nannies and having a look around Christina's bedroom at the house in High Wycombe.

'I'll take care of that,' said Nightingale. 'I believe you have a family engagement to go to.'

'What about Tyburn?' I asked.

'They released Olivia on police bail over an hour ago,' said Nightingale. 'She's to return here first thing tomorrow morning. I thought Cecelia took it rather well – considering. I believe we may be safe from cataclysms along the Tyburn for tonight at least.'

'Did Olivia change her story?'

'No,' said Nightingale. 'She still claims to have supplied the fatal drugs. Although frankly I don't believe a word of it and more to the point neither did Miriam. Not least because she's remarkably vague about where she obtained the drugs in the first place.' He nodded at Stephanopoulos' desk. 'Miriam said she'd be back later if you need her for anything.'

It didn't help that there wasn't any physical evidence, beyond her presence at the party, to corroborate her confession. That had to be nagging at Stephanopoulos, but I doubted that if Olivia had been some seventeen year old off an estate somewhere we would have been spending this much time on the case. We had a confession and I suspect we would have charged her and let the Crown Prosecution Service sort it out.

'I did have a moment to see if the parents were on any of our lists,' said Nightingale.

Meaning, to check if any of them been members of the Little Crocodiles dining club while at Oxford University. Unlike other similar clubs this one had eschewed smashing up restaurants in favour of learning magic, courtesy of a former colleague of Nightingale's called Geoffrey Wheatcroft. In this he broke the law and, more importantly, the social conventions of the Folly – he was probably lucky he died in bed before Nightingale found out.

We had several lists of names to work with, one of confirmed members in the early 1980s – provided by Lady Ty who'd been getting her double first at the time. And one of suspected members from the late fifties onwards – collated from various reliable sources. Then people who might have been members and/or were close associates of people we knew were members. As you can imagine, the last list was huge and pretty much covered everyone who'd gone to Oxford since the end of the Second World War. Unsurprisingly Martin Chorley and Albert Pryce were on that list. Pryce had gone to Geoffrey Wheatcroft's old college – Magdalene – while Chorley had been at Oriel. One critical overlap was Chorley's time with that of Robert Weil, who even now was doing life for the murder of an unidentified woman he'd been caught dumping in the woods near Crawley. We were as sure that he had a connection to the Little Crocodiles as we were that he hadn't killed the woman, but we couldn't prove either.

And the Little Crocodiles had spawned Albert

Woodville-Gentle, otherwise known as the First Face-less Man, who'd done unspeakable things to people in Soho during the 1960s and then in turn helped another man who kept his face hidden. I'd met the new boy on a couple of occasions and he'd nearly killed me on both. And Nightingale, who I knew for a fact had gone toe to toe with a pair of Tiger tanks, was worried about which of them would come out on top in a straight fight.

Not that we had any intention of letting it come to a straight fight – us being coppers and all.

The connections so far were pretty bloody tenuous. Victim's posh dad and victim's best friend's posh dad both went to a posh university – hold the press. Some-one was going to have spend some time drilling into the data to see if there was a deeper connection – guess who that was going to be. But not tonight.

'Are you sure I've got time for that?' I said to Nightingale.

'I assured your mother that if you failed to arrive it wouldn't be my fault,' he said.

'You talked to my mum?'

Nightingale grinned – he has a surprisingly mischie-vous grin.

'As your . . .' he paused, he always does at this point. 'As the one responsible for your apprenticeship, it is expected that I keep your parents informed as to your progress.'

He saw the look on my face.

'Only in the most general terms,' he said quickly. 'For the purpose of reassurance.'

'Did you talk to my dad as well?'

'I have spoken to your father, yes,' said Nightingale.

'And?'

'I never knew that Tubby Hayes was also a virtuoso on the vibraphone. In fact, he once played with Charles Mingus in that capacity.'

I was relieved – at least my father was reliably uninterested in my career.

'Wait,' I said. 'What exactly did you talk about with my mum?'

'She evinced a great interest in the Thames family,' he said.

I resisted the urge to curl up and hide under Stephanopoulos' desk.

'I suppose some emergency overtime is out of the question?' I asked.

'And cross your mother?' said Nightingale. 'Not likely.'

If you live beside the river, Beverley says, you're going to get flooded – that's the cost of doing business, the price you pay for the blessing of the waters. A lot of the London Borough of Barnes sits inside a northern loop of the Thames that stretches from Putney Bridge to where the railway crosses the river. One day, says Beverley, she and her Mama are going to pinch it off at the base and make one big island. I asked her when she thought this was going to happen and she just shrugged.

'Sooner or later,' she said.

There's nothing like having your girlfriend talk in geological time to make you feel insignificant.

The Bull's Head sits safely above, and a road width

back from, an artificial embankment on the south side of the river. Just around the corner from where Holst composed *The Planets* – I know this because there's a blue plaque on the house and Bev once made me wait half an hour while she checked on some nearby trolls.

The pub itself is an early Victorian mansion with French windows and wrought iron balconies to give it that sexy New Orleans look. Despite being hemmed in by later buildings it retained its courtyard and coach house round the back, which is where, these days, they keep the jazz. Coleman Hawkins played at the Bull, as did the multi-talented Tubby Hayes, beloved of my dad and Nightingale, until the early 1970's when he popped his clogs. Other visiting greats included Shorty Rogers, Bud Shank and Ben Webster. And during the jazz revival of the noughties, rising young stars like Jamie Cullum and Simon Spillett made The Bull's Head the groovy place to be – man. My dad had played there in the past and now it was marking the start of his fourth attempt at jazz stardom – however far that went. It was also the debut of his brand new teeth, paid for by yours truly with the help of a Kickstarter campaign and what was left of my savings.

I'd been there when he'd tested his new embouchure, watched him as he lifted his trumpet to his lips, paused to nervously wet them with his tongue and then blow a single pure note. I'd watched him stop and stare at his trumpet in disbelief and then at my mum who'd pinched the bridge of her nose to hide her tears. Then he smiled at me and for that moment, and just that moment, I forgave him everything – everything – because now I knew what joy looked like and I was part of it.

It wore off fairly quickly in the days after that, but the music stayed and my mum was happy.

I was less happy with the amount of interest my dad's gigs were getting in the demi-monde, but as Nightingale had pointed out it was my own damned fault.

'You did rather insist on that open day at Casterbrook,' he'd said. 'Your father's performance there must have caught their imagination.'

That's the trouble with community policing – strangely, people start expecting you to be part of the community. Fortunately my dad's brand of soul jazz wasn't Goth enough for the wilder shores of the demi-monde, so I expected the mundane to weird bollocks ratio to be quite high.

It was dark by the time I parked on the embankment and there was a cold wind racing up the Thames bringing threats of rain. The tide was turning and I could feel the Thames pushing upstream and slapping at the exposed shingle. I was early enough that Beverley was still in the main bar.

I spotted her by the window, waving at me. She was wearing a purple knit top with a neck wide enough to slip off her shoulder and had her dreads tied back with a matching purple woollen scarf. An oxblood leather jacket was draped over the back of her chair. She'd managed to score a table despite the crowd and even had a free seat waiting for me. As I slid in beside her a complete stranger put a half of lager down in front of me and walked away.

'Do you even pay for these?' I asked.

She leaned close to murmur in my ear. 'This close to high tide I'm not sure I could make them stop,' she said and then she kissed me on the lips before introducing me to the others at the table. She'd brought a couple of her white friends from Queen Mary's where she'd started reading — you don't study at uni, you read — Environmental Science. She'd sold this to her mum on the basis that while it wasn't the law or medicine it was a little bit like engineering, if you squinted. And even Lady Ty couldn't argue with Queen Mary for university snob value. Bev's friends included Douglas, who would have been a hipster cliché had he been able to manage the beard, and Melanie, who was one of those round perky people who give the impression that it's only a great effort of will stopping them from bouncing around the room. I'd once asked Beverley whether she told them she was a goddess of a not-so-small river in South London and she said – sure, course she did.

'And?' I'd asked.

'They think I'm some kind of New Age weirdo,' she'd said. 'The dreads help.'

Beverley said that she found that people stuck the first vaguely appropriate label on, whether it fit the facts or not.

'It's too much effort to tell them otherwise, isn't it?' she'd said. 'Besides, then you've got to explain stuff . . . And aren't we supposed to be keeping a low profile?' Then she'd done a Nightingale saying – 'I'm keeping to the agreements and trying not to scare the horses.'

Beverley had a ton of friends at uni, but these were

the only two that were interested in jazz. Not enough to know who my father was without looking him up on Wikipedia, but interested all the same.

'And it's in a good cause,' said Melanie, which was news to me so I looked at Beverley.

'Help for the Ebola crisis,' she said.

Help for mum's extended family, I thought. But since this seemed to constitute at least a quarter of the population of Sierra Leone, the effect was going to be much the same. It was odd, that, because for a Fula my mum didn't half have a lot of Temne and Susu relatives.

Melanie said that she'd always wanted to work somewhere like Sierra Leone once she was qualified – somewhere she could really make a difference – what did I think?

'The beaches around Freetown are brilliant,' I said, which got me a blank look.

But you can only tease white people for so long before the universe punishes you for it – in this case when my mum came into the main bar, spotted me and waved me over.

She was dressed like something out of an old photograph – black long-sleeved roll neck jumper and grey slacks. Around her neck hung a couple of thick gold ropes that I was amazed had made it through the family lean patch, and a high quality wig cut in an eighties bob. All she was missing was a beret.

When I joined her she pecked me on either cheek – continental style – which was just disturbing.

'*Peter kam ya, are wan talk to you,*' she said.

I sighed and let myself be drawn to quiet corner.

When I was younger she only used to lapse into Krio with me when she was angry or she wanted me to do something like fetch her a cup of tea or go to the shops. Nowadays it's a sign that she's about to discuss something I don't want to talk about.

'*You en Beverley don begin for lay down wit each other en?*'

'Mum,' I said, with an involuntary whine.

'*Are hope say u dae use protection ooh.*'

'Of course we're using protection,' I said. 'And it's none of your business.'

'*U get for take tem en be careful.*'

'We're always careful.'

My mum looked suddenly disappointed.

'*So you want tell me say e go tay before are see me gran pekin dem?*' she said.

'I'm not sure that we're quite at that stage yet.'

'*But Aunty Kadie en borbor get two pekin dem already,*' said my mum.

'I know – you made me go to the christening, remember?'

'*An you big for ram.*'

'He has more time on his hands,' I said.

'*E bette for born pekin way you young,*' said my mum. 'It's scientifically proven.'

'Yes mum.'

'I'd look after them,' she said.

'What?'

'*If you born now are go mend dem,*' she said. 'That way you could both be about your business.'

I suddenly wondered if my mum could swim and

61

whether I dared tell Beverley about the offer. Not now, I thought, not a good idea right now.

Luckily it was time to go out through the side door and follow the black arrow painted on the white brick walls marked JAZZ ROOM. According to my dad it had just been refurbished and the acoustics were much better, though he missed the proper sized piano.

'Joe Harriott would have loved it,' he'd said.

Despite its role in jazz history it was a small space, with its own bar and triangular stage in the corner opposite the entrance. Bev made sure she was front and centre with her friends tagging nervously behind. She cast a look over her shoulder at me, her eyes dark and sly and her beautiful wide mouth twitching up at the corners, but I wanted to stay by the door – where I could keep an eye on who was coming in.

The wizards of the Folly, or the Society of the Wise, back when there was no chance of taking the piss out of them on Twitter, have never really got the hang of the demi-monde – that strange collection of people and things-that-are-also-people tied into the magical world. Following the predictable mania for classification that gripped them during the seventeenth and eighteenth centuries, they spent a lot of time talking about proportions of human and good- and bad-faerie blood and then assigning names to the result. Most of it was as useful as the theory of luminiferous aether, but it did explain why calling someone a goblin in some London pubs could get you a smacking. Still, after two years and change at the Folly I knew them when I saw them – most of the time.

I knew this one as soon as he entered. A short young white man with a pointy chin and rust coloured hair slicked back with gel. He wore a tweed countryman's jacket over a black T-shirt, a pair of zombie hunter cargo pants and hiking boots. Not DMs, I noticed, something Swiss and military. I knew instantly that he was at least part fae and a wrong-un. Partly because of my long experience as a copper, partly because of his expression of beatific innocence, but mostly because I'd last met him trying to chat up my thirteen year old cousin and as a result had run a comprehensive record check on him.

His name was Reynard Fossman and he was dismayingly pleased to see me.

He raised his walking stick in salute and I saw that it was made of hickory and its head was a knot of roots smoothed down and polished to bring out the grain. I considered having him for carrying an offensive weapon, because it doesn't have to be offensive *per se* – it's the intention to use it as such that counts in law.

'Mr Fossman,' I said.

'Excellent,' said Reynard and gave me a vulpine smile, 'you remember me.'

'Yes, I do,' I said.

'And how is your lovely cousin?' he asked. 'Still gorgeous, I hope.'

'What do you want?' I asked.

'Oh, so many things,' said Reynard. 'But in this instance I bear a message for your master.'

People don't like it when you don't react to this sort of shit. They can get frustrated and escalate out of their own comfort zone. You can end up with some useful information that way, or an excuse to arrest them for assaulting a police officer. I gave Reynard my blandest expression, but he just cocked his head and gave me a calculating look. He had a reputation for being cunning, as well other words starting with C.

'Tell him,' said Reynard, 'that I can put him in touch with a certain someone who has an item he might well like to purchase.'

'What's that?'

'Jonathan Wild's final ledger,' he said.

'So?' I said.

'You do know who Jonathan Wild was?' asked Reynard.

Jonathan Wild – self-styled Thief Taker General who cut out the criminal middle man by arranging to have your property stolen, fenced and sold back to you in-house. It was a wonderful scam – if you wanted your stuff back, you had to deal with him. And if you were a thief and you didn't play ball it was a long walk to a short drop at Tyburn. Of course, this was back in the eighteenth century when a gentleman might have a good meal, a little professional company and still have enough left out of a fiver to bribe a high court judge.

'Is he part of One Direction?' I asked.

Reynard sighed theatrically and proffered his business card.

'Just make sure you tell the Nightingale,' he said and then, pausing only to doff an imaginary top hat at my mum, he slipped back out the way he came.

I looked at his card. White high quality stock, a stylised fox's head in embossed red-gold and below that a single mobile number – a disposable, I found when I checked it the next morning.

'Ah,' said Nightingale when I stepped outside and called him. 'That is indeed an item we might want to acquire.' Which was Nightingale speak for: grab it with both hands. 'We shall have to discuss this tomorrow.'

Later that evening my dad and the Irregulars struck up 'The Sidewinder' and I got to spend a good thirty seconds admiring the way Beverley moved before she dragged me out and made me dance with her. When the set finished she put her arms around me and kissed me – she smelt of new mown grass and heated car wax, like old deckchairs and plastic hosepipes – like a hot summer's day in a London garden.

These days my mum doesn't let my dad hang around after a gig, so I stuck them in an Uber and joined the Irregulars, plus girlfriends and boyfriends, plus Beverley and her friends in the bar. The manager of The Bull's Head had been a fan of my dad's almost as long as my mum, so we were treated to a lock-in and drinks at cost. The band, or at least Daniel and Max, predictably took this as a challenge, as did their and Beverley's friends – musicians and students – you'd think the manager would have known better.

'Given he's such a skinny lad,' James said after watching Daniel's boyfriend sink yet another Guinness, 'you've got to ask where it's all going.'

James was the drummer and so by tradition it was his van that the band tooled around in – this was causing some friction.

'I don't want to invoke national stereotypes but I'm

65

bloody dying for a drink here,' he said staring meaning-
fully at Daniel and Max. They were less than sympathetic.

'You should have taken up the sax,' said Max.

'You only dare say that cause you're pure steamin',,'
said James. 'The world's full of wannabe sax players,
but jazz drums – that's a vocation.'

Bev's friends tried to match the jazzmen drink for
drink, and as a result had to be poured into the back of
James' van with the rest of the band plus hangers-on.
James promised faithfully to see them safely back to
their digs. As the van lurched off I noticed that it was
riding well low on its suspension and hoped, ironically
as it turned out for me, that they didn't get stopped.

It was breezy out by the river, the cold finding its
way down the back of my jacket. It was high tide and I
could practically feel Beverley's mother slapping at the
embankment, looking for cracks – nothing malicious,
you understand, just doing what comes naturally – so
it didn't surprise me when Bev vaulted onto the parapet
and started taking off her clothes.

She turned to look at me, wearing just her knickers
and the red silk bra that I knew for a fact she'd nicked
from her sister Effra and was two sizes too small.

'Race you home,' she shouted and, turning, dove into
the river.

I gathered up her clothes and threw them onto the
passenger seat of the Asbo before setting off down
Barnes High Street at a swift but totally legal speed.
I considered using my blues and twos but that would
have been cheating. I'd have beaten her home, too, if
I hadn't been pulled over by a pair of uniforms on the

Kingston Road 'on suspicion' and had to flash my warrant card.

'What were you thinking?' I asked. 'Me in a Ford Focus – what was it? The colour?' I'd stopped using the Orange Asbo for covert work – for obvious reasons – so it had become my off-duty transport.

'To be honest,' said one of the uniforms, 'you just looked so bloody cheerful – it was suspicious.'

I stayed polite, although I did make a note of their collar numbers because you never know.

Driving while cheerful, I thought, that's a new one.

Still, it did mean Beverley was waiting for me in bed when I arrived.

4

Obligatory Audience Participation

The next morning it was my turn to slip out of bed leaving Beverley behind, invisible under the duvet except for a spray of dreadlocks across the pillow. I had a text from Stephanopoulos – *My office @ 7 briefing TST Albertina Pryce*.

The police are well aware of the subtle degrees of intimidation they can exert, from the veiled menace of the 'friendly chat' to turning up at dawn with a battering ram, a van full of TSG and a documentary TV camera crew. Being asked to show up at a nick first thing in the morning to 'clarify a previous statement' is a signal that the police have reason to believe that you are a lying little toerag, but are willing to give you a second chance to come clean. It's also a signal that a sensible body would bring a brief – just to be on the safe side.

So it says something about Albert Pryce, multiple Booker Prize shortlistee and a man whose appearances on Radio 4 were so frequent that Broadcasting House had given him his own entry pass, that he decided that he himself would be an elegant sufficiency with regards to legal representation for his daughter.

Stephanopoulos and Seawoll, ever alive to the nuances of interpersonal dynamics as they pertain to screwing evidence out of potential suspects, decided to send me in alone.

Normally when you're handling the rich and powerful you stick them in the ABE (Achieving Best Evidence) suite, which is fitted with pastel furniture and throw cushions designed to make vulnerable witnesses feel more comfortable. But either they were all in use or Stephanopoulos had actually read *A Filthy Trade* – Pryce's Booker shortlisted novel of crime and punishment. Which, according to the *Times Literary Supplement*, beautifully inverted Dostoyevsky's premise in its portrayal of a man who, having murdered his wife out of sheer exasperation, proves to have a higher degree of morality than the corrupt and degraded detectives who pursue him. By another completely unrelated coincidence we ended up in Interview Room Three which was usually reserved for Belgravia's more fragrant customers. I'm not saying you were going to slip on sick when you walked in, but there was a marked old-hospital smell of disinfectant and wee.

We left them in there for half an hour while we – me, Stephanopoulos and Seawoll – discussed interview strategy. 'Go in there and be your usual charming self,' said Stephanopoulos.

'We want the dad to stay nice and smug,' said Seawoll.

So I made a point of carrying in a stack of papers and faffing with them for a bit before introducing myself and shaking their hands.

I was beginning to think that there must be a factory somewhere stamping out dangerously skinny white girls with good deportment and a nervous disposition. Albertina Pryce had long blonde hair framing a narrow face with a pointed chin. She wore a pink sweat shirt that was too big for her and skinny blue jeans. Her handshake was limp and I could feel the small bones in her hand under my fingers.

Mr Pryce was surprisingly short, but broad-shouldered. He had the same fair hair as his daughter but with a square, blunt face. He wore a well-tailored suit jacket over a crisply ironed white shirt but no tie, and his top two buttons were undone to reveal a centimetre of greying chest hair. When he stood to shake my hand I saw he was wearing pre-faded jeans. His shake was firm but the skin of his hand was soft. I knew from my notes that he was sixty-three, but he looked as if he were desperately clinging to fifty with both hands.

'Grant, eh?' he said as we settled. 'Dad from the Caribbean, yes?'

He waited impatiently while I gave his daughter the caution plus two, and interrupted me before I had a chance to ask my first question.

'Can't we just get on with this?' he asked.

'I'm sorry sir. Legally we have to do these things,' I said.

Albertina glanced nervously at my pile of papers and then off to the left – away from her father – as he gave me a sympathetic nod.

'Bureaucracy,' he said sagely.

'Sir,' I said, because Stephanopoulos wanted me to encourage him but not too much.

'I know it's hard, Peter,' she'd said. 'But if you could

contain your erudition and ready wit for just a little while we'd be most grateful.'

'Am I allowed to be cheeky?' I'd asked.

'No you're fucking not,' said Seawoll.

'I'm afraid it has to be done, sir,' I said to Albert Pryce.

'Does it? Or do we just think it does?' he asked. 'Did you join the police to do paperwork? Of course you didn't.'

I made a show of straightening my papers and looked at Albertina, who was resolutely staring at the point on the table where her phone would have been if we hadn't asked her to leave it in her bag.

'Would you say you were Christina's best friend?' I asked.

'Maybe,' she said.

'Oh, come on,' said her father, 'you practically lived in each other's pockets.'

Albertina glared at him, but either long exposure had rendered him immune or, more likely I thought, it didn't even register. Seawoll had told me not to be cheeky, but there's cheeky and then there's *cheeky*.

'Did you see a lot of Christina Chorley, then, sir?' I asked him.

'Oh, very clever,' he said. 'Middle aged man, young girls, let's have a little dig, see what we can find? Is that it?'

'We're merely looking to establish a timeline,' I said.

'Interesting that you refer to the collective "we" there,' he said. 'Is that why you joined the police? To find an identity? You've got an old fashioned working class London accent, so I'm betting your mum was a native, south of the river, maybe Deptford, maybe from an old Southwark family.'

God help me, but I couldn't stop myself saying, 'Pretty much.'

'So there you were, growing up stuck somewhere between black and white,' said Mr Pryce. 'Never really one thing or the other. I mean . . . absent a father figure for you to build your black identity around and, being a proper working class bloke, not comfortable with your feminine side. I'll bet you didn't do well at school – right? Bit of a rebel, acting up.'

'I had my moments,' I said, thinking of the time me and Colin Sachlaw borrowed a lump of dry ice from the chemistry lab and slid it into the girl's toilets. I didn't mind the week of detention, but they called mum at work. And that didn't end well.

'So, hello police,' said Mr Pryce. 'A nice uniform identity, a little authority and, god knows, after Macpherson they'd be desperate enough to recruit you to overlook any educational deficiencies.'

That, as they say, is fighting talk. But, as Nightingale once told me during boxing practise, the best blow is the one your opponent doesn't even notice until he keels over.

'I don't blame you,' said Mr Pryce, not noticing his daughter's look of disgust. 'Scrabbling for some structure in the wreckage of the permissive society to make a meaningful connection with other people. But we don't do that anymore, do we? Listen to other people. The mighty Self has obliterated our ability to communicate.'

'Dad,' said Albertina.

'You're lucky, though,' he said. 'It could have been Islam, couldn't it? The siren song of the mad mullahs, or the rough fellowship of the gang. Did smiting the infidel not appeal? Did you have something against drugs?'

'Dad!' screamed Albertina. 'For god's sake shut the fuck-up.'

Her dad's mouth closed with a click and he looked guiltily at his daughter in a way that suggested to me that things like parent-teacher conferences and the like might have followed a similar pattern.

Albertina turned to me, controlled her breathing, and asked whether it was alright if she could choose her own responsible adult – thank you very much.

Her dad was a lot of things, but he wasn't stupid. So the next responsible adult was a suspiciously competent criminal solicitor whose parents might have been from the Kashmir but who spoke with a Bradford accent. He also slicked his thick black hair back with gel and, I suspected, wished he could wear his aviator sunglasses indoors. We got on famously.

Stephanopoulos took the opportunity to get a separate statement from Albert Pryce and sent in Guleed to do the honours. I wondered what she was going to make of the mad mullahs.

'I'm sorry about my dad,' Albertina said as soon as we sat down.

I'd fetched in some coffee for me, a bottle of iced tea for her and a plate of biscuits to add to the whole *we're just having a chat* vibe and Stephanopoulos gave me permission to take off my jacket and roll up my sleeves.

'Mine always talks about jazz,' I said.

'You have it easy,' she said and we both turned to the solicitor who gave a little shake of his head.

'Can I remind you that we're conducting an interview here,' he said.

'Come on,' said Albertina. 'You have a go, too. Then we can get all serious.'

'Politics,' said the solicitor finally. 'He goes on and on about the partition.'

Albertina asked what partition that was.

'The partition of India,' said the solicitor. 'Now can we get on?'

Albertina sighed and asked me what I wanted to know.

'When was the last time Christina stayed the weekend at your place?' I asked.

'Three weeks ago,' she said. I looked up the dates and confirmed them.

'And before that?'

Albertina had to think about it, but she thought it was probably three or four weeks before that.

'Do you know if she was telling her father that she was staying with you, but then staying with somebody else?' I asked.

'Definitely,' she said. 'I had to cover for her.'

'Do you know who Christina was staying with?'

'Some man,' she said with a definite emphasis on the word man – as opposed to a boy.

I asked if this man had a name.

'Raymond,' she said. 'No wait. Reynard – like he was French.'

'Did you ever meet him?'

She shook her head.

'So you never met him?' I asked this to avoid the whole *for the record Miss Pryce has shaken her head,* which can come back to bite you in court.

'I never met him,' she said.

'But you knew he was an adult?'

'It's not like Christina ever shut up about it,' said Albertina. 'Although, to give her her due, unlike Dad, she didn't feel the urge to write it all down and publish it for everyone to see.'

Albert Pryce's last book but one, *An Immovable Subject,* had been a semi-autobiographical account of how he'd left his second wife – Albertina's mother – after falling in love with an American intern half his age.

'You're sure his name is Reynard?'

'Oh, definitely,' she said.

'Was there anything unusual about him?'

'Like what?'

'Did anything Christina said about him strike you as unusual?'

'She said he was a prince,' said Albertina.

I asked whether Christina had said where Reynard was a prince of.

'Not that kind of prince,' said Albertina. 'Chris said he was a fairy tale prince.'

'Interesting,' I said, and asked if Albertina knew how Christina and her 'prince' had met. While I did that, I wrote the word NIGHTINGALE on my pad in large enough letters to be picked up by the camera and then I underlined it twice.

The word 'bollocks' is one of the most beautiful and flexible in the English language. It can be used to express emotional states ranging from ecstatic surprise to weary resignation in the face of inevitable disaster. And Seawoll was definitely veering towards the latter when we all sat down in his office to talk about Reynard Fossman.

'Bollocks,' said Seawoll.

'And he came to see you last night?' asked Stephanopoulos.

I read them in on my brief encounter with Reynard at the gig and his message to Nightingale.

'This can't be a coincidence,' said Stephanopoulos. 'Him turning up just as he becomes a person of interest.'

'Bollocks,' said Seawoll, allowing a tinge of melancholy to enter his tone. 'I was hoping to wrap MARIGOLD up – I've got a nice stabbing in Fulham which would be much better use of our Miriam's professional time.'

'Then I suggest that we apprehend him as swiftly as we can,' said Nightingale. 'So we can rule him in or out of your inquiry.'

Stephanopoulos glanced down at her tablet where I knew she had the latest IIP on Reynard Fossman. I also knew there were some things in there she didn't like, because she'd actioned Guleed to get the information and Guleed had glared at me until I'd handed over the file I'd already compiled on the red-headed little toerag.

'Fossman,' said Stephanopoulos, 'from the German *fuchs* for Fox, so Foxman,' she caught my eye. 'Reynard the Fox.'

'Nasty little sociopathic trickster who turns up a lot in fourteenth century French literature, sort of like Brer Rabbit but without the redeeming sense of humility,' I said.

Reynard Fossman had a string of convictions, the most serious of which was ABH for biting the ear of a member of the Old Berks Hunt during an anti fox-hunting demonstration, and a couple of assaults against similarly hunting-orientated gentlemen. Beyond that it was all trespass, public order offences – also hunting protest related – and an alleged indecent exposure when he was found running naked across Wimbledon Common which, according to Reynard, was a prank gone wrong. The arrest report was a fun read and the arresting officers had lent him some trousers and dropped him off at his house.

'So he's a French fairy tale,' said Seawoll and turned to look, thank god, at Nightingale instead of me. 'Is he?'

'That's a difficult question, Alexander,' said Nightingale.

'I know it's a difficult question, Thomas,' said Seawoll slowly. 'That why I'm fucking asking it.'

'Yes, but do you want to know the actual answer?' said Nightingale. 'You've always proved reluctant in the past. Am I to understand that you've changed your attitude?'

'You can fucking understand what you bloody like,' said Seawoll. 'But in this case I do bloody want to know because I don't want to lose any more officers to things

I don't fucking understand.' He glanced at me and frowned. 'Two is too many.'

'Well, he's definitely associated with the demimonde,' began Nightingale.

'The demi-monde?' asked Seawoll, who didn't appreciate being unhappy and liked to spread it around when he was.

'It's what we call all the people involved in some way or the other with weird bollocks,' I said, in an effort to head them both off. 'Some of them are just people that know things and others are people who are a bit strange in themselves.' Out loud it sounded even weaker than it had in my head. But Seawoll nodded.

'Individuals like Reynard are not uncommon,' said Nightingale. 'And it's hard to tell whether they have, consciously or unconsciously, sought to mimic a figure from folklore or myth, or whether they are indeed an incarnation of that figure.'

'And the difference being?' asked Seawoll.

'The first is relatively innocuous,' said Nightingale. 'But if Reynard is the story made flesh, then he's as dangerous an individual as you are likely to meet.'

'More dangerous than you?' asked Seawoll.

'Perhaps we shall find out,' said Nightingale.

Stephanopoulos heaved a sigh that they probably heard upstairs in the Outside Inquiry Office.

'Not that I'm not enjoying the spectacle, lads, but what if we drag this back down to the practicalities,' she said. 'Reynard had a message for you – one he was sure you'd be interested in.'

I checked my notes to make sure I got the phrasing

right – 'He said he could put us in touch "with a certain someone who has an item he might well like to purchase". I asked him what, and he said Jonathan Wild's final ledger.'

You can't be a London copper and have any interest in history and not know the story of Jonathan Wild – neither Stephanopoulos or Seawoll had to ask who Wild was. But, being police, they did want to know exactly why it would be of interest to the Folly.

'Aside from its obvious historical value, the ledger is thought to reveal the whereabouts of some of Sir Isaac Newton's lost papers,' said Nightingale. 'The ones that Keynes couldn't get hold of.'

'Are you telling me that Sir John Fucking Maynard Keynes was one of your lot?' said Seawoll.

'An associate,' said Nightingale. 'Not a practitioner.'

'And Isaac Newton is significant to the Folly why?' asked Stephanopoulos.

'Because he founded it,' said Nightingale.

Because, back in the go-ahead post-Renaissance pre-Enlightenment days of the seventeenth century there was no science or magic as such – it was all Natural Philosophy and people hadn't quite got round to deciding which was which. Back then chemists hadn't had that dangerously foreign 'al' removed and Sir Isaac Newton wanted all the answers to everything – how long the universe was going to last, the exact date of god's creation, how to make the Philosopher's Stone, and why do things that go up have to come back down again.

In those days the idea that large celestial bodies might influence the trajectory of other bodies without an actual material connection of some kind *was* the stuff of magic, not rationalist thought. Vast, invisible spheres of crystal – it was the only rational explanation. Next you'll be claiming diseases aren't caused by bad smells – a lavender nosegay, that's your friend.

Sir Isaac Newton legendarily wrote the famous *Philosophiæ Naturalis Principia Mathematica*, which gave us principles that a couple of hundred years later were good enough to land a man on the moon. Then he wrote the slightly less well known *Philosophiæ Naturalis Principia Artes Magicis*, which codified the magical techniques that allow me to inconvenience paper targets and Nightingale to demolish small agricultural buildings.

'There are suggestions that there might have been a *Third Principia*,' said Nightingale. 'This one dealing with alchemy.'

'Don't tell me,' said Seawoll. 'Lead into fucking gold?'

'He was Master of the Royal Mint when he wrote it,' said Nightingale. 'He might have considered that a viable way of revaluing the currency.'

'No wonder Keynes was a fan,' said Stephanopoulos.

'Quite,' said Nightingale. 'However, if Wild's ledger does exist, and if it does contain details of Newton's lost papers, then we have to acquire it.'

Seawoll narrowed his eyes.

'Why's that?' he asked.

'Because we are the rightful owners,' said Nightingale. 'And if it really does contain the secret of transmutation or, god forbid, of the philosopher's stone – then it has to be kept out of the wrong hands.'

'That's as may be,' said Seawoll. 'You want Wild's ledger. We need Reynard because he's a material witness. What you do with him afterwards is your business. Can we agree to that?'

'Absolutely,' said Nightingale.

'I don't suppose we have a current address for Mr Fossman?' said Seawoll.

I told him nothing more recent than five years old, and he nodded absently.

'In that case I suggest we set up a meet as soon as poss, and arrest the little fucker before this case gets any more fucking complicated,' he said.

The rule of thumb in this kind of negotiation is that the negotiator stays as junior as you can get – that way you have somewhere to escalate for extra leverage – so I made the call.

'Are you ready to do a deal?' asked Reynard.

'I'm ready to talk,' I said.

'Do you know the Montreux Jazz Café in Harrods?'

'Not really,' I said.

'Yeah, well, it's a café in Harrods,' said Reynard. 'Meet me there at ten tomorrow morning. Just you, nobody else.'

I agreed and he hung up before I could wangle anything else out of him.

We spent a happy couple of hours that afternoon working through the logistics of the meet, after which I might have managed to slope off to see Bev that evening if Nightingale hadn't reminded me that I owed him some practise and a translation of Pliny the Younger.

'I don't trust this situation,' said Nightingale. 'I want you to be sharp.'

Bollocks, I thought, or *testiculi* or possibly *testiculōs* if we were using the accusative.

Established in 1851, Harrods is the world's largest family owned corner shop. Although I suspect it's pretty unlikely that any of the Qatari Royal Family are doing a stint behind the counters. It covers twenty thousand square metres of some of the most expensive real estate in the world and, I couldn't help but notice, was less than three hundred meters down the Brompton Road from our crime scene at One Hyde Park. Even at ten o'clock in the morning it was going to be full of members of the public. Rich, influential members of the public, many of them foreign, a lot of them with some level of diplomatic immunity.

'What I'm saying here,' Seawoll had said, 'is try to limit the amount of damage you do to none fucking whatsoever.'

I don't know where I got this reputation for property damage, I really don't – it's totally unfair.

Harrods has ten public ways in and out, not counting staff and goods entrances – providing a potential fugitive with a wide selection of rapid getaways at an affordable price. Inside, it was a warren of showrooms, staircases and escalators, making it a good place to meet if you're up to no good, and in our estimation the only question was what kind of no good Reynard Fossman was up to.

I went in, as we had agreed in the planning, through the main entrance on Hans Crescent. The morning clientele was mostly well dressed white women with the occasional upmarket burka thrown in for variety.

Following the route we'd thrashed out the night before, I went straight up two sets of escalators – past zig-zag mirrors and wall-sized adverts for Dolce & Gabbana and Jimmy Choo's *Eau de Parfum* – and a couple of big rooms full of expensive furniture. Most of which was cheaper and nicer than the stuff in One Hyde Park, but still a bit out of my price range. I've worked in retail, and I've got to say that the Harrod's staff were all ridiculously attractive, well dressed and happy. Either the management were paying them way over the odds, or their HR department had been outsourced to Stepford, Connecticut.

A scary white waitress was waiting by the 'Please Wait Here To Be Seated' sign. Behind her was a blasphemously bad sculpture of Aretha Franklin that would have caused my father to have a word with the management.

I told her that I was meeting that guy over there and she waved me cheerfully past.

Inside were rough grey walls, interspersed with black and white tiles, stainless steel shelves and counters, with round PVC chairs at the tables. There were antique Revox reel-to-reel tape machines randomly placed on shelves. It really wasn't authentic enough to be a Disney theme park version of a jazz café.

A pair of wide screen TVs mounted on the walls were showing clips from the Montreux Jazz Festival. They were playing Mélissa Laveaux doing a live set, so they couldn't be all bad.

Reynard was the only customer, sitting at a six person table that gave him a view through the café to the corridor and gift wrap department opposite. He was wearing the same tweed jacket, only this time over a black T-shirt with MY SPIRIT ANIMAL IS A GOTH TEENAGER printed in white on the front. I couldn't see a bag on the table or by his chair, but then we'd all thought it unlikely he'd bring the ledger with him.

He stood when he saw me and waved at a seat opposite. This left me, I noticed as I sat down, with my back to the entrance.

'Where's the Nightingale?' he asked.

'He's working,' I said. 'Have you got the ledger with you?'

'Now, that would be foolish of me, wouldn't it?'

The waitress asked if I wanted to order anything.

'Black Americano,' I said and looked at Reynard. 'You?'

'I'm good,' he said and watched the waitress' bum all the way back to the counter. 'A bit mature for my taste,' he said.

'We get it,' I said. 'You're a class act.'

'I am what I am,' he said.

'How much do you want?'

Reynard raised an eyebrow.

'That's your opening position?' he asked. 'Hardly a sound negotiating tactic.'

'This isn't a negotiation,' I said. 'I'm not a private individual or some covert spy or something. I'm police and you're in possession of stolen material of consider-able value which we want to return to its rightful owners – that being us.'

'You have no evidence that it's stolen,' said Reynard.

'No. But then you are what you are,' I said. 'Aren't you? At the moment, you see, it would be more effort to arrest you, statement the information out of you, seize the ledger and then throw you in prison.'

'Arrest me for what?'

'There's bound to be something,' I said. 'You and Christina were not being particularly law abiding, that's for certain.'

But Reynard had started at Christina's name and I really don't think he heard the rest of the sentence at all.

'That had nothing to do with me,' he said.

'Oh, yeah,' I said, and I was just about to say some-thing clever when a white woman sat down next to Reynard. She was dressed in a pastel yellow blazer over a white blouse and black leggings. Her face was very familiar.

'Hey Peter,' said Lesley May. 'What's up?'

Reynard had gone as pale as semi-skimmed milk – I swear his hands started shaking.

It was her old face, from before the Royal Opera House and Mr Punch.

'So,' she said. 'You wearing a wire or not?

'Hello, Lesley,' I said – slightly louder than I meant to.

'Well, that answers that question,' she said. 'I'll bet you're surprised to see me.'

Twenty seconds, I reckoned, that's all I needed.

'What do you think?' I asked.

Lesley smiled and I saw the skin of her face was smooth and clear, like that of a child.

'Got my face fixed,' she said.

'So I see.'

Ten seconds.

'You didn't think it was possible,' she said.

'Obviously I was wrong,' I said.

'So the question is,' said Lesley, 'did Nightingale lie to you, or is he just ignorant?'

'This is nothing to do with me,' said Reynard and started to stand.

Lesley balled her fist and I felt the little flicker that warns you that a practitioner is summoning up a *forma*. If you want to do the counter spell, then you have to guess the *forma* and then cast faster. This is what Nightingale calls the *lutte sans merci* and surviving one requires sensitivity, foresight and lightning fast reflexes.

Or you can lean back in your chair, brace yourself against the wall, get both feet up against the table and shove with all your strength. The edge caught Lesley in the stomach and Reynard across the thighs. Lesley went with the blow – I saw her allow herself to be pushed backwards, finishing her spell as she tipped over. Not an easy thing to do, I can tell you. Reynard screamed with pain and then did a neat little standing jump that left him crouched on the table.

On the sound principle that whatever Lesley had cast I didn't want to be in front of it, I threw myself diagonally across the table top and while I slid down it I conjured a couple of delayed action fireballs that I call, much to Nightingale's annoyance, skinny grenades and lobbed them in the Lesley's general direction. John Woo would have been proud.

I made a half-hearted grab for Reynard but he sort of bounded off the table, through the slot in the wall, and out into the corridor. I let him go – Lesley was my priority now. But before I could roll off the other side, the bloody table lurched and shot straight upwards. I flattened myself as the ceiling came rushing towards me, but there was a bright flash, like a professional standard flash gun, and the table lurched to the left and tipped me off.

I hit something with my shoulder – I think it was Aretha – and smacked face first onto the floor tiles. What with one thing and another, I didn't think having a rest was a good idea, so I rolled in a random direction and scrambled to my feet. Just in time to see Lesley vault through the slot in the wall and tear after Reynard who was vanishing up a cross corridor marked HAR-RODS' TECHNOLOGY. I went after them, but I had my shield up because I really didn't think this was going to have a happy ending.

It might have been a Wednesday morning, but there were enough punters around to give a working copper conniptions. There are rules about putting the public in danger during a chase – the principle one of which is *don't* put members of the public at risk.

'Police,' I shouted as a member of the public bounced off my shield. 'Everybody out.'

Which had the effect of making some people stop,

some people reach for their phones, and the rest to carry on shopping regardless.

I shouted again – which at least cleared enough of a hole for me to spot Lesley turning left into the next room. I followed and felt my shield ripple as I veered past a triple-screened games console with built-in racing car controls. There was a smell of burning plastic and I hoped it hadn't been me.

Just ahead Lesley and Reynard were in a three-way struggle with a solidly built white man in a beige raincoat. He had an army surplus crew cut and narrow little eyes. He didn't look like store security and I felt a flash of irritation because have-a-go heroes are all very well until they get themselves killed, and then guess who's left explaining themselves to the subsequent inquiry.

At least this room was narrow, with Spyware counters on the right and Vodafone on the left – small enough that all the potential collateral had had the good sense to clear out.

I was less than two metres from the struggle when something hit me in the back and knocked me forward on my face. There was a sudden smell of candle wax and hyacinth and a rope of crimson smoke shot overhead and smacked Crew Cut in the face. As he reeled backwards, the smoke fluttered like silk in the wind before slapping Lesley in the chest hard enough to knock her backwards over a counter top. I winced as I heard glass break under her back and saw fashionably black spy gear scatter behind her.

Despite the blow Crew Cut hadn't let go of Reynard and he quickly regained his balance, tightened his grip on the young man and started dragging him away.

I tried to scramble to my feet, but another blow on my back put me down. A second crimson rope rippled overhead like a vintage special effect from the 1980's.

'Is Nightingale doing that?' yelled Lesley from somewhere to my right.

Hyacinth and candle-wax? I thought, not likely.

Nightingale should have arrived by now, though, and I suspected the delay was something to do with whoever was flinging ropes of magic smoke around. Still, I doubted he was going to be long.

'Stay down,' I shouted.

'You first,' she shouted back.

I rolled left through a gap in the Vodafone counter to see if I could avoid another smackdown and found myself face to face with a very well dressed but terrified Asian guy. I motioned frantically for him to stay down and he nodded.

The counter I was behind had a transparent top which gave me a chance to see out without getting my damn fool head blown off. The rope of crimson smoke had wrapped itself around Reynard's neck and was dragging him back-up the aisle despite Crew Cut's best efforts to pull him the other way. Even as I looked back to see if I could spot where the rope was coming from, a pulse of light raced up its length in a blaze of petrol bomb yellow, vaporising the crimson smoke as it went. It roared past me and then, as it reached Crew Cut and the struggling Reynard, the pulse slowed and dissipated the last of the smoke with a gentle pop, leaving the pair temporarily frozen – and staring in amazement.

Now, that was Nightingale.

Reynard recovered first, and with a snarl buried his teeth in Crew Cut's neck. The man screamed and beat at Reynard's head with his fists. Lesley hadn't emerged from hiding yet. And she was still my priority, so stalemate suited me. Every second of status quo meant more members of the public evacuated, a tighter containment perimeter, and more chance that Nightingale was going to arrive to back me up. And if Reynard got a bit of a smacking in the meantime, I could live with that.

Unfortunately, this plan went to shit when Crew Cut fumbled inside his jacket, pulled out a compact semi-automatic pistol and bashed Reynard on the head with it.

From a policing point of view, guns are a pain. Once someone is known to be tooled up, your operational priorities are suddenly fucked up. It all becomes about managing whoever was stupid enough to pull a gun in central London and your number one priority is public safety, followed closely by officer safety and then, not so closely, by the safety of the moron with the gun. Any other operational considerations, such as arresting former colleagues, don't enter into it.

'Gun!' I shouted as loud as I could.

Crew Cut whirled to point his gun in my direction in a professional, albeit one handed, firing stance. I crouched down and threw up my shield – but he didn't fire. While he was aiming at me, Lesley launched herself out of her hiding place at him.

He was fast. Before Lesley was half-way to him he'd turned and fired – a flat loud popping sound – and then again and again. There was ripple in the air in front of Lesley's chest and something small and fast whistled over my head.

He didn't get in a fourth shot because Lesley swung at his wrist with what I recognised as a police issue extendable baton. There was a crack and the pistol fell out of his hand. He gasped at the pain and Lesley followed up with a sharp blow to the head then a third to his face – another crunch and a spray of blood from his mouth.

I used *impello* to flick the gun as far up the room as I could, and then I jumped up and yelled, 'Armed police, stop fighting and drop your weapons.'

All three of them stopped and turned to look at me – and for a moment I thought they might actually comply, if only out of sheer incredulity. But then Reynard gave Crew Cut a swift knee in the bollocks, wriggled free and legged it.

Traditionally, the weapon of choice for a classically trained wizard is the fireball – I'm not kidding. And in some respects, from a policing point of view, it's not a bad weapon. Being by definition a soft and low velocity projectile, you can loose them off in the knowledge that it's not going to blast through your target, the wall behind them and the bus queue of blameless OAPs behind that. However, this means that – unless you're Nightingale – the bloody things can be stopped by modern ballistic armour, my metvest and, in some cases, a thick woolly jumper. At the same time, they remain potentially lethal, which means you've got to be careful who you lob them at.

So I water bombed Lesley instead.

It's a harder spell, third order, based on two *formae* – *aqua*, *impello* – and a couple of extras we call *adjectivium* which modify the way other *formae* work. The result generates a ball of water the size of a party balloon which, when properly applied to a suspect's face, often causes them to cease and desist in their activities – whatever these might be. Fireballs are much simpler and easier to cast under pressure, but I'd been practising the water spell by playing dodgeball with one of Beverley's younger sisters and, trust me, if you do that with a hyperactive nine year old river goddess then you pick up the skills fast.

Nightingale says that one of the prefects at his old school claimed there was a variation that created a ball of gin, but try as they might nobody ever found the spell or worked out how to recreate it.

'And, as you can imagine,' Nightingale told me, 'a great deal of effort was expended in that direction by the sixth form.'

Water was fine for my purposes, and I'm sure Lesley appreciated the elegance of my approach when it smacked her in the face. She went down swearing and I ran forward, flicking out my baton as I closed the distance.

I didn't make it because, when I was almost there, Lesley threw Crew Cut at me. It was *impello*, of course, but that didn't make 140 kilos of bad suit any less painful when it sails through the air and hits you in the chest – especially when you also have a duty of care and have to catch the bastard. So, while I was putting Crew Cut in the recovery position, Lesley went haring after Reynard.

Not far away I heard shouting and the sound of things breaking and, because I'm police, that's the direction I ran in.

Guleed met me in the next room, running in with David Carey and a bunch of uniforms. He peeled off to deal with a member of the public who'd obviously been knocked down.

Guleed pointed to a ramp.

'That way,' she shouted.

'Unconscious suspect on the floor back there,' I said to one of the uniforms. 'White male, cheap suit. Non-life-threatening injuries. Had a firearm but now disarmed, check for other weapons, hold him for assault and check welfare.' I told him he needed to find and secure the firearm so an AFO could bag it. He nodded and sensibly grabbed a mate before heading back the way I'd come.

Me and Guleed advanced cautiously up the ramp – there was a short corridor at the top with entrances to the public toilets.

'They didn't stop,' said Guleed.

'Where's Nightingale?' I asked.

'Back at the café,' she said. 'Dealing with something Falcon.'

Presumably whoever had been throwing the crimson smoke around.

We navigated the corridor and looked out onto a long, wide room filled with flat screen televisions lined up like the suspiciously convenient cover in a third person shooter. It was empty of staff and customers and Guleed said that Stephanopoulos had moved her troops in from the other side as soon it all went pear-shaped.

'We should have a security perimeter,' said Guleed, which meant that Reynard and Lesley were somewhere in there amongst the Panasonics and Toshibas.

'Was that really Lesley?' asked Guleed.

'Large as life,' I said. 'And twice as beautiful.'

'How is that possible?'

'You grab Reynard,' I said. 'I'll grab Lesley and then we can ask her.'

Which is what we in the business call an operational plan.

'Okay,' said Guleed. 'Slow and quiet, or fast and loud?'

'Loud,' I said.

So we marched out amongst the televisions bold as brass, although both of us had our batons resting on our shoulders and left arms extended in the recommended manner. Around us the big LCDs showed Jeremy Kyle getting self-righteous with Sharon and Darren, although a couple near the end of a row were showing *Alpha and Omega 2*. I couldn't tell which was worse.

'Lesley,' I shouted. 'You know how this works, you know you've lost your opportunity to escape, so you might as well put the fox down and show yourself.'

Guleed snorted quietly.

'Come on, Lesley – do us a favour.'

A couple of uniforms appeared in the archway opposite, but Guleed signalled them to stay put. Others took up positions at the remaining exits. Near the centre of the room where the aisles from one exit to another formed a crossroad was an old fashioned jukebox, which I noticed wasn't turned on. As we approached the centre, me and Guleed let the distance between us widen. I swear I could almost hear Lesley breathing.

In the corner to my left I noticed that one of the TVs was off. So was its power indicator and that of the Blu-ray player below it.

'Hey, Peter,' called Lesley from behind the TV. 'Heads up.'

Something small, flat and metallic flew through the air to land where I'd have been standing if I hadn't immediately jumped backwards. It was an iPhone, and from its screen came a little wisp of blue flame. I opened my mouth to shout 'Get back!' But of course by then it was too late.

The phone exploded in a most peculiar way.

I actually saw the pressure wave, a hemisphere of distorted air that expanded out in a lazy, unstoppable fashion. And, as it did, everything with a microprocessor blew out. And then the wave reached me and knocked me on my back.

There was a sensation like static electricity and the smell of ozone and the taste of lemons.

Fuck me, I thought, she's weaponised her iPhone.

And then the lights went out.

5

Mother's Little Helper

When we briefed Seawoll later all he said was 'That could have gone better.' Which, as portents of disaster go, is pretty fucking portentous.

The blast didn't knock me out. I've been unconscious before and this was different. It did knock out every light in a thirty metre radius, plus the CCTV and everyone's Airwave. Not to mention a couple of million quids' worth of top of the line consumer electronics.

Seriously, I thought, we couldn't have met in a Greggs? I really hoped that Harrods' insurance covered them for Acts of Lesley.

What CCTV we had left showed Reynard making his escape down the central stairwell and out through the Food Hall. There was no sign of Lesley and, although Stephanopoulos shut down the store for a thorough search, nobody had any doubt that she was long gone. *How* was another question.

Crew Cut had escaped as well, but we did recover his pistol which turned out to be a suspiciously clean Glock 17 with the serial numbers erased and no matches in our or Interpol's databases. Seawoll thought it stank of spook, but nobody was in a hurry to get CTC involved – we figured they'd be along soon enough.

It wasn't a total loss, because back at what was left of the Montreux Jazz Café Nightingale had a strangely familiar suspect in custody.

'Did you use the proper caution?' I asked.

'I believe so,' said Nightingale.

Lesley May's name hung between us but we had other things to deal with first.

Even though she was sitting down on a plastic chair salvaged from the café, the suspect was still obviously very tall – taller than me, in fact. She was dressed in an expensive black wool suit jacket – a Stella McCartney, we learned when Guleed surreptitiously checked the label later – a white male dress shirt and pre-faded skinny jeans. She'd dropped her chin down to her chest as I approached and let her long straight weave fall over her face but it was too late – I'd recognised her.

'Hello,' I said. 'Obviously the cleaning gigs are paying well.'

Guleed asked if I knew her.

One thing you acquire as police is a good memory for names and faces, not only because of the long parade of villains you encounter but also because most of them are repeat offenders. It's considered bad form not to know someone's name when you're arresting them for the fourth time. I'd met this one while raiding a County Gard office near Liverpool Street the year before. Just before I was distracted by the whole being on the roof of a tower block when it was demolished thing.

'She gave her name as Awa Shambir,' I said.

'I seriously doubt that,' said Guleed and then spoke

to the woman in a language I assumed was Somali or a dialect thereof.

The woman kept her face down but I could tell she was smiling.

'You couldn't repeat that, but a smidge slower,' she said. 'I'm a little rusty.'

'Not Somali,' said Guleed. 'Ethiopian maybe.'

Pure Home Counties, I thought, with a side order of posh school. Not the accent she'd used to talk to me when we last met.

'What's your real name?' I asked, but the woman kept her head down and refused to speak. Nightingale and I left her with Guleed and retreated into the café for a quick bit of post incident assessment.

'There are undoubtedly going to be consequences,' he said. Which was Nightingale for: Look out, here comes the shit avalanche. 'We need to make good use of our available time.'

We decided that I would stay with our mysterious not-Somali and bang her up in one of the special cells back at Belgravia.

'Be careful,' said Nightingale. 'I didn't recognise the *formae* per se, but her technique was very clean – I'd say she's been training for a long time.'

I asked how long.

'Difficult to say,' he said. 'But since she was a child for certain. Stay behind her and keep your hand on the cuffs.' During the war, the Folly had developed techniques for dealing with captured practitioners – Nightingale had dusted off an old manual, I kid you not, complete with cheap khaki cardboard covers and line drawings. Basically it amounted to keep an eye on them and don't let them get anything started.

'I don't think she's going to be very co-operative,' I said.

'You don't get that well trained without a master,' said Nightingale. 'Let's keep her under lock and key and see who comes to fetch her.'

So while Nightingale and Stephanopoulos stayed to face the music, me and Guleed took our prisoner and legged it back to Belgravia to see whether a Sith lord turned up to bail her out.

The custody sergeant gave us a strange look when we booked her in.

'How many more of these posh young ladies are you planning to bring in?' she asked. 'Or are we going to have start sending out to Fortnum and Masons for refs?'

'This one has to go in a Falcon cell,' I said, which wiped the smile off her face.

The same wartime manual with the prisoner management rules also contained instructions for creating cells for magical POWs. Nightingale decided that it would be an interesting way to combine training and necessity if we were to enchant the 'wards' together. These proved to be strips of iron inlaid with a crude copper filigree in loops and whirls. You enchant them as you beat them into shape – it's very therapeutic and good for your upper body strength. We selected two cells in Belgravia's custody suite and fused the strips across the front of the doors and then painted them over with institutional blue paint. Nightingale did the fusing and I did the painting.

I then spent a fun afternoon locked in one of the cells trying to magic my way out – followed by an unpleasant evening when I realised that I'd been abandoned by Nightingale, who'd put the fix in with the custody sergeant. I had just resigned myself to a night in the cells and was wondering what time refs were up when Guleed took pity on me and let me out.

When the custody sergeant asked for a name I expected our suspect to refuse but to my surprise she gave the sergeant a cheerful smile and said – 'Lady Caroline Elizabeth Louise Linden-Limmer'. She turned that smile on me and Guleed. 'Mum's a viscountess.'

'Very nice,' said the custody sergeant. 'And mine's a Jaffa Cake.'

Thirty seconds looking for Caroline's mother on Google led to the Lady Helena Louise Linden-Limmer, or rather to a famous picture of her wearing nothing but a leopard skin fur coat taken by David Bailey in 1964. After that in the listing came her autobiography, *Growing up Wild: A Childhood in Africa*, and a scanned article from the Observer Colour Supplement circa 1988 about her menagerie – as she called it – of adopted and fostered kids. There had been six at that point. All girls. I looked at the photographs. Two were black, one was brown, one was possibly Chinese or South East Asian. Of the white girls one had cerebral palsy and other had been a victim of thalidomide. According to the article, Lady Linden-Limmer had run a health clinic in Goa and then in Calcutta, and had worked with people suffering from leprosy.

You can't just return home and stop caring, she told the interviewer.

One of the black girls in the photographs was about four, wearing a grubby blue smock and a sly expression that was an echo of the woman we had in the cells – Caroline, I presumed.

I attached the article to Caroline's HOLMES nominal and was about to request an IIP on her mother when Guleed kicked me under the desk and jerked her head in the direction of the door. Just coming in was a tall white DI from the Department of Professional Standards called William Pollock – SIO for Operation Carthorse, the hunt for Lesley May. He saw me, made sure he'd caught my eye and beckoned me over. I gave Guleed a cheery wave and off I went. Guleed, who knew she was going to be next, sighed and turned back to her work.

In the initial months following Lesley's defection to the dark side I was treated with a certain amount of suspicion. Yes, she had tasered me in the back of the neck just as I was about to arrest the Faceless Man. But they only had my word for it that things had gone down the way they had, and the ABC of policing literally goes: Assume nothing, Believe no-one, Check everything. Still, about a year of continuous suspicion had convinced DI Pollock that it was just possible I wasn't as bent as a threepenny bit and so instead of an 'interview' in an interview room, I got what's known as a hot briefing in a meeting room. I'd know my rehabilitation was complete when DI Pollock had me in the local for a chat over a pint.

He asked me whether we'd had any prior intelligence that Lesley might turn up at the meeting or even that FAM ONE, which was how Operation Carthorse referred to the Faceless Man, had an interest in Reynard Fossman.

I told him that had we had any fucking inkling whatsoever we probably would have revised our operational plan for the meeting.

'In what way?' asked DI Pollock.

'We would have held it in a more secure location,' I said.

'Why didn't you?' asked DI Pollock.

'Our assessment was that any potential additional security provided by a new venue was outweighed by the risk that Fossman wouldn't show,' I said. 'In which case we would have had to mount a resource intensive search for him – particularly since he'd become a person of interest to Operation Marigold.'

'And you received no intelligence, no intelligence at all, that Fossman was connected to Lesley May or FAM ONE?' asked Pollock.

'None whatsoever,' I said.

'And you're certain Lesley May wasn't there because of you?' he asked.

'Sir?'

'Perhaps she was there to see you,' he said. 'Have you considered that?'

'She went after Reynard at every opportunity,' I said. 'She was there for him.'

'And you yourself have had no contact with Lesley May since Herefordshire,' said DI Pollock.

'No,' I said.

'Were you aware of any links between Reynard Fossman and Lesley May?'

Round and round and round we go and where we stop nobody knows.

He was particularly interested in my identification of Lesley – was I sure about her face or was I unconsciously picking up cues from her voice or body language.

'It was definitely her face,' I said. But smoother, paler, unblemished and disturbingly like the skin of the Faerie Queen – when she was on this side of the border.

Because I'd graduated to 'briefings' rather than 'interviews', DI Pollock actually fed some information my way – almost as if we were colleagues.

'We can't find evidence of her entering or leaving the store,' said Pollock. 'Security there is tight and the CCTV coverage is extensive, it covers all points of entry both public and staff – we've done a preliminary check and she's not there.'

Pollock wanted to know whether someone could magic themselves invisible or teleport themselves from one place another. He even asked if there were 'roads through other realms' that a practitioner could walk, the better to pass unseen. Which shocked me because I didn't have DI Pollock pegged as a romantic. I swear he was going to ask about hyperspace next, but I made it clear that as far as I knew practitioners couldn't teleport or walk faerie roads. As for invisible, I thought of the unicorns I'd met in Herefordshire. Still, I didn't think it was feasible, at least not without shutting down the CCTV cameras as a side effect.

I asked if I could review the footage myself and he said he'd see what he could do.

'How did it make you feel?' asked DI Pollock.

'How did what make me feel, sir?'

'Seeing Lesley again?'

Shock and anger and betrayal and vain hope that she'd changed her mind and anger at myself for having that hope.

'I was surprised, sir,' I said. 'I thought she'd know better.'

They let me out midafternoon and I was hoping for a fry-up, but Nightingale and Stephanopoulos intercepted me and guided me into the ABE suite where Lady Helena Linden-Limmer had been stashed.

'Guleed will interview the daughter and you can use your charms on the mother,' said Stephanopoulos.

I looked to Nightingale, who just nodded in agreement.

I did manage to grab an emergency sandwich, which I stuffed down during my truncated pre-interview strategy meeting with Guleed, Stephanopoulos and Nightingale. Basically our plan was to see how both of them reacted to an initial set of questions, then stop for a break and then base further sessions on their responses. These were also going to be what Stephanopoulos called 'Falcon interviews' – ones where we would decide after the fact if they officially took place or not.

Guleed passed me the completed IIP on Caroline Linden-Limmer and pointed out a note which registered that she'd been granted a Gender Recognition

Certificate when she was eighteen – changing her legal gender from male to female.

'So . . .' I started, but was cut off by the vast silence emanating from Stephanopoulos behind us.

I looked over at Nightingale, who looked quizzically back, and decided to explain the implications later. Surprisingly, when I did, his reaction was outrage that somebody had to apply to a panel to determine what gender they were – he didn't say it, but I got the strong impression that he felt such panels were intrinsically un-British. Like eugenics legislation, banning the burka and air conditioning.

I thought of the little girl in the blue dress – you can't get a certificate until you're 18 – it must have felt like a long wait.

Her mother, when I met her, didn't strike me as someone who liked to wait.

In the black and white world of the David Bailey photographs, Lady Helena seemed taller than she was in real life. In the photos she'd had a pixie bob haircut that had emphasised the smooth oval of her face, and her large eyes with their drag queen lashes. Now her face was in colour, with the wrinkly brown chamois leather complexion that white people get if they spend their lives under a hot sun. The bob was longer, shaggier and streaked with grey.

'You've seen my glamour pics haven't you?' she said before I could introduce myself. 'I can always tell.'

She stood up to greet me and held out a hand. It was slender but her palms were rough and her grip was strong.

She sighed. 'What a difference a lifetime makes, eh?'

We sank down onto the chairs which, this being the ABE suite, were low-slung 1970's wooden frame things with square foam cushions zipped into hard wearing pastel covers. Very useful if you have to crash some-where over night – although you generally have to beat the CID nightshift to them first.

'Where's my daughter?' she asked as soon as I'd fin-ished the caution plus two.

I explained that Caroline was along the corridor being interviewed about her role in this morning's Harrods incident. I prefixed it with the word 'serious', which usually gets a reaction, but Helena seemed a bit too san-guine for my taste. Generally when you're interviewing somebody and they seem remarkably calm about one crime, it's because they're relieved you haven't found out about something else. You hope this is going to turn out to be some major case-breaking bit of information but, people being people, it's often the most mundane shit – affairs, porn stashes, secret second families, that sort of thing.

'What is she supposed to be responsible for?'

'Assault,' I said, 'assault on a police officer, criminal damage, obstruction, assisting an offender and wasting police time.'

Lady Helena gave me a long look.

'Assault?' she asked. 'Did she physically assault someone?'

You see, even the clever ones can't resist being clever and the next move, if you want them to stay being clever, is to play dumb.

'In a manner of speaking,' I said.

Lady Helena leaned forward and looked me in the eye.

'Did my daughter at any point physically strike another human being?'

Which answered my and Nightingale's first question – did the mother know about the magic?

'Assault doesn't actually require physical contact,' I said.

'So how exactly did my daughter assault a policeman?' she asked. 'Was it you, by the way?'

'Your daughter gave your house in Montgomeryshire as her home address,' I said. 'Does she still live with you?'

Lady Helena settled back in her chair. 'That's children these days,' she said. 'They don't ever seem to want to fly the nest. I blame the parents.'

'How about the rest of your kids?'

'Why do you want to know?' she asked.

The other five members of the 'menagerie' had all shown different addresses on the DVLA.

'They all moved out, didn't they?'

'I raised them to be independent.'

'But not Caroline?'

'Caroline is joining the family business,' she said.

'And what is the family business?' I asked.

'Helping people,' she said. 'We run a retreat for those who need to rebalance their lives.'

'Rebalance in what way?' I asked.

She tilted her head and narrowed her eyes before answering.

'Mind, body and spirit,' said Lady Helena. 'For a person to be healthy each must be in balance with itself and with the others. We help people restore those balances.'

'And how do you do that?'

'Mostly by providing them with a bit of peace and quiet,' she said and then shrugged. 'And charging them vast sums of money – the money is an important part of the process. People don't appreciate things they don't pay for.'

I asked whether Christina Chorley had ever attended her clinic, but she said she didn't recognise the name. I ran through the names of the attendees at the ill-fated party and threw Reynard's name casually in the middle. She denied knowing any of them but there was definitely a response at Reynard's name – a twitch of her eyes to the side.

My phone buzzed against my leg.

'Okay,' I said. 'I'm just going to get myself a cup of coffee. Would you like one? Anything else?'

'Would you recommend the coffee?' asked Lady Helena.

'Only as a last resort.'

She declined and I popped out into the corridor where Nightingale met me with a cup of coffee. Guleed and Stephanopoulos hurried to join us.

I sipped the coffee – I hadn't been kidding, it was terrible.

Guleed hadn't been making much headway with Caroline – she claimed she'd been out shopping and had been minding her own business when Nightingale had physically overpowered her and falsely arrested her. She also denied ever meeting me and Lesley on the premises of County Gard the year before. Her lawyer was asking to see evidence that her client had been involved and if none was forthcoming etc., etc. Since the lawyer was working for the mother it was decided that Guleed would keep plugging away to keep daughter and brief pinned in place while I took a more robust approach with Lady Helena.

'Meaning what?' I asked.

'Meaning, Peter,' said Stephanopoulos, 'that we want you to go in there and put your foot in it.'

As Guleed said – it's always good to be playing to your strengths.

So back I went and sat down across from Lady Helena and said, 'Okay, tell me – how long have you been practising magic?'

Judging from her long hesitation before answering, Lady Helena hadn't been expecting that question. Which told me quite a lot. One thing being that she didn't know who I was. In fact, she might not even know about the Folly – which meant that she wasn't connected to the demi-monde, who definitely knew who we were.

Or she'd just remembered that she'd left the gas on.

'When you say magic,' she asked, 'you mean what, exactly?'

'The creation of physical effects through the casting of spells,' I said.

'My god, you're serious,' she said.

I have a nice low powered *werelight* that I can conjure in an interview room without blowing all the surveillance – you'd be amazed how often I have to use it. My latest refinement was to add a *scindere* forma so that I can park it over my shoulder and use it as a reading light.

When I started my apprenticeship it took me the better part of two months to learn how to cast a simple *werelight* – now I barely have to think about it. If you're an experienced practitioner you can sense another practitioner in the initial stages of spell casting. The more experienced you are the more sensitive and the quicker your reaction.

Lady Helena reacted before I'd finished the metaphorical first syllable and, by the time my *werelight* hung over the coffee table between us, she knew that I knew and that she was well and truly busted.

'So, it's true then,' she said. 'The magical gestapo is alive and well.'

You go ahead and liken Nightingale to the gestapo, I thought, and see what that gets you.

'I take it you're a practitioner yourself,' I said.

'A practitioner,' she said. 'Is that what you're calling yourself?'

I said it was the official term.

'My,' she said. 'What an ugly term. I suppose I should have expected the establishment to try and suck all the joy out of magic. God knows they try so hard with everything else.'

'What do you call yourself?' I asked.

'Oh, I'm a witch, darling,' she said. 'Or a sorceress – depends on my mood.'

'And who trained you?'

Lady Helena smiled.

'Who do you think trained me?' she said. 'My mother, of course. As her mother trained her and hers before her. It all goes back to Queen Caroline, you know.'

Back to the court of Caroline of Ansbach, who was famously brighter than her husband – the future George II. Caroline, who kept company with Walpole and Leibnitz and did medical experiments on condemned prisoners and orphaned children.

'Early form of vaccination, darling,' said Helena. 'And they all lived happily ever after.'

She also had Phillip Boucherett, former protégé of the great Isaac Newton, as a regular guest at court. There he was happy to impart what Nightingale is pleased to call 'the forms and wisdoms' of magic to others in her circle – male and female.

'Of course,' said Helena, 'in those days your lot were hardly what you'd call a reputable bunch.'

According to Lady Helena, the Folly at that time had been reduced to a bunch of quacks, grifters and near charlatans meeting at a floating coffee house moored outside Somerset House. The true intellectual heirs of *The Second Principia* grew out of Caroline's salons and later those of Elizabeth Montague and her fellow bluestockings.

They called themselves *La Société de la Rose* – The Society of the Rose.

'Why was that?' I asked.

'I have no idea,' said Lady Helena.

But this alliance of posh women and pushy middle class entrepreneurs wasn't going to last. By the end of the century the need for an organised response to all things magical had become obvious to the state – even one as cheerfully laissez-faire and corrupt as the British.

The Scottish led the way, with many from the famed Edinburgh Club arriving in London. And, by the 1760's, they were calling themselves practitioners, greasing up their patrons and hoovering up the cash.

'As soon as they got a whiff of respectability they couldn't dump the women fast enough,' said Lady Helena. Being a female practitioner became as disreputable as being a female . . . well, anything not connected with maintaining a household. The men moved into their brand new club house on Russell Square and slammed the door in the face of the women following behind.

Actually, I had noticed that the Folly's lecture hall had a separate 'Ladies Gallery' which you reach via a back passage off the east staircase. Presumably it was there so proud mothers, sisters and wives could watch their menfolk demonstrate particularly clever new *formae* or spells. There was a discreet brass plaque and everything.

I decided not to mention this.

'Women carried on "practising",' said Lady Helena, 'just as they carried on composing, painting and all the other professions from which history has erased them. Mother taught daughter, who passed on the skills through the generations – just as women have always had to do. My mother petitioned the War Office to be allowed to serve. Do you know what they said?'

I admitted that I did not.

'Nothing,' said Lady Helena. 'Not even a polite "piss

off." It's no wonder she buggered off to Kenya, a new country with new possibilities.'

'Did she practise in Kenya?' I asked.

'No,' said Lady Helena, 'Mum was so good at that point that she didn't have to practise.'

'And you?'

'I was mother's little helper,' said Lady Helena. 'We used to find wounded animals and nurse them back to health.'

'Using magic,' I asked, trying to be casual.

'That would be telling,' said Lady Helena. 'Although if you really want to know, I'm sure we can come to some sort of arrangement.'

She'd been working towards this, I realised, dangling her information in front of us in the hope that we'd bite. I was willing to bet cash money that she had known all about the Isaacs and the Folly and probably about Nightingale before she so much as set foot in Belgravia nick. We'd been outplayed. But that's the beauty of being the police – you get to cheat.

'First you're going to tell me what your interest in Reynard Fossman is,' I said. 'Then I might go to talk my governor about how we're going to sort this out.'

Lady Helena made an airy gesture.

'He offered to sell us something,' she said. 'An antiquity.'

'What kind of antiquity?' I asked. 'A family heirloom, a genuine Chippendale, a licence to crenelate?'

'Jonathan Wild's final ledger.'

'And why would you want that?' I asked.

'You know damned well why,' she said.

'Yes,' I said. 'But I want you to say it out loud.'

'*The Third Principia*,' said Lady Helena.

'You're that keen to turn lead into gold?'

'Never mind filthy lucre,' she said. 'The philosopher's stone, eternal life and therefore by extension a cure for all that ails you.' She leant back in her seat and folded her arms. 'And that's enough for the starling. You want more, send in the Nightingale.'

'Do you think there's more?' asked Nightingale.

We'd left Lady Helena and the Right Honourable Caroline to stew, on the general police principle of when in doubt keep them waiting. You never know when something incriminating might turn up – it's happened before, even if you sometimes have to nudge the process along.

Nightingale and Stephanopoulos had made themselves comfortable in her office and sent me off for coffee and biscuits. Once we'd divided up the chocolate hobnobs we got down to the business

'She knows who we are,' I said. 'Which means she probably walked in with a plan.'

'To what end?' asked Nightingale.

'It can't be to spring her daughter,' said Stephanopoulos. 'Her brief's going to have her out in less than two hours. We don't have enough to charge her with anything more than making an affray and she's going to maintain that she was out shopping when she was caught up in a police operation.'

'That's unfortunate,' said Nightingale.

'That's the consequence of having a branch of the

Met operating without statutory authority,' said Stephanopoulos. 'We can't really explain to a jury that she obstructed the police in their lawful activity by shooting smoke out of her fingertips – can we?'

'Quite,' said Nightingale. 'Which is why I'm going to take a leaf out of Peter's book and invite them round for tea.'

'Sir?' I said and looked at Stephanopoulos, who shrugged.

'Lady Helena clearly wants something from us, and equally clearly she has information it could profit us to know,' he said. 'I suggest we ask her – politely – what it is.'

'So, tea this afternoon then?'

'Good Lord no, Peter,' he said. 'Tomorrow afternoon at the very earliest. For one thing we need to gather as much intelligence on Lady Helena as we can, and I need to brief Postmartin about the ledger. But, most importantly, we must give Molly time to prepare for guests. If we spring a member of the aristocracy on her without warning it could go very badly for us indeed.'

So, in the classic manner of a swan, the top half glided effortlessly across the police work while below the surface me and Guleed scrambled to pull together a decent intelligence assessment of a woman who, if I'm any judge, learnt how to be bureaucratically invisible on her mother's knee.

And how to heal with magic – possibly.

With all that implied.

And having made sure my attention was focused in one direction the universe, which likes a good laugh, smacked me in the face from the other side. Just as I was considering calling the Foreign and Commonwealth Office, formerly the Colonial Office, to see if they had anything on Lady Helena's activities in Kenya, my phone rang and an American voice said, 'Hi Peter, how you doing?'

It was Kim or, more formally, Special Agent Kimberley Reynolds of the FBI. We'd met a couple of years back when we'd engaged in competitive car tracking, suspect-losing and the world's first three-person sewer-luge team. We'd exchanged maybe five emails apiece since then – mostly at Christmas. One had been to alert her to the change in Lesley May's status.

'Hi Kim,' I said. 'What's up?'

'You never write me, Peter,' she said. 'You never call – so I thought I'd see how you were doing.'

This seemed unlikely. Now, she couldn't be worried about being bugged because if you're taped then someone's listening and probably isn't going to fall for 'this is a casual chat about the snow being particularly severe in Moscow this year' – so this was more of a plausible deniability sort of phone call. Kimberley wanted to be able say it was a friendly call with no 'policy' implications. The question was who she would be plausibly denying it to – a question that, obviously, you couldn't ask over the phone.

'You know how it is,' I said. 'Fighting crime and stuff.'

'Well, anyhoo,' said Kimberley. 'A real interesting thing happened to me the other day. I was working at my desk when a couple of gentlemen walked up and introduced themselves and started asking after you.'

'Agents?' I asked.

'That was the interesting thing,' she said, maintaining her bright tone, 'they had visitor passes. But, you know what, their escort must have wandered off and left them to their own devices.'

'Is that so?' I said. Visitors that could wander around an FBI office without an escort had to have some official status, or at least sanction from somewhere. 'What did they want to know about?'

'Who you were. What office you work from.' Kimberley paused. 'Had you ever done anything extraordinary.'

'Extraordinary?'

'Yep, that's what they asked.'

Fuck, fuck, fuckity fuck with extra fuck.

'What did you tell them?' I asked.

'I said you were a perfectly nice young low-ranking police officer who was on the task force investigating the murder of a US citizen abroad,' said Kimberley.

'And?'

'They weren't buying.'

'Did they ask about anyone else?' I said, meaning Nightingale.

'No,' said Kimberley. 'They only seemed to know about you.'

Kimberley had left Nightingale out of her – already heavily edited – report when she returned to the US. Operation MATCHBOX, the investigation into the murder of James Gallagher Jr, had left him out too, along with the community of magical folk that lived under the streets of Notting Hill – that was standard policy.

'Did they say why they wanted to know?'

'Strangely, they didn't,' said Kimberly. 'But I did get the impression that they might be coming to visit you in the near future, so I thought I'd give you a heads-up.'

'Thanks for that,' I said.

'My pleasure, and you take care now,' she said and hung up.

'What was that?' asked Guleed from the other side of our desk.

'Big trouble,' I said. 'Right here in River City.'

6

On the Comparing of Watches

Nightingale is big on the whole healthy body, healthy mind thing and, given that he looks good for a man who should have got a telegram from the queen more than a decade ago, I tend to follow his advice. Which is why when I'm working out of Belgravia I sometimes leave one of the Asbos there so I can run over the next morning. It's a good route, down St Martin's Lane still dirty from last night's theatre crowd, across the top of Trafalgar Square before dropping down onto the Mall and giving her majesty a quick wave if she's at home.

That morning it was cool and despite the smell of rain the sky was clear and the predawn light turned the roadway a nice shade of pink. I'd just passed the ICA when Beverley rang me – she does most mornings if I don't stay the night at her place.

'I don't want to be funny babes,' she said without preamble, 'but when were you going to tell me you'd run into Lesley?'

I slowed to a walk, then stopped and took a deep breath of chill air.

'Well, for a start, I wasn't going to do it over the phone,' I said. 'Where did you hear that from?'

'Tyburn ran into me "by accident" yesterday,' said Beverley. 'Couldn't wait to tell me. And what have you done to piss her off?

'I didn't fulfil my wool quota,' I said.

'And Lesley?'

'Tried to kill me a couple of times,' I said. 'But I don't think it was personal.'

'Wait,' said Beverley. 'Was that Harrods?'

'Maybe,' I said.

'So you roughed up the top shop,' she said. 'No wonder Ty is pissed. Did you get me a present?'

'I was busy at the time,' I said. 'Was there something you wanted?'

'Always,' said Beverley. 'You chasing Lesley now?'

'Not my job,' I said. 'The DPS is responsible for Lesley, and they don't want me anywhere near the case. And if you like being police – and I do – then you don't mess with the DPS.'

'And the real reason?'

'She's taunting me,' I said. 'What with the texts last year and popping up at Harrods like that. I think she's trying to pull me off balance.'

The breeze down the Mall was making the sweat chill on my legs and back. I started walking again.

'Maybe she's trying to tell you something,' said Beverley.

'Then she can send me a letter,' I said. 'Or, better still, turn herself in.'

'Hey,' said Beverley. 'Just saying.'

'Sorry, Bev,' I said.

'Are you coming over tonight? I've got to do an essay

on the atmospheric carbon cycle for tomorrow – you could help me with my chemistry.'

'Can't,' I said. 'I'm planning to blow up some phones for science.'

Someone had left a copy of the *Sun* on my desk. It had a good photograph of some TSG officers milling about under the Harrods awning – the headline read HARRODS HORROR. A quick flick through indicated that they didn't have the faintest idea what had happened, but that wasn't going to stop them from devoting six pages to it. It turned out to be the lead with most of the papers except for the *Express* which went with UKIP TO ROCK WESTMINSTER.

I knew Stephanopoulos and Seawoll were shielding me from a ton of shit already, but after the mess at Trafalgar Square Seawoll had admitted that my career's strange ability to survive its excursions into major property damage owed more to the fact that – should the Met actually get rid of me – they couldn't guarantee my replacement wouldn't be worse.

'Nightingale is fucking untouchable,' Seawoll had said. 'And you're the lesser of two evils.'

Still, I happened to know for a fact that the whole of Belgravia nick were running a pool on how long I would last and how I would go – the options being death, medical discharge (physical), medical discharge (psychological), indefinite disciplinary suspension, sacked for misconduct, secondment to Interpol and, with just one vote, ascension to a higher plane of existence.

I suspected the last one was a bit unlikely.

Guleed turned up a few minutes later wearing her leather jacket, the Hugo Boss she said her mum had bought her, which meant she'd been out doing some serious police work.

'Entry codes,' she said when she saw me. According to their statements, the kids had gained access to One Hyde Park via the underground staff tunnel that ran from the Mandarin Oriental Hotel next door. Two of them had identified James Murray, the victim's official boyfriend, as the one who'd possessed the passkey and security codes. There had been multiple actions including one to re-interview James Murray re: where he got the codes, but it was still pending until Guleed pre-empted it that morning.

'Christina Chorley gave him the codes,' said Guleed. 'And the passkey.'

Since James didn't know where Christina had got them, and she was seriously dead, Guleed decided to work the other side of the problem and find out who owned the flat.

'I thought all those things were actioned already?' I said.

'I don't know if you've noticed but just about everyone else is off working that murder in Fulham,' said Guleed. 'It's basically you, me and whatever time we can bully out of David.'

'I hadn't noticed,' I said, although it did explain where everyone else was that morning.

'Not surprising,' said Guleed. 'You were too busy blowing up Harrods.'

'Are we getting leaned on?' I asked.

'What do you think?' asked Guleed.

I didn't ask who by and I was pretty certain that the 'how' was Deputy Assistant Commissioner Folsom, he of the unfortunate eyebrows and midlife opera crisis. He was one of Tyburn's circle and, while he didn't have any direct influence over Belgravia MIT, he'd know a man who did – probably the Assistant Commissioner.

The AC would be asking whether this particular suspicious death was worth the resources, what with the current government cutting budgets and the sudden proliferation of expensive historical abuse investigations.

And you couldn't argue, because deciding on resource allocation is what ACPO officers are all about – and, let's face it, there's always more crime than budget. So Seawoll and Stephanopoulos had pulled most of their team off Operation Marigold, but left Guleed. Because, while those two liked a result as much as the next copper, they preferred it when it corresponded with your actual truth – they were very modern that way.

So, actions were still being actioned and me and Guleed were actioning them, and the wheels of justice ground on. Albeit in first gear.

So the low ratio wheels had taken Guleed to a civilian employee at Serious Fraud who was a friend of her brother's who had helped her untangle the – deliberately complex – web of fronts and shell companies that surrounded the flat at One Hyde Park.

'And then one name tripped a flag to a certain Operation Wentworth.' She smiled brightly. 'Sound familiar?'

Wentworth was the investigation into the illegal demolition of Skygarden Tower, with me on it I might add, and the activities of County Gard Ltd which, along with County Finance Management and The County System Company, was a known front organisation for the Faceless Man.

'Which ties Christina Chorley and Reynard Fossman to the Faceless Man,' I said. 'Serious Fraud have been banging their heads against that for a year – this could be their way in.'

'And it was at County Gard's offices,' said Guleed, 'where you first met the Right Honourable Caroline Linden-Limmer.'

'Yes.'

'Who's linked to Reynard Fossman, who is linked to Christina Chorley, who is linked back to County Gard.'

Unless Reynard was the link to County Gard, I thought. And we knew the Faceless Man loved his hybrids, his tiger-men and cat-girls. So why not a fox?

'So the Right Honourable Caroline has conveniently turned up at both ends of that trail,' said Guleed. 'What I'm asking is, do you really think it's a good idea to invite her into your secret hideout?'

But invited in they were, and at the appointed time I was in the entrance foyer in my second best suit, waiting for them to knock on the door. They were fifteen minutes late.

The doorbell rang and I triggered the counterweight mechanism that causes the doors to swing open impressively on their own – well, it impressed me once. They opened to reveal Lady Helena waiting with a half-smile on her lips. She'd deeply invested in the ageing bohemian look, with a quilted burgundy jacket and corduroy slacks. Her daughter was dressed in a conservative navy skirt suit that fitted her tall frame too well to be anything but bespoke.

Apart from my mum and certain senior aunts and uncles, I don't do deference as a rule. And certainly not to inherited titles. But I also believe in making people comfortable enough to make mistakes, so I smiled and called her Lady Helena.

I noticed that she didn't tell me to call her 'just Helena please'.

I invited them inside and let the doors close behind them.

Lady Helena paused in front of the statue of Sir Isaac Newton and read the inscription.

Nature and nature's laws lay hid in night;
God said 'Let Newton be' and all was light.

'"I do not know what I may appear to the world",' she said and I recognised the quote, '"but to myself I seem to have been only like a boy playing on the seashore".' She looked at me and raised an eyebrow. 'Where would be without the "great men" of history to guide us.' And with that she swept, unprompted, into the atrium.

I caught Caroline's gaze and she rolled her eyes.

We use the atrium for afternoon tea because Molly won't let us use the breakfast room for anything but breakfast, and the main dining hall is, despite having a high ceiling decorated with a fine Enlightenment mural of Newton bringing light to the world, actually a bit dingy.

Still, the green leather armchairs had been artfully re-arranged so that the comfy one with the severe cracking on the armrests was not amongst those arrayed in a loose u-shape around a couple of walnut coffee tables. I noticed that both the table tops and the green leather gleamed and there was a definite lingering smell of polish.

The silver tea service, which I'd only ever seen decorating a dresser in the small dining room, was assembled upon those coffee tables. On the service were a selection of biscuits, cakes and iced delights in pink and yellow. Enough, I was to learn much later, to make a Swedish housewife proud. Molly had been baking all night and in such quantity that Toby had fallen into a diabetic coma around dawn and was currently lying in the kitchen with his legs in the air.

Nightingale had stood as the women entered and he waved them towards the chairs. I'd been hoping that Molly would suddenly materialise behind them, but instead she came gliding in from the direction of the kitchen stairs bearing a silver tray and a squarish art deco teapot in white china with gold trim.

Lady Helena watched Molly approach. She looked interested but not surprised. I wondered, what did she know about Molly? And what had she heard about the internal disposition of the Folly?

Once we were seated, and Molly had poured the tea, Nightingale gave a little formal nod in the direction of our guests and invited them to eat and drink without fear of obligation.

'Thank you,' said Lady Helena. 'But I'm curious as to whether you believe that sort of thing is really necessary.'

'Between us?' said Nightingale. 'Among practitioners I doubt it's necessary. In the Court of the Rivers or amongst the High Fae I'm not sure I'd be willing to take the chance.'

Lady Helena took a sip of her tea.

'You don't think it's based on an atavistic fear of the feminine realm?' she asked and, when Nightingale looked politely blank, added 'Food and sustenance traditionally being a woman's responsibility.'

'I have no idea,' said Nightingale. 'But I've always liked to err on the side of prudence.'

They fenced along these lines for a bit while I had a slice of strawberry lattice tart and Caroline ate two pink angel cakes in quick succession.

'I gather you were taught by your mother,' said Nightingale. 'Was this the usual practice?'

'I don't think there was such a thing as a "usual practice",' said Lady Helena. 'My mother was taught by her aunt, and her aunt by a friend of the family.'

'A female friend?' asked Nightingale.

'Naturally,' said Lady Helena. 'But I think we may have exhausted that topic – shall we get down to business?'

'By all means,' said Nightingale. 'What would you like to discuss?'

Lady Helena put her tea down – she'd barely touched it.

'Jonathan Wild's Ledger, *The Third Principia*, alchemy, the secret of eternal life.' She smiled – a bright echo of the young woman in the photograph. 'Is that enough to be going on with?'

'We're always interested in information leading to the recovery of stolen goods,' said Nightingale.

'Is that the case here?' asked Lady Helena.

Nightingale glanced my way.

'*The Third Principia* was definitely stolen in 1719,' I said. 'The Master of the Royal Mint at that time was one Sir Isaac Newton, who was busy sending counterfeiters and coin clippers to the gallows for crimes against the currency.'

'Stolen by Jack Shepherd himself according to legend,' said Nightingale. 'So, yes, I believe it counts as stolen property.'

Lady Helena held up her hand to surrender the point.

'We are both the true heirs of Isaac Newton,' she said. 'Whether you're willing to recognise it or not. We can't ignore each other and I'm sure you'll agree that any conflict between us would be both pointless and counterproductive. Which leaves us where?'

Nightingale nodded slowly.

'You think we should work together,' he said and then he looked at me and laughed. 'A stakeholder engagement,' he said.

Oh, he looks like he stands still and lets the modern world flow around him, I thought. But he's always watching and when something useful catches his eye, he merely reaches out and takes it – things, ideas, people.

The smile vanished as he looked back at Lady Helena.

'Let's leave the question of a common cause aside for

a moment,' he said. 'And start by clearing the air. Have you ever heard of a wizard who conceals his identity?'

'Does he use a glamour and mask to hide his face?' asked Lady Helena.

'We call him the Faceless Man,' I said and Caroline didn't exactly snigger, but I could tell she wanted to.

'We believe there might have been two of them,' said Nightingale. 'One active during the sixties and seventies and a second, a successor if you like, active since the mid-nineties.'

'The older one is dead,' I said.

'If we're talking about Albert Woodville-Gentle,' said Lady Helena, 'Then I should bloody well hope so – since I killed him.'

Nightingale was so stunned he looked shocked for almost half a second before moving on to ask quite when that might have happened.

'August Bank Holiday, 1979,' said Lady Helena.

'And you're sure he was dead?' asked Nightingale.

'Are you saying he wasn't?' asked Lady Helena.

'He turned up alive and well and living in the Barbican Centre,' I said. 'Under the care of a Russian woman.'

'Wait,' said Lady Helena. 'Not Varvara Sidorovna Tamonina?'

'That's the one,' I said.

'That lying witch!' said Lady Helena and turned to her daughter. 'You said she was lying, but I didn't want to believe you.'

'So you know each other?' I asked.

'Our paths have crossed,' said Lady Helena. 'But fuck her. Is Albert still alive?'

Nightingale told her he wasn't, which was an obvious relief. He gave some of the background, that he'd been disabled by brain damage, by hyperthaumaturgical degradation, but I noticed that he didn't mention that Varvara Sidorovna had located and arranged for Albert Woodville-Gentle's care on behalf of the second Faceless Man. Like me, he wanted to see if Lady Helena knew this already.

'Perhaps you should start by telling us why you tried to kill him in the first place,' said Nightingale and this, I realised, was why he had opted for tea in the Folly. In here we were all like-minded individuals of quality and learning, not police officers and suspects, and Lady Helena was about to regale us with an interesting story and not implicate herself for an attempted murder. Which was why I didn't have my notebook out.

But I was recording the conversation on a transistorised Dictaphone I'd picked up on eBay for exactly this purpose, and taped to the bottom of the coffee table. Transistors don't last much longer than microprocessors when exposed to magic, but magnetic audio tape does. Which meant that even in the event of a major disagreement I'd still have a record. And that, boys and girls, is why we spend so much time in the lab doing experiments.

'I grew up on a farm in Africa,' said Lady Helena. 'My father had inherited a title and not much else from *his* father and so after he was demobbed from the RAF he sought his fortune there.'

There hadn't been any other kids and she'd grown up

'like a weed' she said, the only child for a hundred miles around.

'This was in the old days before the poachers decimated the local game,' she said. 'You still got animal attacks on the livestock, and once a leopard took a couple of village children.' Her father had led the hunting party that had tracked it down and killed it. He'd sold the skin to help support the farm, but had kept the head as a trophy.

'She still has it,' said Caroline. 'In a box in the attic – we used to spook ourselves by sneaking up to look at it.'

'I wondered why things in the attic kept moving about,' said Lady Helena. 'I thought it might be a poltergeist. You lot are lucky I didn't put down a trap.'

I glanced over at Nightingale, who was probably thinking the same thing I was: what kind of trap, and where did you learn how to make one?

Her mother hadn't approved of the killing. As far as she was concerned, man was the interloper in Africa and shouldn't be surprised when the animals merely followed their instincts.

'If people aren't willing to pay the price, my darling,' her mum had said, 'then perhaps people should live somewhere else.'

Not that she feared for her daughter, who was left to explore on her own. Although generally speaking one of the houseboys would be told to keep an eye on her.

'She'd already taught me the snapdragon by the time I was seven,' said Lady Helena. Nightingale asked for a demonstration; she made a flicking gesture with her hand and there was a flash and a loud crack that echoed

131

off the walls and caused Molly to suddenly appear behind Nightingale's chair.

It was too fast for me to read her *signum* but I got the same hint of burning candlewax that I'd felt in Harrods during the fight.

Nightingale asked Molly if we might have a fresh pot of tea. Caroline nodded enthusiastically at this and helped herself to a Manchester Tart – or it might have been a Liverpool Tart, I can't always tell them apart.

'What did the locals think about the magic?' I asked, thinking of my mum, who has definite views about spells, witches and where they fit into a well organised society – i.e. not around her.

'These were tribesman,' said Lady Helena. 'They already believed in magic. I don't think they saw anything strange in it – even if we were *wazungu*.'

They were much more enthusiastic about her mother's ability to set bones and treat injuries. Nightingale asked where she'd learnt those particular skills.

'The basics were handed down,' said Lady Helena. 'But she refined the techniques working on her animals.'

'What about the natives?' I asked.

Lady Helena glared at me and then looked away.

'You have to understand,' she said, her eyes on Nightingale. 'There were no hospitals or clinics nearby – she couldn't turn people away.'

Nightingale nodded understandingly.

There were limitations to what her mother could do. Gross physical damage, broken bones, cuts and abrasions were easy enough. But not diseases or chronic conditions.

'Cancer,' said Lady Helena bitterly. 'Obvious tumours she could excise and then promote healing at the site. But she couldn't reach anything systemic. Including her own leukaemia.'

She hadn't told her family either, until it was too late for chemotherapy.

'This was after the Emergency,' she said, 'after we'd moved to Uganda.'

I wanted to ask what kind of *formae* her mother had used to knit bones and heal tissue, but Nightingale had discussed this with me in advance.

'Please try not to be distracted by the details, Peter,' he'd said. 'We want to know about her connection to Fossman and what she knows about the Faceless Man. If all goes well, there'll be plenty of time to satisfy your curiosity later.'

My curiosity? I thought, as Lady Helena talked about bones healing in days not weeks. Dr Walid's going to break his Hippocratic oath and kill us because we didn't invite him along. Thank god I'll have the recording to keep him sweet.

After her mother died, her father packed her off to posh school to finish her education. But this was London in the sixties and there was no end of mischief a fearless young woman could get up to in those days. Stripping off for David Bailey was the least of it.

'You know the list, darling,' she said to Nightingale. 'Sex, drugs, rock and roll. But of course I found myself drawn into what they call the demi-monde.' She looked at me. 'French for half-world,' she said, obviously unaware of the existence of Google. 'A bit more exclusive in those days, less fashionable.' She grinned. 'Less safe.'

She met a young man called Albert Woodville-Gentle there, who could do magic.

'Not as well as me,' she said. 'He was all bash, bash, bash – no finesse.'

'You were lovers?' asked Nightingale.

'On occasion,' said Lady Helena. 'When the mood took us.'

'Friends with benefits,' said Caroline.

'Such a vulgar term,' said Lady Helena.

Caroline caught my eye and mouthed *fuck-buddies* behind her mum's back.

Magic was what drew them together. They spent the summer of '66 breaking the bank in Monte Carlo and then wintered in Tangiers spending the proceeds. All the time teaching each other magic and refining their technique.

'And having spectacular sex on the roof,' said Lady Helena. 'With Chris Farlowe and Procol Harum on the radio.'

Caroline winced.

They arrived back in London on a grey day in October '67 and found everything had changed.

'You could practically feel it oozing out of the stones,' said Lady Helena. 'And there were new faces in the old haunts. It wasn't the London we'd known; it felt dangerous, alienating. At least that's how I felt.'

Albert Woodville-Gentle seemed to find it more agreeable.

'By that time I'd already set my sights on India,' she said and off she went, although via BOAC rather than the hippy trail. 'I studied at an ashram, got myself a guru or two.' But she couldn't find an indigenous magic tradition. 'Although I got the strong sense that there was something going on under the surface. I didn't know about the Rivers in those days, or I might have looked in somewhat different areas. They knew about your lot, though,' she nodded at Nightingale. 'I'm not sure you left a good impression in India.'

'So you didn't find what you were looking for?' asked Nightingale.

'Yes and no,' said Helena. 'I never found an Indian magical tradition, at least not one based on what we might understand as magic.' But she did find a vocation, a sense of purpose, in the slums of Calcutta.

'Unless you've been there you can't believe what it's like,' she said. 'That vast press of humanity crowding in from all sides, the noise, the colour, the chaos, the smells and the pain, the suffering. If you plan to stay you either hide behind walls or you roll up your sleeves and try to help.'

She helped set up a free clinic in a poverty stricken suburb and there she found a use for the magical techniques that her mother had developed in Africa. 'At first I kept it simple,' she said. 'Broken bones and physical injuries, but in Paikpara that's just the tip of the iceberg. You could work yourself to death just dealing with the diarrheal conditions.' And she wanted to, because these were things that were killing the kids. But the real problem was poor sanitation and poverty.

'There was nothing I could do about either, but I thought I might be able to do something about leprosy,' she said and I almost dropped my second slice of Bakewell tart.

'Did you?' I asked, which got me a frown from Nightingale.

'For the disease, no,' she said. 'For the symptoms, for the nerve damage, sometimes. But not remotely reliably. I thought I saw a way it might be done, but I needed money, for medical supplies and equipment.' And to meet the huge need that pressed in around her every day.

So she returned to London to set up a fundraising arm for her charity, and ran straight back into the arms of Albert Woodville-Gentle who was just as charming as he'd ever been. After getting reacquainted they came to an arrangement – Albert would provide seed funding and run the London end of the charity, and in exchange Helena would share the techniques she'd developed in India.

I thought of the Strip Club of Doctor Moreau where Albert Woodville-Gentle had created real cat-girls and tiger-boys and other things that Nightingale wouldn't let me see. And I thought of the smooth new skin of Lesley May's face, and found it suddenly hard to keep an expression of polite interest on mine.

'You never suspected how he might use it,' said Nightingale.

'I received a phone call in May 1979,' said Lady Helena. 'The caller asked me if I knew what my "good friend" was really up to. They gave me the address of a club in Soho. I believe you know the one I'm talking about.'

'On Brewer Street,' said Nightingale.

'Do you know who made the call?' I asked.

Lady Helena did not; she'd been busy when she'd taken it and hadn't understood the implications.

'A woman,' she said. 'English certainly, or at least she didn't have an accent.'

A woman with a posh accent, I thought. Because people always think their own accent is universal.

'Did you visit the club?' asked Nightingale.

'I'd been due to visit London that summer, so instead of calling Albert to let him know I'd arrived I popped in on my way to my hotel,' said Lady Helena. 'Do you know what was in the foyer?'

Nightingale nodded.

I certainly remembered, the disembodied head of Larry 'The Lark' Piercingham, petty criminal, grass and object lesson in why you didn't cross the Faceless Man. He'd been done up like a fortune-telling machine and, as far as Dr Walid could establish later, kept in a semi-state of aliveness for over thirty years.

Lady Helena smacked her palm on the coffee table making the china rattle.

'I developed that technique,' she said and her face was suddenly flushed. 'In an emergency you can use it to stave off brain death.' She raised her hand again, but hesitated and then dropped it into her lap.

'Have you taught it to anyone else?' I asked.

'You mean, why haven't I given it to the drug companies?' asked Lady Helena. 'Because it's difficult, dangerous to the witch, and has a one-in-twenty success rate. I'd used it in extremis and tried to refine it, but the most common result is a type of terrible half-life.'

'Zombies,' said Caroline, which got her a glare from her mother. 'What? I'm just saying – zombies. That's what you get when it goes wrong.'

'I decided I couldn't trust anyone with the technique,' said Lady Helena. 'Least of all the medical establishment. God, can you imagine what the military might do with it? It doesn't bear thinking about.'

It was after her encounter with Larry the Lark that she concluded the medical knowledge she'd developed was too dangerous to be passed on.

'I've decided that it has to die with me,' she said.

'What about Albert?' asked Nightingale.

'Quite,' she said. 'What about dear old Albert?'

She'd arranged to meet him at her hotel, but he must have heard that she'd visited the club because he turned up ready to fight.

'It was a sort of mutual ambush,' said Lady Caroline. 'He had first go, but I always was faster than him. Things got rather disagreeable and I'm afraid the hotel rather bore the brunt of it. So it's just as well I always stayed under an assumed name.'

'Was this the Pontypool Hotel on Argyle Square?' asked Nightingale.

'As a matter of fact it was,' said Lady Helena.

'I was called in to investigate that,' said Nightingale. And, to me, 'They thought it was a gas explosion at first, then arson and then the IRA. Only once they'd exhausted those possibilities did they think of me, and the trail had grown somewhat cold by then.' He looked at Lady Helena again. 'Thank you for clearing that up.'

Not to mention thank you for adding attempted murder, gross negligence and identity fraud to your charge list, I thought, or explaining your cheerfully relaxed attitude to medical ethics.

'You do understand what happens when you overuse magic?' she asked.

'We call it hyperthaumaturgical degradation,' said Nightingale.

Lady Helena nodded.

'Useful term,' she said. 'That's what happened to dear Albert. Which I thought a fitting punishment. I didn't have time for a *coup de grace* – the police were practically knocking on what was left of the front door when I made myself scarce.'

Nightingale nodded thoughtfully in a way that made me think that somebody was going to be digging out incident reports from 1979, and just for a change it wasn't going to be me. There was a good chance it would be a big box full of papers – which would suit Nightingale much better anyway.

Without Albert, the charity funding evaporated and, in any case, she'd begun to have doubts about the ethics of her work.

'But you must have saved lives,' I said.

'World ill-health is like world hunger,' said Lady Helena. 'We could end both tomorrow if we wanted to.' And she'd become terrified of the potential abuse. 'Imagine what the military industrial complex would do with animal hybrids,' she said. 'Better that the knowledge dies with me.'

Nightingale glanced my way and gave his head the

almost imperceptible tilt that meant it was time for the children to wander off and entertain themselves. I had a number of incentives lined up to coax Caroline away, but in the end I just asked if she wanted a tour and she said yes.

We were followed by Toby, who'd shaken off his sugar induced lethargy and had obviously decided that he wanted a bit of attention.

I started with the lecture hall, where generations of practitioners had snoozed their way through demonstrations and lectures, then the smoking room with its art nouveau trimmings and into the mundane library where we could slip up the ladder to the top stacks and step through a concealed doorway onto the landing. Then up another flight of stairs to the main lab.

'What are you doing here?' asked Caroline.

I had a pile of modified first generation smartphones at one end of the lab and a noticeably scorched sheet of metal on a bench at the other end. I'd painted distance markers on the metal and on the floor around it. The remains of a couple of cheap pocket calculators were still welded to the innermost markers – I hadn't had a chance to scrape them off yet.

'Remember when the lights went out at Harrods?' I asked.

'I remember your master knocking me off my feet,' she said.

'He's not my master,' I said.

'Well he's not your dad, is he?' said Caroline and then looked at me sharply. 'He's not, is he?'

'He's my boss,' I said. 'My governor.'

'I see,' she said. She looked at the bench. 'Magic interferes with technology – do you know why?'

'No,' I said. 'Do you?'

'No,' she looked at the pile of smartphones. 'But I think you know more than I do.'

So I explained that, as far as I could tell, magic had a serious degrading effect on microprocessors, and a lesser effect on transistors. 'But not on thermionic valves,' I said, 'or simple circuit boards.'

'I know about that,' she said and held up her wrist to show off a silver stainless steel Classic Ladies Fireman from Balls – which was at least eight hundred quids' worth of watch.

'I've shown you mine,' she said, so I held my wrist to show my black and silver Omega.

'Damn,' she said and grabbed my forearm and pulled it up for a closer look, 'Where did you get this?'

'Christmas present,' I said.

'What about your boss?' asked Caroline. 'Your *guvnor*? What's he got?'

'Depends on what he's wearing,' I said. 'I think he's got a drawer full of them alongside the cufflinks.'

'Sharp dressed man,' she said. 'Bit old fashioned for my taste.'

Oh, you don't know, I thought, but you suspect. And you can just go on suspecting.

'It's hard to stay current working in a place like this,' I said. 'What's your mum have on her wrist?'

'Just skin,' said Caroline. 'She says "clock time is an imposition of industrial capitalism and should be resisted if not ignored". Besides, she thinks it interferes with the flow of energy around her chakra points. And you still haven't said what all the phones are for.'

'Somebody,' I said, meaning Lesley May, 'has found a way to tap directly into the energy potential of a smartphone.'

'Does it have to be an Apple or will an Android do?'

'Anything with a chip-set,' I said.

'Wait,' said Caroline. 'Are you saying magic doesn't just destroy the chips – you can actually get power out of it as well? How do you know that?'

Because I'd trained myself to do a very consistent *were-light* for testing purposes and then measured the output while feeding calculators, phones and, once, an obsolete laptop into the spell. Then I measured it with an antique optical spectrometer that I'd found in a storeroom. It was a beautiful brass and enamel thing that looked like someone had bolted two telescopes to an early turntable. It had taken me another two weeks to find the prism which was in a different box with some notes handwritten in Latin which I hadn't dared show Nightingale in case he confiscated them. I hadn't translated them yet, but from the diagrams I was pretty sure the author had been conducting experiments similar to mine.

'How do you feed a calculator to a spell?' asked Caroline.

'Same way you'd do a ritual animal sacrifice, except without the animal,' I said.

This amazed Caroline, not least because she hadn't known you *could* do ritual animal sacrifice – which really shouldn't have surprised me, what with her mum being her mum.

'Ten points to Ravenclaw,' she said.

'Really?' I said. 'I always fancied Gryffindor.'

'Dream on,' she said. 'Definitely Ravenclaw.'

'I think,' I said, 'that it might be possible to trigger a sort of magic chain reaction that feeds off the chipset without the practitioner having to do anything else.' I nearly said it was like setting a phaser to overload, but I've learnt to keep that kind of joke to myself, even with people who make Harry Potter references – especially with people who make Harry Potter references.

'To do what exactly?' asked Caroline.

'Magically it just makes a lot of "noise", but the side effect is to dust every microprocessor in about twenty metres.' I'd gone over the Harrods crime scene that morning with a laser rangefinder and a pocket microscope and found that every chip within ten metres was toast, damaged beyond repair out to twenty, and showing signs of damage out to thirty. I was hoping that further research would reveal it was following the inverse square law, because otherwise I was going to have to call CERN and tell them to take a tea break.

'I've got a similar spell I use to knock out electronic ignitions,' I said. 'I call it the car killer.'

'Oh, that's a great name,' said Caroline.

'Alright,' I said. 'What do you call the smoke rope thing that you do?'

She said it had a name in Sanskrit or Bengali or one of those but she just called it the smoke trick.

'We've got a firing range downstairs,' I said. 'Want to show me how it's done?'

*

And it wasn't as easy as she made it look. I showed her the car killer and the skinny grenade but I kept the water balloons to myself, because a man's got to have a few secrets. We both managed to do some serious damage to the NATO standard cardboard cutouts and we might have moved on to the paintball gun but the grownups came looking for us and said it was time for Caroline to go home.

I walked them round the corner to where their car was parked. It was an honest to god early model MG MGB, a 1968 judging from the dashboard instruments, although at some point it had been re-sprayed a hideous lime-flower green, once again proving that nine out of ten classic motors are wasted on their owners. As I waved them off I made a note of the car's index to add to their nominal file.

Nightingale said he'd come to an arrangement with Lady Helena. They would track down Fossman while I worked Operation Marigold to see if I could firm up his involvement from that direction. And, if I could discover who'd supplied the fatal drugs to Christina Chorley and get Tyburn's daughter off the hook at the same time, so much the better.

'Just to clarify one thing,' I said. 'When you find Fossman, he's going to be cautioned and interviewed on the record – right?'

'Do you think that's wise?' asked Nightingale. 'Considering?'

'Either we're the law or we're not,' I said.

Nightingale nodded gravely and then he looked away and smiled.

'Agreed,' he said.

'Right,' I said, but the smile worried me.

I'd expected there to be some cake left over, but I'd arrived back in the Folly to find Molly packing up anything that didn't have a bite out of it into professional looking cake boxes. She couldn't possibly be planning to store them – we'd never finish them before they went stale – and Molly never froze anything.

'Homeless shelters,' said Nightingale when I thought to ask. 'I found out when a nice young woman turned up at the gate with a van.'

'We should find out who she's liaising with there,' I said.

'Whatever for?' asked Nightingale.

'Basic security?'

'But Peter,' said Nightingale, 'if we do that Molly might discover that we know what she's up to.' He picked up a forlorn slice of Liverpool Tart. 'She's enjoying sneaking around behind our backs far too much for us to spoil it.'

7

The Intrepid Fox

I arrived back at the Belgravia Outside Inquiry Office to find everyone else working the Hammersmith stabbing.

'Poor sod was standing outside a pub having a drink,' said Carey. 'And a bunch of guys just stroll up and stab him.'

There was already a row of white faces pinned to the whiteboard because, while they'd been sensible enough to wear hoodies to mask their identities from the CCTV, somebody in the pub had recognised them.

'Had it away with one of the suspects' girlfriends,' said Carey. 'We're not sure which of the suspects' girl-friend she was and, get this, two of the other suspects are her brothers. If they'd been Muslim I'd have said this was an honour killing.'

The media always calls this sort of thing senseless, but the motive made sense – it was just stupid, is what it was.

Still, this was the kind of case that Seawoll liked — simple, straightforward and easy on the clear-up rate. They were going to go in and grab all six suspects the next morning in a series of raids. Carey had been given responsibility for one of them, which was pissing

Guleed off no end, because she was stuck on my Falcon case. You can always tell when you've pissed Guleed off because of the bland look of polite interest on her face whenever you speak to her. This was why when she announced that she was going to head over to St Paul's School for the effortlessly posh to put the frighteners on the sixth form, I decided to stay where I was and work my way through Operation Marigold's action list just to see if anything popped out.

What popped out was a cross-reference from Bromley Crime Squad who had busted someone with a suitcase full of Magic Babar pills. Not just the same brand but, according to the lab report, from the same batch as those found at One Hyde Park.

So the next morning I actioned myself to take a little trip across the river.

Bromley nick is, like Belgravia, a redbrick 1990's build resembling an out-of-town Morrisons that was repurposed at the last moment and fitted with offices and a custody suite. A middle-aged PC from the local Case Progression Unit met me in the reception and walked me into the interview room where Aiden Burghley, wannabe suburban drug dealer, was waiting with his solicitor.

Aiden was a young white man, about my age, but smaller with a soft bland face, brown hair and watery blue eyes. He looked like he should be selling insurance or houses rather than drugs, but according to his nominal a sad second from Warwick University had landed him back in his parents' semi in Bromley. No record of a job but he did own an ancient Vauxhall Vectra, so I could see he might be desperate enough to turn to crime.

You can understand the temptation – you pop over on the ferry to Holland, pick up some pills, drive around, visit a dope café, go clubbing, hop back on the ferry. It's pills, so the dogs don't smell them. You're not buying in huge bulk, so your shipment's not going to show up on police intelligence. Shit, you're practically at personal use levels anyway, and the chances of a random search picking on you at customs are thousands to one, really hundreds of thousands to one.

Had Aiden Burghley been sensible enough to pop the pills himself or just share them with his friends he'd have been alright, but no – he had to try to flog them to a pair of surprised off-duty female police officers at Glitrrz, a club just off Bromley High Street. After weighing up whether an easy collar would be worth the stick they'd get for frequenting a notorious trouble spot, they went for the collar and now Aiden had spent a night in the cells and was looking at a long list of charges with words like 'intent' and 'supply' in the title.

He had an equally young and fresh-faced solicitor from the local Legal Aid specialist firm at his side. You always have to be careful around legal aid solicitors because not only do they spend more time in police interview rooms than you do, they're also usually in a really bad mood because their clients are idiots and because the government is always cutting the legal aid budget. This one was a white woman with slate-grey eyes which she narrowed at me when I introduced myself.

One way or another Aiden was going up the steps. But, as a young white middle class first offender, if he pleaded guilty there was a good chance he'd walk away without a prison sentence. My strategy was simple – I threatened to add him to the suspect pool in the death of Christina Chorley.

'The pills that killed her came from the same batch as those you brought back from Holland,' I said. 'And that puts you in the frame for manslaughter—'

And that was as far as I got before the solicitor objected to the evidence that Aiden's drugs had been the same drugs that allegedly may have caused the death of Christina Chorley. Thank god she didn't have access to the PM report yet. Had she known about Christina's pre-existing condition it might have been all over. I waited for her to wind down, suspended the interview and then asked the solicitor if I might have a word in private.

The solicitor, whose name was Patricia Polly – seriously, Patricia Polly – said she needed a cigarette anyway, so we repaired to the car park.

'Look,' I said. 'I don't want your boy for this, but it's a high profile case and someone is going to get done for it. Even if I walk away now, any review team that comes in is just going come to the same conclusions I have.'

Which, while not an out and out lie, was probably at the far end of wishful thinking.

Ms Polly took a deep drag of her Silk Cut and nodded.

'So what do you want?' she asked.

'I know he claims that he did the run for his own personal use and that he wouldn't have sold any except he was unexpectedly skint,' I said. 'But I reckon he sold a big bag to somebody else – I just want to know who.'

'I'm not going to have him admit to that,' she said. 'Even if it is true.'

Wait for it.

'Unless there was a bit of mutual consideration.'

'Why don't you ask him in confidence if he can help,' I said. 'Because if there's somebody else, not only will he be volunteering vital information but he'll be making sure somebody else steps into the frame for the manslaughter.'

I could tell she was doubtful, but I reckoned she'd figure it was worth a punt.

I gave her my card and had time for a full English in the canteen before she called me back.

Apparently there'd been this posh girl.

'Did she have a name?' I asked – we were on the record because he was still under caution, and I might need the evidence for court. There's no point knowing who done it if you can't prove it.

'Don't be stupid,' said Aiden.

I asked what she looked like.

'I don't know,' he said. 'Curly hair and . . .' Aiden made chest expanding gestures with his hands. 'You know.'

'Black or white?' I asked.

'Maybe.'

'Maybe?'

'Maybe tanned?' said Aiden. 'I really wasn't looking at her face.'

I asked if he'd seen her car.

'Oh, yeah,' he said. 'BMW X5, the one with the three litre turbo diesel.'

'What colour?'

'Imperial blue.'

'Imperial blue?'

'That's what that colour is called – Imperial Blue,' said Aiden.

'Can you remember what she was wearing?'

'No, mate. Sorry.'

Which is a good demonstration of why eyewitnesses have all been a caution since Marc Anthony said *'I dunno mate, they were all wearing togas.'*

'Did you notice the year on the plate?' I asked.

'Yeah,' he said. 'It was a 63.' But crucially he didn't remember the area code or the rest of the index. Some things are more important to some people than they are to others. 63 meant the car was registered between September 2013 and February 2014 – which might narrow it down a bit.

I terminated the interview and gave him back to Bromley CID and told them what a good boy he'd been – for whatever good that might do him. Then I headed back across the river and settled back at my corner of the desk at Belgravia nick. Carey grumbled and shifted over, but he was too busy doing the metric ton of paperwork involved in organising a raid to chat. Guleed was out – presumably still terrorising the sixth form at St Paul's.

As soon as Aiden Burghley had mentioned the blue BMW, there'd been a little tickle in my brain. And when I logged into HOLMES and a did a word search through the Marigold nominals there it was – a blue 63 reg BMW X5 registered to George Thames-McAllister. On the off-chance I ran an ANPR sweep on Bromley and there was the right BMW, tooling down the A21 towards the town centre and then back again. Exactly the right time window for Aiden Burghley to sell its occupant some MDMA.

I hesitated before I added this to HOLMES – I didn't want to firm up the case against Lady Ty's wayward daughter, but the whole point of a collation system is that you feed in information to collate. Still, with her mother's influence putting the brakes on the investigation I figured that Olivia was safe for the moment. With a bit of luck that would give me time to sort things out using the time-honoured tradition of exploiting family connections.

In days of old, a stout yeoman would set out from Aldgate along the road to Colchester in the full knowledge that just a mile up the road was a small hamlet where he could stop for a pint and a cheeky pie. This rest stop was called Mile End from *Le Mille End* which is your Norman French for a hamlet a mile up the road. The road from Aldersgate was called *Aldgatestrete* and then, because that was considered too on the nose, the Mile End Road. It's where young Richard II signed the peasants' charter with his fingers crossed behind his back and the first ever V1 cruise missile to land in London hit. It's also where Queen Mary University teaches Environmental Science, so it was there that I had lunch with Beverley Brook.

Now, just up the road are some of the best curry houses in London. But no. Bev, who's gone all outdoorsy since Herefordshire, wanted to go picnic up on the Green Bridge. This is a foot and cycle bridge that crosses the Mile End Road linking the two halves of Mile End Park. Since the bridge was constructed this side of the year 2000 it has a ton of retail space built into its base and one of these places was called Rooster Piri Piri, where you can get a reasonably priced double chicken burger and chips. Even if me and Beverley both agreed that their extra hot Piri Piri sauce was a bit mild by our standards.

We found ourselves queuing behind a bunch of young men with matching beards and black framed Malcolm X glasses who were making a complicated bulk order. Their fathers might have been from Bangladesh or Pakistan, but their accents ranged from local London to Glasgow with, I noticed, a side trip to France on the way.

'Engineering students,' said Beverley as they argued about how to divide up the bill.

Once they'd finished constructing their order we got ours and took it up the steps to the bridge and then across to where there was a decent bench and, importantly, we couldn't see Regent's Canal.

'It's bad manners for me to sit too close to the canal,' said Beverley, 'without asking Mrs Canal's permission.' Which Beverley reckoned was more trouble than it was worth, given that she didn't think it was that scenic a canal.

'There are swamps with a better flow rate than hers,' said Beverley.

Now, I've met the Goddess of Regent's Canal. And she's perfectly nice, you know, providing you bring her a banana – preferably free trade.

So once we'd stopped fighting over the remaining chips I asked Bev whether she could maybe see her way to facilitate an off the record meeting with her sister.

'Can't you just go around and talk to her?' asked Beverley.

'Even if I make an unofficial visit,' I said, 'she won't talk to me without her brief present.'

If she's sensible, I thought, which she is.

'I am not getting involved in this,' said Beverley.

'I'm not asking you to get involved,' I said.

'Yes you are.'

'Okay, yes I am.'

'And I'm not going to get involved.'

'Olivia's your niece,' I said. 'And she's sleepwalking her way into a serious drugs charge.'

'And Tyburn is my sister,' said Beverley. 'My older sister, and she holds grudges forever. And I mean forever. Besides, it'll never get to that – Tyburn will fix it.'

'And how will she do that?'

'If it comes to it you know she's going to march to Fed HQ and tell your boss to lay off – who's going to stop her?'

'I'm going to stop her.'

'Why?'

'Because it's my job – that's what the Folly is about.'

'No,' said Beverley. 'That's what you've decided the Folly is about. I wonder if the Nightingale thinks the same as you do.'

'I don't know,' I said. 'But that's not the point.'

'Really?' asked Beverley. 'You can't let this case go – not even for a quiet life?'

There was a long pause while Beverley looked me right in the eye and I was suddenly worried that she was going to ask me to cease and desist as a personal favour to her. And if she did, I wasn't sure what I was going to say. But then she shook her head and waved her burger at me.

'Alright, I'll do it. But it's going to cost you,' she said.

'What is it this time?'

'Maksim's putting in some baffles where I run across the common,' she said. Maksim was the administrator and sole employee of the Beverley Brook Conservation Improvement Trust. He was also a terrifying former Russian mobster who'd come into Beverley's 'service' via a complicated and morally ambiguous route. 'He needs a hand.'

'Fine,' I said. 'As long as you come and watch.'

Beverley grinned. 'You know I like it when you do improvements,' she said.

I know she liked to get me in the water with my clothes on – I blame Colin Firth for that.

I had a sudden brainwave while driving back west, so when I got to Belgravia I hunted down Guleed, who was typing up that morning's statements from St Paul's school for girls with rich parents. I showed her the picture I'd taken of the collage on Olivia's wall, with the young curly haired woman who had cropped up so frequently.

'Spot this one?' I asked.

'Oh yes,' said Guleed and checked her notebook. 'Phoebe Beaumont-Jones – shared a couple of classes with your Olivia.'

I thought of the picture of them standing together in France, arms comfortably around each other's waists.

'Not best friends?' I asked.

'Nobody said anything,' said Guleed. 'Least of all Phoebe herself.'

'They definitely look like friends in the picture,' I said.

'Do you think she was at the party?' asked Guleed.

None of the witnesses had identified her, but if she was Olivia's friend rather than theirs they might have overlooked her. Or were they scared of Olivia, or of Phoebe Beaumont-Jones?

You can't go by appearances – I once helped put away a gang of steamers who'd been working Oxford Street at the behest of an OAP with a dodgy hip and pipe cleaner arms. They were so terrified of him that not one of the gang would grass him up. I asked one of them why – off the record – and he told me that the geezer had no off switch, and once he started in that was it. You were dead meat.

It was just possible that her fellow Paulinas feared to mention Phoebe. Was she the one who supplied the drugs?

I looked at Guleed, who was obviously thinking the same thing.

So we called up Bromley and sent them Phoebe's picture to show to Aiden Burghley.

Less than an hour of paperwork later, Bromley called back and said that it was just possible that Phoebe might be the young woman he'd sold the drugs to – maybe. We passed Phoebe's details on, but asked Bromley to let us know before they took any action.

'Follow-up?' asked Guleed, meaning let's go find Phoebe and put the frighteners on her, on the off-chance she might cough right there and then. It's always a good tactic – turn up like a horrible surprise. But since she was seventeen we'd have to faff about getting her a responsible adult and everything, and that would take the edge off.

'What do you think?' I asked.

Guleed bit her lip.

'Let's see if we can't lean on Olivia a bit more first,' she said. 'If Phoebe was supplying the drugs, I wish we knew why Olivia is covering for her.'

'Perhaps she doesn't think there will be consequences,' I said. 'Maybe she thinks her mum's going to get it sorted.'

Guleed sighed.

'She's a fool if she relies on that,' she said.

'Her mum seems to be doing quite a good job at the moment,' I said.

'When I was a little girl,' said Guleed, 'I lived in a great big house with marble floors and servants to clean them. I remember the marble floors because you could get a rug, do a run up and slide all the way down the hall and into the dining room. There was a garage with five cars including a beautiful bright green Mercedes and every morning my father would climb into the back of that Mercedes and be driven to work.'

Guleed tugged at her hijab, adjusting the fit slightly.

'Then one morning my mother woke all us children up and bundled us into the back of that green Mercedes and my father drove us to the airport. The next day I woke up in a B&B off the Euston Road. There were seven of us in two rooms and the toilets smelled.' She made a note in her daybook. 'My father was somebody important right up to the day he was nobody at all,' she said. 'Power in the material world is fleeting.'

'And yet you became a police officer,' I said.

'I said it was fleeting,' said Guleed. 'Not that it wasn't important.'

'So what did your dad do that was so important?' I asked.

Guleed snapped her daybook shut. 'Are we going to lean on Olivia or not?'

'Just waiting on a location,' I said, which was sort of true. 'Where's David?'

'He's out doing a recce on his target,' said Guleed. 'He managed to dig out floorplans on Zoopla, of all places, and now is checking to make sure he'll have all the exits covered.'

'Pays to be thorough,' I said.

Guleed shrugged and I could see that she was going to push the Olivia issue again when I was saved by my phone ringing – it was Beverley.

'You so owe me for this, babes,' she said and gave me the details.

When she was finished I hung up and told Guleed. Who was not happy.

'Just you?' she said.

'If you're there, then it becomes sort of officially official,' I said. 'This might be our best chance to find out who supplied the drugs.'

'And if it turns out to be Olivia Thames-MacAllister?'

'Then at least we won't be wasting our time looking for someone else.'

'All right,' she said. 'But I'm sitting outside while you're in there.'

So, back to Mayfair where the constant flow of money keeps the streets clean and free of unsightly poor people. It was just as well one of us was staying in the car, because we couldn't find a legal parking space.

'Be careful,' said Guleed as I got out.

'Hey, if I'm not back in an hour,' I said, 'call the President.'

Lady Ty met me at her front door and for once she wasn't wearing a suit. Instead she wore a pair of jeans and a loose green Arran jumper. Her hair was wrapped in a faded green and gold African print scarf which meant that either she was between hair conditionings or she was reverting under stress – neither was a good omen.

Her gaze flicked over to Guleed and then back to me.

'I see you've left the secret policeman's daughter in the car,' she said.

'Ty,' I said, 'you're better at sarcasm than I am – I concede. Whatever. Can we just get this done?'

The idea that I was more reluctant to meet up than she was threw her off long enough for me to get inside the house, and we were back in the kitchen where the wheels had come off the first time. Olivia was waiting for us in the same seat as before, but there was no caution this time, plus two or otherwise. This was off the books – I was not here, this never happened – the spice must flow.

Since she was sitting, I stayed standing – so did her mum.

'We know about Phoebe,' I said.

A little jerk of the head as Olivia tried to hide her reaction, not helped by having her mum ask, 'What about Phoebe?'

I looked at Lady Ty, but made sure I could still see Olivia's reaction.

'Your husband George drives a blue BMW?' I said and quoted the licence number.

'What about it?' asked Lady Ty who had probably been planning to hold my feet to the fire but now had something else to worry about – thank god.

'Do you know its current whereabouts?'

'George has a space at the car park at Marble Arch,' she said. 'He always leaves it there when he's away working.'

'A car matching its description was used to buy the drugs that killed Christina Chorley,' I said.

'That's not possible,' said Lady Ty and strode across the kitchen to where a surprisingly unbranded clutch bag was sitting on the counter beside the microwave. From it she pulled a set of keys and dangled them at me. 'There are only two sets of keys,' she said. 'George has the others.'

'Then it must have been you who drove down south to buy drugs,' I said.

'That's absurd,' she said. 'You know that's absurd.'

'I have a dealer who can identify your car and I can prove that it was in the right place at the right time – I've got the CCTV,' I said. Which was a total lie. At best there was a fifty-fifty chance that should I spend five days tracking down cameras I might find one that had recorded the event. 'If it wasn't you, who was it?'

'I've told you,' said Olivia from behind me. 'It was me.'

'Olivia can't drive,' said Lady Ty. 'I offered to pay for lessons, but she can't even be bothered to apply for a provisional licence.'

This I knew – just as I knew that Phoebe Beaumont-Jones had a brand spanking new driver's licence, issued just a month previously. Obviously she was better motivated than our Olivia.

'So it must be you,' I said to Lady Ty, who raised an eyebrow in reply. I drew myself up and said in my most serious voice – 'Cecelia Tyburn McAllister-Thames I—' It's a long name and I drew it out as much as I could, but you've got to wonder what might have happened had Olivia been made of sterner stuff.

'Fine,' said Olivia. 'Fine, okay, I wasn't alone.'

Lady Ty met my eyes before I turned to face her daughter, and her gaze was cool and ironic and terrifying.

'Was it Phoebe?' I asked.

'Yes,' said Olivia.

'Did she buy the drugs?' I asked.

Olivia hesitated.

'Did she?' said her mother.

'Yes.'

Lady Ty asked if buying the drugs had been Phoebe's idea and, when Olivia hesitated again, asked the question again in a tone I recognised from my own mum. The one that says: Yes there's going to be trouble, but that is as nothing to the trouble you are about to be in if you continue to cross me.

'Yes,' said Olivia. It had been Phoebe's idea because Phoebe was fun and exciting and didn't spend her whole life trying to conform to other people's expectations. Phoebe was a rebel.

'Yes, yes,' said Lady Ty. 'She's a rebel, good for her. And you're planning to go to prison on her behalf why?'

'You forget I've seen you at work,' said Olivia. 'I knew you'd get me out of it.'

'I understand that,' said Lady Ty. 'What I'm asking is why you're even risking it for this girl. God knows I've got close friends, but I wouldn't go to prison for them – not for a packet of dodgy E's.'

I've seen enough of these rows to know that we were winding up to DEFCON 1 and that my window for getting any coherent information out of either of them was small.

'Whose idea was it to go to the party at One Hyde Park?' I asked.

Mother and daughter turned to look at me.

'What's that got to do with anything?' asked Olivia.

'You said you weren't friends with Christina, so was it Phoebe that suggested you go to the party?'

'I don't have to answer that,' she said, but I was pretty certain she already had.

'Why are you doing this?' demanded Lady Ty, turning back to Olivia. 'What could you possibly owe this . . . girl.'

'I love her,' said Olivia quietly.

'What?'

'She's my girlfriend,' she said and then, to clear up any semantic confusion, 'My lover,' and then, because her mum was still staring at her with a stunned expression on her face, 'we have sex, we're lesbians, queer, dykes, we get out of the left side of the bed, we dance the face fanny fandango—'

'All right,' said Lady Ty. 'I get it – you're a lesbian.'

By this point I was eager to emulate Guleed and merge unobtrusively with the imitation French farmhouse fitted cupboard and counter unit behind me.

Lady Ty took a deep breath.

'So,' she said. 'Since when?'

'Since about I was eleven.'

'And you didn't tell me?' Lady Ty turned to glare at me. 'Does he know?'

'Why the fuck would he know?' asked Olivia.

'Why the fuck don't I know?' said Lady Ty.

'Because I thought you might react like this,' said Olivia and, when her mum continued to just stare at her dazedly, continued, 'Aunty Fleet said I should tell you.'

'Fleet knows?' said Lady Ty. 'Of course Fleet knows! Why am I not surprised?'

'I had to tell someone,' said Olivia and then stopped

mid-sentence to stare at me. Her mum turned to face me as well.

'You've got what you wanted,' she said in a strangely distant tone. 'Now piss off.'

And off I pissed.

I found Guleed still in the car reading something off her phone. She'd taken the opportunity to change her hijab, the new one being electric blue with silver and black details. Hijabs, Guleed once told me, were like T-shirts – you could choose ones that uniquely expressed your personality. But, unlike a T-shirt, you could wear them with the sort of conservative suit that was *de rigueur* for serving police officers.

'Do you get the impression that this Phoebe is more involved with the dead girl and Reynard than Tyburn's daughter is?' asked Guleed, once I'd filled her in.

'Just a bit,' I said. 'We'll have to ask.'

We were already heading for Phoebe Beaumont-Jones' address in St Johns Wood. She lived just west of Primrose Hill, part of that band of posh that runs down from Hampstead Hill in the north to Mayfair in the south. Along the line, I couldn't help notice, of the hidden river Tyburn. My dad says that when he was younger these areas used to have all sorts of people, but the artists, musicians and other undesirables had been leached out by London's continuous house price boom.

I was pretty certain that, ten seconds after I'd left her house, Olivia would have phoned or texted Phoebe to let her know we were on our way, and we needed to at least have the house under surveillance in case she tried to leg it.

But before we got there Nightingale called and said that he and Lady Helena had found Reynard Fossman.

'Where is he?' I asked.

'He's gone to ground in Archway – at the Intrepid Fox.'

'Seriously?'

'Perhaps,' said Nightingale, 'he felt that its very obviousness would be deception enough.'

Obviously not very experienced with the police then – we like obvious. Obvious is our middle name.

Since this was going to be an all-Falcon, plus ambiguous auxiliaries, operation Nightingale needed me immediately. Guleed promised she'd sit on Phoebe's house until I had a chance to get back.

'It's all go in the Isaacs, isn't it?' she said.

'Where'd you get that name from?' I asked.

'Isn't that what the Folly is called?' said Guleed. 'I'm sure I heard that somewhere.'

'You've been talking to Bev, haven't you?'

'That would be telling,' she said. So, yeah, she'd been talking to Bev.

God, I *hoped* it was Bev. Because if it was someone else—

Guleed dropped me off at Warren Street so I could get the tube to Archway.

When I was a kid, the Intrepid Fox was called the Archway Tavern, a notorious pub that stood at the centre of the Archway circulatory system and was definitely not a place where a well brought up Kentish Town boy would go drinking. The original Intrepid Fox was a famous metal pub stroke music venue which was driven out of Soho as an early casualty of the blandification of the West End. The venue moved briefly to St Giles and then to the unlamented Tavern and proceeded to paint the inside and outside as black as a teenager's bedroom and stuck a ton of Goth iconography on the walls in the hope that Marilyn Manson would pop round for a pint. It actually closed down not long after we raided it, but just for once I can say with a clear conscience, it wasn't my fault.

Archway is where the post-war dream of the urban motorway died in the teeth of local opposition and the inability of the designers to answer basic traffic management questions. Thus the A1 remained unwidened and what was then the Archway Tavern stood proudly like a combination tank trap and brick shithouse in the way of progress. Famously, the planning inquiry got so unruly that the Planning Inspector fled through a fire escape to escape the protestors.

I've often wondered if such 'awkward' spots in London are somehow sacred to Mr Punch – the spirit of riot and rebellion – and maybe that was why I thought I heard him laughing the afternoon we nicked Reynard the Fox.

Or it might have been carbon monoxide poisoning because me and Caroline were stuck on a strip of pavement thirty centimetres wide with nothing but a safety barrier between us and three lanes of congestion. We were there because this was where the Intrepid Fox had its back door, and where we expected Reynard to make his egress, at some speed, about two minutes after Nightingale and Lady Helena went in the front.

'Whatever you do,' I told Caroline, 'don't put your hands on him – if you physically touch him it gets legally complicated. If you think he's going to get away see if you can trip him up with your magic rope trick and I'll go sit on him.'

'Do you like being a policeman?' asked Caroline.

'Love it,' I said. 'Why do you ask?'

'You're a bright guy – it just seems like a waste.'

'You think I should be a stockbroker instead,' I said. 'Or a celebrity chef or something constructive like that?'

'Oh,' she said. 'You're an idealist.'

I asked Caroline what she planned to do with *her* skills, then.

'I'm going to teach myself to fly,' she said.

'With magic?'

'Of course with magic,' said Caroline. 'I already have a pilot's licence.'

'And when you learn to fly,' I said, 'what are you going to do with that?'

'What am I going to do,' said Caroline, 'is I'm going to fly.'

I felt rather than heard a thump from inside the Intrepid Fox and caught the scent of candlewax.

'That was Mum,' said Caroline.

I motioned her to stand to one side of the doorway while I took the other.

'It pays to be careful,' I said.

There was the distant crash of breaking glass that was definitely not *vestigium* and then a series of high pitched barks.

'Reynard?' said Caroline.

I shrugged.

There was a sound like somebody running the tape of a Michael Bay action sequence backwards and something thumped into the door with enough force to make the frame rattle.

'Nightingale,' I said.

Then it went suspiciously quiet and we both tensed, and then forced ourselves to take deep breaths to clear our minds. Nothing fancy, I thought. Water balloon in the face and then knock him back into the arms of Nightingale, who would likely be just behind.

We waited what seemed like a long time while the congestion roared past and the carbon monoxide infiltrated our red blood cells – then the door opened and Nightingale stuck his head out.

'You can come in now,' he said. 'We've got him.'

Reynard was not a happy fox as we manhandled him through the gloomy halls of Gothdom and out the front door to where Nightingale had left the blue Asbo, the Jag being a bit conspicuous, and plonked him in the back. Then, once he was sure Reynard was safely hand-cuffed, Nightingale cautioned him – using the proper modern caution, I noted.

To give him his due, Reynard looked like he was going to go for defiance – before suddenly deflating and dropping his chin onto his chest.

'So where you taking him?' I asked – while technically

the Folly is a nick, it bears the same relationship to basic human rights legislation as Camp X-Ray.

'Belgravia,' said Nightingale and, smiling, held up an honest to god sky blue Metropolitan Police issue Evidence & Actions Book and flipped it open to the PERSONS CONCERNED/ARRESTED page to show me where Reynard Fossman's name had been filled in in nice clear capitals.

I wondered what Reynard was going to ask to put in the self-defined ethnicity slot – there wasn't enough room for 'anthropomorphic fairy tale animal'.

'Stephanopoulos said she wanted to be present for the interview,' said Nightingale.

I glanced over to where Lady Helena and Caroline were standing, just within not-too-obvious eavesdropping distance.

'And our friends?'

'They're waiting for Harold, who's making haste from Oxford even as we speak,' said Nightingale.

'So you found it?' I asked. If Harold Postmartin was abandoning his Oxford comforts it could only be for *The Third Principia*.

'We've found something that might be it,' he said. 'With luck Harold can verify it.'

'You seem to have everything sorted,' I said.

'You don't need to sound quite so disappointed,' said Nightingale. 'I've always been a quick study, Peter. But if you wish to keep an eye on my progress you're welcome to come along.'

'Nah,' I said. 'Anyway, I promised Guleed I'd be back before dinner.' I explained where we were on Phoebe

Beaumont-Jones and her upcoming involuntary stint helping the police with their inquiries.

'In that case,' said Nightingale, 'would you like any assistance with that?'

'Don't worry,' I said. 'I think we can handle it.'

Famous last words.

8

Uninvited Guests

So I headed back to the improbably named Woronzow Road in St Johns Wood, home of the mysterious Phoebe Beaumont-Jones. On the way Stephanopoulos called me.

'You haven't disappeared a suspect have you?' she asked.

We better not have, I thought.

'Not that I know of,' I said in the vain hope that Stephanopoulos wouldn't notice the plausible deniability aspect.

'Only Bromley Crime Squad have lost track of a minor little scrote called Aiden Burghley who they said was talking to you this very morning,' she said.

I assured her that not only hadn't I disappeared him, but the last time I saw him he was in the care of said Crime Squad and in the presence of his lawyer.

'His brief says she took her eyes off him for five seconds and he was gone.'

'Wasn't me, boss,' I said.

'Was it *your* boss?' she asked because she's police and had spotted the plausible deniability bit.

I said it wasn't him either because, *au contraire*, he was bringing in Reynard the chicken worrier even as we spoke. In that case, Stephanopoulos decided, Aiden Burghley had gone walkabouts on his own recognizance and it was Bromley's problem not ours.

It was a couple of hours past the school rush and the sun was setting and the four by fours were nestled up against the pavement. I spotted the Asbo hiding amongst them two doors down from the Beaumont-Jones house and headed over. I saw Guleed's face reflected in the wing mirror as she clocked my approach – nobody sneaks up on the Muslim ninja.

I climbed in beside her and traded the chicken kebab I'd picked up from a Halal café in Tufnell Park for her tablet. After a slow start the police have taken to mobile technology in a big way – mainly because it means you can pretend to work anywhere: at home, the canteen, the local boozer. Senior officers favoured using iPads because the *find* function allowed them to track how much time you spent in the boozer, and to find lost tablets before they're picked up and their contents sold to the *Guardian* newspaper.

So, even sitting in the car, Guleed had been busy collating.

'It turns out the father is really rich,' she said.

'What's he do?'

'Invests,' she said.

Jeremy Beaumont-Jones had been lucky enough to be born rich. He wasn't in the mad oligarch class but once you're past a certain point, the sheer weight of your money sucks in wealth like a financial singularity. If you're sensible enough not to blow it on race horses, cocaine or musical theatre, then it becomes a perpetual-motion money making machine.

He'd also been to Oxford, although he wasn't on any of the Little Crocodile lists.

'Where is he now?'

'The Bahamas,' said Guleed. 'Business convention.'

'Do you think he's on his way back?' I asked. Having the daddy arrive with a legal posse would put a crimp in the investigation. Since Lady Ty had all but shut us down, I really didn't think we wanted another pile of influence landing on our heads.

'He's at least five hours away,' said Guleed. Although apparently there was a private jet.

I eyed the, it had to be said, fairly nondescript late Victorian terrace – even in this area it couldn't have been worth more than three million, four million pounds tops.

'This is a bit pokey for someone with big money,' I said.

'It's one of five,' said Guleed. 'Oh look, there goes the maid.'

A thin, washed-out white woman with sandy hair opened the front gate and headed up the road towards Swiss Cottage. Probably Polish or Romanian. Mum said the rich private clients always preferred to use white cleaners rather than Africans. Actually they'd prefer Filipinos or Vietnamese or, well, anyone really rather than Africans. Mum said she preferred offices anyway, because you didn't have to deal with some posh woman standing over you and telling you your business.

And the way she said it was a lot ruder in Krio – trust me.

Guleed hadn't spotted anyone else going in or out, and if it turned out Phoebe was currently residing at one of the other four properties – Lombardy, Ireland, the Cotswolds or Santa Barbara – then there was no point us sitting outside like muppets.

We were just gearing ourselves up to leave the car when Crew Cut from Harrods arrived.

I recognised him immediately and so did Guleed, who was calling for back-up before I'd finished swearing.

Crew Cut had come with friends, three other white guys with the same army-surplus muscularity and haircuts. They all wore off the peg black suits cut baggy for comfort, and all the better to cover any concealed weapons.

En masse they couldn't have stood out as Americans more if they'd painted their faces red, white and blue. They went up the steps and paused in front of the door; two kept watch while a third bent over to do something to the lock. I couldn't see what, but I doubted it was anything legal. Whatever it was, it was quick. The door opened and the whole group slipped inside with a practised lack of fuss.

I had a horrid feeling I'd just met the 'gentlemen visitors' that Kim had warned me about.

Where had they come from? I doubted they'd sauntered here from the tube station. I glanced up the road and spotted a black Ford Explorer hiding amongst the other Chelsea Tractors. It had the traditional tinted windscreen but we could still make out the figure of a white guy in the driver's seat.

'Can't leave him there,' said Guleed.

She was right. If we went in after the goon squad, their man in the Explorer would tip them off. So we quickly concocted one of our better plans – better insofar as that just for once it went as planned.

I approached on the pavement while Guleed strolled up the middle of the street and caught the driver's attention. As soon as she had it, she pulled out her warrant card and held it up as she advanced. We'd both decided that when dealing with a possibly armed American it was better to avoid any potential ambiguity.

'Especially since I'm the one being ambiguous,' said Guleed.

The driver might have sussed me for police as well, but it didn't matter. He hesitated for long enough for me to slap a car killer into the bonnet of the Explorer and that's all she wrote for that particular electronic ignition system. I kept it low key enough to avoid frying any phone he might be carrying – just in case we might need it later.

Because he was American, he instinctively kept his hands on his steering wheel where we could see them.

'Good evening, sir,' said Guleed. 'Would you step out of the car, please?'

And that was that.

He got out and we conducted a search in full compliance with Code A, Paragraph 3.1 of the Code of Practice – to whit, that all searches must be carried out with courtesy, consideration and respect for the person concerned.

Apart from, sensibly, keeping his mouth shut he co-operated with the search. Which was just as well because he was tall and fit and carrying a semi-automatic pistol in a shoulder holster. He also had a Samsung Galaxy with a retro modded hard 'off' switch not entirely unlike the phones me and Nightingale carried. And when I checked his wrist I saw he had a wind-up diver's watch. It was practitioner's gear and, coupled with the absence of anything identifiable on his person – not even a driver's licence – pretty much confirmed that these were magic spooks. They might even have some legal standing in the states.

But not in London, so Guleed arrested him for carrying a firearm, driving without a licence and being suspiciously foreign in a built-up area. By the time we had him cuffed, the first IRV had arrived and we cheerfully handed him over to be tucked up in the back.

And I was quite happy to wait for back-up at that point – up to and including SCO19, the SAS and/or Nightingale in full tank-destroyer mode – except I got a blast of *vestigia* from the house. Nothing I could identify beyond a whiff of oily water and a chill across my back.

According to the Human Rights Act (1998) as interpreted in my dog-eared copy of *Blackstone's Police Operational Handbook: Practice and Procedure*, I had a 'duty of positive action' with regards to protection of the public. This meant I had to at least make a token attempt to make sure Phoebe Beaumont-Jones was not this moment being waterboarded by the Jack Bauer wannabes I'd watched walk in not five minutes previously.

Assuming, of course, that they weren't in league with

our Phoebe and even now sitting down for a nice cup of tea and conspiracy. And assuming that she was inside the house in the first place.

Normally the Metropolitan Police frowns on its officers rushing in without a risk assessment and/or the appropriate specialist unit. Unfortunately in this case I was the appropriate specialist unit, and the firearms officers who were on their way were unequipped to deal with a Falcon scenario. Not least because the first draft of *Procedures Relating to Serious Falcon Incidents* a.k.a. *How to Deal with Weird Bollocks* was currently sitting as a half-finished Word document on my hard drive back at the Folly.

I called Nightingale, who said he was fifteen minutes away and asked him to authorise a little look.

'Yes,' he said immediately. 'But carefully, Peter.'

I told Guleed that it was standard procedure for a second officer to stay outside the immediate Zone of Potential Magical Effect (ZPME) in order to facilitate communications should my Airwave and personal phones be compromised. Guleed was rightly suspicious.

'Is that true?' she asked.

Just as soon as I get back to the Folly and add it to the Word document, I thought.

'Just make sure nobody rushes in,' I said. 'Especially you.'

'And when things start to explode?' she asked, but I didn't dignify that with an answer.

'I'm coming at least as far as the door,' she said.

As we approached the front door I saw that there were strips of thick perspex or glass embedded into the front lawn – skylights for a basement. I pointed them out to Guleed, who frowned.

The very rich, having fundamentally missed the point of urban living, have long been frustrated by the fact that it's impossible to squeeze the amenities of a country mansion – car showroom, swimming pool, cinema, servants' quarters etc. – into the floor space of your average London terrace. Those without access to trans-dimensional engineering, a key Time Lord discovery, have had to resort to extending their houses into the ground. Thus proving that all that stands between your average rich person and a career in Bond villainy is access to an extinct volcano.

They are also a bugger to raid, because you need twice as many bodies to secure the premises. Stephanopoulos once told me that it was like watching a clown car in reverse. Once, during a raid in Kensington, she said that after waiting outside for half an hour she went in herself to make sure none of the entry team had got lost or, worse, been distracted by the bowling alley that reputedly occupied the bottommost level.

The front door was ajar – the lock had been drilled.

Not a friendly visit, then.

I put the Airwave in my pocket on open mic. Before I could move, the door was opened from the inside. They'd left someone to guard the perimeter – of course they had.

He was shorter than the driver, blond haired, oval faced with a surprisingly weak chin. He only opened the door half-way and he kept his right hand hidden behind it so I didn't think trying to nut him was a viable tactical option.

'Hi,' he said brightly. 'Can I help you?' I'm not that good at American accents but I guessed East Coast.

For a mad moment I was tempted to ask him if he had a personal relationship with Jesus and, if not, would he like one? But I think that was the adrenaline talking. The pistol I suspected he was concealing behind the door was weighing heavily on my mind.

'Hi,' I said. 'My name's Peter Grant. I'm with the police. Is Phoebe Beaumont-Jones available for a chat?'

'Sure,' he said. 'Come on in.'

He opened the door wider and stepped to the side to let me in.

Guleed, who'd slipped to the side and out of sight when the door opened, tapped her fingernail twice on the wall to let me know that she wasn't happy – but she stayed out of sight.

There was no sign of a pistol in either hand when I stepped inside. I figured he might have stuck it into the back waistband of his trousers, but I couldn't be sure. And, from an operational standpoint, you generally want to avoid uncertainty about where a firearm is before you do anything stupid.

I asked for his name and he said 'Teddy', which made him a bloody liar.

Inside, the house had obviously been gutted, stripped down and rebuilt in the last five years. The narrow stairway typical of a London terrace had been replaced by the spiral staircase with marble risers so beloved of people who don't have to lug their own furniture up to the floors above. It also extended down into the basement and I caught a whiff of chlorinated water that indicated a pool. I'm not very fond of the combination of under-ground and water, so of course down we went.

It wasn't that super, by the standards of London super-basements, being mostly swimming pool, fitness centre and wine cellar. And it wasn't that big a pool either, since it had to fit into the narrow footprint of a terraced house – less than ten metres long and three wide. It was lit by underwater lights that cast ripples on the ceiling and pale red marble walls. The designer had probably been going for Turkish Bath but had hit Czech Porn Shoot instead.

There was a tiled space at the near edge of the pool which sported a couple of white plastic chairs, a match-ing round table and, redundantly, a sun lounger. A young white woman in a blue string bikini was reclining on the lounger. I recognised her face from the pictures on Olivia's wall – Phoebe Beaumont-Jones. One of Crew Cut's buddies, jackets unbuttoned, hands loosely held ready by their sides stood on either side of her.

Crew Cut was sitting at the table as if expecting a waiter at any minute.

'This is unfortunate,' he said. He still had a wicked bruise across the side of his face – it was going a nice mottled purple and must have really hurt.

I considered telling the lot of them they were under arrest, but even I'm not that stupid. Phoebe was staring at me with a fixed expression but I could see her legs trembling.

'Hello Phoebe,' I said. 'How are you doing?'

She bobbed her head nervously but she couldn't seem to open her mouth to speak.

'Why don't you have a seat?' said Crew Cut. His accent was Southern-ish but not the caricature I'd heard on TV – it was the deliberately cultured accent of someone working hard to convince you they were a reasonable and civilised man. I was immediately on my guard. Well, even more on my guard, given the room full of armed men.

'What's your name?' I asked.

'Let's not worry about that for the moment,' said Crew Cut.

'What should we worry about instead?'

Crew Cut tilted his head slightly.

'I'd say we've managed to get ourselves into one of those unfortunate situations,' he said, 'where two parties that should be allies find themselves in a confrontation.'

'Allies?'

'We are both the heirs to Isaac Newton,' he said. 'A product of the same enlightenment.'

Which made them, after Lady Helena, the second lot of heirs we'd met this week. Now personally I didn't think of myself as the great man's heir so much as somebody who'd wandered into his house to borrow his lawnmower, but as Stephanopoulos has indicated, on more than one occasion, sometimes my cheek is inappropriate in a modern policing context.

'Just to be clear,' I said, 'you're the American wizards?'

Crew Cut shook his head slowly.

'Specialists, son,' he said. 'Our job is to deal with the problems, not create new ones.'

That was bollocks from where I was standing, but I was perfectly happy to keep Crew Cut chatting shit until

Nightingale turned up to put him out of my misery. But Crew Cut had to guess back-up was on its way by now, and that it was only a matter of time. He looked a bit too relaxed to me, and it was making me nervous.

'I think you're a little bit out of your jurisdiction,' I said.

'The whole world is our jurisdiction, son,' said Crew Cut. 'And I have the executive order to prove it.'

I looked over at Phoebe who was still shivering – it was noticeably chilly down here and I wondered if the heating had been turned off.

'I'm going to take off my jacket,' I said. 'Nice and slowly.'

Crew Cut told me to go ahead and then he let me pass it to one of his men who passed it to Phoebe who put it on. She was much smaller than she looked in the pictures and seemed even more childlike as she tried to tuck her legs up inside the jacket.

'Pity,' said Crew Cut as Phoebe stopped visibly shivering. 'Another fifteen minutes and she might have told us something useful.'

I told him I thought it might be better if Phoebe were allowed to leave.

'Better for who?' he asked.

I wondered again what he was waiting for – what did he think was going to happen?

'Better for her,' I said. 'And, in the long run, better for you.'

Crew Cut made an elegant shooing gesture at Phoebe, but she just stared at him.

I told her that it was going to be all right and was amazingly convincing, all things considered.

Phoebe hopped up smartly and, keeping an eye on Crew Cut, edged past me.

'Go out the front door,' I said. 'And keep going until you see someone in uniform.'

She nodded and headed for the stairs. Just to try my luck I turned to amble after her, but Crew Cut shook his head.

'Not you, Peter,' he said and then lifted his wrist to his mouth and spoke into his sleeve. 'Teddy – we're letting the shade go.'

That he knew my name pretty much confirmed that these were Kim Reynolds' visitors, but I did wonder what a 'shade' was – and how come this lot were so relaxed. Crew Cut didn't strike me as stupid. He had to know we would have the house surrounded, and that an armed breach would be next – if they were lucky. If they were unlucky, one of the Met's highly trained negotiators would turn up and be aggravatingly reasonable to them until the Americans a) surrendered or b) shot themselves in the head in an effort to make it stop.

'What's a shade?' I asked.

'A creature that looks like a man but walks in the shadows,' said Crew Cut.

Police doctrine is, even if you're waiting for someone to do something violent to your suspect, you should de-escalate the situation because at the very least a peaceful resolution produces a ton less paperwork.

'Am I a shade?' I asked.

'The jury's still out on you, son,' said Crew Cut, and

then spoke into his sleeve again. 'Okay Teddy – time we were leaving.'

I wondered what the hell they thought they were going to do – was there a rear exit, a helicopter on the roof, or had they contracted with International Rescue to lease The Mole and drill their way out?

I never did get to find out, because about then was when the lights went out.

All at once.

I dropped to the floor, on the basis that I was in a room full of excitable men with guns, and I thought it might not be a bad idea to get my centre of mass out of the line of fire. As I went down I heard a cracking noise, a muffled grunt and a rushing sound. A terrible and familiar smell rolled over me, the liquid shit stink of the sewers. Something slapped my leg so I pulled it in under me.

I heard the Americans shouting and something heavy – I hoped it wasn't a body – hitting the pool with a splash. I needed some light, but I wasn't stupid enough to want it anywhere near me. So I cast a *werelight* over at the far end of the basement where it wouldn't blind or illuminate me. Even as I released the spell I lined up the *formae* for a shield and had that ready to go.

The *werelight* popped up, strangely blurred and wavering.

There was a series of painfully loud bangs as the Americans opened fire.

The light flickered and cast rolling shadows across the walls and ceiling.

'Cease fire,' I yelled. But, just in case they didn't, I put up my shield.

A cold and stinking wind struck me in the face, and with it I realised what was wrong.

My *werelight* had materialised inside a rolling wall of water stretching from the base of the pool to the ceiling. It was racing down the length of the basement towards me, and that's what was causing the wind.

Oh shit, I thought as I raised my shield. Wrong spell.

I noticed the shield *did* slow the water down a fraction before it swept me, the Americans, and the cheap plastic garden furniture down the remaining the length of the basement.

Which, incidentally, saved our lives.

Not that I appreciated it at the time, you understand.

My shield bought me enough time to take a breath, but then it was a cold, wet, spinning darkness enlivened only by the occasional violent blow and the constant distraction of my own screaming terror. My shoulders hit something and, despite having my chin tucked into my chest, my head snapped back and slammed into a hard surface. I lost my air, and my *werelight*, darkness crashed in and I heard a voice from far away, shrill and terrifyingly cheerful, start to chant.

Right fol de riddle loll
I'm the boy to do 'em all.

Breathing – it's an autonomic function and, past a certain point, your body is going to take a breath whatever your consciousness says and regardless of what you're actually going to be breathing in.

I saw light – pale strips wavering in the darkness – the

185

skylights embedded in the front garden. I needed a way out and I didn't have time to be subtle.

Here's a stick!

Magic is not about passion or anger or the power of friendship. Magic is about control, focus, and being able to concentrate when you're drowning to death.

To thump Old Nick!

Training helps, as does experience. But the key is preparation. I'd once spent a fun afternoon buried under the eastbound Central Line platform at Oxford Circus and subsequently made a point of getting Nightingale to teach me something simple and effective for breaking architecture. It's an *impello* variant with a lot of complicated little twists and curlicues. Not a spell – Nightingale said – normally learnt by apprentices. It's also a bit limited in its applicability to everyday policing.

I picked a spot half-way along one of the skylights.

If he, by chance, upon me call.

I'd done a lot of practise – and I was motivated.

And anything to get Mr Punch to shut the fuck-up.

Only it didn't work.

There was enough light for me to see the puffs of dust across the ceiling. Fine cracks shot out in a star shape from the focal point I'd picked, but the basement was well built and the ceiling held. I tried to gather up the *formae* for another go, but my mind was filled with the need to breathe and a long ululating laugh of triumph.

Suddenly there was a terrible pain in my ears and a burst of light from above and the section of the ceiling I'd been casting at seemed to blow upwards. I kicked and swam towards the light. But when I was almost at the lip, the water suddenly dragged at me as if I was caught in an undertow. And back down I went.

There was a thudding hollowness in my chest and I figured I had seconds before I took an evolutionary step backwards and tried to breathe water, but my feet hit solid floor and I kicked as hard as I could back-up towards the light.

The water around me boomed and rumbled and suddenly I was flying upwards. I burst out into the air and took a breath before I could stop myself and choked on a face full of water. Somebody grabbed my arm and held me up while I coughed desperately and took a second, proper, breath.

I blinked and saw brown eyes framed by black cloth, blinked again and saw that it was Guleed with the bottom of her hijab pulled up to cover her nose and mouth. I figured out why she'd done that when I took another breath and started coughing again. The air was so brown with brick dust that I couldn't see the street lights.

I was at the edge of a surprisingly smooth-sided hole in the garden about a metre and a half across. Dirty water was welling up over the edge in rippling pulses. Obviously my spell had weakened it before something had raised the water level with enough force to punch it out.

I'd have liked to ask what that something had been, but just then I was too busy breathing.

But not too busy to yell when something grabbed my leg and tried to drag me down. I kicked frantically as Guleed tightened her grip on my arm and shoulder and attempted to heave me up over the lip of the hole.

A head broke surface next to me and did the whole emergency air sucking thing. It was one of Crew Cut's boys. A second head bobbed up, retching and gasping – that was two.

'I need some help here,' shouted Guleed, bending over our impromptu garden pond as she tried to keep all of us afloat at once.

A pair of uniforms appeared out of the dust and helped pull me out.

'That way,' said one and pushed me gently towards the street.

A slim, unexpectedly elegant, paramedic pounced on me as I cleared the dust and threw a space blanket over my shoulders. He wanted to know if I was in pain and I told him I was just happy to be breathing.

He wanted to drag me away to his ambulance and do medical things, but I waited until Guleed emerged from the dust cloud trailed by the two uniforms and, suitably searched and handcuffed, the two Americans.

I asked Guleed if she'd seen 'Teddy' or Crew Cut himself.

'I jumped Teddy as soon as Phoebe cleared the front gate,' she said, pulling her hijab off her lower face.

'We'd better get back in there and find their leader,' I said.

'I don't think that's a good idea,' she said.

The dust was clearing and I looked back at the house and saw it wasn't there anymore. The whole front had collapsed into the basement, leaving the floors open and exposed like a vandalised doll's house. It looked like something from the Blitz, with broken floorboards and haphazard piles of brick. One room near the top had cheerful yellow wallpaper – a cot teetered precariously on the edge of what was left of the floor.

The weight of the initial collapse must have caused the pressure wave in the water which blew out the hole I'd being trying to magic in the skylight. A second collapse had squirted me out.

Barring a miracle, Crew Cut was probably under that lot.

Uniform was pulling back to be replaced by the Fire Brigade. They'd have the dogs and thermal sensors out as soon it was safe.

'Oh, shit,' I said.

Guleed looked at me, at the remains of the house, and then back at me.

'Not one word,' I said. 'Not one.'

The Custody Sergeant sighed when she saw the remains of Crew Cut's crew.

'I should have known when I was well off,' she said.

The Americans all maintained a stoic silence, which bothered the Custody Sergeant not all. She just wrote 'refused' in every box, made sure they were all DNA'd and live scanned and banged them up. To avoid confusion they were marked up on the electronic white board as *Male: anon – 'Teddy'*; *Male: anon – blond*; *Male: anon – eyebrow scar*.

The Americans were all adults, foreigners, and had been caught red-handed – so they could wait. Phoebe Beaumont-Jones being seventeen and – since we didn't have direct evidence of her drug dealing yet – a witness rather than a suspect, had to be interviewed immediately. So, after I'd pulled some dry clothes from the emergency bag I keep under the shared desk in the Outside Inquiry room, I joined Guleed in the Achieving Best Evidence suite to do just that. Anyone looking for a place to kip tonight was going to have to snooze at their desk like everybody else.

Phoebe had refused her stepmum as her responsible adult.

'Frankly I'd rather go to prison,' she'd said. And her dad was still abroad, so we ended up with a young solicitor from the local criminal law specialist. The solicitor was white, presentable and spoke with an affected South London accent that didn't fool anyone, except maybe Phoebe.

After caution plus two we could have gone straight to the business with the drugs. But our priority – as determined by the senior officers even now monitoring us from the video suite – was to find out what the fuck the Americans had wanted.

Phoebe said she had no idea.

'I was downstairs by the pool,' she said. 'And they just appeared.'

'They' being Crew Cut, who finally identified himself as Dean, and his merry men.

They'd asked her about her eBay activities.

'What about your eBay activities?' I asked.

'I don't know,' she said. 'I never use eBay.'

'Do you have a PayPal account?' asked Guleed.

'No, I have a credit card,' said Phoebe, who was perfectly happy to buy online and perfectly happy to buy second-hand – just not at the same time.

'It's so much more fun getting clothes from charity shops,' she said. 'I once almost grabbed a genuine Nicole Farhi jacket in a charity shop in Chelsea but this woman beat me to it.'

She wasn't sure what she was supposed to have done on eBay, but Dean, formerly known as Crew Cut, seemed to think she'd tried to sell a book.

We asked what kind of book.

'An old book,' she said. 'Really old, like centuries old. A ledger – that's what boss American called it.'

'Did he mention a title?' I asked.

Phoebe said not, but when we pressed she thought that Dean might have referred to it as the 'Last Ledger'. This all seemed a bit pat to me – suspects often can't resist dropping in little bits of detail in the hope that it adds veracity to their statement, when all it actually does is make us more suspicious. I made a note to pursue this question in a later interview and we retraced the timeline leading up to the Americans' arrival.

'I was in the kitchen getting a drink and—' Phoebe frowned. 'Then I went downstairs. Somebody knocked on the door.'

She didn't know the exact time, but it wasn't that long before the cleaner left. We'd had the door under observation by then and definitely hadn't seen anyone. Nobody sneaks past Guleed – she says it's a talent you acquire if you're the eldest child in a big family.

'Was the knock at the front door?' asked Guleed.

'Must have been,' said Phoebe, but she didn't seem so sure.

'Did you answer it?' asked Guleed.

'No,' said Phoebe.

'Was it a knock or the doorbell?' I asked.

'It was a knock,' she said hesitantly and then, with more confidence, 'definitely a knock.'

So it could have been the back door, not the front – perhaps that's how Dean and co planned to make their escape.

'What did you do next?' asked Guleed.

'I went downstairs,' said Phoebe.

'Did you go for a swim?' asked Guleed.

'I must have done,' said Phoebe. 'Why else would I go down there?'

She'd looked bone-dry to me when I'd seen her.

'What were you wearing when you were in the kitchen?' asked Guleed.

'Is that important?'

'Helps us establish a timeline,' said Guleed.

'Jeans,' said Phoebe. 'Or maybe tracksuit bottoms and a sweatshirt.'

'Not your bikini?'

'No,' said Phoebe.

'Not under your other clothes?' asked Guleed.

Phoebe looked at me and rolled her eyes at Guleed.

'No,' she said.

'Do you keep it downstairs by the pool?' I asked.

'Don't be silly,' said Phoebe. 'It's a Sofia by Vix – Ollie bought it for me in Nice – I wouldn't leave it downstairs where *she* could get her hands on it.'

'She' being Victoria Jones – Phoebe's stepmother.

'So you must have gone upstairs to your room before you went down to the pool,' I said.

Phoebe shrugged.

'Yeah,' she said. 'Must have.'

Memory is unreliable, and it isn't unusual for a witness to forget big chunks of the events that led to them answering your questions – even when things were fresh. Still, the obvious hole in Phoebe's timeline was beginning to worry me.

'Before the Americans turned up,' I said, 'was anyone in the basement with you?'

'Like who?'

'Like anybody.'

Phoebe frowned. 'I was talking to someone,' she said.

'Do you remember who?' asked Guleed.

'Someone from school, I think,' she said.

'A school friend?' asked Guleed.

'No,' said Phoebe and bit her lip. 'An old person.'

'Man or a woman?'

'Man.'

'A teacher?' I asked.

'No,' said Phoebe firmly. 'Not a teacher. You know, it's funny, but I think he was a parent . . .' she said.

'What makes you think that?' asked Guleed.

'He was familiar – like I totally knew him from some-where – but definitely not a teacher.'

'And yet you didn't recognise him?' I said.

'I did, but not so I could tell you who he was.' She made a waving motion with both hands. 'It's like when you're half-way to school and you can't remember what you had for breakfast. You know you had breakfast, you know what you usually have for breakfast, but you cannot for the life of you remember what you actually had today.'

Doing a two-hander during an interview is all about rhythm; you and your partner shift backwards and for-wards to keep the interviewee ever so slightly off balance. If they don't have time to think about their answers, then they are more likely to blurt out the truth. Or at least contradict themselves enough for you to figure out what they're lying about. Good cop/bad cop is the Holly-wood version, simplified and sexed up for maximum drama in minimum screen time. Me and Guleed had spent a year, off and on, interviewing everyone from mad mechanics to surly bouncers – not to mention the thing with the police horse which I've promised never to bring up on pain of ninjutsu – so she knew that the next line was mine, which would have probably been me asking what his voice sounded like.

But my mind, ironically, went blank. Because all at once I knew who had been in the basement swimming pool with us that evening.

'What did his voice sound like?' asked Guleed.

If Phoebe answered I wasn't listening, because I was thinking that the subset of St Paul's parents that Phoebe

194

knew personally was going to be finite. Maybe as low as ten to twenty males, and they'd all be on a list at the school. And that list could be cross-referenced with the list of Little Crocodiles and whittled down by finding out who had a reliable alibi for certain important dates. He'd been good at covering his tracks. But like Nightingale had said, he's not Moriarty. He's just another criminal and sooner or later he's going to make a mistake.

And I was fairly certain that the Faceless Man had just made it.

9

The Tiger Hunting Committee

The main purpose of an administrative meeting is to establish collective guilt for whatever fuck-up arises out of its decisions. That way, when the wheels come off you can't pretend you didn't know what was happening – because you were there, weren't you? – when those decisions were made. And we've got the minutes to prove it.

In the normal course of events a lowly PC like me, if they're sensible, finds themselves something better to do – paperwork, house to house inquiries, searching a landfill. Anything. Unfortunately, the Folly's flat management structure, viz there only being two of us, and its specialist nature, meant that not only was I at the meeting, but I was expected to make a valuable contribution.

So here we were, in a sparsely furnished meeting room on the fourteenth floor of the Empress State Building at Olympia with representatives from the DPS, Belgravia MIT and the National Crime Agency. All chaired by one Deputy Assistant Commissioner Richard Folsom, who apart from being a wholly owned subsidiary of the Tyburn Preservation Society had it in for me personally on account of that business at Covent Garden.

Ask not for whom the buck stops, I thought, it stops for thee.

I noticed that Guleed had made herself scarce.

Folsom glanced at me – the tic over his right eye causing a twitch – before turning to Seawoll and asking him to bring us all up to speed on the current state of the investigation and our operational posture.

Which could be summarised as 'confused' and 'ready to spring into action' – just as soon as we had the faintest idea where to spring.

We'd held Phoebe Beaumont-Jones on Friday night because Bromley Crime Squad wanted a word about the MDMA. But since they couldn't lay their hands on Aiden Burghley, the guy who allegedly sold her the gear, she walked out of the nick on Saturday afternoon without a charge.

DAC Folsom, to nobody's surprise, suggested that since there was no indication that Christina Chorley had been coerced into taking the pills and that Olivia Thames-MacAllister had retracted her statement, not to mention the complete lack of corroboration that she or her friend Phoebe had been involved, it was probably best to close down Operation Marigold and pass the file to the CPS.

'Especially given the number of other pressing concerns that have come to light,' said Folsom.

For a second, I thought Seawoll was going to fight it just on general principles, but then he shrugged. You don't get to DCI without knowing a losing proposition when you see one, and Folsom was right – there were more important things to worry about.

'*La majestueuse égalité des lois, qui interdit au riche comme au pauvre de coucher sous les ponts, de mendier dans les rues et de voler du pain,*' said Nightingale later when we were preparing our case notes. Which is French for 'Them that has, gets.'

So, goodbye Operation Marigold.

Which left Operation Carthorse, the hunt for Lesley May, Operation Wentworth, which was the fraud investigation surrounding the illegal demolition of Skygarden Tower and Operation Tinker, which was the still open murder inquiry into the unpleasant death of George Trenchard. Bromley MIT, which owned Tinker, was notably absent from the meeting, having dumped their files on us on Sunday afternoon and scarpered. The SIO had given up her Sunday just to get them off her hands.

And then there were the Americans.

It took the Fire Brigade a day and a half to secure the remains of the house enough to recover Crew Cut's body, which was described by Dr Jennifer Vaughan as 'suffering from crush trauma' and by Dr Walid as 'mostly flat'. Fortunately no other bodies were recovered and the neighbouring houses, while damaged, were declared safe. The neighbours themselves were spooked in a way that only watching three million quids' worth of equity sink into a hole in the ground can do, and it was only a matter of time before they tried to blame us for it. Even as we met at the Empress State Building, a crack team of police lawyers were figuring out how to blame it on the contractor who'd built the basement.

Crew Cut's *compadres* refused to talk when interviewed, and even refused the routine offer to contact the American embassy. None of them had been carry-ing ID and those who'd joined me in the twenty metre underwater dash hadn't been carrying weapons when they were fished out. I was pretty confident that when the weapons were recovered they would be the same scrubbed and anonymous Glocks that Teddy and the driver had been caught with.

'Have we contacted the American Embassy our-selves?' asked Folsom.

The woman from the National Crime Agency said they'd asked Belgravia not to do that just yet.

'We want to know if anyone official already knows they're here,' she said.

I wondered if it was safe to contact Agent Reynolds, but I didn't want to drop her in the shit unless I had to.

Folsom went back over my actions in the basement.

'Why didn't you wait for back-up?' he asked.

'I had reason to believe a Falcon incident was under-way and that a member of the public was at risk,' I said. 'I believed that a careful approach would help calm the situation until the appropriate Falcon resources could be deployed.'

Folsom asked what 'appropriate Falcon resources' might be when they're at home.

'I rather think that would be me,' said Nightingale. 'And Peter cleared the action with me before proceed-ing. It was the right thing to do and I believe that had external factors not intervened then a peaceful resolu-tion could have been effectuated.'

Folsom nodded as if squirrelling away the word

'effectuated' for use at future meetings. Then he gave me a thin lipped smile.

'This is not the first time Peter here has been put into a position of potential harm because of a shortfall in Falcon capable resources,' he said and made a show of a consulting a list. 'These incidents include a severe RTI involving an ambulance, a near drowning in the Thames, a confrontation with armed men in a sewer, being buried under rubble at Oxford Street station and, if this report is to be believed, surviving a fall from a thirty storey block of flats while it was in the process of explosive demolition.'

I opened my mouth to say it was more complicated than that, but he held up a hand to silence me.

'He was involved in an unauthorised hostage exchange in Herefordshire, an armed standoff in Essex and let's not forget the business at the Royal Botanical Gardens in Kew.'

Which was totally not my fault, I might add, although I probably shouldn't have used the word Krynoid in my official report.

'Then, this week alone, there have been two confrontations with armed men. The second one culminating in yet another building collapse and fatality.'

I noticed he hadn't mentioned his own glorious contribution to the Bow Street riots.

'All of these incidents,' said Folsom, turning back to Nightingale, 'were exacerbated by the current operational bottleneck caused by lack of suitable Falcon capable resources.'

'It takes time to train new apprentices,' said Nightingale. 'It's not a process that can be rushed.'

'So, you agree that there is a shortfall in appropriate resources?' asked Folsom, who was obviously looking to get an admission from Nightingale that the Folly wasn't up to the job – and one that was nicely minuted at an official meeting.

'If I can speak to that, sir,' I said. 'The Special Assessment Unit has recently instituted a programme of capacity expansion in order to build greater operational robustness and provide a more efficient service to our partner OCUs when dealing with both Falcon and pseudo-Falcon incidents. The first phase of which is already underway.'

I noticed that Stephanopoulos was hiding her mouth with her hand.

Folsom, who should have known better, took the bait.

'The first phase being?' he asked.

'Strengthening our specialist support, particularly in the forensic and medical area, with a view to providing a continuous on-call service to investigation teams that might need them, coupled with the development of a best-practice guide for use in dealing with suspected Falcon related incidents and investigations,' I said, and heard Seawoll smother a cough – at least I assume it was a cough.

'In tandem with phase one implementation, the SAU is also developing a consultation document that will be sent out to all priority Falcon stakeholders prior to being submitted to the commissioner's office for approval.'

'Why was phase one implemented without a consultation paper?' asked Folsom or, in other words, how did you manage to spend money without clearing it with the commissioner first.

'Phase one was implemented under existing Home Office guidelines,' I said. Last updated in 1956 – during the Suez Crisis, no less, which must have been a good week to announce bits of political housekeeping you might not want to attract too much attention. 'In addition, phase one was financed entirely from within the current SAU budget.'

In other words, we have our own money so you can stick your oversight in your *La Traviata* and smoke it.

Folsom hesitated and then shrugged. He wasn't happy, but he was playing a long game. Besides, he was right – the current Folly operational structure was archaic and not fit for purpose. It was just that I didn't trust him or Lady Ty to fix it.

Of course, now I was going to have to deliver a consultation paper pretty damn sharpish or I was going to be in major trouble.

So we moved onto what seemed like five days, but was actually just a couple of hours, of wrangling about who was going to do what. Which in the end boiled down to deciding that the NCA would carry on investigating the Faceless Man's shadowy commercial empire, CTC would handle the Americans and the Folly would handle the Falcon related stuff with support from Belgravia MIT.

'It's a good thing that was sorted out,' said Seawoll. 'I was beginning to worry.'

We were still running short-handed because Belgravia was busy mopping up their stabbing, but at least we had Guleed who was, I felt, going to be thrilled to bits.

Before we could escape the building a DS Kittredge from CTC took me and Nightingale aside and said that there were some people we needed to talk to first. Kittredge had had the misfortune of getting tangled up with a Folly case a couple of years previously and had obviously got himself on a list as a result. No doubt a senior officer had told him that since he'd dealt with us weirdos before, he was perfectly placed to do it again. His expression was bland but I could tell he'd much rather be out arresting medical students in Ladbroke Grove.

He took us up to the twenty-ninth floor of ESB which, along with the twenty-eighth, was the domain of CTC – Counter Terrorism Command – which is the long spoon by which the Met deals with political crime and the security services.

There, in a conference room, Kittredge introduced us to a couple of officers from MI5. The spooks were a man and a woman, both white, both with deliberately suppressed posh accents and carefully nondescript off the peg suits. He was in his thirties, rugby player fit, with pale blue eyes and a tendency to squint. She was a bit older with auburn hair in a neat bob, grey eyes and gave her name as Finula – no surname. Blondie didn't give his name at all and spent most of the meeting squinting at Nightingale.

One of them had brought along a fully rugged Tough-book, presumably so they could play Angry Birds under battlefield conditions. Finula saw me looking and gave a rueful shake of her head.

'Don't ask,' she said.

'Does it self-destruct?' I asked.

The blondie gave me an irritated look, but DC Kittredge's lips twitched.

'No,' said Finula. 'But in a pinch you can beat someone to death with it.'

'I'd like to know how you disabled their vehicle,' said Blondie.

'I could show you,' I said. 'If you don't mind me demonstrating on your laptop.'

Finula put her hand on top of the case, an unconscious protective movement and I thought: You totally know what I'm talking about, don't you?

'I believe the purpose of this meeting,' said Nightingale, 'is to pool information regarding our American friends.'

'What with all the new Islamist franchises springing up,' said Finula, 'not to mention the hardy perennials on the far right and the unrepentant Fenians, we're a little bit too stretched to spare much attention for our closest allies.'

'Do you know who they are?' asked Nightingale.

'We do now,' said Finula. 'They're a PMC based outside of Charlottesville, Virginia. They've done a few small scale contracts in Afghanistan and Iraq – which is how we know them – but nothing like as active as Blackwater. Their official name is Alderman Technical Solutions but that was registered in 2005. Before that it gets murky, but we think they were probably known as The Virginia Gentleman's Company.'

Nightingale stirred.

'That name is familiar,' he said. 'I believe I met them during the war.'

According to Nightingale, they'd formed the second wave of American practitioners who'd joined the war effort following Pearl Harbour. The first wave had consisted of a hundred or so volunteers from the University of Pennsylvania, the so-called Printer's Men, who'd arrived in 1940 and worked directly with the Folly or in conjunction with Special Operations Executive.

The Virginia Gentlemen, inevitably nicknamed 'The Virgins', had kept themselves separate from the British and Commonwealth practitioners.

'They mostly operated out of Istanbul,' said Nightingale. 'I got the impression that they had a rather low opinion of us, and of course there was the little matter of our allying with Tecumseh in 1812.'

Blondie perked up and asked for a clarification.

Apparently back in 1812, when the special relationship was special in a whole different way, British policy had been to support the creation of a Native American confederacy as a buffer between an aggressively expansionist United States and the completely peace-loving and not in any way land-grabbing bit of the British Empire soon to be known as Canada.

When the Treaty of Ghent ended the War of 1812, the British, in time-honoured fashion, abandoned their allies. Who were subsequently wiped out by the Americans along with any other tribes that happened to be in the same general vicinity – even those that had actually been allied with the US government during the war. It's exactly this sort of thing, of course, which gives colonialism a bad name.

Nightingale had gained the impression that the Virgins had never forgiven the Folly for its role in providing Tecumseh's medicine men with modern Newtonian techniques.

'They rather avoided having anything to do with us,' said Nightingale.

'Were they involved in the attack on Ettersberg?' asked Finula.

'No,' said Nightingale. 'They were . . .' he paused, looking for the right word, '. . . contemptuous. They didn't believe the research the Germans were doing represented a significant threat to the Allied cause. I thought they were wrong about the threat, but right about the dangers of launching a major operation so deep into enemy territory.'

Dangers that were realised when the cream of British wizardry was cut down in the forests of Grosser Ettersberg.

'Of course we didn't know about the Manhattan Project at that time,' said Nightingale, 'although I rather suspect *they* did.' There was a definite note of bitterness there. Personally, I thought it was probably better that parts of Southern Germany didn't glow in the dark . . . but then I didn't leave most of my friends in that forest.

Nightingale shook his head and gave the spooks a tight smile.

'Of course, none of this is relevant to the present case,' he said.

'Did you know the Americans were on their way?'

'I was given a heads up last week,' I said.

'This would be a phone call from Agent Kimberley Reynolds of the FBI,' said Finula. 'Yes?'

I said it was and they asked if I'd been in contact with her since.

'No,' I said. 'I didn't want to land her in it.'

'So you don't know she boarded an American Airlines flight from New York last night,' said Finula. 'That can hardly be a coincidence now – can it?'

We agreed that it probably wasn't, but it also wasn't anything I'd done.

'Tell me, officer,' said Nightingale. 'Which worries you the most – the idea that we have our own channels of communication with the Americans, or that we don't?'

'What worries us,' said Finula, putting the emphasis on the plural, 'is that as the agency charged with the defence of the realm we are only hearing about this now.'

'We didn't feel it was required,' said Nightingale. 'We rather thought you had your hands full, what with the Irish Republicans and the like. And there was a clear agreement in 1948 that magic and the demi-monde would remain our responsibility.'

'That was half a century ago,' said Finula. 'In those days we didn't officially exist and we took a man's word that he was playing a straight bat. Now we run recruitment ads in the *Guardian* and have a mission statement and everything. Things have moved on a bit, the world has changed and we with it – you have not.' She glanced at me. 'Or at least not noticeably. We cannot ignore the potential damage that could be inflicted by an individual armed with your suite of capabilities.'

I squirrelled away that last phrase for my upcoming briefing document.

'Especially,' said Finula, 'when we don't have an effective counter.'

'Shoot them in the head with a rifle,' said Nightingale. 'Or a pistol from close range if the practitioner is not on guard.'

'Would that work on you?' asked Finula.

'It *has* worked on me,' said Nightingale. 'Twice. You see, you can train an irregular in a couple of weeks and you can learn how to make a bomb by reading a book. But it takes years to become even somewhat useful in a fight using magic.' He nodded in my direction. 'Unless you're a particularly gifted student and even then . . .' he shrugged.

'And its use in interrogation is limited,' I said. 'Because training someone to resist the glamour is easy.'

'All of this is beside the point,' said Nightingale. 'We shall of course include you in the latest round of consultation papers, given that you are—' he looked to me for help.

'Stakeholders,' I said and he gave me the ghost of a wink.

'But unless you have anything useful to tell us, then I'm afraid you'll have to excuse us,' said Nightingale and stood. I dutifully followed him up.

They didn't have anything useful to say after that, so we took ourselves off.

'Another feint by Tyburn, do you think?' asked Nightingale as we drove back to Belgravia.

'No,' I said. 'We're just out in the open these days. I'm amazed the media haven't jumped on us yet.' I'd expected Tyburn to at least think about using the media as leverage in her long running campaign to 'reform' the Folly. I had to assume she was being blocked by her sister Fleet, or possibly even by her mother.

Beverley had wanted to know if the whole collapsing house thing had been down to Tyburn. She'd asked about it as we'd shared a bath on Sunday morning – her version of tea and sympathy.

'Don't you know?' I'd asked. 'She's your sister.'

The Tyburn ran right behind Phoebe Beaumont-Jones' house, in the direction that the first burst of water had come from. And we were still waiting for the Thames Water engineering report as to where the flood had originated.

I said I didn't think she was that angry with me.

'Maybe not with you,' said Beverley and walked her toes up my chest. 'But she's been backing up pipes from Westminster to Hampstead since you arrested baby Ollie. Lesbian she can cope with, drug dealer she can cope with – Ollie grassing herself up to cover for her girlfriend? That had to piss her off big time.'

'Seriously?' I asked.

'Well, if it was her then she definitely wasn't after you.'

I asked how she knew.

'You're still breathing,' she said.

I didn't think it was Lady Ty either – even though

she'd joined her daughter as a person of interest in the house collapse, with her very own nominal node in HOLMES and a set of actions aimed at eliminating her from the inquiry.

I figured that Phoebe Beaumont-Jones had been talking to the Faceless Man when they'd been interrupted first by Crew Cut and his American Virgins and then by me and my unfailing ability to be in the wrong place at the wrong time. The flood had just been to cover his escape, or I doubt any of us would still be walking about. He might have hoped that Lady Ty would get the blame, although *why* he might have thought that was a bit of a mystery – maybe he knew something we didn't, or perhaps he was getting bad advice?

And if Phoebe was right – that the Faceless Man was a parent of a student at St Paul's, even better, a parent that she'd met personally – then the haystack he was hiding in was finally getting shrunk down to a manageable size.

Once we were at Belgravia we measured up our haystack and looked for shortcuts.

Guleed was back at St Paul's to gather up the names of the parents or guardians of all the students. Stephanopoulos went with her to provide some senior rankage in case they faced any upper-class fuckery. While they did that, I drilled down into the reams of stuff we had on the parents of the kids who'd attended the unfortunate MDMA-and-brain-damage party. I considered disregarding the mothers, but it occurred to me that we didn't know for certain that the Faceless Man was male. I also started going back over all the cases with suspected links to the Faceless Man to see if any of their faces fit. So to speak.

A year ago Richard Lewis, a planning officer with Southwark Borough Council, had thrown himself in front of a tube train at Paddington station. We'd always suspected that he jumped under the influence of a glamour and had pinpointed the moment we thought the glamour had gone in. Since it occurred just short of the ticket barrier in a London Underground station, it happened in one of the most CCTV saturated places in the world. And since glamour was not something you did from a distance, the Faceless Man must have been caught on camera. Along with about a thousand other people.

So I reckoned it was worth a punt and I spent some time with pictures of the parents, seeing if I could match any of them to faces in the crowd. And because magical facial recognition systems have yet to be invented, it had taken me most of the weekend. Except for the bits I spent at Bev's and the two hours magic practise that Nightingale insisted on.

'We need to work on your precision,' he'd said.

I didn't spot anyone on the CCTV but I did catalogue most of the likely targets to make it easier for whatever poor sod got lumbered with the job of checking them against the parents of the entire school.

'Plus staff,' said Guleed. 'Phoebe might have confused the two – children often do.'

That search was going to stay a low priority because we had a key time frame, the collapse of the house on Friday evening, to check alibis against. Phoebe

Beaumont-Jones' dad's alibi being that he wasn't in the country at the time, although it turned out he had gone to Magdalene College Oxford in the early nineties. Roughly the same time as the known Little Crocodile Richard Lewis, he who threw himself under a tube train, and Christina Chorley's father Martin had been there too.

It would have been nice if just one of them had gone to Cambridge or, god forbid, Bristol, which was where, according to Guleed, posh students went when they failed to get into Oxbridge.

There was always the cheerful thought that the Faceless Man, in proper Sith Lord fashion, had trained up someone as his apprentice. But I didn't think that was likely. If he'd had a fully trained apprentice he wouldn't have needed Varvara, and if they weren't trained then I could probably take them.

But if that apprentice was Lesley May?

Which one of us would hesitate the longest, I wondered.

Normally when you TIE a nominal you send the lowest ranking member of the team round to flat out ask the subject to account for their whereabouts. Then, usually, the same lowly minion does all the cross referencing with CCTV, mobile phone records and/or actual living breathing witnesses to verify the alibi. We couldn't do that with the Faceless Man because we couldn't predict what he might do if he was tipped off. Since his capability envelope stretched from levelling a house to causing luckless members of the public to throw themselves off tall buildings it was, as Nightingale said, like hunting big game. We needed to stay downwind and un-detected until we'd lined up our elephant gun. Since the elephant gun in question was Nightingale, this meant I had to wait until he was free before we could beard any suspects in their lairs.

We started with Albert Pryce. And, because there was an off-chance that Nightingale's mere presence might spook our quarry, he would remain hidden nearby ready to rush in and put the boot in. My role in *that* scenario was to race for the exit as fast as possible – taking any potential collateral with me.

Unless Lesley was there, in which case I was sup-posed to grab her.

As it was, when we tooled up outside Albert Pryce's six bedroom semi in St John's Wood he wasn't even there – which was a bit of an intelligence failure. Fortunately Albertina answered the door and, without prompting, invited me in. I left Nightingale in the Jag contemplat-ing the infinite, doing the crossword in the *Telegraph* and keeping an ear out for screams.

The house was early Victorian enough to retain some Regency class. Inside it still looked like a place where people actually lived, with framed prints on the walls and bookshelves and furniture that had its corners smoothed off with use. There were signs that money had taken hold in the kitchen, though, sprouting han-dleless brushed steel cabinets, randomly deformed sink units and work surfaces as cheerfully domestic as a pa-thology lab.

Albertina was doing her best to humanise it by spreading empty cups, jars with the tops off and knives sticking out, a dealer's shuffle of brown bread spilling out of its packet and a recyclable plastic bottle of guaranteed organic semi-skimmed milk thoughtfully left in a patch of sunlight.

'He's gone to Aberystwyth to see grandma,' said Albertina and offered me a marmite sandwich. 'She's not very happy with dad at the moment.'

I wanted to ask where her dad had been on Friday evening, on the off-chance he'd been dropping a house on me at the time, but I couldn't think of a way of slipping it into the conversation. Instead I asked why Albertina's grandma wasn't happy with him.

'She doesn't like the idea of him moving to America,' said Albertina. 'She says that she's only just got used to him living in London.'

'When did he move to London?' I asked.

'Forever ago,' said Albertina.

Actually, according to my notes, it had been just after he graduated in 1972. But when you're seventeen forever isn't a very long time at all.

'Aberystwyth is miles,' I said. 'That's a bit of a drive isn't it? Or did he take the train?'

'Dad doesn't take the train anymore,' said Albertina. 'He says he's allergic to other people. He drives up – takes him ages.'

'So when did he set out for Wales, then?'

'Friday morning,' she said. 'To avoid the traffic.' She said it so smoothly I wondered if she'd been coached – but to what end? Still, some poor sod back at Belgravia was going to be spending some time with the ANPR logs to see whether Albert Pryce's Mercedes M-class had been spotted on the M4, and if so at what time. I hoped it wasn't going to be me.

'When are you moving to the States?' I said, wondering whether we were going to have to ask them politely to stay in the country and what earthly pretext we were going to justify it with.

'Not until the spring,' said Albertina. 'And I'm not going with – this is totally just for him, the Intern and the Replacements.'

The Intern being the woman featured in her father's acclaimed semi-autobiographical novel, wife number three and mother of the two 'replacements' – even now, hopefully, vomiting all over the back seat of their mother's Toyota as she ferried them from playgroup to kaffeeklatsch to ballet for tiny tots.

'She's the one that's desperate to move back to States,' said Albertina – and had persuaded her husband that he'd be treated with the respect he deserved there. Not like in London, where no one fully appreciated his genius.

'Dad's always been a bit insecure about that,' said Albertina.

'He won the Booker prize,' I said. And had pretty much made the shortlist every year he had a new book out.

Albertina shrugged.

'He's haunted by a deep dark secret,' she said.

'Yeah?' I said, trying not to sound overly interested.

'Yeah,' she said, and then asked if I liked sci-fi.

I suggested that I was occasionally partial to a bit of SF – you know – when the mood took me.

'Then you'll love this,' she said and took me to see her dad's study.

If the kitchen had been colonised by the money, then the study had been irretrievably lost to literature a long time ago. Every spare centimetre of the wall space had been covered with shelves, all of which were stuffed with books. It reminded me of my dad's record collection, which had filled up my parents' bedroom and pushed every other activity except sleeping out into the rest of their small flat. Which was why my old bedroom was now my mum's walk-in wardrobe and shoe store. But unlike my dad's precious vinyl, which has to be stored vertical and absolutely upright in exactly the right sized shelves, here books spilled out onto the floor and across the big hardwood dining room table in the middle of the room that substituted for a desk. Albert Pryce wasn't averse to using his books as coffee coasters, or to weigh down piles of hardcopy or even as an impromptu building material for shelves where they served to support even more books, an old fashioned boombox and a row of withered potted plants.

'Have you spotted them yet?' asked Albertina.

Since I was looking for signs that her dad was an ethically challenged practitioner, I doubted I was looking for whatever she was talking about, and I was just about to say no when I did spot them.

Most of the shelving had enough horizontal spacing to take quite tall books but one unit had clearly been custom built to take small, old fashioned paperbacks. The spines were colourful, smooth and uncracked. I knew the signs – this was a collection, not a library.

I looked at Albertina, who grinned back and said that it was OK for me to touch them.

'The Intern is totally desperate to leave these behind,' she said. 'She had someone in to value them – on the sly.'

I pulled out a book at random – it had a solid yellow spine and a DAW logo. The cover looked like a classic Frazetta or a good imitation – all muscular white men and women in implausibly tight spacesuits with bubble helmets. The title was *The Crystal Spires of Mazarin* by T.J. Morton. I checked the next book along and found it was the same title – this time the New English Library edition with a cover depicting a strange alien land-scape with globular trees and improbably low-hanging planets. A random sample of the rest of the bookcase revealed multiple first paperback editions of three SF writers I'd never heard of – although I was pretty sure I'd read at least a couple of the books – the aforemen-tioned T.J. Morton, Allen Vincent and Carter Houston. There was a lot of Carter Houston, who apparently spe-cialised in mighty thewed barbarians and, if the quotes on the front were to be believed, was favourably com-pared with Howard's *Conan* and John Norman's *Gor*.

'Interesting choice of authors,' I said.

'Not authors,' said Albertina. 'Author – they're all pen names.'

'Not your dad?' I said. It couldn't be, because some of the books dated back to the 1950s – although he could have been a teen prodigy like my father.

'Close,' she said. 'It was Granddad.'

Who, according to my obviously flawed IIP report on

the Pryce family, had led a blameless life teaching Military History at Aberystwyth University. And, according to Albertina, who was obviously a fan, also had a sideline as a prolific pulp SF writer until the early seventies – just about the time his son Albert had picked up his first literary award for his debut novel *Cunning Men*.

And I thought of the person who had written, in Elvish script, the words *If You Can Read This You Are Not Only A Nerd But Probably Dead* across the face of a Demon Trap.

I was trying to think of a way of segueing the conversation around to asking whether her dad ever talked about magic or ghosts or anything of that ilk, when my phone rang. It was a call from Bromley Crime Squad regarding Aiden Burghley.

'Have you found him yet?' I asked.

'Sort of,' said Bromley. 'Bits of him, anyway.'

10

Picking Up the Pieces

Everybody's a slave to their habits, little behavioural tics that we're often barely conscious of – and even if we are, we probably couldn't change them if we wanted to. Bev always sleeps on the left side of the bed, Guleed always puts three sugars in her black Americano, and the Faceless Man has two ways of killing people he wants dead. If it's just business then he favours the quiet and forensically invisible approach – an apparent suicide or a sudden heart attack. If he's pissed off or wants to make an example, then it gets very messy indeed. Having your dick bitten off or your bones set on fire from the inside are only a couple of the merry ways that we know of for certain.

We'd been reluctant to employ a forensic psychologist because of the well-founded fear that they might section us for believing in fairies. But you didn't need a degree to figure out that the whole 'making an example' aspect was actually bollocks. It was simply an excuse to do horribly inventive things to his fellow human beings.

You certainly had to wonder what poor Aiden Burghley had done to justify having his face nailed to a tree in a small park in suburban South London.

Well, not nailed exactly. Removed from his skull and

attached to the trunk at head height – my head height, I noticed – not Aiden's, who had been shorter.

Downham Fields was a low green mound that formed the centrepiece of Downham Estate – a 1920s housing estate in Lewisham. Built by the London County Council as a low-rent version of the then-fashionable garden city idea, it was to house the 'respectable' working class of Bermondsey and Rotherhithe in six thousand unremarkable semis. Unremarkable, of course, providing you'd grown up with such luxuries as indoor plumbing and back gardens. To ensure that the hoi polloi were properly appreciative of the largesse bestowed upon them, the LCC employed inspectors to enforce acceptable standards of cleanliness and order. Although this wasn't enough reassurance for the residents of a nearby private estate, who insisted on a two metre wall topped with broken glass to maintain a suitable degree of separation.

The low hill in the park was crowned by a Catholic church and attached school and further down the slope was a rectangular copse of trees which I totally failed to identify. Just inside the treeline, in a surprisingly compact area, was what was left of Aiden Burghley.

Bromley MIT had already done a preliminary canvass of the area, plus house to house and CCTV, before gleefully dumping it all on Nightingale, me and Stephanopoulos and skipping away with happy cries. They wanted nothing to do with it. I could empathise – neither did I.

According to Bromley's timeline, the murder had taken place in a fifteen minute window between when a couple of schoolkids had walked past the trees on their way to the leisure centre next to the church and a Mr Thomas Gantry had noticed Chuck, his Irish Setter, bounding towards him with what turned out not to be a stray leg of pork.

Chuck really hadn't wanted to relinquish his prize, and finally had to be distracted with a piece of cheese to make him let go. Dr Jennifer Vaughan found the whole thing very educational.

'I didn't even know dogs liked cheese,' she said, and took saliva samples from Chuck for elimination purposes.

In that fifteen minute window Aiden Burghley had been dismembered at every major joint – ankle, knee, hip, shoulder, elbow and wrist – leaving just his head and torso lying at the base of a tree. That part was still dressed in the jeans and sweatshirt he'd been wearing when I interviewed him. Later stress analysis determined that this was because his limbs had been torn out of their sockets by an extreme axial force strong enough to rip skin and snap tendons.

'Not something that's easy to do,' said Dr Walid. 'Particularly with a young person,' he added, and then had a discussion with Dr Vaughan about whether the victim's youthfully stretchy skin would have made that much difference to the level of force required.

Aiden Burghley's head was a nightmare, the skin of the face having been neatly removed to reveal the dried-meat coloured muscles and tendons beneath. It looked almost surgical, although later microscopic inspection revealed that the tissue had been torn rather than cut.

His face had then been mounted on a tree so that it looked out over the curving rows of identical semi-detached houses that stretched away to the horizon.

I sighted along the direction of his gaze, but saw nothing remarkable. It had been raining off and on, and the clouds were low, so the visibility was crap. The wind kept picking at the corners of the white forensic tents that the SOCOs were trying to jockey into position to cover all the bits.

'I'm not sure I like the implications of this development at all,' said Nightingale, and I knew he was thinking of Lesley's new face and the medical miracle magic of the Viscountess Linden-Limmer.

'This is him talking directly to us, you know,' I said.

'Yes,' said Nightingale. 'That's what I don't like.'

The Doctors Walid and Vaughan agreed that the Faceless Man might be showing off, especially when Dr Vaughan reported that the skin of the face had been fused to the bark. And, more importantly, that the wood itself had been subtly reshaped to substitute for the bones and cartilage that normally gives the face its shape.

'Otherwise I seriously doubt you'd have recognised him so easily,' she said.

It still seemed unnecessarily flashy. And why Downham Fields, when there were half a dozen open green spaces further south – much closer to Bromley and Aiden Burghley's old stamping ground?

'There's a chance that this may have very little to do with Mr Burghley at all,' said Nightingale. 'At least nothing personal, *per se.*'

'Shit,' I said, because if there was something the Faceless Man liked better than a dismemberment then it was creating a distraction in one place while he sneaked in and murdered whoever his real target was.

I looked at Nightingale, who frowned back.

'Reynard,' I said.

It's amazing how fast you can cross London in a vintage Jag if you put on blues and twos and your governor drives like a maniac. Although there's still nothing to be done about the gridlock on Vauxhall Bridge in the evening, except invest in a Sherman tank. We'd called ahead to Belgravia to tell the custody sergeant to put the custody suite on lockdown and I mentally added 'Falcon Lockdown Procedures' to the ever-growing consultation document.

I had the Jag's Airwave set to Belgravia's channel and Nightingale drove in silence through the grey drizzle as we listened out for screams and lamentations. But these didn't start until we arrived back to find half a busy Monday night's customers piling up in the corridor, and the shift duty inspector waiting for us with a dangerous gleam in his eye and a metaphorical rolling pin in his hand. After him was the custody sergeant who pointed out that her duty of care extended to *all* the prisoners in her cells, thank you. She'd heard the rumours of collapsing houses, burning markets and what really happened at the Saville Row nick a couple of years back. She wanted a pretty comprehensive risk assessment or, failing that, we could take our suspect somewhere else – thank you very much.

We couldn't take Reynard to the Folly because, never mind that we weren't PACE compliant, we didn't even have any cells – although I suppose we could have put him in one of the disused servant's rooms in the attic. The custody sergeant suggested that Paddington Green, it being where we lock up the terrorist suspects, would be a more suitable location. But Nightingale didn't agree.

'A prisoner's always most vulnerable when he's being moved,' he said. 'And, in any case, if our adversary was truly planning an attack I believe he would have done it by now.'

But I noticed he arranged to spend the shift in the custody suite. Which meant I got sent off to fetch refs, make a formal note of our actions and catch up on the paperwork. David Carey asked if I wanted to go to the pub to celebrate his successful raid which had netted two butcher's knives, a bag of slightly doubtful skunk and, the reason for the celebration, three thousand quid in used readies that had 'intent to supply' written all over them. Beverley was babysitting her sister Brent that evening so a bit of moderate police boozing seemed appropriate . . . right up until FBI Agent Kim Reynolds rang me on her disposable pay as you go.

'I thought I'd finally take you up on that kebab,' she said.

It actually took me a couple of seconds to process that. To remember Shepherd's Bush Market in the snow, Zach having the snot kicked out of him and me knocking Kimberley down with *impello* because I thought she was reaching for a gun.

Then we'd gone round the corner for a kebab – or at least I did – Kimberley had stuck to Coca Cola despite the fact that the coffee hadn't actually been that bad.

'There's always time for a cheeky kebab,' I said. 'When are you going to be hungry?'

'About an hour,' she said.

'Kebab it is then,' I said, and then popped down to tell Nightingale where I was going.

The Uxbridge Road was full of hunched figures hurrying for the Tube station as I found a rare parking space down a side street and hunched my own way through the irritatingly persistent rain to the other side of the bridge.

It was your classic Kurdish kebab place in that it looked exactly like the Greek kebab places I'd grown up with, only now the meat was guaranteed halal. Just to shake things up, Kimberley had gone for the coffee while I, as a mark of respect to the late Aiden Burghley, had a falafel.

Kimberley had eschewed the mandated FBI agent-in-a-suit look for a pair of off-duty black jeans, an orange and grey sweatshirt with OSU embossed across the front, a blue quilted jacket and, as far as I could tell, no shoulder holster.

'You stopped dyeing your hair,' I said.

'Since I was already knee deep in *The X-Files*, I gave up trying to hide the colour,' she said.

'So the X-Files are real?'

'You'd love that, wouldn't you? But I'm sorry to disappoint you,' she said.

'What, no UFOs?'

'Not yet,' said Kimberley and sipped her coffee with every sign of pleasure. 'I'll be sure to let you know if they turn up.'

I asked what had dragged her back across the Pond.

She waved her hand around at the worn Formica and easy-clean plastic interior of the kebab shop.

'This is all your fault,' she said.

'I really don't think it is,' I said.

Kimberley begged to differ.

'After our little adventures underground I was curious,' she said. 'It didn't seem likely that you Brits had a monopoly on . . .' she hesitated.

'Magic?'

'It seemed unlikely,' she shrugged. 'That's the trouble with being law enforcement – you can't let things go.'

So she dug around and was probably not as subtle as she thought she was, because the next thing she knew she was sitting in her supervisor's office with a Deputy Assistant Director who'd flown in specially from Washington that very morning just to have a conversation with her.

'He had my London file open on the desk and looked me in the eye and said "Do you have anything else to add to this report?" And I said I may have, but that I wasn't sure he was going to like it.' She grinned. 'I'm paraphrasing here you understand. He said, "Why don't you just tell me and I'll be the judge of that."'

'So what did you tell him?'

'Well I started out small – just testing the waters. A little bit about how you seemed to be able to do some things I wasn't sure I could explain. He just nodded at me and asked if I'd encountered other instances of magic during my investigation.'

'And?'

'I told him everything. About you, Nightingale, Lesley, the Folly – even the people living under the city – didn't seem to faze him at all.' She was offered a transfer to Washington within a week.

'I say offered,' said Kimberley. 'It was more *ordered*.'

To the Office of Partner Engagement, which handles co-operation between the FBI, 'partner' agencies and local law enforcement.

'So is that where they keep the X-Files?'

'Yeah,' she leant back on her chair. 'There's a big secret warehouse.'

Mostly she worked a regular shift engaging with the FBI's partners.

'Whether they wanted to be engaged with or not,' she said.

The weird shit she was supposed to deal with in her spare time.

'Like what?'

'They've had me looking into the possibility of demonic possession of active shooters,' she said. Active shooters being individuals who arm themselves and then pop out to kill as many innocent bystanders as possible. There had been a definite upward trend in both incidents and casualty rates since the turn of the century, and since gun control was off the table the FBI had been looking for other preventative measures. Kimberley had actually found literature on the subject from, of all places, the Centers for Disease Control. They'd commissioned a 1995 study that hinted, very obliquely, that some incidents of mass murder could not be solely attributed to normal criminality or psychological conditions. The study had never been officially released and no follow-up had ever been authorised. So Kimberley had gone on a road trip around the US interviewing all the surviving gunmen that would talk to her.

I thought of Mr Punch and the trail of bloody mayhem he'd left behind him and asked if she had any confirmed cases.

'That's hard to say,' said Kimberley. 'Half the time the shooter kills himself or is shot dead by first responders. And the rest all have their own sad stories.' They'd been abused or victimised or they just plain didn't like the way the world had treated them and had decided to teach it a lesson.

But there had been one interview Kimberley had conducted in Florence, Arizona. A thirty-six year old white male who'd inexplicably woken up one morning, shot his wife and then driven over to his mother-in-law's house to shoot her, too, and only missed making the FBI's list of mass killers because he'd been tackled by the postman before he could open up at the local 7-Eleven.

He claimed, during his interview with Kimberley, that he'd been possessed by the spirit of a bear.

'"An old bear," he said. From a time before the arrival of the white man – an angry old bear,' said Kimberley.

I asked if she'd believed him.

'Have you ever heard a bear?' she asked. 'One that's really angry? Nothing else sounds like a bear. It's got that kind of deep breathy bark. Let's just say I have heard it twice. Once when I was out hunting with my dad and again when I was talking to the shooter in Florence.' She paused – to see how I was taking it, I think – before continuing. 'Not literally, but like an echo or . . . I'm not sure.'

'A memory?' I said, and Kimberley gave me a hard look.

'You *do* you know what I'm talking about,' she said, 'don't you?'

'It's called *vestigia*,' I said. 'It's sort of like an afterglow from magic. Although, to be honest, sometimes it's just stuff you make up in your head . . . or even a memory triggered by an association with something somebody says or does.'

'So, is it real or not?' said Kimberley.

I told her it was real, but learning to differentiate the real from the unreal was one of the things you needed a teacher for, although an annoying dog can be of some help. When she asked what breed of dog I recommended, I realised I might have been leading her a bit astray.

'Forget about the dog,' I said.

'I liked the dog,' said Kimberley.

'The dog is a distraction,' I said.

Kimberley's lips twitched.

'You don't say,' she said. 'So do you think my active shooter was possessed or not?'

'He might have been,' I said. 'But that doesn't mean that whatever got into his head made him kill those people. It might have wanted something else, but your

229

shooter misinterpreted it. Or it might have been influenced by the shooter's own personality. And even if it unequivocally did influence him to shoot his wife, that doesn't mean that any of the other "active shooters" suffered the same thing.'

'That's unhelpful,' said Kimberley.

'It is, isn't it?' I said. 'I can scan some of the basic textbooks we've got back at the Folly, but really they're not that useful, either. At least, I haven't found them that useful.'

Kimberley nodded and stared at her empty coffee cup.

'You know the coffee in this place is terrible,' she said.

So we walked further up Uxbridge Road until we found somewhere with decent coffee and Kimberley finally told me what she was doing in the UK.

'Now, since I have become the Bureau's go-to girl for things both English and supernatural, I have been tasked to try and smooth the repatriation of my fellow citizens –' she gave me an arch look, '– those that are still alive, back to the United States of America where they belong.'

'You could just leave them to us,' I said. 'They're facing some serious charges. False imprisonment, possession of a firearm with intent.'

'Intent of what?'

'Just general intent at the moment,' I said.

Kimberley said that if it were down to her she'd be happy to let them enjoy Her Majesty's hospitality, but there was the pesky detail of their quasi-official status and the US Government being loath to rinse out its undies in the British courts. In order to facilitate a happy outcome she'd be sent over with a grab-bag of low level secrets and concessions to tempt the palate of the British security establishment.

'Not to mention save the taxpayer some money,' she said.

'Did it work?' I asked.

'Yes and no,' said Kimberley. 'Everybody agreed in principle.'

'But?'

'Only if your boss says yes,' said Kimberley.

'My boss?'

'Yes.'

'Nightingale?'

'Do you have another boss?'

No, I thought, but I didn't think his influence stretched that far.

'Did they say why?' I asked.

'They said there was an arrangement,' she said.

Of course there is, I thought.

'And you want me to persuade Nightingale,' I said.

'Would you?' said Kimberley. 'Because that would be swell.'

'So what do you plan to offer us?'

Kimberley smiled.

'I thought you'd never ask,' she said, and pulled out a USB pen and put it on the table between us. 'I've got their names, the organisational structure and history of the Virginia Gentleman's Company and, most importantly, details of what got them over here in the first place.'

'And what was that?' I asked.

Kimberley said she had never driven out to Fort Meade, Maryland to gaze upon the collection of gargantuan modernist blocks that made up the headquarters of the National Security Agency. But she liked to imagine it a honeycomb of bland little cubicles. All the cubicles would be almost identical, but to the trained eye there would be subtle variations of status and purpose. Those cubicles tasked with monitoring global communications for unsuspecting terrorist suspects would have bigger, flatter monitors, nicer desk calendars, maybe the ones with a humorous daily proverb, and first crack at the sandwich trolley when it came past.

'How much sleep have you had recently?' I asked.

'Bear with me,' said Kimberley, and described the cubicles furthest from the canteen, the ones with the worrying smell from the pipes overhead, whose inhabitants walked the furthest to find their cars at home time. This was where the information gathered from open sources on the internet, twitter, eBay, Facebook, Tumblr and the like was processed. It was flagged by machine, of course, but some poor schlub still had to go through the items and decide which organ of the state might want to know who was selling a used pink bathrobe for suspiciously large sums of money – possible money laundering – or a rare mint snow globe – potential hazardous material transfer. There was a list, Kimberley imagined, and in an obscure subsection of that list, a section that had not been properly updated since George Bush was President, was the government contractee Alderman Technical Solutions, AKA the Virginia Gentleman's Company.

So when the right flag was triggered the cubicle jockey dutifully notified an organisation which should have been taken off that list ever since an unspecified disaster in Fallujah had got them struck off another list – that of approved contractors.

I asked what had happened in Fallujah, but Kimberley shook her head.

'That information was so redacted that I only know it happened in Fallujah because someone missed a reference in the document authorising the redaction,' she said. She couldn't even discover what they were doing in Iraq although there were references to something called 'area shade suppression' and 'TechSub'.

Whatever it was they were doing, Kimberley didn't think it was very successful because their contract was terminated in 2009 with two years left to run. Given the low, low standards for success applied to private military contractors in Iraq, the fuck-up that got them fired must have been spectacular. Not that Kimberley used the words fuck-up, you understand.

She didn't seem surprised that they were still tangled up in the byzantine coils of the American intelligence establishment.

'People still know people who know people,' she said. 'You should know that.'

I asked what she thought had triggered the cubicle jockey to contact them in the first place – what had brought Alderman Technical Solutions across the pond.

'Your late friend Christina Chorley tried to sell something called *The Wild Ledger* on eBay with a reserve price of twenty grand,' she said.

'We knew they were after that,' I said, and wondered why Crew Cut hadn't just paid for it – probably cheaper than flying all his guys over and smuggling their guns in, not to mention hiring the SUVs with the suitably sinister tinted windows.

'Ah, but did you know about something called the Mary Engine?' said Kimberley. 'She was selling that on eBay too.'

She showed me a picture taken from eBay on her tablet – a dense cube of steel and brass gears.

'A difference engine?' I asked.

'That's the advantage of having the NSA looking at something like this,' said Kimberley. 'Those guys know the difference between their difference- and analytical-engines, and apparently this is neither.'

I asked what they thought it was.

'They couldn't lift enough detail from the photographs to determine what it was supposed to do, but they think it's genuinely Victorian. Mid 1840s they reckon. In fact, if you run it down and you want to generate some good will with the NSA you might want to send it over as a gift.'

'You think I'm going to need goodwill at the NSA?'

'Peter,' said Kimberley, 'the way your life is going you're going to need all the goodwill you can get.'

There were other items of interest, too. A 1920s anthology of Victor Bartholomew's work on spirits which I recognised from a particularly tedious Latin lesson, and a *Genuine Wizard's Staff* that had, according to Kimberley, a British Army serial number stencilled along its length.

The attached NSA report indicated that there was no coherence to the collection and posited a high probability that it was just that – a collection. Items acquired by an individual who had a high degree of access but limited understanding.

'Access to what?' I asked.

'They didn't know,' said Kimberley.

And where it all came from was a mystery, I thought. Like the changing of the seasons and the tides of the sea.

Kimberley and the security arm of the American military industrial complex might not know, but I thought I knew a fox who might.

Still, I didn't think there was any point interviewing Reynard the wannabe fox that evening. So I stopped off at Belgravia to brief Nightingale and make multiple back-ups of the USB pen. Since I was there, I also scanned the files and dumped most of them on the Inside Inquiry Office for assessment and entry into HOLMES, including the real names of our American friends. Crew Cut's name turned out to be Dean Miller, a former reserve Captain in the 29th Infantry Division who had served in Kosovo and Iraq. The 29th was a National Guard unit, but there was no official word on what his day job had been. After leaving the National Guard he was listed as a 'consultant' with Alderman Technical Solutions. A sour little note appended by some anonymous security apparatchik complained that just about everybody at ATS was listed as a 'consultant'. His military record in Iraq was heavily redacted and what wasn't missing was written in an impenetrable mix of jargon and acronyms – I thought the Met was bad but they were as nothing compared to US Military. It was going to take some serious Google-hours to translate.

Captain Dean Miller's *compadres* all had similar backgrounds in the military and law enforcement and were noticeably from the American south and south-west. I wondered if that might be significant, but it was a small sample size. I added 'hire a civilian analyst' to my list of things to go into the growing Word document and moved onto the action list for what was still called operation MARIGOLD because no-one had got round to officially deactivating it yet.

I also thought I might as well work my way through my email backlog, which was just as well because an annoyingly unflagged communication from the Border Agency informed me that Jeremy Beaumont-Jones had flown in from the Bahamas two days before his daughter thought he had. Which meant he had no alibi for our suspected Faceless Man incident involving the collapse of his own house.

Which in turn meant that he was going to have to be TIEd all over again. And since he was back on our Tiger list, that action would fall to me and Nightingale.

I stuck it on our long list of urgent actions before heading back to the Folly and the next morning I got in bright and early to prepare for the interview.

So far, all the earlier interviews with Reynard had gone along the traditional lines of us saying he'd done it and him saying he hadn't – in continuous variations. This is not an uncommon type of interview, and so over the years police have come up with a number of techniques for breaking the impasse. Some of which are still even legal. One of the techniques not outlawed by human rights legislation is the horrid surprise. So I printed up some crime scene images and took them into the interview room with me.

We're not allowed to let our prisoners fester, so Reynard was washed and dressed in clean clothes. He was beginning to show a little bit of that fraying around the edges that people get after a couple of nights in the cells. For all the fact that he had villain tattooed on his forehead, Reynard hadn't put in the hours on the judicial/criminal coal face I had, hadn't developed that dogged patience that separates the police and the professional criminal from ordinary members of the public.

The fact that he hadn't asked for legal representation was another dead giveaway.

'When was the last time you were in Bromley?' I asked, once we'd finished the ceremonial putting of the tapes in the machine and intoned the ritual opening litany of the police interview.

'Bromley?' said Reynard. 'What about Bromley?'

'When was the last time you went down there?'

He smiled, showing white teeth.

'Can't say that Bromley's the sort of place I rush to embrace,' he said. 'I believe I may have passed through once or twice – on my way somewhere else.'

'So you never stop off to see your good friend Aiden Burghley?'

'Who?' asked Reynard.

'White middle class drug dealer,' I said. 'Your kind of people.'

'My kind of people?'

'You know,' I said. 'Pretend-criminals, love breaking the law, hate taking the consequences.'

'I think you've just described the human condition there,' said Reynard smugly.

I wasn't going to get a better cue than that – I laid out selected pictures of the Aiden Burghley crime scene – saving the artfully framed close up of his detached face until last.

'Nice,' he said, but behind his casual tone I caught a whiff of real fear when he asked who it was.

'Don't you recognise him?' I asked.

He said no, shaking his head, but his gaze skittered away from the picture.

'That's Aiden Burghley,' I said, and was surprised by a hint of relief in the set of Reynard's shoulders. Either because he didn't know who Aiden was, or merely because it happened to somebody else.

'What about this?' I asked and laid down a picture of the Mary Engine next to the face. Reynard glanced at it and shrugged.

'What is it?'

'You don't recognise it?'

'Puzzle box?' he asked.

'It's one of the items Christina Chorley was selling on eBay,' I said. 'Along with the item you were trying to sell us.'

238

'On eBay?' said Reynard, too outraged to keep his mouth shut. 'The little bitch.'

'So you're telling me you didn't know?' I asked – making it a challenge.

'You don't put things like this on eBay,' said Reynard. 'Everybody knows that.'

'Everybody but Christina,' I said. 'And why not sell stuff on eBay? Everybody else does.'

'Because there are some things that are just not done,' said Reynard.

'Even by the likes of you?'

'Especially by the likes of me,' said Reynard. 'One does not piss in one's own pool, after all.'

'But Christina did, didn't she?' I said. 'Not quite the compliant little bunny you were hoping for, was she?'

'Well, they're no fun, constable, if they don't wriggle a bit under the claw – are they?' His smile was vulpine and humourless, but now he was talking about the things that floated his particular boat, and once they've started doing that it's just a matter of hopping on board and sailing them down the river.

'You like the thrill of the chase, then?' I asked.

'Don't we all?'

I gave him a half shrug that implied that I would love to agree with him, but I was constrained by the iron hand of political correctness. Which was all it took for Reynard to pick up the paddle and push us out into midstream.

He leaned forward and looked me in the eye.

'Most men do,' he said. 'But they've been conditioned not to admit it – even to themselves.'

'So where do you like to go hunting?' I asked.

'I don't go looking for them, Peter,' he said. 'They come looking for me.'

Presumably with torches and pitchforks.

'All the little bunnies do it,' said Reynard. 'Even the Germaine Greer wannabes. There they go, backwards and forwards right under your nose,' he said. 'While making sure everything is bouncing away in the most appealing fashion.'

'It's those little fluffy tails,' I said before I could stop myself, but fortunately Reynard was too deep into his happy place to notice.

'When little Christina came hop hopping past,' I said, 'where were you?'

'The Chestnut Tree,' said Reynard.

Which was a famous pub in Marble Arch where denizens of the demi-monde hung out after doing a hard day's whatever it is members of the demi-monde do. Zach the goblin boy was a periodic patron when he wasn't barred. I'd been in a couple of times to show my face and reassure the community that I was bloody well keeping an eye on them – the thieving gits. It wasn't the sort of place that checked IDs once you were visibly old enough to do a paper round.

It also wasn't a pub you wandered into by accident – I pointed this out to Reynard.

'She was there with company,' he said.

'What sort of company?'

'The deified sort,' he said. 'Or at least one of their offspring.'

'That's quite a lot of kids,' I said. 'Which one?'

He hesitated; I suspect he was considering whether he could use the name as a bargaining chip. But then, sensibly, he told me.

'Lady Ty's little girl,' he said. 'Olivia.'

And round and round we go and where we stop nobody knows.

11

Under the Spreading Chestnut Tree

While I was talking to Reynard the Unreliable, Nightingale had popped out with Guleed to extend Jeremy Beaumont-Jones, and his lovely daughter Phoebe, an invitation to help the police with their inquiries. That way they could run the whole Trace Implicate or Eliminate routine free from the fear that he'd turn up and drop another building on us. And, should that or any other equally gruesome thing happen elsewhere while he was with us, we could safely eliminate him from our inquiries.

By agreement we all paused for coffee and scheming, and I asked Guleed what she thought of Phoebe's father.

'Actually he comes across as a bit dim,' said Guleed

'A perfectly pleasant fellow,' said Nightingale. 'But not what you'd call a world-class brain.'

Which just goes to show that all a degree from Oxford guarantees is that the recipient went to Oxford and turned up for some lessons.

'And it was a rather poor second at that,' said Nightingale.

It seemed that our Mr Beaumont-Jones had been more interested in the Oxford Revue than his Philosophy,

Politics and Economics, although he'd also failed to generate a career in cutting topical satire.

By the end of the morning, while we'd confirmed that he'd been booked in at an exclusive West End hotel at the time the Faceless Man was subjecting me to an involuntary swimming lesson with the Americans, we couldn't confirm that he'd actually been in the hotel. Not only did the hotel in question not CCTV its visitors going in and out, discretion being part of the service, but we also hadn't managed to track down 'Anna' the 'open minded blonde' that Jeremy Beaumont-Jones claimed to have bunged a grand to for a night of if not passion then a really good simulation of it. It didn't help that he couldn't remember which escort agency she'd come from, and had paid in cash so there was no electronic record. He hadn't booked this young woman of negotiable affection on his own phone, and there was no record of his making an outside call from the phone in his room.

It was a fair bet that someone at the hotel knew exactly which agency represented the young women who came and went, and David Carey had been actioned to take 'statements' from the staff until such time as someone coughed. Once that happened, Carey had declared, he was willing to work all hours tracking down escort agencies and taking statements from 'the girls'.

'That's just how dedicated I am to this job,' he'd said.

'Rather him than me,' said Guleed. 'That's a dreary job.'

Jeremy Beaumont-Jones' alibi for this Monday afternoon's dismemberment in the park was equally porous.

But walking around without an alibi was not sufficient grounds to charge either father or daughter. Or at least, it isn't if the suspect has a decent lawyer.

I reported Reynard's assertion that Olivia had introduced Christina Chorley to The Chestnut Tree, and thus to the wonders of the demi-monde.

'So Olivia McAllister-Thames was lying to us,' said Seawoll. 'Again.'

'Somebody's lying,' I said, which got me a look of amused indulgence from Stephanopoulos and a snort from Seawoll. Of course somebody was lying – we were the police – somebody was always lying to us.

'We have Olivia's girlfriend,' said Stephanopoulos. 'We can always ask her.'

'No,' said Seawoll. 'I don't like the way these posh buggers have been pissing us about.' He looked at me and Nightingale. 'Do you know this place?' he asked, meaning The Chestnut Tree.

Nightingale said we did, and Seawoll asked if we wouldn't mind popping over and seeing if we couldn't scare up some witnesses who could tell us exactly who had taken whom to where and what they were doing while they were there. Armed with that information we could then go back into an interview and nail said posh buggers' hands to the table.

Metaphorically. Or at least I hoped he meant metaphorically.

You can't take Nightingale to The Chestnut Tree, because by the time you've walked in the front door most of the clientele will have run out the back. In fact, on the off chance that this might prove useful one day, I once spent a fun morning trying to find the back door but to no avail. Rumour was that it opened into a secret subterranean passage which emerged in the Hyde Park car park. On this visit I did take Guleed, because Seawoll was more likely to believe her report than mine, and also I don't go into The Chestnut Tree without someone watching my back.

The place itself is on a windswept alleyway in Marble Arch just short of, and not to be mistaken for, the famous City of Quebec pub. There's no sign on the door, but I've been told that the frame is made of genuine chestnut cut from the original tree. Inside is a short corridor painted that strange green colour that I assume someone, somewhere, once persuaded the brewery chains looked wholesome, inviting and encouraged people to drink to excess.

At the end of the corridor there's a short flight of stairs into the main saloon bar. That's where the actual chestnut tree that presumably gave the pub its name grows out of the wall behind the bar. Or rather doesn't grow, because it's been dead for more than a hundred years, but its branches spread out in a tangle of bare limbs across the width of the saloon where they merge with the wooden booths that lurk in the gloom on the other side. Amongst the branches hung dusty iron and glass lamps holding what I really hoped were fake gas mantles, because using real ones would have been a bit of a health and safety violation.

As I walked in, I caught a whiff of old sweat and hot pie which might have been bad ventilation or the memory of the crowds that flocked to this end of the Tyburn Road to watch the felons morris at the end of the rope.

Morris being an old word for dance, by the way – it's amazing what you pick up on the job.

The woman behind the bar was reassuringly Romanian and didn't flinch when I showed her my warrant card and asked to see the manager. The barmaid explained that she was out getting her lunch, but was expected back any minute. In the meantime would we like a drink?

Not being tied to a brewery chain, The Chestnut Tree offered a range of beers in the mid- to totally obscure CAMRA range. I had a half of Sambrook's Junction Ale, just to keep everything friendly and relaxed you understand, and Guleed had an orange juice and Perrier.

It wasn't easy, but we managed to find a table from which we could keep an eye on most of the saloon bar. The table top was made from planks of wood that had grown pitted with use and warped with age, possibly before being lacquered with what looked like about half a centimetre of varnish. Despite the ancient beer rings worn into the surface there was a printed sign in a freestanding iron frame which requested patrons to preserve the natural beauty of the genuine antique furniture, thank you – the management. In front of this was a stack of mismatched beermats. When I had a flick through, I found they were all from different breweries and, where marked, from different pubs. I learnt much later that it was considered good form for patrons to nick beermats from other pubs and donate them to The Chestnut Tree. The really rare ones from places like Tibet or obscure bars in Abeokuta ended up pinned to a cork board behind the stage in the adjoining public bar.

'They have live music here,' said Guleed, who'd found a leaflet stuffed into the iron frame. 'Someone called the "Shanren Mountain Men Band" tonight – ever heard of them?'

I said I hadn't, nor had I heard of Lol Robinson or Laura Marling who were headlining the coming weekend.

Guleed used an apparent interest in the playbill to give the room the once over. Places like The Chestnut Tree don't get much of a lunchtime crowd. As a rule, the demi-monde doesn't work nine to five, and so doesn't need to get them in before heading back to the office for a couple of hours of pretending to work.

That said, there was a bunch of young men in white shirts in a nearby booth, blue pinstripe jackets flung over the backs of their chairs – two white, one darker who might have been Turkish or somewhere equally Mediterranean. They looked like they might work in an office and I wondered if they knew where they were drinking or if they had wandered in by accident.

In another booth two middle aged women were sitting hunched over their table so that their faces almost touched. One of them was so pale as to be actually white white with platinum blonde hair swept back behind reassuringly unpointed ears. Her friend was pinker, dark haired but with an upward curve to the corner of her eyes that I recognised from some of Edward Linley Sambourne's illustrations for Charles Kingsley's monograph on the taxonomy of the Fae. They must have spotted us watching because they both turned to frown at us – I saw their eyes were an unsettling hazel brown. The last time I'd seen eyes that colour I'd been the wrong side of the faerie veil, where I would have stayed if Bev hadn't turned up in a traction engine and given me a lift out.

Me and Guleed pretended to be interested in our drinks because, you know, it's rude to stare.

We gave it ten minutes, enough time for me to finish my half, before I went back to the bar and asked after the manageress again. While I did that, Guleed went to stand in the archway that linked the saloon bar with the public bar beyond. We'd decided that was her best position to cover what we reckoned was the door to the staff area and also the steps back-up to the street. This way, should the manageress, or anyone else, make a sudden break for it, Guleed could intercept.

'She texted me,' said the Romanian barmaid and held up her phone for me to see. 'She says she'll be back soon.'

I looked back and saw that Guleed was talking to a young Chinese guy in a purple open necked shirt, pre-faded jeans and leather trainers. He was short but broad-shouldered, his black hair cut with a long fringe. In his left hand, as if glued in place, he carried a slim bamboo and leather case which I couldn't definitely identify as a sword scabbard only because of the blue drawstring pouch covering the pommel.

He leaned forward like a bird dipping for fish and said something that made Guleed laugh. I saw her eyes flick in my direction and so did his. He turned to look at me, grinned, and gave me a polite nod and a mocking salute before turning and walking away.

'That was interesting,' said Guleed when she joined me. She showed me his card. It was expensive in its simplicity, a good card stock and superior printing. It read MICHAEL CHEUNG in black ink and, in smaller print underneath – LEGENDARY SWORDSMAN, and under that two clusters of Chinese characters. Guleed was reluctant to hand over the card, so I took a picture to send to Postmartin for translation and analysis.

'He said that he was the new guy in Chinatown,' said Guleed. 'And when you had a moment he'd like you guys to drop in at the usual place for dinner. He said Nightingale would know which place.'

'And it took him ten minutes to say that?'

'He also gave me his phone number,' she said.

'You going to call him?'

'Probably,' said Guleed.

'And if he draws that sword, are you going to arrest him?'

'That depends, doesn't it,' said Guleed. 'On what he does with it.'

Which was Guleed for 'mind your own business', but I might have pursued the matter just a little bit further in the interest of intra-collegial due diligence if the manageress of The Chestnut Tree hadn't chosen that moment to come back from lunch.

She was a white woman in her late thirties with an oval face atop a rather long neck which she grew her light brown hair long enough to partially disguise. She was wearing a no-nonsense, easy to clean, light pink blouse with black jeans and nice comfortable flat shoes. Her eyes were light brown, but even before I got close enough to see the flecks of hazel-gold around the iris I had her pegged as being fayer than the client list of a New Zealand casting agency.

Her name was Wanda Pourier and she had the kind of Estuary accent that says she could have grown up in London, only her parents moved to the Thames Valley when she was young – presumably to find work in the boredom mines.

'We'd better talk in my office,' she said. 'We don't want you lot scaring the punters more than you have already.'

The staff area was unkempt and vaguely depressing in the way that staff areas always are. The punters get the gloss and the staff get scabby, peeling walls and lockers that looked like they'd been salvaged from a sunken U-boat. The manager's office was just a spare bit of space randomly separated off with drywall and fitted with a long shelf down one side that served as both desk and storage space. There was a serious looking free-standing safe as far from the door as possible and the obligatory year planner taking up the free wall. Wanda sat in a battered operator's chair and motioned us into the two grey stackable polyurethane seats that were the only other furniture.

One thing that was missing was a computer – or even a desk calculator. Instead, an old fashioned gunmetal blue mechanical adding machine stood next to a stack of cheap ledgers, the type with carbon paper interleaves for the keeping of multiple records.

I realised that we didn't actually know who or what owned The Chestnut Tree and its prime bit of super-expensive London real estate. I put finding out on the long list that I carry around in my head, about two thirds of the way down – between rustproofing the Jag and taking Toby to the vet to get his nails clipped. Fortunately I didn't have to fish for Wanda's background because she volunteered it upfront.

'My mother was a Falloy,' she said. 'Do you know what a Falloy is?'

'Irish surname,' said Guleed.

'That too,' said Wanda.

A Falloy, according to Joseph Malzeard in his work *On the Natural Order of the Unnatural*, was a creature one half human, one eighth unseelie fae and three eighths seelie fae. Malzeard described them as *'pleasant fellows in the main albeit shiftless and prone to small mischiefs'*. I didn't mention this to Wanda because it's good practice not to let on how much you know about a particular witness, and also because I know racist bollocks when I read it.

'What's a Falloy?' asked Guleed.

'We're a little bit of this, a little bit of that,' said Wanda. 'My parents were originally from Brittany.' Which explained the surname as well.

I said that we were looking to check whether she'd

noticed certain people visiting the pub in the last six months.

'This is purely for elimination purposes,' added Guleed.

I took out my official police tablet and showed her some pictures.

'That one looks familiar,' she said when I showed her Jeremy Beaumont-Jones.

'Has he been in here?' asked Guleed.

Wanda shook her head.

'Shit,' she said. 'Wait, I have seen him. He was much younger. Was he a student at Oxford?'

I said he had been, but I was careful to keep it vague. Once you get them talking, witnesses like to tell you what you want to hear. It's depressingly easy to lead them astray – just asks the inmates of any remand wing.

'I did catering at Oxford College in the early nineties,' she said. 'I used to do silver service jobs to pay the bills. There was plenty of work around the colleges; they always seemed to be stuffing their faces for one reason or another.'

I nodded – Jeremy Beaumont-Jones had been at Oxford at that time.

'I remember him because we did a couple of jobs for this dining club,' she said. 'And they were a bit odd, if you know what I mean?'

'Scientology odd?' asked Guleed. 'Or *My Little Pony* odd?'

'Our kind of odd,' said Wanda, making a little swirling gesture with her hand that took in all three of us. Guleed frowned at that and gave me an accusing look.

'Magic, right?' I said.

Wanda gave me a small smile and tilted her head to one side.

'Or are we talking fae?' I asked, but I knew exactly who we were talking about.

'Wizard stuff,' said Wanda. 'You know, spells and wheels and compasses.'

I rummaged around on the tablet until I found a student photograph of Jeremy Beaumont-Jones that I'd lifted off his Facebook Page.

'Definitely him,' said Wanda.

I found similarly youthful pictures of Martin Chorley and a couple of other suspected Little Crocodiles, but she didn't recognise any of them. She did identify a contemporary picture of Geoffrey Wheatcroft, DPhil, former wizard, theology lecturer and the man stupid, or wicked, enough to teach magic outside the formal structure of the Folly.

'That's one of things that made them unusual,' said Wanda. 'He was there for a lot of the gigs.'

Wanda said it was important not to get carried away with mystique around the dining clubs.

'It's just like your average Saturday night in Reading city centre, only wrapped up in a ton of money,' she said. 'Well, most of them, anyway . . . not this lot – ah!' She stopped and tapped the table. 'Little Crocodiles,' she said. 'That's what they were called.'

And since Geoffrey Wheatcroft turned up to most of the events, that at least kept the student projectile vomiting to a minimum. Although the wandering hands were still a nuisance.

'Like Greenford disco all over again,' she said.

'How did you know they were doing magic?' asked Guleed.

Because people were popping off spells all through dinner, especially *lux* which, as anyone will tell you, is the first spell you learn. And there was a drinking game where each contestant conjured a *werelight* and then saw how many shots they could knock back while keeping it up.

She didn't recognise the young Martin Chorley or Albert Pryce – which Wanda freely admitted didn't mean they weren't there. Silver service is hard work and, like most of the young women doing the dining club circuit, she concentrated on getting through the night with the maximum of tips and the minimum of manhandling.

'But you haven't seen Jeremy Beaumont-Jones since Oxford?' asked Guleed, bringing us back to the case at hand.

'No, sorry,' said Wanda. But when we showed her pics of Phoebe, Olivia and Christina she sighed and said the last two had definitely been in. She didn't know who Christina was, but she remembered Olivia's name on account of her having to call her mum to take her away.

'Why was that?' asked Guleed.

'Do you see where we are?' asked Wanda. 'Do you know what was standing here before they started hanging people behind closed doors? Do you know the real name of this place?'

'Tyburn,' said Guleed, who'd obviously been paying more attention to me than I thought.

Because back in the days of yore, when Oxford Street was the Tyburn Road and the city had only just started its mad rush to cover all the west in desirable redbrick and stucco terraces, it was the main route out of London to the little village of Tyburn that sat just beyond where the road crossed the river.

Condemned prisoners were loaded onto tumbrils at Newgate Gaol, and would wind their way through the streets of London, past the rookeries at St Giles, before hitting the long straight road into the open countryside and the Tyburn Tree.

And it was a busy place, the Tyburn Tree. Because markets were *laissez-faire*, every Englishman's home was his castle and what passed for law and order was largely privately run. Back then the gentry lived in fear of the London mob and, to keep the masses in check, made sure that stealing bread or your employer's linen was a topping offence.

So they came in numbers, the tragic lads and lasses, the local boys and the immigrants from Yorkshire, Cornwall and Berkshire, from Strathclyde and County Clare. Some weeping, some defiant, and most of them pissed out of their box because the whole sad procession from Newgate Gaol would make periodic pauses for refreshments.

'This was the last stop,' said Wanda.

A last drink under the spreading chestnut tree, perhaps a chance to unburden yourself of any secrets or things you might not be able to take into the next world. And so The Chestnut Tree became the repository of final bequests.

Or a final offering, a tradition from back when the river ran free and its god walked amongst men.

Jonathan Wild went to the tree in the spring of 1725. I wondered whether this was where he'd left his final ledger. And if he had, was it a coincidence that Christina Chorley and Reynard Fossman happened to meet up here?

Coincidence, I thought. Like fuck.

So I asked about Reynard.

'Oh yeah, Reynard,' said Wanda. 'We know all about the Reynards.'

'We?' I asked.

'My family,' said Wanda. 'We know all about him.'

'Reynards you said,' said Guleed. 'Reynards plural.'

'And his family,' said Wanda. 'From France. They're a long line of total Reynards.'

And because in my line of business it pays to be sure, I asked – 'Just so we're clear, when we're talking about a line of Reynards, are we talking multiple members of one family with the same name, or the same guy changing his identity with each generation.'

'Oh he's a nasty piece of work, but he isn't that nasty,' said Wanda. 'Different guys with different names – Reynard's more of a title, an appellation, a *nom de bastard total*.'

'And he's a regular here?' I asked

'Well, we can't bar people just for being unsavoury, can we?' said Wanda. 'We'd be out of business.'

I asked who, exactly, would be out of business. Wanda gave me a card with her area manager's contact details and the name of the company who owned

256

the business: CHIPMUNK CATERING.

'Not that we see that much of them,' she said.

I handed the card to Guleed, and while I asked about Reynard's comings and goings Guleed texted the Inside Inquiry Office. I'd love to claim that I'd had a gut feeling about the owners, but really it was following routine. In policing, your gut might point the way – but it's the shoe leather that catches criminals.

I showed Wanda Christina Chorley's picture again and asked if she had ever seen her with Reynard. I used a different picture and made sure that I didn't cue Wanda that this was a repeat viewing – if you can shift the context, people often remember new facts.

This time Wanda thought it was possible that she might have seen them together, but she was hazy on the details. In just about any other pub in London I'd have asked about CCTV footage, but me and Guleed had noted the lack of cameras on the way in.

I was going to roll the conversation back round to Olivia when Guleed showed me her phone and the answering text from the Inside Inquiry Office – CHIP-MUNK CATERING DIRECTLY LINKED TO COUNTY GARD.

And County Gard belonged to the Faceless Man – shit.

'How often do you see your area manager?' I asked.

Wanda said she didn't think she'd ever met him in the three years she'd been running The Chestnut Tree – which was entirely a good thing from her point of view. 'It's not like area managers ever have anything useful to say about running a pub,' she said. 'Is it? Especially a pub like this.'

She had interviewed for the job, here in this very room, and could provide us with a name and description but she didn't understand why. I was tempted to tell her it was just routine but literally nobody ever believes that – even when it's true.

'It's part of an ongoing inquiry into property fraud,' I said, which *was* true, as far as it went.

'Are there any storage areas in here?' asked Guleed.

Wanda said that obviously they had food storage, dry goods, bottle storage, wine racks and a separate cool room for those casks that needed it.

'Do have any storage you've never been in?' I asked.

'I don't know about storage as such,' said Wanda. 'But there's a couple of rooms we don't use.'

'You couldn't give us a look, could you?' I asked.

There was a corridor that was 1930s brick down one wall and 1970s breezeblock on the other. There were two doorways in the newer wall with cheap red doors made of medium density fibreboard and the kind of stainless steel lever handle and lock combination that you find fitted to schools and council buildings from John O'Groats to Land's End.

Wanda opened them both with one of the keys from the bunch she kept in her pocket on a hoop key ring. Inside the first were a ton of stackable polyurethane chairs and, in the second, modular steel frame storage shelves that, judging by the dust, hadn't held anything for years.

'See,' said Wanda locking them back-up. 'Nothing extraordinary at all.'

'What about that one?' I asked.

. There was a third door, this one in the old side of the corridor and made of what looked like wooden planks. It looked suspiciously as if one of the artfully rustic tables from the saloon bar had been hauled upright and jammed into the doorway.

'Ah,' said Wanda, looking over at the door. 'Yeah.' She bit her lip and looked back at us.

'Do you have a key?' said Guleed.

'Yeah, I'm pretty certain we do,' said Wanda and shuffled backward a couple of steps – away from the door. 'But I don't think I should let you open that door.'

I exchanged looks with Guleed. We both knew that the words 'search warrant' were heading for Wanda's lips and we'd both been around enough weird bollocks to be suspicious as to why.

I suggested that we make our way back-up to the end of the corridor, and as we did Wanda became noticeably calmer. She asked if we'd seen everything we wanted to?

I suggested that perhaps I might borrow her key ring, just to do a security check you know, for advice purposes you understand, can't be too careful, can you, don't worry about it, it's all part of the service.

Guleed rolled her eyes, but I got the keys and Wanda got to stay at the end of the corridor where things were less likely to disturb her. I left Guleed with her and walked back to the door, carefully, with all my electronic devices switched off and my tray in the upright position.

After a build up like that, the old wooden door was

bound to look a bit sinister. But even up close I wasn't sensing anything unusual.

There's a device that Nightingale calls a demon trap, a sort of magical IED but with added animal cruelty. The Faceless Man has made use of them in the past, often to deadly effect – just another in a long list of things that my Governor would like to have a word with him about. A demon trap can be set to have a number of effects ranging from *dead* to *really wishing you were dead* via spending time at the secure mental institution of your choice.

Nightingale has taught me the basics of demon trap detection – the magical equivalent of carefully sliding the blade of your knife into the ground and waiting to see if it goes 'ting'.

The visual inspection divulged nothing, no circles or enclosed shapes incised into the surface of the wood, no disguised metal plates inlaid underneath. The lock itself, a heavy iron thing, revealed no intaglio or pattern when I brushed my fingertips across it.

But there it was . . . just at the cusp of sensation, a whiff of gunmetal and the strop strop strop of the straight razor against smooth leather. It was a *signum* I had come to recognise as belonging to the Faceless Man.

It felt dusty and airless, like an old garden shed. Certainly I wasn't feeling anything that would explain Wanda's obvious psychological aversion to opening the room. Perhaps it only worked on fae . . . perhaps that's why Wanda had been employed in the first place. That part of my mind that is forever a total bastard wondered if we could recruit some fae and map out all the places that they didn't want to go. In the interests of science and public safety.

The lock was the obvious seat for any defence so, after a moment to warn Guleed to stand clear, I sheared the hinges and, nipping up the corridor myself, knocked the door in with *impello*.

Normally when I do a forced entry like that, the door twists as it pivots around the lock, but this door just fell inward with a crash and a backwash of dust. When I gingerly advanced to find out why, I saw that the lock's bolt had been cleanly sheared off level with the strike plate, with the end still inside the socket. It had already been forced – and not by me.

'Is it safe to come down yet?' called Guleed.

I told her to give us a minute while I had a look round. It wasn't that I was worried about her coming in – I was suddenly more worried about Wanda the manageress doing a runner. I pulled on my evidence gloves and went inside – cautiously.

Frank Caffrey, fire investigation officer, former para and Folly liaison is very clear that when entering a room you think might be rigged, the first thing you *don't* do is automatically reach out and flip the light switch.

As he points out, that's got to be one of the cheapest and most reliable triggers an IED can have. 'I mean, it's even got its own power supply,' he said. And he likes to point out that the Faceless Man may like his magical weapons, but he's not so stupid as to rely on them alone.

You know . . . I used to be worried that they were

going to assign me to undercover work in Operation Trident – I obviously didn't know when I was well off.

It was another store room with metal frame variable-height shelving lining the walls from floor to ceiling. About half the shelf space was occupied – mostly those at waist height for easy access. There was a thin layer of dust over the shelves and the floor. It's hard to tell with dust, but I'd spent enough time on the job with my mum to reckon a couple of months' worth. On the shelf closest to the door was a row of standard seventy-five litre plastic storage boxes with red clip-down lids. Their contents were a collection of angular shadows visible through the semi-transparent sides. The dust around them had been disturbed and there were clear hand-prints on the edges of the lids.

Staying on the fallen door to avoid contaminating the floor any more than I had to, I carefully levered the lid off the nearest box and had a peek inside. It looked suspiciously like old hardback books with stiff cloth-covered covers. The topmost book had the rough green cover I associated with the limited editions published by Russell House Press – one of the Folly's own publishing arms. I picked it up and flipped it open to the title page.

It was a 1912 reprint of Meric Casaubon's *A true and faithful relation of what passed for many years between Dr John Dee and Some Spirits*. And, yes, at the bottom *Russell House Press*. A second edition – obviously Casaubon had been popular amongst British wizards.

I was willing to bet real money that Jonathan Wild's last ledger had once languished in one of these boxes. The Mary Engine too, not to mention the genuine wizard's staff and the bloody tedious Victor Bartholomew book. Which begged the question why the Bartholomew had ended up on eBay and not the Casaubon. From a magical perspective they were both about as useful, although as cures for insomnia the Bartholomew had a slight edge.

Because the Casaubon was a second edition?

Carefully I checked the other books in the box. All of them were either second editions from the 1920s or the 30s or had significant damage to their covers or their interior pages. I was pleased to see that even back in the glory days of the Folly people left their mugs of tea on their magical textbooks.

At the bottom of the box I found part of a map that had been ripped down its centrefold – a 1:40,000 scale depiction of a place called Ootacamund, which turned out on later research to be a British Hill Station in Tamil Nadu. A Hill Station being a place where colonial administrators and the like could use altitude to avoid the oppressive Indian summer heat, since the sensible solution, i.e. abandoning colonialism and moving back to Surrey, obviously never occurred to them.

I considered checking one of the other boxes, but my mystic powers of precognition bestowed a vision upon me of a full forensic search with noddy suits and fingerprint powder and people taking their sunglasses off in a dramatic fashion.

I did stop on my way out to examine the lock a bit more carefully. Again I felt the razor strop of the Faceless Man's *signum* and it was definitely centred on the point where the bolt was sheared right through.

A hypothesis was forming in my mind. If County Gard belonged to the Faceless Man, then The Chestnut Tree did too. Perhaps it was even an asset inherited from his predecessor, which meant that, possibly, this was his storeroom – these had been his things.

Which had been looted by Christina Chorley and Reynard Fossman.

Did they know who they'd stolen from?

He was bound to be a bit miffed . . . I've only met him a couple of times, but he didn't seem the type to take that sort of thing with a light and forgiving heart. Which might explain why Aiden Burghley's face got laminated to a tree and what the fucker had been doing in Phoebe Beaumont-Jones' basement . . . looking for accomplices?

Presuming he wasn't her dad.

Christina and Reynard – they'd taken the stuff that looked valuable – possibly over a period of weeks. Then one day the Faceless Man pops down to check on his booty, or maybe he had a burning desire to brush up on his basic thaumatology, and finds that the door is locked.

Let's assume the key he's got doesn't work for some reason – he burns the lock, steps inside and finds half his stuff's been jacked. So Action 1 for me – fingerprint team for the corridor and the room, because nobody wears gloves all the time.

Next the Faceless Man's going to go ask Wanda the manageress just who she's been letting into the storerooms, possibly using *seducere* to fog her memory, or maybe she's a much better liar then we thought. So

Action 2 – re-interview Wanda, this time under caution plus two, which leads us onto Action 3, trace the rest of The Chestnut Tree's staff and interview them as well.

Rule of thumb for lowly constables – once you're up to three actions it's time to kick the buck upstairs.

12

The 100 Metre Nonchalant Stroll

'And you didn't think to try pushing the door open first?' asked Professor Postmartin.

I said nothing, mainly because he was the fourth person to ask that, after Guleed, Nightingale and Stephanopoulos.

Postmartin looked remarkably dapper in his noddy suit and was supervising approvingly as the SOCOs carefully catalogued the evidence with their hoods up and their masks on. Mind you, the Professor probably thought all books over five years old should be handled in this fashion – particularly by undergraduates.

I stayed in the corridor and tried not to get fingerprint powder on my sleeves.

'Have you found anything else interesting?' I asked.

'Interesting, yes,' said Postmartin. 'How significant – I don't know. Your hypothesis that this was the repository for the last offerings of the hanged is charming, but unsupported by the evidence so far.'

'Any copies of the *Principia*?' I asked.

'Two in fact,' said Postmartin. 'One of them quite rare.'

'But physically damaged?'

'I've seen better kept copies,' said Postmartin. 'But the marginalia in one edition is quite fascinating.'

'Christina Chorley and Reynard Fossman couldn't read Latin,' I said. *The Second Principia*, the *Philosophiæ Naturalis Principia Artes Magicis*, had never been published in English – as a deliberate policy to ensure that only people of the 'right' sort read it. 'They didn't recognise it for what it was – it probably just looked like a tatty old book to them.'

'They understood the importance of the ledger,' said Postmartin.

'Yeah, they did, didn't they?' I said. 'Which implies an outside source of information, doesn't it?'

'I'm afraid it does,' said Postmartin and went back to his cataloguing.

I found Nightingale in the manageress' office. He was leaning against the wall, arms folded, as he watched a DC from Intelligence triaging the papers on the desk and packing them into evidence boxes that looked remarkably similar to those the Faceless Man had used to store his goodies in. I hoped they didn't get them mixed up.

I asked where Guleed had got to.

'Finishing the interview with the manageress,' said Nightingale. 'She seemed to think she'd get more out of the poor woman without me hovering in the doorway.'

'You know she's demi-fae,' I said.

'So Sahra explained.'

'You don't seem very surprised.'

Nightingale shrugged.

'If Abdul ever gets his wish and finds a reliable . . .'

He frowned. 'What does he call it – a genetic marker?'

Determining whether there was an actual genetic basis to being a fae was one of Dr Walid's research priorities. I'm pretty certain that his keenness to employ Dr Vaughan had come from a desire to have more time to pursue it.

I confirmed that Nightingale was right and it was indeed a genetic marker. Although, of course, it was all much more complicated than that, genetics-wise. It always is.

'Should he ever find his marker,' said Nightingale, 'and conduct his survey, I believe he will find that fairy blood is far more widespread than previously assumed.'

And most of them passing, I thought, like Wanda the manageress.

'None of the items listed on eBay have been sold yet,' I said. 'So they must be stored somewhere.'

'Indubitably,' said Nightingale. 'I think we must assume that our tricky fox has a hideaway he hasn't told us about.' All of Reynard Fossman's last known addresses had already been searched over the weekend as well as a few likely lock-ups that had, as Nightingale admitted, quite tenuous connections to the man. Not to mention that we still hadn't found the antique Renault 4 GTL that, according to the DVLA, was registered in his name.

'It would be nice to find the Mary Engine,' I said. 'It could be the only original difference engine in existence. We could flog it to the Science Museum.'

'You'd have to fight Harold for it,' said Nightingale.

Postmartin took his role as archivist very seriously.

'But it's not a book, is it?' I said. 'That means we get first dibs. Do you know if they made any more – did anyone at the Folly have one?'

'There was always a rumour that Babbage had worked on a mechanical device of some kind for the Folly,' said Nightingale. 'One which might have had applications in the practise – but it was just a rumour.'

'Was there anything about Ada Lovelace?' I asked.

Nightingale gave me a funny look.

'Byron's daughter?' he asked. 'I'm not sure I understand the connection.'

'She worked with Babbage on the difference engine,' I said.

'In what capacity?'

'She was a famously gifted mathematician,' I said. Who I mostly knew about from reading Steampunk, but I wasn't going to mention that. 'Generally considered to have written the first true computer program.'

'Ah,' said Nightingale. 'So now we know who to blame.'

'Reynard's not going to tell us where his real lock-up is,' I said. 'And I don't think he's stupid enough to lead us to it. He must know we're going to tail him once we release him. I suppose we could still charge him with whatever we've got lying around. Or ask for an extension.'

'No,' said Nightingale. 'I think we let the fox run. But not before we inform him that the Faceless Man might have him in his sights.'

'He might bottle it there and then, ask for protective custody.'

'So much the better,' said Nightingale with a smile. 'Because then we can extract a price for his protection. And if he doesn't, then fear might just drive him back to his den. Might it not?'

'And if we hang him out as bait and the Faceless Man offs him?' I asked.

Nightingale put his hand on my shoulder and leaned forward.

'I thought I might intervene before that happened,' he said softly and then, straightening, said, 'Besides, it will do Reynard good to play the hound not the fox for a change.'

I was thinking that it sounded like a fucking desperate plan to me, but Nightingale was the man who had walked home from Ettersberg and struck awe into the breasts of classically educated wizards from Herefordshire to Vladivostok.

'Do you think you can take the Faceless Man?' I asked.

'He's started making mistakes,' said Nightingale. 'Something has put him off his game. And, if he's scrambling, we might be able to bring him down with a good tap.'

He *is* making mistakes, I thought, but why? Yes, Reynard and Christina had pilfered his goodies from under his nose. But I couldn't see any connection between that and Aiden Burghley. Especially not one which warranted that flashy dismemberment. And what was he doing questioning Phoebe in her underground pool? Unless the Faceless Man was her father,

Jeremy Beaumont-Jones, and he thought Aiden Burgh-ley was another link in a conspiracy that encompassed Christina Chorley and Reynard the Suspicious ... In which case Olivia McAllister-Thames would be a target too.

'We need to close down the other loose ends,' I said.

'Agreed,' said Nightingale. 'Let's see how Sahra is doing.'

So we divvied up the jobs, subject to Seawoll's agreement of course. Guleed would action a TIE on the 'area manager' who'd interviewed Wanda the manageress for her job.

'I'm sure Carey will have finished with his escorts by then,' she said.

Then both of us would head out to the fabled lands beyond High Wycombe to see whether Christina stashed her stolen goodies at her father's house.

'Isn't Martin Chorley on the Tiger list?' asked Guleed.

'Our target's made a big thing out of his anonymity,' I said. 'So assuming for a minute that he is Christina's dad – which is unlikely, but possible – then he's not going to reveal himself just because we want a look at his daughter's room. Especially if we let him know we're coming up.'

Guleed frowned – it's bad practise to give people warning before you turn over their house, but if Martin Chorley was the Faceless Man, I reckoned the room would have been cleaned out by now anyway. It's also bad practise to startle dangerous armed suspects – better to slowly and calmly take control of the situation. At least that's the theory.

'He's not going to blow his cover if he thinks he can fob us off,' I said. 'And if he's not our man then he won't know what we're looking for, so he won't have a reason to hide it.'

Nightingale offered to authorise Guleed to carry a taser but she claimed to have never done the training course.

'In that case you might want to carry a screamer instead,' said Nightingale.

'As long as you carry one too,' I said.

'What's a screamer?' asked Guleed.

I said I'd show her when we got back to the Folly, because Postmartin wanted us to cart a couple of crates over there and lock them in our secure evidence room. Actually, he meant the library because there was no way he wanted 'his' books stashed downstairs in the basement armoury.

Molly came out to meet us as we drove in the back gate. She glared at me and then tilted her head up towards the top floor of the coach house where I keep my widescreen, my desktop and any other bits of the technology that, for one reason or another, don't work well in the Folly proper.

We left the boxes in the car and me and Guleed climbed the spiral stairs to find Caroline inside playing *Shadow of Mordor* on my PS4. Toby was curled up at her feet, thus once again demonstrating his true worth as a guard dog.

'Thank god you're here,' she said, putting it down. 'I was about to go mad with boredom.'

I did a quick inspection of my stuff, but nothing seemed out of place. I haven't got so paranoid that I've started sticking hairs across doorjambs but between Nightingale watching the rugby while I was over at Bev's, and Molly sneaking in whenever she thought I wasn't looking to swap recipes on Twitter, I've taken to securing anything important in filing cabinets.

I asked how long she'd been hanging out on her own.

'We came over to talk to your experts,' said Caroline, who made it clear that she'd been dragged over as reluctantly as any child to an art gallery. Despite tea and cakes Caroline thought she'd just about reached peak boredom when Professor Postmartin was called away.

'You're not interested in *The Third Principia?*' I asked.

'It's not going to have anything about aerodynamics in it,' she said. 'Is it?'

'Aerodynamics?' asked Guleed.

'Caroline wants to fly,' I said.

'Does she know about your swan dive off the top of Skygarden Tower?' asked Guleed.

She does now, I thought.

'The one that was blown up?' said Caroline.

'As it came down,' said Guleed, who wasn't making any friends just then.

I busily rooted around in the equipment rack for a couple of screamers while Caroline fished for information. Had I actually been flying, or gliding, or otherwise retarding my fall through the use of magic and if so – how?

'Retarding,' I said while I checked that the screamers were working. 'Only it was the Faceless Man doing it, not me.' I handed the screamer to Guleed and showed her how to use it.

Caroline wanted to know whether I'd seen how the Faceless Man was controlling his descent, and I remembered the tower falling, the screaming, the smell of brick dust and the whole wide world rushing up to smack me in the face.

'I was a bit distracted at the time,' I said. 'But he had to concentrate to maintain it.'

'So what happened to Dr Walid and Lady Helena?' said Guleed who always liked to keep things moving along.

'After the professor rushed off, your pair of mad pathologists asked my mum whether she'd like to see their unparalleled collection of horrible things,' said Caroline. She explained that she hadn't really fancied it herself. She would have done a bit of exploring around the Folly, only Molly kept on following her, so she came into the yard and found the tech cave.

'It wasn't locked?' I said.

'No,' she said, and smiled innocently. 'Was it supposed to be?'

'Generally I keep it locked.'

I chivvied her out and she ended up helping me and Guleed carry the boxes of books up to the library.

'Anything in these for Mum?' asked Caroline.

'She can take that up with the Professor,' I said. But that's when I decided to take Caroline with us to check Christina Chorley's room.

It was all going perfectly fine until I noticed Martin Chorley's watch. After that, as Nightingale might say, it all rather went downhill.

The Chorley house was just the other side of Lane End, itself a village just the other side of High Wycombe which could, I suppose, be described as a small town just the other side of London. Since we'd managed to catch the M40 during a rare moment of decongestion we made it there in less than an hour, not counting the stop off at Marks and Spencer's for snacks.

We'd checked the location on Google Earth, so unless there'd been some drastic landscaping in the last couple of years, the house had two L-shape wings and was situated just below the brow of a wooded hill that overlooked the valley and the motorway that snaked through it. It was reached by a private driveway that peeled off the main road and looped up through the woods – Martin Chorley certainly liked his privacy.

We stopped off at the entrance to the drive for a quick pre-arrival conference and the last of the Percy Pigs.

I didn't want Caroline to come up to the house.

'On the remote chance he is the Faceless Man,' I said, 'then he might know about you and your mum. Better if he doesn't know we're working together.'

'You expect me to wait in the car?' said Caroline

'Actually, no. Because we're going to park the car right outside,' I said. 'I thought you could wait in the pub we went past back there.'

'Back there?' said Caroline.

'About five hundred metres,' I said. 'It looked like they did food.'

'And you didn't think to stop when we went past?'

'I didn't think of it until we got here,' I said. 'Look, we'll drive you back down the road and come back.'

I expected a longer argument but Caroline gave me a look, put up her hands and said she'd walk.

'Can you bag us a table for when we're finished?' I asked as she started back down the road – she didn't answer.

'And that was in aid of what, exactly?' asked Guleed.

'I don't trust them,' I said. 'I don't trust her or her mother. I couldn't leave her rattling around the Folly and I definitely don't want her getting first dibs on anything Christina has stashed at her dad's house. Particularly if she had a copy of *The Third Principia*.'

'You think Caroline'd try and steal it?' asked Guleed.

'Believe it,' I said.

'What does Nightingale think?'

'Maybe he just likes having someone to talk shop with, but he seems a bit too trusting to me.'

'Maybe he's picked up some bad habits,' said Guleed.

'Yeah – who from?'

Guleed looked down the road to where, despite the curve, we could just see Caroline trudging back towards the village.

'Is there some reason why we're still standing here?' she asked.

'I want to make sure she doesn't double back,' I said. 'Also, she might fly.' I got out of the Asbo for a better look.

'When you're finished I'll be in the car,' said Guleed.

Disappointingly, Caroline didn't launch herself into the air. So I climbed back into the car and we drove up the winding drive to Chorley central.

It was a beautiful house, if you like fine detached William and Mary villas in the middle of nowhere. Still had a lot of its original features, and I was surprised it wasn't at least Grade II listed, but that hadn't shown up on the IIP check during the initial stages of the investigation. It had a nice sensible tarmac drive with discreet drainage channels built into verges – not that they were going to flood this far up a hill, but Bev would have approved.

Checking the roof, I spotted solar panels on the south facing slopes and I was willing to bet the gutters directed rain into storage barrels against the possibility of hosepipe bans. I pulled up next to the BMW 5 series that was parked outside the garage that made up the ground floor of the barn conversion next door. Presumably the Ferrari 288 GTO also registered in Martin Chorley's name was kept inside. I spotted what definitely looked like an office attached to one end of the garage and made a mental note to check it – if only to sneak a look at the Ferrari.

'What do you think?' asked Guleed as we approached the door.

'Puzzled but co-operative,' I said.

'Resigned but obstructionist in a passive-aggressive fashion,' said Guleed.

'That's very precise.'

'I've done more notifications than you,' she said and rang the doorbell.

It turned out we were both wrong.

Martin Chorley, knowing we were coming, had had time to clean the kitchen, tidy the living room and hide his porn stash. I'm kidding about the cleaning because after five seconds in that house it's clear he had a cleaner in three days a week at the very least.

He looked less haggard when he opened the door, the smudges under his eyes having receded and the pain lines around his mouth seemed less prominent. It looked like he was beginning to settle into his grief, but there was a feverish aspect to his eyes that I didn't like. He was dressed in khaki chinos and a white and black check shirt with the sleeves rolled up to his elbows. There was a smudge of something black, oil or ink I couldn't tell which, on his left shoulder.

'Please,' he said when he saw us. 'Come in – make yourselves at home.'

Guleed gave him a sharp look.

'Can I ask how you're feeling, sir?' said Guleed.

Mr Chorley gave her a puzzled glance and then shrugged.

'Bloody awful,' he said. 'But thank you for asking.'

The entrance hall was low ceilinged, made lower by the original roof beams that crossed it. There was a staircase with bare wooden risers varnished a dark brown leading upstairs, a square archway into what I learnt later was called the snug, with a real fireplace, old leather furniture and the sort of worn throw rug that really needed to have an Irish wolfhound curled up asleep on it.

I glanced at the staircase and Guleed took up the cue

– asking whether we could see Christina's room first. Mr Chorley was welcome to supervise, she said, although in reality we were both hoping he didn't.

In the end he led us upstairs to the first floor where the hallways were covered in a thick cream carpet that must have been a bugger to clean.

'She pretty much had the run of this floor,' he said, although officially the main bedroom with its en-suite was hers and the other rooms were for guests. Then he left us to it, thank god, and said that when we were finished there was coffee in the kitchen.

The main bedroom and bathroom were far too neat, the modern reproduction brass bed was neatly made, a ghastly pink vanity and matching wardrobe had their drawers closed and when we opened them to look inside we found the clothes neatly folded – even the underwear. Guleed tutted. The room had been practically scrubbed clean, probably since Christina's death. That was odd. Grieving parents often put off making any changes to a lost child's things. But grief smacks everyone in the face in a different way, so I didn't read anything into it.

There was no school work – presumably that had all been in her dorm room back at St Paul's – but there was an interesting collection of books. Lots of YA in the American 'drown the sister' school of social realism, plus various Malorie Blackmans, Shirley Jackson's *We Have Always Lived in the Castle* and *Land of Laughs* by Jonathan Carroll.

'A bit more Goth than I was expecting,' said Guleed, and I remembered that we'd collared Reynard in that

Gothic paradise in Archway. Perhaps that's what they had in common.

There was nothing under the bed, inserted into the mattress or taped into an envelope under the knicker drawer. The lone stuffed animal propping up the headboard had no suspicious lumps, zips or loose seams, and valuable seventeenth century magical artefacts were definitely not lodged under any loose floorboards.

We widened our search, softly stepping out into the corridor and moving as quietly as possible into the bathrooms and guest bedrooms. It's not that we were creeping about, but we figured what Mr Chorley didn't hear us doing wouldn't worry him – us police are thoughtful that way.

We also have no shame, so once we'd found nothing of note on the first floor we split up, Guleed to check the second floor, where Mr Chorley had his domain, while I went downstairs to keep an eye on the man himself and, with a bit of luck, look at his motor.

I found him in the kitchen where he offered me tea, but I asked if I could see the garage. He asked if I liked cars and, when I said I did, he gave me a wan but genuine smile.

'Then you're going to like this,' he said.

The garage was clean and, judging from the perfectly balanced temperature and humidity, had the sort of environmental control system that Postmartin demands for his most fragile historical documents. The brickwork was painted a bright glossy white with just the Pirelli Calendar and an immaculate tool rack to break up the sterility. All the better for us to appreciate the car.

The Ferrari was a ridiculously beautiful motor, fire brick red with proper sleek 70s sci-fi lines so that it looked like any second the wheels would fold down to become lift engines and the vehicle would launch itself back to the future that never was. It also had a completely insane de-bored 2.8 litre V8 engine that could do nought to a hundred in less time than it takes to say it. And, from the point of view of the magic police, no electronic transmission — which meant you couldn't accidentally wreck your own motor when in hot pursuit. I'm not saying that Nightingale should have traded in the Jag, but would it really have killed him to lay down a couple of Italians from the golden age of supercars? Just as an investment, if nothing else.

I asked Mr Chorley if he ever took it out for a spin.

'Absolutely,' he said. 'There's no point owning a car like this if you never drive it.'

I was just wondering if there was a way I could wrangle a ride or, failing that, just a go in the driving seat with the engine on when Martin Chorley checked his watch. It was a slim steel coloured Montblanc Timewalker, two grand and change from reputable stockists and the sort of high quality wind-up that any practitioner would be proud to wear.

I literally nearly shat myself.

I was suddenly certain that I was bonding over a motor with the Faceless Man, and if it was him then he already knew who I was. Which meant that either he was just playing with me or was still hoping to maintain his cover. I considered whether I could tackle him right then – but he was fast and ruthless, and if I didn't take him down with the first blow I probably wasn't going to get a second attempt.

He didn't turn his back on me or lift the engine cover and conveniently bend over so I could concuss him with the first blow and, to be totally honest, I bottled it – which, surprisingly, is approved police procedure.

Evacuate, report and contain – that's what I was going to say in the ever-expanding Falcon Operations Manual – assuming I lived long enough to finish writing it.

I sighed, trying not to make it theatrical, and said that I would love to stay and talk about cars but we had to get back to London. He asked whether we'd found anything useful and I explained that we hadn't but you had to cross your I's and dot your T's.

'I'm just pathetically grateful that you haven't closed the case,' he said.

I assured him that the full might and majesty of the Metropolitan Police was focused on finding the truth behind his daughter's death. If he would like a Family Liaison Officer to be assigned to him I'd be happy to oblige.

And I was thinking that now I understood the ferocity with which Aiden Burghley had been dismembered. Not because he was an obstacle, or as warning to others, but because Martin Chorley held him responsible for his daughter's overdose.

Damn, but Phoebe must have been seconds from death – the arrival of the Americans had saved her life.

He shook my hand; his palm was warm and dry, his grip firm but not macho. A salesman's shake, a grifter's shake, a psychopath's handshake. He gestured for me to proceed him through the garage door. A line of sweat ran down my back as I turned away and stepped outside.

'I'll just call my colleague and let her know we're going,' I said and thought, shit, shit, shit, over-thinking it, stupid, stupid, stupid. I pulled out my phone and called Guleed.

'Yeah, they need us back at Belgravia,' I told her.

The garage was parallel to the back edge of the house and there was a good six metres of drive between me and the Asbo. I lurched at a sudden grinding sound but it was only the motorised garage door closing. I disguised it by converting it into a half turn and cheery wave for Mr Chorley who stayed by the garage and watched me go.

Ahead of me Guleed sauntered out of the front door and over to the Asbo where she leaned against the bonnet. She raised a hand in a lazy salute, aimed behind me so presumably it was for Mr Chorley, who I deduced was still watching me go. I slipped my keys out of my pocket and, without pointing them at the car or doing anything else obvious, I pressed the unlocking remote.

Nothing happened.

I tried again and still no clunk or beep or flashing tail lights.

Either the remote had chosen that exact moment to break or the electrics in my car had been nobbled – no prizes for guessing which. And that meant the fucker had disabled the Asbo while me and Guleed had been upstairs in his daughter's room. My guess was that in his head I was going to point my fob at the car, it would fail, I would click it again and again before futilely trying the door handles.

How he would chuckle as puzzlement turned to stricken realisation, I would look over at him and our eyes would meet. Then he would strike, nothing fatal to start with, so probably *impello* to knock me down, or something fancy and fifth order that I'd not even heard of.

The way the Asbo was parked meant that there was a two metre gap between the driver's side door and the corner of the house. So two metres to put us out of his line of sight. Once we'd managed that, I'd worry about what do next.

I picked up my pace. I didn't want our friend getting impatient and kicking off early.

I called out something to Guleed but I can't remember what I said. It was enough to get her off the bonnet and meet me in front of the car. There we stopped as if having a quick chat before leaving.

'Martin Chorley is the Faceless Man,' I said.

Guleed's eyes widened and her head jerked back as if trying to escape the news, but she kept her body language neutral and disguised her reaction with a tolerably convincing laugh.

'Shit,' she said. 'Nightingale is an hour and a half away. Does Chorley know we know?'

'I think so,' I said.

'Plan?'

'I'm going to walk to the car,' I said. 'You keep going round the corner until you're out of sight, then chuck the screamer and run like crazy.'

'What are you going to do?'

'I'm going to do exactly the same thing but in a different direction,' I said. 'I'll keep him occupied. You organise the perimeter.'

If Guleed was going to say anything along the lines of 'No, no, I can't let you sacrifice yourself for me,' it was too late, because we'd reached the car and in any case she knew it had to be this way.

Careful not to look, I heard the tempo of her sensible shoes as, once out of Mr Chorley's sight, she took off towards the treeline.

I took out my key-fob and pointed it at the car. Nothing happened. I made a show of trying it a couple of times more, tried the handle and then, with a quick prayer to Sir Samuel, the patron saint of policemen, I looked back at Mr Chorley.

He was still standing in front of the garage, hands casually in his pockets.

He nodded amiably at me and I saw his eyes flick to my right – he was wondering where Guleed had gone.

And while he was distracted I gave him everything I had.

Now, I'm not up to Nightingale's standards and 100mm of case-hardened steel is a bit beyond me, but I have progressed a bit from that first time we met on a rooftop in Soho when the Faceless fucker snatched my fireball out of the air. The flash git.

What he got was a flashgun bright fireball followed by an *impello palma*. The idea is that the target spends all his time worrying about the bright light coming at his face and doesn't notice the invisible wall of force rushing along at waist height.

It might have worked, for all I know, but I didn't stick around to find out. As soon as the spells were loosed I turned and legged it for the trees.

You don't run straight away from someone with a ranged weapon unless you want to get shot in the back – you're supposed to zig-zag at random intervals to present a constantly shifting target. It's one of those things I've always known intellectually but, fuck me, it's difficult to do in practise.

So I went left as if I was trying to get out of sight around the house and then right, picking a number at random and counting down the paces, eleven, ten, nine and then a horrid thought that maybe eleven was too high. So I turned at six and had gone one pace when something huge and orange shot past my head, close enough for the wind of it to stagger me. As I recovered, I looked up long enough to see the Asbo go tumbling into the trees, splintering branches and spinning round as the front clipped the trunk of a full grown oak.

I thought I'd been running flat out . . . but, you know, I think now I added a couple of kph and shaved some time off the world record. I feinted right again, went left and suddenly I was in amongst the trees and the under-growth and running downhill towards the main road.

The previous summer I'd done the exact same thing while being chased by an invisible unicorn – so at least

I had form. I fumbled my screamer out of my jacket pocket, pressed my thumb hard against the activation slot and threw it as far as I could to the left.

The hardy men of the Bow Street Runners were used to working alone and thus relied on a loud voice to raise the hue and cry, alert the populace and, occasionally, scream with pain as they were savagely beaten by a criminal gang. The new men of Peel's innovative civilian police force were, in contrast, equipped with the latest in communications gear – the hand rattle. A Peeler could summon aid by shaking his rattle while in hot pursuit of a felon and hoping that people would stop laughing long enough to help. The rattle was soon superseded by the whistle, whose principal advantage was that, not only could you have a number of prearranged signals for a variety of situations, but you didn't look like a total tit using it.

Once the telephone had been invented, it was only a matter of time before the police got in on the new technology and, first in Glasgow and then in London, the police box was born. Here a police officer in need of assistance could find a telephone link to Scotland Yard, a dry space to do 'paperwork' and, in certain extreme cases, a life of adventure through space and time.

Finally, radios got small enough that a constable on the beat could carry one on his person, call in back-up, report crimes and lie about how long he was taking on refs. Then we got Airwaves, which could be integrated with every other emergency service network all over the country – now a copper under threat can get help anywhere from anyone. There's even a panic button that opens your mic and broadcasts everything it picks up over the emergency channel. It's the sort of thing that saves the lives and, even more frequently, the tender parts of police officers.

But then along comes magic, and suddenly we're supposed to go back to rattles and whistles. Not this PC – I like my tender parts abrasion free.

So I invented the screamer, patent pending. Built around the guts of a disposable mobile phone, it has a felt cover for grip and is weighted for throwing. It's got a recessed hook slide – you thumb it sideways and release and a clockwork timer starts. Then you throw the bloody thing as far as you can, hopefully outside the area of immediate magical effect, where two minutes later it basically phones the Met control room and screams help, help, serious magic shenanigans here – send help – preferably Nightingale.

I have a guy in Leominster who makes them for me, although he still thinks I'm using them to track UFOs.

As the screamer went flying into the undergrowth I shifted axis again, caught my ankle on something unseen and collapsed, flailing, into the bushes. Against my instincts, I stayed down, face pressed against the layer of decomposing leaves that Beverley assures me is a vital part of the arboreal ecosystem, and forced myself to take deep and regular breaths, even as random spores made my nose tickle.

There was wind in the treetops and I heard a vehicle go past, no more than twenty metres downhill – the main road. The trees around me were tall, with straight trunks supporting wide deciduous canopies ... judging from the variation in colour and density there were at least two or three different species, not that I could identify them. Their lowest branches were too high up for me to climb and, apart from the bush I was lying behind, there was little ground cover.

I considered bolting for the road, but then what?

This wasn't a unicorn I was dealing with. Martin Chorley wasn't going to be stopped by any landscape feature short of a three metre concrete wall, and even then it would only slow him down for two, three seconds tops. Better, I decided, to rely on stealth – at least until I had a better idea of where he was.

'Peter,' said a voice far too close by. 'This really is an exercise in futility.'

It sounded like Martin Chorley, only richer and with the timbre of confidence that posh people put on to convince themselves they know what they're talking about. There was money in that voice, and breeding, and behind it all the mace, the whip and the bowler hat. I also didn't think it was entirely natural.

'I've done a deal with Lesley,' said the voice. 'I promised that no permanent harm will come to you.' It seemed very close now – metres, spitting distance.

He had to know that I got a message out, and that it was only a matter of time before Nightingale descended on him in all his glory. Likewise he had to know that it was goodbye Faceless Man, hello plain old Martin Chorley, nominal and prime suspect.

'Look Peter,' said the voice. 'I don't have all day, so why don't we get this over with?'

How not to be seen, lesson number one: Don't stand up.

It started to rain, a persistent invisible drizzle that worked its way through the canopy and started soaking the back of my jacket and trousers. What with being overcast, it was beginning to get dark and I wondered who that would favour – me or him.

'We both know the only reason you're still alive,' said Martin Chorley, a couple of centimetres from the back of my head, 'is because I have a soft spot for Lesley May.'

God, it was hard not to move. But I knew that Nightingale could throw sounds about the place. And if Chorley had really been behind me I doubted he would have been so chatty.

'What I don't understand, Peter,' said Martin Chorley – but now his voice seemed to be coming from a spot three or four metres to my right – 'is your loyalty to these institutions. The police, the Folly – you swore an oath to the crown for god's sake – institutions with hardly the best track record with regards to you people.'

Because the alternative is you, I wanted to shout back. But the second lesson on how not to be seen is: Don't answer back.

He knows he's short of time, so he's trying to provoke me, I thought. Next, escalation – threaten somebody else.

'I've got your Muslim partner,' he said. And this time I spotted the voice wow-wowing back and forth through the trees. I thought I might even be able to sense, just a little, the *formae* he was using to do it. 'You have a reputation for gallantry – are you perpared to do the gallant thing now?'

Now, he might have Guleed, although I doubted it. But even if he did, I knew he wasn't going to just swap me for her. He was trying to provoke a response so he could zero in on me.

And if he *did* have Guleed?

I thought it better to establish the facts before I started worrying about that.

I decided to give him a response.

Lux is really the most ridiculously versatile of the *formae* and it has been the subject of experimentation by literally thousands of practitioners since the Folly was a bunch of likeminded weirdos and charlatans meeting in a London coffee house. As a result, a young person with an inquiring mind can find the most extraordinary things written in the margins of his textbooks. Now, I have the advantage over my nineteenth century peers of knowing what infrared is and how it relates to imparting heat energy to a small cloud of gas so that it expands with a humorous farting sound – oh, how they must have laughed. Thus I can make my farting sound louder and funnier – to the point where it can shake the branches on a small bush.

Ipsa scientia potestas est.

I call them noisemakers because I haven't thought of a decent Latin tag yet.

So I flipped one as far to my right as I could, where it made a sound like a deflating bellows and made a bush shake.

Let's see what you make of that, I thought.

A tree five metres to my right exploded. I was look-ing right at it when the trunk shattered at head height and blew out in a cloud of pale brown dust and splin-ters. Even as I clamped my arms over my head and tried to burrow my way into the leaf mould, chunks of wood were thudding down around me. I yelled into the ground as a heavy bit bounced off my back.

Another tree exploded, closer; I knew it was a tree because I heard the top half of the trunk crash through the surrounding branches before smashing into the hillside with a sound that went vibrating up through my chest. A third explosion followed the crash so quickly that the sound became one long physical blow. A fourth and fifth followed, but further away to the right – below the pain threshold.

I risked lifting my head a fraction. The air was full of yellow and brown dust and the sick smell of broken wood. Flames were visible through the murk, licking up the shattered stump of a tree. Less than ten centimetres from my face a rough splinter the size and pointiness of a fencepost had been driven into ground.

I couldn't stay where I was. Martin Chorley might not know I was here, but one more near miss by whatever he was exploding trees with and I was going to look like an involuntary hedgehog. I drew my legs up and braced to scramble towards the road.

Another couple of explosions – much further to my right.

Sometimes courage is easy, and sometimes you have to scream at your own body to act in its own bloody best interest, and sometimes it refuses the call altogether.

And the pisser is that you never know which one it's going to be until you try.

This time my body was in full agreement with flight mode and off we went.

We got maybe five metres before a weight landed on my back, wrapped something solid around my chest and hoisted me into the air. I would have screamed like a little girl but whoever had a grip on me had their hand clamped over my mouth. There was the scent of saffron, the sharp bite of clean sunlight over a windswept hillside and the sight of far horizons.

You lying little toerag, I thought, you *can* fly.

The soaring effect was ruined by the leafy twigs that smacked me around my head and shoulders and then we stopped in a green space and I was dumped onto a branch next to the tree trunk which, while being alarmingly thin at this altitude, I grabbed hold of gratefully. Caroline's hand squeezed my mouth for emphasis before letting go.

I looked around – Caroline sat casually, legs swinging, on a branch on the opposite side of the trunk and Guleed was on a branch a metre below. We were near the top of the tree and the branches below us had been bent back and up to create a sort of natural hide. Suspiciously, none of them had broken in the process and I couldn't see any string or wire holding them in place.

I looked at Caroline, who gave me a bland look in return.

Then I flinched at a nearby explosion, then another and another and then two more moving away.

We sat in terrified silence for another half an hour, but heard nothing more.

The likelihood was that Martin Chorley had cut his losses and scarpered, but none of us felt like betting our lives on it. Besides, he could have left booby traps and/or weird hybrid things behind.

So we waited quietly in the gathering dark for someone to come along and rescue us.

13

Angry Birds

We waited largely in silence and stillness, except for a furious unvoiced argument about whose turn it was next to play *Angry Birds* on Caroline's phone, which only really ended when the phone in question buzzed and we got a text saying – *You may alight whenever you feel ready.*

'He took his time,' I said.

'Does this happen a lot?' asked Caroline.

'Nope,' I said. 'Sometimes Beverley rescues me, sometimes Lady Ty, occasionally Molly – I think there's a rota.'

'Shit,' said Caroline. 'You're not joking, are you?'

'Don't be daft,' I said. 'There isn't really a rota – we're not that well-organised.'

Guleed snorted.

Caroline carried Guleed down first – just wrapped an arm around her chest and stepped off into thin air. It was hard to tell in the dark but it looked to me like they dropped smoothly and at a steady pace. As they fell, the branches that had been curled over to hide us from the ground began to unbend and return to their original positions. When I told Bev about that later she said that was more impressive than the flying.

'Wood not being notably motile,' she said.

When it was my turn I closed my eyes and tried to get a sense of the *forma* Caroline was using. When you're learning a new a *forma* it can take dozens, sometimes hundreds, of demonstrations before you can even start to replicate it in your mind. But you can still learn something from a brief encounter, if you pay attention.

Not that this is easy when you're dropping twenty metres with nothing holding you up but Caroline's contempt for the laws of motion.

I felt it, floating in the non-space where these abstractions catch hold of the fabric of the universe – and it was different. I mean really different. Now, I knew there were different magical traditions, but I'd always assumed that they shared common characteristics. Sensing the *forma* Caroline invoked to defy gravity was like listening to Yusef Lateef take his flute into the pentatonic scale, still music, still beautiful, but a whole new landscape of sound.

'Can you truly fly?' I asked.

She paused once our feet had settled and whispered in my ear.

'Not yet,' she breathed. 'Soon, though. And then I will be away and free.'

Away from what, I wondered, and free from who?

Nightingale was waiting for us at the bottom of the tree, wearing the oyster coloured Burberry coat that is the closest he's ever going to get to a high-viz jacket.

'How did you find us?' I asked.

'In the first instance the screamers worked as advertised,' said Nightingale. 'Then there were your texts.

Beyond that it was just a matter of following the trail of destruction.'

Up the hill there were flashing blue lights visible through the trees.

Guleed chivvied Caroline towards the waiting paramedics while she protested she was fine – which wasn't the point. As a civilian mixed up in a police operation we had to be able to prove she was uninjured so she couldn't sue us later.

'You understand the implications of Martin Chorley being the Faceless Man,' said Nightingale.

'Which one?' I asked and shivered.

'The revenge aspect,' he said. 'There's a definite cause for concern there.'

'No shit,' I said, and held my right hand in front of my face – there was definitely a tremble. 'Did you warn everyone?'

'Phoebe is with Olivia at Tyburn's house, but I lost Reynard when the screamer alerted me and I had to divert here,' he said. 'Gone to ground no doubt.'

I stopped walking towards the lights and looked around. What was left of the Orange Asbo was sitting on its roof amongst shattered wood. Nightingale stopped to wait for me.

'Is anyone looking in our direction?' I asked.

Nightingale said he couldn't see anyone, so I turned away, found a convenient tree trunk, leaned over and vomited. Once I'd started I found I couldn't stop until what seemed like about a month's worth of dinners had come back-up. I was lightheaded and hollowed out when I'd finished.

Nightingale gave me one of his cream coloured linen handkerchiefs, monogramed and ironed by Molly to such a sharp edge I could have happily used it as a shuriken. I carefully unfolded it and used it to wipe my mouth – he didn't ask for it back.

The Thames Valley Police were out in force at the house, including an armed response unit who slouched against the sides of their Volvo V70 and glared at us on general principles.

Then Stephanopoulos arrived and glared at them until they packed up and left. Allowing me a brief respite before she came and glared at me. There was the requisite three hours of milling around as we waited for SOCO and a specialist search team to go over the house and the inevitable arguments about who was going to find an all-night takeaway in High Wycombe for refs.

Caroline's mum roared up the drive in her MG. Me and Caroline watched from the safety of the kitchen as Lady Helena pulled up and proceeded to castigate Nightingale for putting her baby in danger. While that was going on, Caroline beckoned me over and said she'd rather her mum didn't know about the almost-flying.

'I don't want her to worry,' she said.

'Worry about what?' I asked, but she wouldn't say.

She waved at me as her mum drove her away.

Martin Chorley's utilitarian office turned out to be less interesting than his study. He had every OS Map of the British Isles ever published, going all the way back to the nineteenth century, plus a range of specialist maps and gazettes – some of which I recognised from my post-Herefordshire research. A couple of Edwardian earthwork surveys, the *Old Straight Track* by Alfred Watkins and *The Real Middle Earth: Magic and Mystery in the Dark Ages*, which confirmed that Martin Chorley was an enormous Tolkien nerd. As if the the five or six different editions of *The Lord of the Rings* and the signed first edition of *The Hobbit* wasn't enough proof. He hadn't neglected the other Inklings, though – C.S. Lewis had a shelf. And he didn't have any objection to YA either, judging by the collection of Susan Cooper's *The Dark Is Rising* sequence, again first editions, but these ones far too well read to be worth much, beside similarly worn copies of *The Owl Service* and the rest of Alan Garner's books.

It wasn't exactly screaming 'power mad psychopath', although it was possible that he was modern enough to keep all his vices on a USB stick.

Over the real fireplace, with all its original farmhouse stone trimmings, was a painting that one of the SOCOs assured me was a genuine Pre-Raphaelite masterpiece of the dying king surrounded by weeping queens variety. Painted by one James Archer in the late nineteenth century.

'A romantic,' said Nightingale much, much later. 'The most dangerous people on Earth.'

Finally me and Guleed caught a lift back to London while Nightingale stayed at the house on the off-chance its owner popped back for something he'd forgotten.

I wanted to spend the night at Bev's but I needed to be central in case Martin Chorley did something viciously psychopathic in the middle of the night. As it happened, I got to sleep all the way to nine thirty the next morning before the landline rang and Stephanopoulos told me that somebody had just tried to kill Olivia McAllister-Thames.

The house opposite Tyburn's place had obviously been built post-war, probably to replace bomb-damaged stock. Mercifully it must have been quite late on because it wasn't the featureless box so favoured by the American modernists, and the architect had actually made an attempt to fit it in with the rest of street. It still had a touch of the gun emplacement around the ground floor and a marble floored entrance hallway that managed to be both pretentious and dark at the same time.

Once I was safely cocooned in my noddy suit, Stephanopoulos led me upstairs to the third floor flat where the sniper had made his nest. I'd missed the body, which didn't bother me, but Stephanopoulos had a tablet stuffed full of crime scene photographs.

'We don't know who he is yet,' she said. 'White, mid-thirties, fit, has a Foreign Legion tattoo but that doesn't mean anything.' As police we were always tripping over people with special forces tattoos that were more aspirational than indications of service.

'I'm hoping for distinctive teeth,' said Stephanopoulos, although that was no longer the reliable guide to nationality it once was. I'd been told that American dental work was still distinctively overwrought – whatever that meant with regards to teeth.

'Let's hope he wasn't American,' I said. We didn't

need any more about that complication thank you very much.

The flat was unfurnished, although in a distinctively expensive way with marble flooring in the bathrooms, Italian tile in the kitchen and expensive rosewood parquet in the rest. The nest was in what I'd call a living room but was probably listed by the estate agent as the lounge. The firing position was a good three metres back from the bay windows. The central window had been opened and securely fastened, but with the curtains partly drawn he'd have been in shadow – essentially invisible from across the street.

The lack of furniture meant that he'd had to bring his own stand to rest the rifle on, the heavy duty type serious anglers use for big fish. He'd even brought a campstool, a couple of bottles of water and a packet of Pret a Manger sandwiches. I imagined a couple of DCs were even now pulling the CCTV footage from every Pret within a kilometre.

Damn – that was going to be a lot of Prets.

I glanced around the empty room.

'He knew there wasn't any furniture,' I said.

'Even better, he had a legitimate set of keys,' said Stephanopoulos. 'And this property has had the same owner for five years.'

'Let me guess,' I said. 'Our old friend Mr Shell Company.'

'Oh, yes,' said Stephanopoulos. 'Which is a close relative to A.N. Other Shell Company and a Guernsey registered investment house who bought it on behalf of one James Hodgkins, a.k.a. Martin Chorley.'

I looked across the street to what I'd been assured was Tyburn's bedroom – obscured now by the blue sheeting the forensic people had rigged to cover the shattered window. Less than thirty metres I thought – a good sniper would barely need a telescopic sight.

The gun had been whisked away even before the body. An L96A1 firing a standard 7.62 mm NATO round. It was the standard British sniper rifle as used by the Army, the Navy and the Met's own SCO19. Probably, Stephanopoulos said, one of those guns that occasionally fall off the back of a military supply lorry. A bit specialist for your basic London underworld, who tended to favour cheaper and more personal forms of assassination – although if I'd been planning to take a shot at Lady Ty myself I'd have probably opted for a drone strike from a nice air conditioned Air Force base in Arizona.

And even then I'd do it under an assumed name.

He'd got off only the one shot before he died. It was a bolt action weapon, but still I would have thought he'd have had time to take a second one – just to be on the safe side.

Three hours later they still hadn't found the bullet he'd fired.

'What killed him?' I asked.

'Single stab wound to the chest with a heavy double edged blade,' said Stephanopoulos. 'Through his heart and out the other side.'

'What, through the ribs?'

'Sheared right through two at the front and one at the back,' she said. 'Clean cut.'

'A sword,' I said.

'That's what they think, but they haven't finished the PM yet.'

If I had to guess I'd have said a classic fourteenth century English arming sword like the one I'd once seen worn by a young man in a hallucination I'd had when I was busy suffocating under the eastbound Central Line platform. A young man who styled himself Sir William Tyburn, who had been god of the river from back when it was a wild stream rushing down to Father Thames.

For obvious reasons I kept this intriguing observation to myself.

'Chorley's had this place for five years,' said Stephanopoulos. 'Never had any tenants in here in all that time.'

'He knew about the Rivers,' I said. 'He must have thought it would be handy to have a way of keeping them under surveillance.' Or perhaps he'd known that sooner or later he was going to have to go *mano a dios* with Lady Ty.

'Still not a bad little investment over five years I suppose,' said Stephanopoulos. 'But why a sniper? It's not his MO.'

'If he wanted Olivia dead he knew he'd have to go through her mother first,' I said. 'And he knew he had to take Tyburn down before she was aware of the attack. Otherwise Lady Ty, this close to her river, this close to the Thames – not going to happen.' I looked across at the blinded window opposite.

'He can't possibly have missed at this range,' I said.

'And yet he's the one who's dead,' said Stephanopoulos. 'Could she have thrown a sword across that distance?'

I tried to imagine Tyburn pivoting smartly on her heel, bringing her arm back and flinging a sword across the gap between the houses like a bad special effect. The sniper staggering back, looking down in amazement as half the blade and the pommel vibrate amusingly in his chest. Not enough style points for Tyburn. And anyway, they never found the sword.

'If she threw it,' I said, 'then who pulled it out?'

Stephanopoulos gave the traditional short sigh of the senior officer who is about to explain something they thought was bleeding obvious right from the start of the conversation, but obviously wasn't.

'No offence, Peter,' she said. 'But we were kind of relying on you to provide that information. Us just being normal run of the mill coppers none of who are versed in the mystic arts or currently shagging a supernatural creature.'

'That you know of, Boss,' I said, thinking of Wanda the manageress, who you wouldn't spot as 'special' if you didn't know what to look for. But Stephanopoulos was right. This was the Folly's area of expertise, and it was embarrassing that we were so bloody crap at it.

Assume for the moment that the dead sniper had something to do with laughing Sir Tyburn – thought dead by his father and brothers these last hundred and fifty years.

But we know that apparent remnants of normal human beings can be left behind, and under particular circumstances can physically interact with the mundane world.

Do gods have ghosts? I wondered.

If they did, wouldn't they be much more powerful than those left behind by people? Or was that a typical first order assumption? Probably, I thought. And yet, if we stayed with that idea then surely the world would be full of these powerful ghosts of former gods. Now, I hadn't come across anything like that in my literature and while my predecessors in the craft were often thicker than a bag full of custard I think even they would have noticed something like that.

Perhaps, I thought, the dead god gets folded into the existence of the new god, the way a dormant genetic variation can exist within an organism's DNA – hanging about like an actor's understudy until the right environmental conditions give it expression and – hey presto – suddenly a bacteria is heat resistant, our Chloe gets her big break on Broadway and a sniper for hire gets an unexpected half a metre of cold steel through the chest.

Perhaps that explained why the rivers of London had burst forth with new goddesses so quickly after Mama Thames took up her throne. Perhaps there was more than historical continuity between the dead sons of old Father Thames and the daughters that had taken their place.

And a certain river on the Welsh Borders where me and Beverley had been 'catalysts' in the creation of a new spirit, a new genius loci, a new god.

Shit, I thought, I've just invented *epideism*.

'Peter,' said Stephanopoulos. 'You still with us?'

'Oh, god,' I said. 'I think I preferred being a frog,' And then, before Stephanopoulos had a chance to clip me round the ear for being obscure, I told her I'd have to do some digging on the subject.

'But we still need to see if they find any metal fragments in the wound track,' I said and reminded myself to ask Dr Vaughan to do the most sensitive test she could, because if she couldn't find any then it was possible that the sniper had been stabbed with a sword that didn't physically exist.

What *had* definitely existed was the water that had erupted out of the street in front of Lady Ty's house. A burst water main, according to Thames Water, who said they'd get back to us as to why it had chosen to burst at just the moment Mr Sniper was getting an invisible sword stuck through his chest.

Tyburn's street had a noticeable slope north to south and you could see from the water damage where the flood had risen outside her front door and rolled down hill, across Curzon Street, down the passage under Curzonfield House before emptying out into Shepherd Market. Much to the surprise of the shop workers who'd been sitting on the benches having a quiet fag at the time.

'It was two feet deep,' said Stephanopoulos.

This was confirmed by some of the eyewitnesses, especially those on the dry end of the street. Statements from witnesses downstream were, as Seawoll put it, 'less than fucking useful'.

One woman who'd been carried away and deposited outside the RBS branch on Curzon Street said that the water had been much cleaner than she expected and that she thought she smelt meadowgrass.

'Meadow grass?'

'Meadowgrass,' said Stephanopoulos. 'One word – she was very insistent, and that's not the strangest statement.' Amina Asad, who'd been one of the shop workers having a fag, said she'd sort of 'had a weird vision, you know like a really vivid daydream' that she'd been stood waist-deep in a river washing clothes by hand. 'By hand,' she'd said again and laughed. 'Like that's going to fucking happen.'

Some reported seeing fish in the water, others a young fit-looking white boy in a loin cloth.

'He was laughing,' said David Hantsworth of Charnwood Drive, Walthamstow, who quite fancied getting the guy's number, you know, should we ever catch up with him. 'He had the coolest accent,' according to Mr Hantsworth, who was convinced he'd been part of an elaborate bit of street theatre. 'Like an actor doing Shakespeare.'

'Did he say whether the guy was carrying a sword?' I asked.

'You know,' said Stephanopoulos, 'we never thought to ask.'

I added asking that question and following up the stranger eyewitness accounts to my personal action list.

Martin Chorley must have waited for his chance. At a guess, he'd been downstairs in the foyer of the same building. The sniper would have been instructed to take the shot as soon as he had a clear bead on Lady Ty – the sound of the shot would have served as a signal. Then Chorley steps out onto the street and starts his attack only to, probably, get washed away in the flood.

Thankfully the media were largely ignoring the flood, mainly because of the massive explosion that had blown out the first two floors of Tyburn's house. British Gas, who are a bit sensitive on the subject, were desperate to rule out a gas explosion, but the only alternative the Fire Brigade would commit to involved Semtex and a truly ridiculous amount of fertiliser.

To my trained eye it looked like somebody had tried to unzip the front façade and spray it left and right. They were still pulling bits of brick and rusticated stucco out of basement areas of houses fifty metres to each side. I reckoned I'd actually seen something like it once, in an old barn in Essex, from the other side. It had been terrifyingly impressive sight back then, for all that it meant rescue from certain death.

Once Stephanopoulos had finished with her tour I found Nightingale giving the damage a cool appraisal. He shook his head and looked disapproving.

'See that,' he pointed at a section of first floor window frame hanging suspended from what looked like a curtain rail. 'Very shoddy. I'd say our man was not himself when he cast his opening spell.'

He'd been enough of himself to rip out the base of Tyburn's expensive period staircase, leaving the polished balusters hanging like broken teeth from the handrail. The back wall of the parlour had been smashed into the room behind – the wall mounted TV ripped neatly in half with one part embedded in the ceiling and the other lodged at head height in a kitchen cabinet.

Olivia and Phoebe had been watching *Brooklyn Nine-Nine* on that TV when the attack started and had only avoided serious injury because they'd both happened to be lying prone on the sofa.

'Saved by snogging,' had been Seawoll's verdict. 'Let that be a lesson to you.'

Nightingale's lesson was slightly different.

'He just went straight in with no thought as to where his targets might be,' he said. 'And if you look at the line of his effort there . . .' Nightingale swept his hand to indicate where a wide crack had shattered the delicate Regency moulding in the corner of the room, 'you'll see that it lacks precision. A surefire sign of . . . what, exactly, Mr Grant?'

'One of the underlying *forma* was not properly developed,' I said.

Nightingale's lips twitched.

'Can you tell which one?' he asked.

I studied the crack. I had no idea what the spell would have been, but probably fourth or fifth order given it was doing quite a number of different things at the same time. Since it was shoving masonry around, the spell had to be *impello*-based but not even I mess *impello* up. So it probably had to be one of the modifiers.

'*Temperāre*,' I said – totally guessing.

'Yes,' said Nightingale. 'I think you're right.'

He looked at Martin Chorley's handiwork and shook his head again.

'Definitely off his game,' he said.

Not so off his game that he hadn't managed to do that much damage in the less than five seconds between his casting the spell and a fountain of water bursting up his trouser leg. I'd have loved to have had CCTV of that, but of course every camera within a hundred metres had gone *phut* when he cast the spell.

'Entirely on purpose,' in Nightingale's professional opinion.

'And yet no *vestigia*,' I said. At least nothing I could sense. On a Regency street in central London there should have been at least the background after-glow of everyday magic. But standing in front of the ruined house I could feel nothing. Less than nothing, a vast sucking silence. A great absence of ordinary magic.

I'd felt that before.

At the Coopertown house before Punch took a father and annihilated a family.

Now, what if that was what Punch was – the ghost of a god – literally the spirit of riot and rebellion?

That was a long way to jump from a mysterious chest wound. Still, the case did give me an excuse to investigate.

I asked where Olivia and Phoebe were now.

'At Mama Thames' house in Wapping,' said Nightingale.

'And Tyburn?'

'Still missing.'

But not dead – at least, not according to Beverley.

'We'd know,' she said when I called and asked. 'Mum would know.'

But if not dead, then what?

'Hunting,' said Beverley. 'In her own way.'

So I went hunting too, also in my own way, by adopting the ancient and traditional stance of the lazy copper. Which is in front of his AWARE terminal with a double shot latte and a jumbo-sized pack of prawn cocktail flavoured crisps. I had to hunch up a bit because Guleed was using her own terminal to compile a classically mealy-mouthed Falcon case report.

'Okay,' she said. 'We say he was armed, but what do we say he was armed with?'

'If you put "knowing he was likely armed" that covers a multitude of sins,' I said.

'Armed with what?'

'Weapons with Falcon characteristics.'

'You know, one day this is all going to come out in the open.'

'Don't worry. You'll be a Chief Super by then.'

'Not if I keep writing reports like this.'

'Got him,' I said.

'Got who?' asked Guleed.

Zachary Palmer is a skinny little white boy who is probably half something exotic, which makes him a useful contact when I want to know what's going on in the demi-monde, e.g. where some red-headed fox might be hiding. Less useful of late, because he's been making himself purposefully unavailable on account of him, at one time, being Lesley May's lover. We all suspect he still is or, rather, we think she turns up every so often and bangs his brains out – she wouldn't be stupid enough to settle into anything regular or permanent, nothing that will get her caught. There was a time when tracking him down would have involved more legwork than I'd care to expend, but since the business with the underground pigs – don't ask – he'd become semi-respectable, working as liaison for the Quiet People with Crossrail project managers. That meant regular pay, which these days means a bank account, which we've had passively monitored as part of Operation Carthorse – the hunt for Lesley.

I used to worry that he'd sussed us out because of the way he'd withdraw large amounts of cash and then live off that for a couple of weeks. But soon the siren call of instant card payment caught up with him, and now he chips and pins like the rest of us. I scanned his transactions and noted some regular payments to a branch of Greggs on Kilburn High Road at the same time every afternoon. After that it was a simple matter of 'borrowing' a pool car and having my coffee out.

The only car available was a bloody Silver Astra which was so obviously an unmarked police car that it might as well have had an orange BILL ON BOARD sticker in the rear window. So I parked it around the corner. And, after picking up a coffee and steak slice for myself, took my place at the bus stop opposite. Bus stops are great temporary stops for surveillance since they give you a legitimate reason to be standing around looking bored *and* the adshell shelters you from the rain.

Despite the weather, the High Road was heaving with schoolkids, mums and buggies and people out shopping. Given the rain, I'd swapped out my suit jacket for my stakeout hoodie, which rendered me effectively invisible.

Given that Zach's attitude towards punctuality had

always been one of stunned incomprehension, the time of his daily transactions were remarkably consistent – I suspected that he was on his break from a job. If so, it was amazing he'd held it for the three weeks he'd been making the pickups. Five days having been the longest he'd previously held a job for – at least that we had records about.

Right on time I spotted him coming up the street from the direction of the station. He was the same skinny wretch, hands jammed in the pockets of his worn jeans and, like me, hoodied up against the rain and random CCTV in grey Adidas. I thought he was going to walk right past me, but before he reached the bus shelter he turned sharply and skipped across the road to the Greggs.

I scoffed the last of my steak slice as I waited for him to come back out. I had been planning to catch him in the queue, but now I was curious to know what he was up to.

Whatever it was, it seemed to involve three large carrier bags worth of food. Not even Zach, I thought, can eat that much – or at least not in one go.

I followed him around the corner and down Belsize Road, which runs beside the railway tracks and is one of those places where you can see the industrial heritage of London being swiftly gentrified into luxury offices for hire. Although this process hadn't quite reached the ramshackle collection of one storey garages half-way down the street on the railway side.

Zach stopped outside a side door, turned and waited for me to catch up.

'You can come in,' he said. 'But you've got to keep your voice down.'

Inside it was obvious that, despite the garage doors at the front, the place had originally been built as a workshop with a pitched wrought iron and glass roof designed to let in all that thrifty late Victorian sunlight to save on gas. Age and neglect had yellowed the glass to near opacity, except at the far end where it had obviously recently been cleaned.

The bare brick walls had been whitewashed and then painted pastel shades of pink, green and yellow. There were bookshelves in one corner, a line of sinks and a wet area in another. Underfoot was industrial grade lino and easy to clean carpeting in green and brown. Munchkin sized chairs and tables sprouted in little clusters. A mural on one wall caught my eye – a depiction of an orangutan sitting at a reading lectern in the style of Paul Kidby.

The group of ten or twelve children inside was not a surprise, nor the fact that, having spotted Zach and his armfuls of goodies, they surged forward like a sugar starved tidal wave. What was a surprise was that they did it in almost total silence. They were children of the Quiet People, the people who lived under Notting Hill and Ladbroke Grove, pale-skinned and big-eyed and not normally seen above ground. Many of them had pale blonde hair that had not yet darkened to their usual light brown. As I watched them being marshalled into their assigned seats, all the while stealing glances at Zach as he unpacked the bags, I found myself trying really hard not to think of a brick wall.

The young woman marshalling the children was similarly slender and pale with chestnut coloured hair in a neat French plait down her back. She'd obviously discovered the joys and practicality of skinny jeans, but above the waist she wore a pale yellow high collared blouse and waistcoat. She was wearing dark glasses indoors although, I realised, her charges were not.

Zach had his bags open and was laying out neat plates of rhubarb and custard doughnuts, Belgian buns and iced fingers on undecorated earthenware plates that were beautiful in the simplicity of their curves. There was a low gurgling, rumbling – loud in the unnatural quiet of the nursery. Zach's stomach.

A ripple ran through the children, a whisper of laughter that passed from child to child. Their teacher gave Zach an indulgent smile, and he gave a little wave back. Then I recognised her, Elizabeth Ten-Tons, whose father was King of the Quiet People, or if not king then lead gangmaster or chief mining engineer or something like that.

She was strict, she made those kids wait patiently until everything was ready and then line up neatly to receive their one goody, and one mug of milk, from Zach who beamed like Father Christmas through the whole thing.

'The idea,' said Zach quietly, 'is to get them used to the sunlight.'

The kids had finished their snack and me and Zach were hoovering up the leftovers while Elizabeth Ten-Tons read them a story at the other end of the nursery.

'Are they planning to move to the surface?' I asked.

'Don't be daft,' said Zach. 'But they are looking at acquiring a bit of real estate to serve as an official address.' And then no doubt connect it up to the warren of tunnels they had running under Notting Hill. It was a clever idea since it allowed the Quiet People to bureaucratically integrate themselves into society without giving up their freedom to apply Victorian health and safety standards to their work underground.

'Whose idea was this?'

'Your mate Lady Ty's,' said Zach and explained that she'd also smoothed the way with OFSTED and Camden Council to get the necessary permissions and permits. I've had similar dealings with Camden, so I knew that couldn't have been easy.

I looked over at the kids. It was a sensible, pragmatic solution to the problem of integrating the Quiet People into society. And if those kids started to prefer living above ground, going to uni in far off exotic places like Reading and Cambridge, and marrying out of the tribe? Well then, after a while the whole problem just fades away, doesn't it? Along with the memories of the old people and the unwritten histories. And silence would reign in the galleries of their forefathers. Not that they were exactly noisy now.

'I'm not going to tell you where she is,' said Zach suddenly.

This caused me some confusion until I worked out he was talking about Lesley.

'Is she all right?' I asked.

'What?'

'Is she all right?' I asked. 'Is she OK?'

'Yeah,' he said. 'Considering, you know, one thing or the other. All things being equal.'

Zach thought he had something to hide, which meant Zach probably *was* in contact with Lesley on a regular basis. Good, I thought. Because soon it will be time to pull on that thread and see where it goes.

But not today. Because first there was Mr Fossman.

'I want to know about Reynard,' I said.

Zach hesitated and I could practically hear him weighing up whether to pretend he didn't know, and then thinking better of it.

'What about him?' he asked.

'I need to know where he is.'

'What for?'

'Because the Faceless Man wants him dead.'

'He's probably already dead, then.'

'Not if I can help it.'

Zach licked his lips and glanced over at Elizabeth Ten-Tons before dropping his voice so low I had to lean in to hear him.

'Is it true you know *his* real name now?'

I said nothing, because if I told Zach I might as well announce it on Facebook.

'Have you checked his gaff?'

I said that not only had we checked his gaff, we'd spun his drum and his crib as well. And that we had his ends so thoroughly staked out that street crime had dropped by twenty percent overnight.

'I want to know where he goes as a last resort.'

Zach told me.

'You're shitting me,' I said.

'No lie.'

'That is the stupidest thing I've ever heard.'

'That's the nature of the beast,' said Zach. 'We are what we are.'

14

A Walk in the Park

'The Fox Club,' said Nightingale when I called him.

'In Mayfair,' I said.

'Well, at least he's consistent.'

'He's brown bread if we don't get to him first,' I said.

'Let's see if we can avoid that outcome,' said Nightingale.

Occasionally, when the mood takes us, the police can react very fast to unforeseen events. So we had a surveillance perimeter set up in less than thirty minutes with a pair of PCs in plainclothes inside the club. One of them was PC Omer Kubat from the Mounted Branch whose legendary good looks mean that nobody ever believes he's police.

'Is it true he nearly got arrested while in full uniform?' Guleed asked.

Since Reynard knew me, her and Nightingale, we'd been placed around the corner from the Fox Club. Which was just as well since we were in the silver Astra with the 'My Other Car's an IRV' bumper sticker.

'That's what I heard,' I said. Rumour had it that Kubat plus horse had been deployed as crowd control during the Olympics when a local Inspector had got it into his head that Kubat was an actor involved in an illegal film shoot.

'Didn't believe him,' I said. 'Not even when he handed over his warrant card.'

It was a quality that meant that Kubat was constantly getting poached for side jobs like ours, although his duty Inspector made it clear that anybody, regardless of the rank, who tried to transfer him out of Mounted Branch was going to wake up with a bed full of horse product.

The Fox Club, for all its aspirations and Mayfair address, was less an exclusive gentleman's club and more an expensive bar with some posh hotel rooms attached. Kubat was probably a bit too good looking for its usual clientele, but at least if he were mistaken for something it wouldn't be an undercover police officer.

The club occupied a regency terrace on a street just off Piccadilly, less than two hundred metres from Lady Ty's house and almost on top of the underground course of her river. Curzon Street to the north was still partially closed as the Fire Brigade and Thames Water dealt with the flood damage.

I didn't think it was a coincidence. And the chance that Lady Ty was also using Reynard as bait had been factored into our operational plan, such as it was, and our risk assessment – such as *that* was.

Me, Guleed and Nightingale were designated Alpha. David Carey and a couple of guys from Belgravia MIT were in Charlie covering Half Moon Street at the back of the club. A couple of PCs in plainclothes on ruinous levels of overtime were in what any other nick would call Bravo but inexplicably Belgravia MIT always called the Banana car. I asked them why, but nobody could remember.

Stephanopoulos and Seawoll were trying to rustle up some armed response, but apparently there was some anti-terror operation currently live in East London so we couldn't count on getting them until that was done.

Kubat called to report that he had eyes on Reynard.

'At a table in the main saloon,' he said. 'He's holding some chairs free, too – he must be expecting someone.'

Nightingale told him to hold position and we heard him ordering a pint of lager. A pint is a good drink for undercover work since, unlike a short, you can get away with drinking it slowly, it has low alcohol by volume, and if you keep moving it about people can't tell how much you're drinking.

I suggested that we grab Reynard then and there. But Nightingale said wait.

'I don't think we've played out the line fully yet,' he said.

Poor Reynard, I thought, demoted from fox to fish – he must've done something shitty in a former life. Although how it could be worse than what he was doing in his current life took some imagining.

You don't half end up thinking strange things when you're on a stakeout.

Nightingale was proved right when we got a call from the Banana car saying they had eyeballs on an older IC1 and a younger IC3 female heading for the club.

I asked whether the IC3 female was over six feet tall.

'Definitely,' said the Banana car.

'I thought this might happen,' said Nightingale. 'Lady Helena is still trying to secure *The Third Principia* for herself.'

'Should we stop them?'

Nightingale hesitated – tapping his finger on the steering wheel.

'No,' he said finally. 'If I'm right, then Mr Fossman will either hand it over directly or take them to it.'

'And if Martin Chorley crashes the trade?'

'Lady Helena is more than capable of defending herself and her daughter,' said Nightingale. 'Or at least of fending him off for long enough that we can sweep in heroically like the Seventh Cavalry.'

Burning tipis and shooting women and children, I thought.

And with that cheerful notion I had a root around in the stakeout bag Molly had provided. One of the wrapped sandwiches had a large H written on the outside – I handed it to Guleed as the rest were all unmarked. I played pot luck and got a suspiciously mundane ham salad sandwich. Nightingale said he'd have his later.

Kubat reported that Lady Helena and her daughter had arrived.

'They've sat down at his table,' he said. 'He doesn't seem surprised to see them.'

Nightingale asked if they'd ordered drinks.

'Not yet,' said Kubat.

'Whatever happens, do not engage,' said Nightingale. 'If there's a Falcon incident you may lose radio contact. Don't panic, don't engage the targets. Instead I want you to concentrate on evacuating the civilians.'

Kubat acknowledged and Nightingale contacted Seawoll, who was Gold Commander for the operation.

'Alexander, can you get some men looking for Lady Helena's car?' he said, and rattled off the index from memory. 'Once they have located it, can you disable it in some fashion?'

Seawoll said they could do better than that, and have Vehicle Recovery lift it onto one of their flatbeds and drive it away.

'That should limit their options,' said Nightingale.

Kubat reported that the older IC1 female and Reynard Fossman were having an argument, albeit conducted in angry whispers. The IC3 female, on the other hand, was looking bored and indifferent.

'Well, if this continues,' said Nightingale, 'we might just scoop them all up when they find their car is missing.'

Three minutes later I got a call from an unlisted number – it was Special Agent Kimberley Reynolds.

'Do you want the good news or the bad news?' she asked.

'Bad,' I said, and put her on speaker.

'One of our Virgins let slip some information while I was debriefing them,' she said. 'We think there's a second team operating in London and we think they might have been tasked with the apprehension of Reynard Fossman.'

I would have sworn loudly, but Kimberley had some views about blasphemy and I like to be polite.

'You're cussing aren't you?' she said after a moment. 'Well, stop it because you don't have the time. We think they're running an operation right now, in and around Mayfair.'

'Damn,' said Nightingale. 'That's inconvenient.'

I wanted to know who 'we' were – I suspected Kimberley was drawing on support from both the FBI and the NSA, but it's not like she would tell me if she was and I didn't have time to ask.

'And the good news?' I asked.

'We think it's a small team,' said Kimberley. 'Four people tops.'

'Agent Reynolds?' said Nightingale.

'Sir?'

'Could you liaise with DCI Seawoll, who is Gold Commander on this op.' Nightingale's voice had got very precise and clipped. 'I trust you've informed CTC?'

'Kittredge was with me for the interview, sir,' she said.

'Good,' said Nightingale. 'That should speed things up. Is there anything further your people can contribute?'

'I'm afraid not sir,' said Kimberley. 'Although there may be more intelligence forthcoming.'

'Very good,' said Nightingale. 'Carry on, Agent Reynolds, and keep us apprised.'

'American intelligence,' said Guleed once the phone was safely off.

'Forewarned is forearmed,' said Nightingale.

I asked if it wouldn't be better to cut our losses and grab Reynard, Lady Helena and Caroline before the situation got more complicated. As a rule, the more complex a situation gets the more likely the wheels are to come off. This is why the police strategy with large crowds is to pin them in place until everyone's too desperate for the loo to cause trouble.

'No,' said Nightingale. 'We're going to adopt a flexible doctrine. If we spot the Americans we'll see if CTC can't round them up without disturbing our principals. If Reynard leads us to his hiding place and Martin Chorley makes an appearance, we shall deal with that mob while CTC fends off the Americans.'

'Flexible.' I said. 'Meaning we're making it up as we go along.'

'Quite,' said Nightingale.

There was a click on the Airwave – it was Kubat.

'They're heading for the door,' he said.

'Hand off to Banana Car,' said Nightingale. 'Banana Car, stay in position and tell me where they go.'

The answer was south – towards Piccadilly and Green Park.

Suddenly Nightingale was pulling out of our parking space and accelerating fast enough to push us back hard into our seats. He swung a sudden left into Half Moon Street while simultaneously ordering Banana Car to shift position to the Bomber Command memorial and await further instructions, Charlie Car was to drop two of its watchers off on the Knightsbridge side of Hyde Park Corner.

'And drive carefully,' said Nightingale. 'I don't want you drawing attention to yourselves.'

I hung on grimly to the door handle as he braked hard just short of the corner with Piccadilly and wished he'd take his own advice. We pulled into an insanely unlikely free parking spot and Nightingale looked over and told me to cross Piccadilly and take a position inside the park gate.

'Get yourself twenty yards behind the targets and follow them,' he said. 'Guleed and I will follow ten yards behind you.'

'The targets all know him,' said Guleed.

'They know Peter Grant the dashing constable about town,' said Nightingale. 'In his sweat top they'll take him for an averagely delinquent youth.' He stabbed a finger in the direction of the park. 'Off you go – we'll be right behind you.'

A low cloud had drawn in over London and with it an early twilight. There'd been rain earlier and the smell of wet leaves mingled with the car exhaust. The traffic on Piccadilly was slow and it was easy enough to nip across, vault the safety railings and slip in through the gates.

Green Park had been laid down by Charles II, who nicked the land off a local farmer, laid out the paths and installed an ice house so that he'd never be short of a cool drink after a hard day of amateur theatre. It stayed on the fringes of the city where it served as a convenient open space for midnight liaisons and the occasional spot of highway robbery. It takes pride these days in being the dullest park in London and is noticeably short of shrubs, bushes, kiosks, statues or anything else a dashing constable about town might hide behind.

I should have welcomed the thick mist that seeped in between the upright tree trunks, hazing the street lights and beading my shoulders and the edge of my hood with droplets of water. But I didn't.

Because I recognised that mist. I'd seen it roll up the Thames when Father and Mama held their Spring Court on the South Bank. And the course of the Tyburn ran through Green Park on its way to Buckingham Palace.

I keyed my Airwave.

'Tyburn's about,' I said, my voice dulled by the moisture in the air.

'So I see,' said Nightingale. 'Our fox is certainly living up to his reputation. I doubt Martin Chorley will risk entering the park while she's on the warpath. Reynard's safe while he stays in there.'

'I can't see them,' I said.

'Southeast of your position,' said Nightingale. 'Thirty yards and heading south.'

I stuck my hands in my pockets and slouched off down the path while trying to think delinquent thoughts.

They were a distinctive bunch, so I spotted them walking briskly across the grass towards the centre of the park. I picked up my pace, lifting my knees as if I was doing running practice. I figured I'd look kosher if I stayed on the path. I was crossing their path at a tangent and as I reached the closest approach I forced myself to keep my eyes forward – with luck, even if they looked, my face would be hidden by my hoodie.

Where could they be heading?

South was Constitution Hill Road, notable for not being much of a hill, and just beyond that the walled gardens of Buckingham Palace. Once they hit the road they could go east towards Victoria Memorial and the Mall or west up the hill to Hyde Park Corner.

In my earpiece I could hear Nightingale calmly

ordering units into position around the park, while maintaining his position behind me and working without a map. The mist was thickening, the trees that lined the path I was on were flattening out and fading.

Ten metres further down the path I risked a look and saw that Reynard and co had changed direction. Now they were heading downslope – to the east.

I turned off the path but stayed at a tangent so I wouldn't be obviously following them. But I had to close the distance before they were swallowed up in the mist and darkness. I reported the change in direction.

'You're going to have to risk getting closer,' said Nightingale.

I heard a snarl off to my left and I didn't think it was a dog. I looked and thought I saw movement in the mist, man-shaped but loping like a big cat, picking up momentum as it ran after my targets. I was about to call it in when a long thin shape hissed over my shoulder and slammed into the running figure, which went tumbling with a yowling scream. A naked man ran past me and did a sort of hopping turn to face me. His long rangy body was smeared in blue paint and he held a pair of spears in his left hand. His hair was a spray of spiky black, and gold gleamed at his throat and wrists.

'Did you see that?' he shouted. 'Tell me you saw that – that's got to be a worth a song.'

He turned and ran off, shouting over his shoulder.

'Or at least a memory.' It sounded almost plaintive.

And then with just a few steps he was gone.

I checked Reynard and the others, but they were still

walking calmly in the direction of Hyde Park Corner. Either they were the most focused people on Earth or that encounter had been a lot quieter than I thought it was.

'Boss,' I said into my Airwave. 'It's getting needlessly metaphysical out here.'

'Ignore it,' said Nightingale calmly. 'There's more than one conflict going on at the moment, but only one of them is your concern.'

I realised that despite having two of the busiest roads in London within a hundred metres, the rush hour had faded to nothing. From behind me I heard a stamping, grunting sound and a noise like pots and pans being rhythmically smacked together. A growl, a shout, a scream.

Stay on target, I thought.

'They're definitely heading for Hyde Park Corner,' I said

Nightingale said that he and Guleed were going to get ahead of them and that I was going to be on my own, but I should be quite safe.

'As long as you stay focused,' he said.

Which was easier said than done because that's when Early Tyburn returned.

I smelt him before I heard him, the copper smell of fresh blood and old sweat, wood-smoke and wet dog.

'You should listen to your master,' said a voice by my ear. 'He's a cunning man. And by the way, did you see that sick cast – right through the neck. Never saw it coming. Worth a song right, bit of an impromptu beat box maybe.'

'What's with the woad?' I asked. 'Last time we met you were all medieval.'

Out in the mist the trees had multiplied and the straight London planes and lime trees were sharing space with the shadowy ghosts of oak, beech and poplar.

'Just being true to my roots, fam,' said the former incarnation of the god of the River Tyburn – or maybe a hallucination brought on by way too many supernatural wankers messing with my head. Or possibly both at the same time.

I kept my eyes on my targets ahead and my hoodie was as effective as any pair of blinkers, so I almost screamed when I felt him slip his arm around my shoulders, the spare javelins in his left hand clacking against my arm, the tips pushing into my peripheral vision. I felt my balls and my stomach tighten, the anticipation of action as when you run down a deer in the King's Forest or jack a motor from outside a gaff in Primrose Hill. The defiance of power making the meat taste so much sweeter, the slip into first gear and away so much sweeter.

'I saw your father,' I said. 'He seemed a happy little Roman.'

'And so he was,' said the voice. 'But we are not always the sons our fathers dream of – as you should know.'

As I did know, and all the things sons do to make their fathers proud until you learn to choose your own life for your own reasons. Have your own money, your own car, your own job, you own place, your own life and *fuck* everybody else.

What have they ever done for you?

But I had felt this seduction before. Or something like it. On a tube train between Camden and Kentish Town when old Mr Punch tried to recruit me for Team Riot, and I knew how well that had turned out in the end.

'Lady Ty must be a real disappointment,' I said.

The arm squeezed my shoulders and relaxed its grip.

'Why don't you ask her about the Marquee in '76, the bin bag dress and how she couldn't quite bring herself to push the safety pin all the way through,' said the voice. And before I could reply he was gone.

With him went the concealing mist and suddenly I was standing by the Boris Bike stand at the far end of Green Park and listening to the angry traffic fighting its way around Hyde Park Corner.

Hyde Park Corner is what happens when a bunch of urban planners take one look at the grinding circle of gridlock that surrounds the Arc de Triomphe in Paris and think – *that's what we want for our town.* Inspired no doubt by the existence of the Wellington Arch, George IV's cut price copy of Napoleon's own vanity project, they wrapped seven lanes of traffic around one corner of Green Park, ran a dual carriageway underneath and produced virtually overnight what had taken the French and Baron Haussmann a hundred years to perfect.

I scanned right to left and spotted Reynard, Lady Helena and Caroline waiting for the lights to change at the pelican crossing. There was enough of a crowd to allow me to cross right after them with just a bit of a last minute dash against the red man.

Ahead of us was the Wellington Arch, with Europe's largest bronze statue thoughtfully plonked on top to avoid people getting a good look at it. Nike Goddess of Victory riding the Chariot of War driven by a boy racer. There used to be a mini-police station built into the Arch, which would have been bloody useful right now, but they closed it down in the nineties.

It was full night by the time I crossed the street and the Portland stone of the Arch was bleached white by spotlights, the bronze on top lit up in blue. I let Reynard and his party gain some distance as they passed to the right of the structure. In my earpiece I could hear Nightingale calmly positioning spotters to cover the tube station and all the crossings.

'They're heading for Hyde Park,' I told him and then remembered Reynard's left hand drive Renault 4 that we'd never located. Maybe because it was stashed in a car park somewhere – maybe the one beneath Hyde Park. The one with a reputed tunnel to The Chestnut Tree. I floated the idea past Nightingale and heard Guleed groan in the background. Nightingale punted it up to Seawoll to get some bodies down to the car park to check. If it had been sitting there all this time we were all going to look stupid come case review, but at least we might get there before Reynard.

If they were going for the car park then they'd cross the road and head north up Park Lane or more likely walk along the parallel bridle path.

I veered to the left with the idea of running through the Arch and closing the distance with Reynard, when a young white woman caught my eye. She was slender but toned with strong legs and shoulders under mauve designer jeans and a matching suede jacket. Her face was round and smooth with a snub nose and rosebud lips. Her hair was dark brown and cut into a pixie bob. A pair of pretentious round framed smoked glass spectacles hid her eyes.

She caught me looking and tilted her head in amused recognition before turning and walking away on unexpectedly sensible flat shoes.

I knew that walk, a brisk, business-like walk. A walk to cover the distance quickly without looking hurried or worried.

I keyed my Airwave.

'I've just seen Lesley at the Arch,' I said.

'Are you certain?' asked Nightingale.

'The face is different but it's definitely Lesley,' I said.

'Is it a mask?' asked Nightingale.

'No,' I said. 'Not a mask.'

'Did she see you?'

'Yes.'

'Arrest her,' said Nightingale. 'Now.'

I was wearing trainers – you can run really quietly in trainers if you have to. It's all in the way you roll your feet. I took off as fast as I could, straight for her back. I knew sooner or later she was going to check on my position, but I was counting on her Lesley-esque sense of drama to hold the moment longer than she should. I was three metres short when a white guy in a navy suit jacket over a black Metallica T-shirt theatrically jumped out of my way and yelled, 'Look out.'

The woman who walked like Lesley turned and I saw

the look of surprise on her face. Then I stumbled as the pale skin of her face rippled and her features changed. It started at the bridge of her nose, the skin bunching up and then flopping down horribly, like the wings of a manta or the shroud of a squid. Then suddenly it was Lesley's face again – or rather the smooth pink version of it I'd seen in the Harrods Jazz Café. I was so shocked that I barely registered the raised hand and the shimmer in the air that signalled pain inbound. I forced myself to lengthen my stumble into a fall and a clumsy roll, taking the impact on my shoulders, as something shot through the space I would have been in, with a noise like my mum beating a carpet.

As I climbed to my feet and dodged right on general principles, I heard yells behind me. I had the Airwave off by then and didn't dare to turn it back it on to alert Nightingale to potential collateral. I had to trust to his professional instincts and hope that Lesley wasn't flinging anything too lethal around.

She knew better than to escalate in public in central London – not unless you wanted to take a run up that short ladder that ended with making a personal relationship with the Special Air Service.

I ran through the arch, making my appearance as abrupt as I could, and spotted Lesley heading off towards the Wellington Memorial. She was walking briskly rather than running – hoping, I assumed, to avoid drawing attention to herself.

I flicked an *impello* at her and felt a moment of mad satisfaction as it knocked her legs out from under her. As I ran to close the distance, I pulled my asp from the belly pocket of my hoodie and flicked it out to full length.

But she rolled and was on her feet before I'd got half-way there. She raised her hand – I saw a flash and got my shield up in time to deflect it into the air. I've been training to conjure my shield with an upward slope for use amongst the general public. You don't want any-thing eldritch, or even mundanely pointy, ricocheting into innocent bystanders.

Lesley switched direction and headed for the right of the plinth that held up forty tons of mounted military legend so I went around it on the left just in case she planned an ambush – which is how we came to run smack into each other.

I'm bigger, so she went backwards. But not before her forehead hit me hard enough in the mouth to loosen my one filling and make me taste blood. I swung my baton but missed, and she kicked me in the thigh – which was probably a lucky miss. Then she hit me with something *impello*-ish which knocked me over backwards, but Nightingale has trained me to accept the direction of the blow and roll up so that I regain my feet as quickly as possible.

So far this was all suspiciously non-lethal. Not that I was complaining, mind you, but we were escalating enough for the street lights and spots around us to fizz out. I flung a water bomb in Lesley's general direction but she'd ducked back behind the plinth and I dared not charge after her in case she was waiting around the corner with something unpleasant. I went wide and caught sight of her vaulting a waist-high stone parapet behind the monument and dropping onto the ramp below. I leaned over and watched as she ran down towards the pedestrian subway. I considered following, but instead darted back and ran down the nearby stairs instead – just in case she tried to double back that way.

Hyde Park Corner has some of the cleanest pedestrian subways in the world – this one was decorated with colourful murals depicting the Battle of Waterloo, just in case any French tourists had some doubt about whose capital they were visiting. This time I went for speed and got within two metres. But she grabbed a startled tourist, swung him around as if dancing, and threw him down in front of me. I had to break stride to jump and that gave Lesley enough time to cut right down another passage. I cornered it myself in time to see her skid left and vanish into the ticket office. I followed slower, risking a peek around the corner to avoid any sudden surprises. Hyde Park Corner has a tiny ticket office and Lesley was already through the barrier. She turned to check whether I was following and that's when I knew I was being played.

Still, I charged the barriers to drive her down the escalators. But I didn't follow. Instead, waving my warrant card to reassure the Underground staff, I veered right and back out into the subway. Turning my Airwave back on, I ran up the stairs and found myself at the entrance to Hyde Park. I did a three-sixty scan while waiting for the Airwave to boot up. We used to wait for our electronics to warm up, now it's our software. But there was no sight of any of the targets.

Finally the Airwave connected and I got Nightingale.

'It's a feint,' I said. 'Lesley was trying to draw me away

– which means wherever they're going is close.' And then I looked down Knightsbridge to where the Oriental Hotel was painted a warm orange by its spotlights.

'It's One Hyde Park,' I said. 'Tell me you have spotters there already.'

'But of course,' said Nightingale. 'And I believe you may be right.'

'What makes you say that?'

'Reynard and our friends have just walked in the front door,' he said.

We waited for screams, but none came. That was almost worse.

All of the apartment windows were dark and Seawoll was ninety percent sure that most of the super-rich inhabitants of One Hyde Park were either temporarily not in residence or still living abroad and waiting for property prices in London to peak.

Stephanopoulos and some uniforms in full Public Order kit had sealed off the tunnel from the Oriental Hotel, but David Carey, interviewing staff, was pretty sure at least one group had made it in before it was locked down.

'Four IC1 males in suits,' he reported.

'That will be the Americans,' said Nightingale.

There were reports of burst water mains and flooding from Sloane Street and the Serpentine. I checked my notebook – all along the course of the Westbourne, whose genius loci was otherwise known as Chelsea Thames. I called Beverley and asked if she knew where her younger sister was.

'Here at Mum's,' she said. 'Hiding under Lea's bed.'

'I don't suppose Tyburn's popped in for a visit?' I asked.

Beverley said no and told me whatever I thought I was going to do next I was to be careful.

'Always,' I said.

'I mean it,' she said.

'Tyburn's probably in there as well,' I said, after I hung up.

'Full house,' said Guleed.

We'd escalated up to having a mobile control room, codenamed Broadway, which was parked on South Carriage Drive with a good view of the back of One Hyde Park. The key advantage of a mobile control room is that it gave Seawoll a place to shout at us while sitting in a comfy chair with a cup of tea.

Luckily for us, the postmodern obsession with transparent walls meant that in One Hyde Park nobody could move around the access stairs or lifts without being seen by the spotter teams Nightingale had positioned in the buildings opposite. We'd closed off South Carriage Drive and pushed a perimeter back twenty metres to the south, but Seawoll was reluctant to close Knightsbridge and Old Brompton because the rush hour was still tailing off.

We had about twenty to thirty minutes before the media twigged that a major police operation had descended on the most expensive bit of real estate in London.

Guleed suggested that we leave them in there and arrest the survivors, which earned her a pleased smile from Seawoll. But then he shook his head.

'Somebody,' he said eyeing Nightingale, 'is going to have go in there and clean up the mess.'

'Quite,' said Nightingale and looked at me. 'Peter?'

'Noisy or quiet?' I asked.

'Oh, quiet,' said Nightingale.

And so it was decided. But not before me and Guleed climbed into our PSU overalls and, after a bit of an argument, donned the shin and elbow guards. We didn't bother with the helmets, but Guleed swapped her hijab for a fire resistant hood that made her look like she was about to climb into a Soyuz rocket.

'Practical and modest,' I said and she grinned.

Needless to say we both put our metvests on and loaded ourselves down with CS spray, speedcuffs – I even considered packing a taser which I'm now authorised and trained to carry – but they just tend to complicate things.

Finally Nightingale handed me a stave of varnished wood, the size and shape of a pickaxe handle, one end wrapped with canvas strips, the other capped with iron. Branded into the side was a six-digit number and the hammer and anvil sigil of the Legendary Sons of Weyland.

As I gripped it I felt the hum of the hive and sunlight amongst the hills and hedgerows.

Once more into the breach, I thought.

We paraded round the back of the mobile control centre. Seawoll rolled his eyes at the sight of us, but said nothing. Nightingale was dressed in a leather sapper's coat but thank god not the breeches that went with them. He had donned a pair of serious army boots that had probably only not perished with age because Molly wasn't going to let any of his clothes die on her watch – dammit!

He caught Guleed's eye.

'Sahra,' he said, 'things are likely to get somewhat esoteric before the end, and this is not something you're trained for. I can't, in all conscience, ask you to join us.'

'If it's all the same to you, sir, I think I'm going to have to see this through,' she said. '*Inshallah.*' As God wills it.

'Good show,' said Nightingale.

This is it, I thought. We're all going to die.

15

State Six

A risk assessment is a key part of modern policing. Before diving into whatever crisis is at hand, the modern plod is expected to ask themselves: given the modalities of the current situation would any intervention by myself help promote a positive outcome going forward? And what are the chances of this going well and truly pear-shaped? And, if it does, how likely is it that I will get the blame?

Some people think this makes us risk averse, but I like to point out that a risk assessment is what blonde teenagers *don't* do before heading downstairs into the basement in a slasher movie. Now, I'm not saying I wouldn't go down to investigate . . . but I'd bloody well make sure I was wearing a stab vest first, and had some back-up. Preferably going down the stairs ahead of me.

I reckoned that Seawoll and Nightingale's risk assessment was sound for several reasons. We couldn't just let them kill each other, tempting though that was, because we didn't know how many members of the public were currently in the complex. The owners might not be in residence, but there could still be staff inside – and they counted as people too. That said, there was no point sending in TSG or even SCO19 because Martin

Chorley would just hand their arses back to them. That made it a Falcon job. And, since Nightingale was the most Falcon-capable officer in the Met, I was the second and, god help her, Guleed was the third, we were the logical people to deal.

So in we went, through the back garden past the statues of the two flattened empty heads and entered the wrong way through an emergency fire exit at the base of one of the towers.

Now, personally, I'd have been happier driving an armoured personal carrier in through the front door. But since we're the Met, and not the police department of a small town in Missouri, we didn't have one.

I keyed my Airwave one last time before shutting it down.

'This is Falcon Two,' I said. 'Show us state six.' Meaning, officers at the scene.

Like I said, One Hyde Park had four pavilions with four towers containing lifts and stairs interspersed between them. Two were for residents and two were for service staff, because times might move on but the gentry still like their servants to be invisible.

Despite the transparent walls the soundproofing was good and there was no hint of traffic noise as we stepped out into the wide curved hallway that ran the length of the ground floor. The lights were still on, a good sign, and we could see all the way down three levels of the basement and up to the top floor of pavilions one and two.

Me and Guleed held our position while Nightingale padded off down the hallway to secure the eastern end.

There were exclusive shops for the excessively over-resourced on the ground floor of each of the Pavilions. Nightingale checked the internal doors leading to them to make sure they were secure and free of supernatural taint before moving on.

The curve meant that we lost sight of him when he reached the far end of the hallway. Me and Guleed tucked ourselves into what cover we could find amongst the rent-a-culture statuary and waited. There was a strong smell of lemon floor polish.

Guleed looked abstracted while she listened through her earpiece to the Airwave chatter. Since she wasn't likely to fry her own equipment, she'd been designated communications officer – or, as Nightingale put it, 'radioman' – for the op.

'Stephanopoulos is in,' she said.

It was Stephanopoulos' job to secure the service hub at the eastern end of the complex so that we could evacuate civilians out that way as well. Once Nightingale had declared the ground floor shops Falcon free, she'd go door to door and evacuate them.

The big debate during the planning stage had been whether to then go up to check Martin Chorley's flat, down to check the basement and underground parking area, or head west to clear the entrance foyer.

I signalled Guleed and pointed upstairs, but she shook her head – no reports of movement there. When Nightingale trotted back to our positon he repeated my query and, getting the same answer, led us off towards the foyer. Where we found our first casualty.

He was stretched out, half on the shiny grey marble

and half on the fine silk weave grey carpet in front of the granite reception desk.

Nightingale caught my attention, pointed, and then put two fingers against his throat. As he watched the balcony I scuttled over to do a first aid assessment. I recognised the guy. He was the dark-skinned man in the good suit I'd seen the first time I'd visited. I'd had him pegged as security, and indeed he was holding a compact digital walkie-talkie as used by police, film crews and paramilitary death squads the world over. I shifted my staff to my left hand and found a pulse in his neck. There were no other obvious injuries, so I gently rolled him into the recovery position.

I picked up his walkie-talkie and shook it. It sounded like a rainmaker, with loose bits and sand rattling around inside.

Nightingale signalled Guleed, who spoke quietly into her Airwave then nodded to me. I trotted over to the main entrance to make sure it was open. Then I retreated back to Nightingale and maintained watch while a trio of TSG guys in full riot gear clattered in with a pair of London Ambulance paramedics in tow. The paramedics were public order specialists and had their own riot gear, only their helmets were painted green – presumably to confuse rioters for long enough for them to do their jobs. As the paramedics went to work Nightingale signalled to two of the TSG to take position behind the reception desk while the third escorted the paramedics.

The TSG were under strict instructions not to engage anyone but to contain and report.

Satisfied that the foyer was locked down, Nightingale

led us up a set of grey marble stairs and onto the first floor. Here there was another curved hallway linking the pavilions and the access towers. The flats on these levels were all one- or two-bedroom and mainly owned by shell companies and investment portfolios. What Seawoll called 'corporate jolly pads', and he really didn't need to emphasise that 'jolly' much to illustrate his meaning. Still, they had to be cleared just like the shops. Me and Guleed held the stairwell again while Nightingale did his witch sniffing thing, before signalling Stephanopoulos that her people could go door to door.

Now, I'd wanted to go straight downstairs to the underground car park because, apart from the thought that Reynard might have stashed his car down there, each flat came not only with its own parking space but with an underground storage locker the size of a standard shipping container. But Seawoll and had pointed out that we still had a duty of care to people in the building and that had to be our priority.

'And strangely, Peter, we fucking thought to check it during the investigation.'

'It' being the storage space associated with Martin Chorley's flat.

But not for the Renault 4. Because we didn't know about Reynard's car then.

We'd been inside One Hyde Park for over twenty minutes by now, and I'd expected screams after ten . . . the kick-off was suspiciously late. Martin Chorley had spent the last two years psyching us – from sending a Pale Lady to distract me from the murder in West End Central to Lesley's bit of bait-and-switch that very afternoon at Hyde Park Corner. I figured the very next thing that happened was going to be a feint too.

And so did Nightingale. Because when Seawoll told us that the spotters had seen the lights go on in the Chorley apartment three floors above, he sent me and Guleed down to check the garage while he went up.

Had we managed to make it all the way down to the cars immediately, things might have gone differently. But we ran straight into the Americans on the first sub-level. Below ground the stairs reverted to standard concrete – they were, after all, the service stairs – with the same sort of solid fire door one would expect in any modern building. We were just minding our own business and creeping down the stairs when one of these doors opened. I saw a figure in a dark blue suit framed in the doorway, Guleed yelled – 'Gun!' and I raised my staff and *impelloed* the door shut in his face.

There was a crack as the door trapped his arm, a loud bang as the gun went off and a clang as his pistol hit the concrete floor. I didn't hear Guleed yell over the man's scream – he'd sustained fractures in both bones of his forearm. I let the door loose long enough for him to clear the gap and then slammed it shut again.

'Peter,' said Guleed in a strange voice. 'I think I've been shot.'

I barely had the presence of mind to keep my *impello* up against the door as I turned to stare at Guleed who was plucking at the bottom of her Met Vest.

'Where?'

'There,' said Guleed, pointing at a spot just above her hip. 'Have a look will you?'

This is a thing that both Caffrey and Nightingale have impressed upon me. Most people only fall down when they're shot because the media tells them they're supposed to. Especially with something low calibre like a pistol round. The truth is that unless there's immediate death or gross mechanical damage, people can function quite normally right up to the point where blood loss or shock kicks in. It's known in the police as 'walk, talk and die' – although mostly we run into it when motorcyclists get knocked off their bikes. That's why you've got to check your casualties even when they're standing there with a puzzled look on their face.

There was a definite hole in the heavy material of Guleed's Public Order boiler suit that widened when I stuck a finger in it to reveal a matching slice in the white t-shirt underneath.

'Ow,' said Guleed. 'Careful.'

It would have taken way too long to dig out my pocket knife, so I chopped the cloth with a spell Nightingale had taught me – he'd made me practice on letters and Amazon packaging. I pulled up the T-shirt to reveal a long scrape along her waist. I prodded it, which made her wince – but the skin seemed unbroken.

'It's a scrape,' I said. 'You're going to have a lovely bruise.'

There was a thump on the fire door, followed by gunshots.

I looked at Guleed, and she looked at me, and we both stood there dithering and thinking that about now it would be nice to have a little bit of command and control, when down the stairs thumped DI Stephanopoulos with Bill Conti's 'Fanfare for Rocky' playing in the background, and what looked like half a carrier of TSG piling up behind her.

'Just a scrape, boss,' said Guleed before Stephanopoulos could say anything.

Stephanopoulos looked at the door.

'The Americans?' she asked.

I filled her in.

'But we don't even want to be on this floor,' I said. 'We're supposed to be checking the garage.'

'In that case we'll secure the stairs while you go down,' she said. 'If the Americans try to come in, we scoop them up – otherwise we wait until we get some more bodies in here.'

She stabbed a finger at Guleed.

'You,' she said, 'be more careful. And you,' she turned to glare at me, 'just try to be a little less Peter Grant on this outing.'

I had a witty comeback all ready to go, but at that point the whole staircase shook. There was a shower of fine grey dust all around us as the joists securing the staircase to its frame ground into the concrete.

Stephanopoulos' Airwave squawked and Seawoll reported that Martin Chorley's flat had just lit up like a fireworks display. I could feel it, too, amongst the bangs and shrieks that echoed down the stairwell. *Forma* and counter-*forma*, a full-on magical duel. Nightingale was going head to head with someone formidable – Martin Chorley, at last?

I opened my mouth, but Stephanopoulos put her hand up for silence.

'Wait,' she said.

'But—'

Three gunshots from beyond the fire door, but not that close. Two more further away. Then running feet right outside, five or six shots, loud, rapid, desperate. I tensed, but Stephanopoulos shut me down with another glare.

'Wait.'

Two more shots ... and then it was like being mugged by an old fashioned gentleman's club – a wave of brandy, cigar smoke and pheasant that had hung too long. Then, mixed in with nutmeg and the shine of silver, the heated excitement of the mob, the creak of wood under strain and the smell of old rope, defiance and fear.

And rising above it like a clear note in a trumpet solo, the smell of wood smoke and fresh caught fish cooked over an open fire.

Then silence.

'What was that?' asked Stephanopoulos.

'Okay,' I said. 'We need to get in there now.'

'And the Americans?' she said.

'Yeah, we need to go save them from a fate worse than enforced river conservation,' I said. And then, quickly, 'We have to rescue them from Tyburn.'

Everyone stared at me – strangely they weren't keen. I could tell.

'I'll go in first, check they're okay and then you guys can secure this level and I can finally get to the garage,' I said and Stephanopoulos nodded. Guleed came with me because it's always good to have a witness when

things get complicated – especially one that senior officers trust.

The magical duel was still going on upstairs, I could
feel it, but the crashes and bangs had abated. It was
probably getting subtle – which was all the more reason
for me to stick to the plan.

Me and Guleed eased through the door and out into a
long corridor that ran the length of the complex. It had
a lush grey carpet, cream walls and the same hushed
claustrophobia as a modern hotel. There was a haze in
the air and I thought I smelled gun smoke.

There was tinny music coming from our left so we
went that way, past a pair of lifts and another staircase,
through a fire door that had been jammed open with
a fire extinguisher. There was another corridor beyond
and half-way down its length a pair of open double
doors. I smelt chlorine as we crept along the wall and
the music, from somebody's phone speaker I guessed,
changed track – a mid-'70s band murdering a pair of
guitars and a saxophone. Beside the open doors somebody had helpfully left a Waitrose bag full of Glock 17s.
I kept watch while Guleed checked them out.

'Three,' she said which, plus the one in the stairwell,
should account for all the Americans. Assuming they
didn't have back-up pieces strapped to their ankles.

We slipped inside ever so quietly, into the atrium of
what I guessed was the famed underground swimming
pool. The music was coming from straight ahead and
over it we heard water splashing, shouts and the unmis-
takable sound of somebody smacking a ball around.

Guleed gave me a questioning look, but how the fuck

was I supposed to know what the sounds meant?

The pool itself was a long narrow slot with a high ceiling. Whoever had done the interior design had opted for the upmarket Death's Domain colour scheme – all grey granite walls with ivory details and black marble floors. In the pool a trio of naked white men were batting a ball back and forth. They were all noticeably muscled in that well-fed way Americans can get when they take their training seriously. Another man, also white and naked, sat on one of the redundant purple sun loungers cheering on his friends. His right forearm had been wrapped in a white towel and stiffened with a pair of flip-flops into a makeshift splint. He didn't seem to be feeling any pain.

The Americans stopped as soon as they saw me and Guleed and then turned as one to look at the woman on the other sun lounger. I don't know if I was really expecting woad or spears, or even a bin-bag dress, but it was just Lady Ty in designer jeans and a cream coloured Arran jumper – slightly blemished by grass stains on the left arm. She was staring at us over the top of a pair of completely pointless sunglasses and her phone was playing what I now recognised as *The Day the World Turned Day-Glo* by X-Ray Specs.

She waved airily at the boys in the pool and they went back to their game.

'What happened?' I asked.

Lady Ty propped herself up on her elbow, the better to stare down her nose at us.

'I was trying to kill that bastard Chorley when I was interrupted,' she said.

'You were planning to kill Martin Chorley?' said Guleed.

'Did I say that?' said Lady Ty. 'I meant, of course, that I had planned to discuss his recent actions in a calm and businesslike fashion. I was just coming down the stairs when the goon squad jumped me.' She flicked a finger at the man with broken arm. 'That wasn't me.'

We knew that, of course, but the police never relinquish a psychological advantage when they have one.

'I hope nothing else happened,' I said.

'They're fine,' she said. 'In fact this is probably the first chance they've had to relax since they got here.'

This far underground I couldn't hear the fight upstairs, but I knew I was on a timetable. I told her that we needed to clear the area, but that just made her laugh.

'You know the rules,' she said. 'You have to wait for it to wear off – then you can do what you like with them.'

That was the unwritten and suspiciously voluntary code surrounding the glamour – if you took someone's free will then you became responsible for them until it returned. Like *loco parentis*, Beverley said. That was assuming it *did* wear off and the victim didn't start building their life around their new object of devotion. Some people seemed more susceptible than others. Some day we were probably going to have to set up a support group.

My face must have shown something, because Lady Ty told me to relax.

'I'm not my sister,' she said. 'I have some self-control – they'll be their old all-American selves in a couple of hours.'

As if the business with the fountain and the flowers had never happened.

So Guleed popped back to fetch Stephanopoulos while I crept down the stairs to the garage. You really shouldn't split up during an operation, but sometimes you have no choice. No doubt the blonde teenagers in the slasher movies feel the same way.

It doesn't matter if they're speed-built brutalist tat or expensive air-conditioned stables, underground car parks always smell the same. Damp cement, paint and volatile hydrocarbons. The only variation is whether or not they also smell of wee. Unsurprisingly, the car park under One Hyde Park did not have urine stains in its dark corners – or even have any dark corners that a young man caught short after a night out on the tiles might have a quick slash in.

There were two floors of garage proper but I was heading to the lowest because that's where the parking spaces – plural, since the bigger the flat the more spaces you got – allocated to Martin Chorley were. As was his assigned storage space. Because although POLSA had gone through it during the initial investigation, they hadn't known what to look for.

The stairs I went down were for the delicate feet of residents and thus had black marble risers and point-less art hung at regular intervals. On the bottom landing was a solid fire door disguised by a black stained piano-finish veneer. In a proper, crappy car park there'd have been grimy vertical window slots to look through, but not here. I wondered who was on the other side.

I stopped and tried to clear my mind. The uncanny creates a disturbance in the world. Everyone feels it, the trick is to distinguish it from the all the random noise, the thoughts, memories and misfiring neurons, that fill our heads from moment to moment. It's like everything else – the more you do it, the better you get. I used to think that Nightingale was alerted to Falcon cases by his extensive network of informants. But now I think maybe he's just listening to the city.

Or maybe not. Because that would be freaky.

Nobody was fighting upstairs, or at least not with magic. But beyond the fire door I could feel a little tickle, like mouse claws scrabbling in the wainscoting of the material world. It wasn't Martin Chorley. I know the razor strop of his *signare*. This was more familiar, like listening to an echo of my own voice.

Lesley.

The question was, did she expect me to come through that door? If I went straight in I might be able to catch her off guard while she was concentrating on whatever it was she was doing. Or she might be doing the low level magic to draw me out.

Or, I decided, I could be over-thinking things again.

I pushed open the fire door and stepped into the garage proper.

There were lift doors opposite and an opening to the right. I could smell old petrol and fresh carbon monoxide. Echoing off the clean concrete walls were periodic metal crunches as Lesley used *impello* to rip car doors open. I tucked myself behind a section of dividing wall and tried to work out where the noise was coming from.

Once I had narrowed it down to the left I had a quick look.

On the other side of the garage was a long row of parking spaces, each filled with a couple of tons of high status metal. It was mostly Chelsea tractors interspersed with midlife-crisis-mobiles including an Aston Martin Vanquish Volante that I wouldn't have minded for myself. And two thirds of the way down the line, practically hidden behind an honest to god white Humvee, was Reynard Fossman's ugly red Renault.

Judging by the three cars with their doors open, smoke still rising from the back of one, Lesley was methodically working her way down the line. Currently she had her back to me as she wrenched open the rear door of a Jaguar F-Pace.

I didn't think she'd be that casual about her blind side if she was working alone, so I risked sticking my head out for a quick look left and right. Nobody else was in sight, but even so I started easing myself back towards the fire door and the stairs.

I figured that what with this being a basement and us having all the possible exits covered, it was probably not a bad idea to back off and await reinforcements. If only Nightingale could finish off whatever he was doing upstairs.

I caught movement in the corner of my eye and jumped left on general principles and suddenly found myself suddenly lying on my back with a ringing in my ears and the round white light in the ceiling above me going alarmingly in and out of focus. In policing it's not a good idea to lie down on the job so I tried to roll over, but I'd barely shifted when a blow to my chest pinned me back down.

'Stay down,' said Lesley from outside my view. 'Or Martin here will start breaking ribs.'

'She does like to make me sound gangster, doesn't she?' said Martin Chorley. His voice was coming from the other side of the car park. He must have just come down the eastern set of service stairs. I heard his footsteps as he walked past me to reach Lesley. He was far too sensible to get close enough to look down on me and risk making himself a target – although I could tell he really wanted to.

'We need to get a move on,' he said to Lesley. 'I left a trail of nasty surprises behind me but he won't stay cautious for long.'

Something, *impello* at a guess, dragged me across the concrete and I heard a clattering sound as my staff was dragged behind me by its wrist strap. We both ended up in the middle of the roadway – the decking was strangely warm under my palms.

I felt for the handle of my staff, but it was yanked away, the strap cutting painfully into my wrist and palm until it snapped with a twang. That must have been another spell, because it should have taken my hand off at the wrist before it broke.

'What's this?' asked Martin Chorley. 'Ah, yes. A genuine army surplus battle staff. You don't see many of those these days, do you? I wonder if you've kept it charged up.'

'I wouldn't touch it,' said Lesley. 'It's probably booby trapped.'

What a good idea, I thought, let's add that to the list.

Another clatter as my staff was kicked or spelled off the roadway and, if the sudden echo was anything to go by, under a nearby vehicle.

Great, I thought, that turned out to be useful in the end, didn't it?

'Did you find Reynard?' asked Lesley.

'No,' said Martin Chorley. 'He's a slippery little shit, isn't he? I'm hoping he'll run into Nightingale or the plod and get himself shot.'

I risked turning my head, slowly, to see if I could locate either him or Lesley. He was standing three or four metres away in the centre of the roadway. He was wearing a tailored charcoal pinstripe suit cut in the modern style. He stood, legs slightly apart for balance, arms held loosely by his side – ready for action. I was happy to note that the suit jacket's sartorial perfection had been marred by scorch mark that ran diagonally from shoulder to waist and his trousers were soaked through from the thighs downwards. Nightingale was obviously handing out lessons in appropriate work attire.

Lesley was to his right, continuing her search of the parked cars. I couldn't see the Renault from here but the white Humvee it was hiding behind stuck out half a metre over the line. She continued her search of each vehicle in turn, going round to the back of every car and blowing the lock off the boot, checking inside with a quick scan of the front and rear footwells to ensure nothing was stowed in there. About thirty seconds a car, counting walking time.

'So apart from the face,' I said, 'why are you working with this guy?'

Lesley ignored me, but the question obviously irritated Martin Chorley.

'Because she's properly English,' he said.

'And I'm not?'

'No,' he said. 'Not that I blame you for that, you understand. Your mother was no doubt enticed over to fill some vacancy in the NHS or to drive a bus, or some other job that the working man was too feckless to do himself.'

Or because she was jazz mad and couldn't get a ticket to New York, I thought. He must have known a bit of my family history. I know he'd checked up on me, and had to have asked Lesley what she knew. My mum, who'd had a good job at the American library in Freetown, had unfortunately caught jazz off the radio and headed for the bright lights of the city, any city, and had found London and my father.

Or perhaps he thought being a jazz mad groupie was something only young white women did, or even more likely he just couldn't be bothered to fit his intelligence together into a proper assessment. Thank god, because if he had he would have known about the Renault that was six cars down the line from where Lesley was currently, and carefully, blowing the bloody doors off a rather tasty silver Porsche.

'But Lesley is a proper Brit,' said Martin Chorley, who I realised had probably been waiting years for an audience. 'That wonderful blend of Romano-Celt and Anglo-Saxon with a flavouring of Dane and a pinch of

Norman French. That happy breed that conquered the world and could again if all their children were kind and natural.'

'Henry the Fifth,' I said. 'You're doing the bit where Derek Jacobi introduces the traitors.'

'There was a time when the monarchy meant something more than tea parties and sex scandals,' said Martin Chorley. 'Before the Saxe-Coburgs or the Tudors or anyone else American TV has done a miniseries about.'

'Alfred the Great?' I asked.

'I've always thought you were suspiciously well-educated for a boy from a sink estate,' he said.

'What can I say – I watched a lot of *Time Team* growing up.'

'That's not real archaeology,' said Martin Chorley. 'Talk to any proper professional archaeologist and they'll tell you *Time Team* was a joke.'

'You know a lot of archaeologists, then?' I asked.

'I've read widely,' he said – suddenly cagey, which made me immediately curious.

'What's your favourite period?' I asked.

'What's yours?' he said, dodging the question.

'I like the Romans,' I said.

'But you're a policeman,' said Martin Chorley. 'Of course you'd like your brutality systemic and carefully licenced.'

Actually, I thought, it was the underfloor heating and the regular baths.

'I like the Dark Ages,' said Martin Chorley rolling the syllables around in his mouth. 'When a man could make himself a myth.'

359

I could have talked archaeology and Victorian romanticism all day, but alas work had to take precedence. So while I let Martin Chorley monologue away, I laid my plans against him.

Anyone can sense another person doing magic, if they're close enough and they know what to look out for. In fact you can't learn magic without someone to demonstrate the *formae* first. Right from the start I'd wondered whether some forms were 'louder' than others and it's not a hard experiment to set up. For once Nightingale didn't object, partly because sensing *formae* is the key to winning a magical duel. But mostly, I think, because it forced me to practise producing a consistent effect, which he is very big on.

So we discovered that you can sense loud splashy spells such as *impello* or a fireball from as much as ten metres away. It's down to two to three for normal *were-lights* and things like raising a shield, but less than a metre for certain variations on *lux* – particularly those that pushed the wavelength into the infrared. So while Martin Chorley indulged his strange need to confide in me, I slowly and carefully created a little invisible heat sphere, which I'm really going to have to come up with a name for, and nudged it in the direction of the nearest sprinkler head.

It was a top-of-the-line system and the reaction was almost instantaneous.

A good sprinkler system is gravity fed. The water comes from a big tank mounted as high as is practical and when the valves on the sprinkler heads activate, down that water comes. It's a robust system with a minimum of moving parts and no pumps to malfunction at the wrong moment. The water keeps coming until the reservoir is exhausted.

I knew that and, judging by the peeved expression on Martin Chorley's face, so did he.

I'd love to say I had a plan for what followed, but I'd be lying.

I used the distraction to ease myself into a slightly better position, palms down on the decking ready to lever myself over and up, but Martin Chorley wasn't that distracted.

'Oh no you don't,' he said. 'Face down, hands on your head.'

I complied, linking my fingers in the wet hair at back of my head. When someone's threatening you, you tend to pay attention. Which is why I was looking in the right direction when the Tesla S came drifting around the far corner of the garage and raced towards us.

At first it just appeared, as if a silver shape was silently growing amongst the artificial rain, and I assumed it was someone else doing a spell. But then I registered the distinctive frowny face emoticon grille and realised what it was coming our way.

You'd be amazed how fast you can get to your feet when you have to, and I didn't even bother to go fully upright. I scrambled hand-and-foot to the side like a chimp. I like to think that any remote human ancestors watching from that big savannah in the sky would have given me full points for speed and agility, if not for style.

'Not so fast,' said Martin Chorley before he realised that something was behind him. He spun round to look and that was almost the last thing he ever did. I think he got some kind of barrier up before the Tesla hit him – and I'm certain that the driver corrected their course to make sure they hit him full on. I saw a flash of red hair in the driver's seat – left hand, I noticed, so it was an import – and guessed that Reynard Fossman had wisely decided to get his retaliation in early.

I completely understood his logic – if you go after the Faceless Man you want to make sure he goes down with the first strike. Not that that would stop us from charging Reynard with attempted murder if we thought we could make it stick.

Lesley emerged from the line of cars – she was only one short of the white Humvee – and glanced down the length of the garage just in time to see the Tesla plough into the far wall, the crash strangely muted by the falling water.

Lesley turned to frown at me.

'What have you done this time?' she asked.

I saved my breath for diving sideways, aiming for the gap between a red Mercedes and a forest green Range Rover, where I could just see my staff poking out behind a rear wheel.

I felt Lesley start a spell, but before she could release it Reynard came running out of the falling water and jumped on her back. I tried to change direction but lost my footing on the wet tarmac and bounced face first off the Range Rover. I managed to slide down the side as if that was what I'd planned from the start and scooped up my staff.

Reynard had gone feral, his burgundy button down

shirt in strips and rags to reveal the thick russet hair covering his back and shoulders. His legs were wrapped around Lesley's waist and he had his left arm around her neck while he pounded her head with his other hand. He was snarling, his lips pulled back to reveal his teeth, so that for a moment I thought he might actually be growing a muzzle and I was going to get my first look at a shape shifter.

Still, science had to wait, and I levelled my staff and the wood hummed under my palm as I flattened the pair of them. Lesley twisted going down, throwing Reynard off onto his back. Neither was going to stay down for long, so I had my follow-up ready. But before I could release it, Reynard rolled back on his shoulders and then kicked himself up onto his feet. Lesley was slower and she was still my primary target, so I knocked her down again.

She swore, rolled and I lost track of Reynard as I tried to close my distance with her.

Then I heard Nightingale shout – 'Down!' and threw myself flat on my face.

I only saw it coming because of the rain from the sprinklers. It was a like a lens, an optical distortion whirling through the air – a circular saw three metres across, droplets spraying off the top. Even as I was dropping I saw it slice horizontally through the front of the Humvee. And it was fast. I barely got my face to the concrete before it passed over me with a sound like tearing cloth. I looked up and saw Lesley had dropped as well.

'Stay down!' shouted Nightingale as something zigzagged over my head from behind me, with a noise like a hummingbird ... if hummingbirds weighed twenty kilos and ate rats for dinner.

A second and third super-hummingbird passed me to the left and right. I managed to catch a glimpse of one – it looked like a drill head made of silver snowflakes. Whatever they did when they hit a target, it wasn't going to be a joy forever. I decided to stay down and started wriggling towards Lesley, who was making a spirited crawl for the shelter of the Humvee.

'Get to cover,' yelled Nightingale, which just goes to show that great minds think alike. This obviously applied to Lesley as well, because she scrambled to her feet even as I did. But not to Guleed, who came barrelling out of the rain and smacked Lesley down into the gap between the cars.

I made it into my own gap between a BMW 5 series and a Jaguar XJ, whose resale value Lesley had recently lowered by ripping open the doors, just before a chunk of the ceiling collapsed onto the spot where I'd been lying.

I peered through the windows of the BMW and saw Guleed grappling with Lesley on the other side. I couldn't risk the crossfire on the roadway, so I clambered awkwardly around the back and arrived just in time to see Guleed snap her head forward and land as sweet a Glaswegian kiss as was ever administered outside the National Club in Kilburn. Lesley staggered back, clutching her nose, and before she could recover Guleed had her spun around with her right arm in an elbow lock and I, upholding the fine tradition of the Metropolitan Police Service, piled in behind. I'm sure, had she thought about it, Lesley would have approved.

I hooked her feet out from under her, she went face down and I pulled the speedcuffs off my belt. It wasn't that easy while trying to hang on to my staff, and I only had one of her wrists snapped when the white Humvee lurched half a metre over and squashed us up against the side of the BMW.

'God, Peter,' said Lesley. 'Why are you so clumsy with the cuffs?' And she elbowed me in the nuts. It hurt, but it would have hurt a lot more if I hadn't been wearing the box that's part of my PSU kit. I've been smacked in the bollocks before, and try to learn from my mistakes.

The Humvee lurched again, and we would have been crushed if it hadn't been for its high clearance, which allowed all three of us to slide underneath it.

'Shit,' said Lesley, 'he's getting away!'

I followed her gaze and saw a pair of legs climbing into Reynard's Renault. It was Reynard himself – I recognised the skinny hipster jeans as they climbed through the passenger door. The engine started, no microprocessors to fry on that car, and it started to pull out of the parking spot.

'Where does he think he's going?' asked Guleed, which was a good question because there was no ramp up to the surface. Only the two vehicle lifts, and they were in lock-down.

Lesley wriggled and I was trying to get a grip on her other wrist when she was dragged out from under the Humvee and into the roadway. Since me and Guleed were hanging onto to her, we went too.

The sprinklers had finally stopped, leaving the

decking a wet cold slick and the air full of the smell of stale water. I noticed that some serious puddles had accumulated in some of the parking bays and around the entrance to the lifts. Whoever had put the nice resin coating down had skimped on the drainage system.

We had a good view of the Renault as it accelerated past us towards the far side of the garage. And an equally good look at the bonnet when it exploded in a ball of fire. Exactly the way cars in films do, and cars in real life don't. It scraped forward for a couple of metres before grinding to a stop. Oily smoke poured from the ruined front of the car and, had there been any water left, that would have been a good time for the sprinklers to activate.

Lesley kicked and twisted, but I think me and Guleed had both decided that our operational priority was arresting her which, unlike everything else going on around us, seemed within our performance envelope.

The back of the Renault blew open of its own accord and a couple of storage crates, the same make as the ones back at The Chestnut Tree, bounced out onto the wet tarmac. Lesley made a lunge forward and then recoiled as Guleed sprayed her in the face with her CS aerosol.

'Sahra!' she spluttered.

In the still underground air the smoke was quickly rolling over our heads. According to Frank Caffrey, about a third of fire deaths are down to smoke inhalation and he's a professional so he should know. I wanted out of that basement. Fortunately, so did Guleed.

'The stairwell,' she shouted and we each kept one

hand on Lesley as we crawled towards the atrium with the lifts and stairs. Also, I was thinking of those nice thick fire doors and the strong possibility that Stephanopoulos would be available nearby for tea, sympathy and first aid.

Lesley didn't co-operate.

She somehow managed to roll herself sideways, right over my back, wrenching the speedcuffs out of my left hand and smashing her elbow into the side of my face so that my skull smacked the ground. I really wasn't any good to man or police officer for what seemed like half an hour, but was probably more like ten seconds. The smoke had boiled down to ground level by then and I came to with Lesley gone and Guleed trying to drag me towards where she hoped the stairs were.

I couldn't see more than half a metre and every breath burnt the back of my throat. I was beginning to get seriously worried when I smelt dust and sandalwood and what might have been the hot wind off the desert, or possibly just the car burning a few metres away. Then the smoke blew away like the parting of the Red Sea and Lady Helena walked calmly past us down a lengthening corridor of clear air towards the Renault. She lifted her right hand and made a clenching gesture and the fire that engulfed the engine block snuffed out.

Now that was a spell I definitely wanted to learn.

Me and Guleed took advantage of the fresh air to clamber to our feet and start coughing. I was so busy attempting to expel my lungs that I didn't follow Lady Helena to the back of the Renault. One of the storage boxes was open and on its side and she squatted down and starting picking through the spray of manuscripts and plastic folders.

After a few moments I had enough breath to ask whether she'd seen Nightingale.

She didn't look up from her search but she did shrug.

'I think I might have been fighting him at one point,' she said. 'It all got rather confused. Ah!' She stood up brandishing a package the size of a family sized box of Sainsbury's own cornflakes. 'Not a total waste of my time after all,' she said and then strolled past me back towards the stairs. 'If you're looking to stop our friend Mr Chorley, my best guess is that he'll try break out via the vehicle lifts.'

I briefly considered trying to arrest her. Guleed caught my eye, waiting to follow my lead, but I shook my head. With the fire out the smoke wasn't getting any thicker, but the dense haze remained pretty toxic and whatever air spell Lady Helena had cast we couldn't count on it lasting forever. So me and Guleed gathered up the spilled loot, plonked it back in the storage container and carried it, and the one with the lid still on, back to the stairwell.

There we found Stephanopoulos and a bunch of irate London Fire Brigade in breathing gear. She wanted to know if the garage was clear of Falcon, so she could let the fire officers in. But I couldn't give her that assurance. It took us half an hour to locate Nightingale, who'd chased Martin Chorley through a brand new hole in the vehicle lifts but hadn't dared continue the pursuit beyond the secure perimeter.

'Far too high a risk of civilian casualties,' he said later.

Stephanopoulos didn't look happy.

'We have not exactly covered ourselves with glory,' she said.

'On the other hand,' said Guleed, 'none of us are dead.'

'Just you wait until the Commissioner sees the bill,' said Stephanopoulos.

16

Pleased to Meet You

And so it ended like most Police operations do, not with a bang but with us whimpering over the paper- work. Or at least it would have for me and Guleed, if we hadn't been whisked off to UCH where we snaffled up oxygen and tried not to listen while Dr Walid explained terms like tissue hypoxia to us in more detail than either of us would have liked. Fortunately we responded well to treatment and weren't kept overnight. Beverley popped over to keep me company and then, typically, spent most of the time in Guleed's cubicle gossiping – and not even about me. My mum turned up with a care package which I ate one-handed while fending off Bev, Guleed and Nightingale with the other. Once we were out, Beverley drove me back to her house in her sad little Kia and we shared a bath and then bed.

The next morning Nightingale picked me up from Bev's in the Jag so he could brief me on the way back to Belgravia nick. I was going to take over as Falcon liaison in the hunt for Martin Chorley and Lesley May while he headed back to the Folly to catch up on his sleep.

'He almost got me, you know,' said Nightingale. 'He'd prepared a number of booby traps in the flat upstairs and tried to lure me into the killing zone.'

Fortunately Nightingale still remembered the lessons he'd learnt fighting the Germans.

'They were expert at combining conventional weapons with magical ones,' he said. 'You never knew if you were going to be facing a fireball or a Panzerfaust.'

Martin Chorley was clever and ruthless but his lack of combat experience told against him.

'Set off his first device a fraction too early,' said Nightingale. 'Once I was tipped off it was just a matter of being careful where I stepped.'

Which explained why he'd been slow getting down to the basement. Otherwise both Martin Chorley and Lesley would now be enjoying the simple elegance of our magic-resistant cells.

That they had both managed to get away was the primary failure of the operation, the property damage to One Hyde Park being secondary. Although the fact that we could prove that one of their tenants – Martin Chorley – had instigated the fire was definitely going to help us in the upcoming legal fight.

It would have been even better if we actually had Martin Chorley in custody, or Lesley May for that matter – though we did have Reynard Fossman, who CTC were holding under anti-terrorism legislation at Paddington right across the corridor from Lady Ty's Americans. I know Seawoll would have liked to arrest Lady Helena and Caroline as well, if only on general principles, but Nightingale argued against it even after we'd discovered that they'd run off with the manuscript of the *Magni Operis Principia Chemica*, *'Chymical Principles of the Great Work'*.

Nightingale seemed remarkably relaxed about Lady

Helena half-inching *The Third Principia*, given the grief we'd been through to get it in the first place. Postmartin would have cheerfully sentenced them to a life breaking rocks for crimes against scholarship, but Nightingale merely smiled and said that they were probably better suited to the job of interpreting it.

'I never was one for academic study. And even if you did have time, your Latin isn't up to the job.'

'Thanks a lot,' I said.

'Speaking as one who was obliged to memorise large sections of *The Second Principia*, I think I can say with some confidence that you are not losing out. In any case, while Lady Helena will no doubt do a splendid job teasing out its secrets, I believe relying on the wisdom of the ancients, so to speak, is a mistake.' Nightingale gave a crooked grin I'd never seen before – it made him look all of fourteen. Suddenly I could see him standing on the playing fields of Casterbrook, hands in pockets, school cap pulled down at a rakish angle and looking into a future untroubled by anything more than a couple of world wars, atomic bombs and the loss of everything he held dear.

'In any event, I rather think that Lady Helena is looking to the past whereas I prefer to look to the future,' he said. 'I'm sure if she does discover something worth knowing she'll be only too happy to share.'

I expressed a certain amount of doubt about that, but Nightingale pointed out that Lady Helena had returned to her place in the Montgomeryshire and should we want it, we could always drive out and ask to borrow the bloody book.

'And see if her daughter has learned to fly yet,' said Nightingale.

I asked about Martin Chorley's Ferrari GTO and Nightingale said it was temporarily impounded.

'Why do you ask?'

'I thought they might auction it.'

'And you were thinking of bidding?'

'Just a thought,' I said.

'Alas,' said Nightingale. 'That car will never be sold.'

'Oh.'

'No,' he said. 'I declared it a "magical device" under the terms of the agreement. At least until such time as we can declare it safe for mundane use.'

And he'd stashed it in the coach house where the Orange Asbo used to live.

'How long do you think that will take?'

'Well such an evaluation can take a considerable amount of time,' said Nightingale. 'Especially given our current work load.'

'And we wouldn't want to cut corners, would we?'

'To do so would be irresponsible,' he said.

'Respect,' I said and raised my fist which Nightingale stared at for a moment before raising his own and bumping mine.

Over the next couple of days it became clear that Martin Chorley and Lesley May had gone to ground. We've always supposed he had resources beyond County Gard and its related companies. Seawoll suspects links to organised crime, people smugglers and the like.

I assume that he has links to the shadier parts of the demi-monde as well.

Despite Nightingale's assertion that he's just an ordinary criminal at heart, I think there's something more. There was something of the fanatic about him. I'm sure he has a plan . . . I wish I knew what it was.

We did pick up Reynard, though, and charged him with a miscellany of offences ranging from resisting arrest to handling stolen goods. We're not pushing the Crown Prosecution Service very hard on this case, though. We don't want our fox in prison. We want him to be out and about like a walking lightning rod.

As I promised Beverley I helped Maksim install some herringbone pattern baffles on a stretch of her river. The idea, Bev said, was to break up the flow and ultimately erode the banks into a more natural shape.

'I thought you liked a fast flow?' I asked later that evening.

'It's not the volume,' she said between pants. 'It's how it flows.'

Phoebe and Olivia had joined Beverley on the river bank to watch as we worked and afterwards we had a slightly damp picnic under the protection of a weeping willow. Olivia said that she thought her mum might have forgiven me a little, or at least she'd stopped scowling whenever my name came up. When they left I found myself watching them walking away, hand in hand, and wondering what having kids must be like. Once you're past the nappies and training wheels.

I turned to find Beverley watching me.

'What?' I asked.

'Nothing,' she said and took me home.

Did I mention the paperwork? It took us a couple of days just to pull all the material together, not helped by having DAC Folsom descend on us for a review with the rest of the Tiger Hunting Committee in tow. So it didn't really come as much of a surprise when Lady Ty asked if I could pop in to see her.

'Any time in the next hour would be convenient,' she said.

We met in the saloon bar at The Chestnut Tree which Lady Ty said she was in the middle of acquiring on behalf of her mother's property portfolio. Judging by the way the manageress waited on our table, and hovered attentively until dismissed, that acquisition was a done deal in more ways than one.

Lady Ty had ordered a bottle of red and two glasses, but I shook my head when she went to fill mine.

'Is it true you're writing a briefing document regarding the expansion of the Folly?' she asked after taking a sip.

'Modernisation,' I said. 'To make it fit for purpose.'

'Is there any chance of getting a sneak preview?' she asked.

'You were always on the stakeholder list,' I said. 'And part of the initial round of consultation going forward.'

'Stop that,' she said.

'Stop what?'

'You know what.'

I shrugged and waited to find out what this was really all about.

'Peter,' she said, 'we need to talk about you and Beverley.'

'Is this going to be the big sister talk?' I asked.

'Yes, I'm afraid so,' she said.

'Have you had it with Beverley?'

'Many times,' she said. 'But I promise that this will be the only time I will have it with you.'

'You don't like me seeing Bev – right?'

'It's not the seeing I mind, or the shagging, or the fact that she keeps introducing you to mysteries that you shouldn't be party to,' said Lady Ty.

'Really? Like what?'

Lady Ty grimaced. 'Nice try,' she said. 'You're both young and stupid and nothing I say is going to make you stop. But you need to listen to me carefully. Whatever you think this thing you've got with Beverley is, it's got to be strictly short-term. It can't get serious. And if you're thinking about getting married, it is right out of the question.'

'What the fuck?'

'I'm serious,' she said.

I felt myself flush.

'You don't think I'm good enough?' I said.

Lady Ty sighed and held up a hand.

'You seem to have got the impression that I don't like you,' she said. 'As a person, that is – rather than a fucking impediment to everything I've been trying to build for the last twenty years.' She hesitated and then sighed again. 'Where was I?'

'Fucking impediment,' I said.

'Look, this isn't going to work unless you have a drink,' said Lady Ty and pushed a wine glass across the table at me and picked up the bottle. 'I can't do this with you staring at me like a Methodist preacher.'

'Tyburn,' I said.

She gave me a weary look and then intoned that she, Lady Ty, held me to no obligation and that I could partake freely of her hospitality without obligation.

'Satisfied?' she asked.

I nodded and she poured the wine.

'You remember that Christmas I dug you out from under Oxford Circus?'

'How could I forget?' I said.

'That's what I wondered all last week,' said Lady Ty.

I sipped my wine. It tasted like, well, red wine. Despite Nightingale and Molly's best efforts that's still as far as my palette goes.

'After that Christmas, George and I went on holiday,' she said. 'Stephen was away at uni and we packed Olivia off to go skiing in the French Alps. With Phoebe's family, as it happens.' She shook her head. 'All that needless worry about chalet Romeos – oblivious, that's me. Anyway, we hadn't been on holiday alone together since the kids were born and it was glorious.'

I asked where she went.

'Barbados,' she said. 'I know the Island quite well – he did a sabbatical at Oxford while I was there.'

I drank some more wine while that sank in. I wanted to ask what the Island was like as a person. I really did. But sometimes even I've got to stay focused. Not to mention, you've got to suspect that someone who read Machiavelli in the original Italian is going to be looking to distract you – even if it's only out of force of habit.

'So, you had a good time?' I asked.

'When I came back I felt like was twenty again,' said Lady Ty.

I had a horrible feeling I knew what was coming next.

'You're young, reasonably fit and not bad looking, so the reality of getting older hasn't sunk in yet,' she said. 'As you get older gravity starts to take its toll, especially if you're a woman, especially if you have two kids and then breast feed them.'

I must have squirmed ever so slightly, because she laughed.

'I'm not saying they were heading for my waist,' said Lady Ty. 'Let's just say I wasn't going to go topless on the beach. This is really making you uncomfortable, isn't it?' She pronounced it *innit* – she was definitely taking the piss. 'Scaring you with the thought of my old lady tits.'

'Truthfully,' I said, because sometimes people want a bit of honesty, 'yeah, a bit.'

'Good,' said Lady Ty. 'Then there's stretch marks and moles and these weird flaps of skin and cellulite – let's not forget the cellulite. There's nothing you can do about it and if you're sensible you learn to be comfortable in your skin.'

'And are you?'

'I thought so,' she said. 'Until we were getting ready

for our last night out on the Island and I decided to wriggle into my emergency little black dress and I'm hoiking everything into place when George looks at me and says "Hey, we should do this every year. It really seems to agree with you". And I was feeling pretty damn hot, even if I say so myself, so I sashayed over to the mirror and found my twenty five year old self staring back at me.'

'You'd physically changed?' I asked.

'I closed the bathroom door and had a good feel,' said Tyburn. 'It was all real.'

'You must have known it was a possibility,' I said. 'I mean, look at Oxley and Isis.'

'Peter,' said Tyburn. 'I need you to stop just pretending to be clever and actually be clever. Of course I knew it, intellectually – Mum's looked basically the same since I can remember, and there's Father Thames who doesn't look a day over a thousand. But that's not the same as staring it in the face.' She shook her head.

I nodded my understanding, but she wasn't convinced.

'So when we came back to London I sort of let myself fall back into middle age.'

'Just like that?'

'Well, I stayed away from mirrors and watched a lot of *Antiques Roadshow* – that helped.'

'How quickly did it happen?' I asked.

'A couple of months,' she said. 'Crow's feet, fat thighs and all.'

Fairly unobtrusive crow's feet, I thought.

'And it all just reverted?'

Lady Ty shrugged.

'I may have left out the stretch marks,' she said.

'Did he notice?'

'I don't know,' she said. 'When you're married you get used to each other – you really only see the person you expect to see.'

'Can Beverley make herself look older?' I asked, and then I thought of her sister Nicky who was allegedly nine years old and might just have drowned a man on dry land. 'Can Nicky?'

'There's no manual, Peter,' said Lady Ty. 'There's no self-help group with a Tumblr page and an easy-to-access FAQ. And I'm the oldest, which means everything happens to me first – of course. I have to make all the mistakes, and my first one was thinking I was human and could have a human life.'

I felt a cold clutching in my chest. It must have shown on my face.

'I'm going to outlive my babies, Peter,' she said. 'I'm going to outlive my babies' babies. Barring some radically unforeseen circumstance I'm going to outlive everyone I love, except my family.' She made a strange head bob. 'I want to save my sister some pain – so sue me.'

I didn't know what to say, so I didn't say anything.

'Are you at least going to think about what I've said?'

'Who stabbed the sniper?' I asked. 'Do you know?'

Lady Ty stiffened and she took another sip of her wine before answering with a question. 'Do you have any theories?' she asked.

'I think it was Sir William Tyburn, late of this parish,' I said. 'Do you know who I'm talking about?'

'The son of old Father Thames,' she spoke the phrase in a formal manner, as if invoking a spirit or introducing a judge.

I waited, but she sipped more wine and looked at me over the rim of her glass.

'Was it him?'

Lady Ty shrugged.

'Is he associated with you in some way?' I asked. 'At a spiritual level?'

Lady Ty snorted into her wine, put the glass down and quickly covered her nose and mouth with her hand.

'Spiritual, Peter? Having difficulty integrating this within your rationalist schema, are we?'

'Only because nobody ever gives me a straight answer,' I said.

'That's because they don't know,' said Tyburn. 'It's like economics. Everybody's got a theory, and some people make it their religion.'

'Is he part of you or not?' I asked, louder than I meant to. 'I need to know.'

Lady Ty snorted again, so I defiantly lifted my wine-glass and drained it in one go. I grabbed the bottle and poured myself the last of the wine.

'There,' I said. 'Now I've met you half-way .'

'You and Bev are so suited,' she said. 'It's such a pity you're going to wear out so quickly.'

'Got any Red Stripe?' I asked. 'Kronenberg? Tsingtao? Star? Come on, you must have some Star Beer left.'

'You'd think so, wouldn't you?' said Lady Ty. 'But you haven't seen my mum's friends drink yet.' She sighed.

'Okay. He's there, is Mr William Tyburn Esquire – like a memory, like a story I made up when I was a kid and repeated so often that it's become the truth. He's real, like a photograph of a grandfather who died before you were born.'

'Did he kill the sniper?'

'Well, I sure as shit didn't,' said Lady Ty. 'You know, I've done business with the Public Policy Foundation. They did a study on increasing passenger traffic along the Thames. I must have attended half a dozen meetings and presentations with them, and I never once met Martin Chorley.'

'He was avoiding you,' I said. 'He didn't want you sniffing him out.'

'I nearly got him, you know,' said Lady Ty with a wicked smile. 'I'd have drowned the little fucker if the bloody Americans hadn't got in the way.' She frowned. 'What have you done with them, by the way?'

'Why do you want to know?'

'I have an overdeveloped sense of responsibility,' she said.

'We're flying them home tomorrow,' I said.

There had been a deal, but nobody bothered to tell us what it was.

'A couple of quid for our quo pro,' said Seawoll when I asked him.

I asked Agent Kimberley Reynolds when I saw her and her charges off at Brize Norton, but she said she couldn't tell me. She did ask whether we'd recovered everything on the NSA list. I didn't tell her about Lady Helena walking off with *The Third Principia*, but I did tell her that Babbage's Mary Engine hadn't been recovered.

'We don't even know if it was in the car,' I said. 'I don't suppose you've got it?'

'Didn't it weigh like two hundred pounds?' she asked, and offered to let me carry her luggage.

We agreed to stay in touch and I promised to send her some books. I asked how we might keep our discussions private and she just laughed.

'What do you propose we use – a magic decoder ring?' she said. 'Just don't say anything you don't want the NSA to know.'

I added establishing relations with other national magical policing bodies to the great big fun file of things the Folly needed to do.

Which left a certain hook nosed bastard who didn't know when to shut up.

Early the next morning I drove out to London Bridge and stood about where I judged the centre to be, turned my back on the river and leaned against the parapet. Even at six in the morning the commuters were streaming past me in the darkness, shoulders hunched, hands in pockets or clutching umbrellas against the chill drizzle.

'You've been bugging me for a year now,' I said. 'You want to talk? Let's talk.'

A couple of people gave me a strange look but, I suspect the majority thought I was on my phone, hands free. Of course some of them detoured to avoid me, but they would have done that even if I'd been silent.

'You see, the thing is I'm still alive,' I said. 'Martin Chorley could have killed me a number of times during the fight in the garage. Fuck, he could have killed me at Phoebe Beaumont-Jones' house. Now he says that he's got a deal with Lesley, which he doesn't want to break. But, you know what? I think there's more. Because there's half a dozen ways that Mr Chorley could have offed me and gone "Whoops, total accident, wrong place, wrong time". And he didn't. Which he means he doesn't dare risk pissing Lesley off, which means she's not just important. She's vital to his plans.'

And there, very faint, like a whiff of shit in a posh restaurant, I caught the off-key jangle of bells, the rustle of jester's motley and a snatch of familiar verse – *He lives, while he can, upon clover. And when he dies it's only all over.*

'It can't be access to the Black Library,' I said. 'Because she's off the guest list and she's picking up magic. But I reckon he could find a replacement without too much trouble. Shit, he could train someone himself if he needed to. It's not to get a psychological advantage over the opposition. Because I might hesitate when it comes to Lesley, but Nightingale will not – trust me.'

The press of commuters crossing the bridge grew until it was a continuous hurrying river of people streaming past.

'So, I wondered what might be special about Lesley,' I said. 'Beyond all the things I think are special about her. And, you know what? And this is going to make you laugh . . . the answer is *you*, isn't it? Some special knowledge she got while you were in her head. Or maybe a connection to you. Is that it? A connection.'

And then a voice, like a breath in my ear.

384

If I had all the wives of wise King Sol, I'd kill them all for my Pretty Pol.

'You better watch it, bruv,' I said. 'Because you and I ain't finished.'

And I thought I heard laughter echoing out of the city, but it might have just been the traffic.

Acknowledgements

Ruth Goldsmith and Harry Shapiro of DrugScope, Nial Boyce of the Lancet Psychiatry, Bob Hunter formerly of the Metropolitan Police now keen-eyed gumshoe and wicked piper. Andrew Cartmel for tirelessly keeping me from making a fool of myself and James Swallow for tirelessly allowing me to go on about totally imaginary people. Simon and Gillian for just letting me go on – period. John for not screaming even when he had cause. Anne Hall for being calm.

Technical Note

As keen-eyed readers will know, *The Jeremy Kyle Show* would have finished by the time Peter confronted Lesley in the Harrods Technology Department. I did consider substituting that day's episode of *Homes Under the Hammer* but I couldn't resist Sharon and Darren – I mean, could you?

Nightingale's bit of French erudition is from *Le Lys Rouge* (*The Red Lily*) written by Nobel Prize winning author Anatole France and can be loosely translated as – 'The majestic equality of the law forbids rich and poor alike from pissing in the streets, sleeping under bridges and stealing bread.'

Please turn the page for a Waterstones exclusive
short story from Ben Aaronovitch:

King of the Rats

King of the Rats

By Ben Aaronovitch

'This is discrimination,' said Melvin.

'No it isn't,' I said – although technically speaking I suspected it was.

'It's because I'm a rat,' he said. 'Isn't it?'

'You're not really a rat,' I said.

'I'm a rat and this is a violation of the Human Rights Act.'

I really wish members of the public would bother to read that bloody act before quoting from it.

'No it isn't,' I said. 'Apart from anything else, if you really are a rat then the Human Rights Act doesn't apply.'

'Typical,' said Melvin.

I suppose he did look a bit rat-like, being a small white guy with a scraggly beard, and big yellowy front teeth which he persistently displayed by exaggerating his overbite. Personally, had a simile been required, I would have gone with ferrety. But that would have been to ignore the rat costume he was wearing. It was like an adult-sized pyjama suit complete with a hood and fake ears. It looked like it had originally been made of felt but had since been covered in so many layers of shit that it was impossible to tell for sure. Literally shit – judging from the smell.

Melvin's head twitched from side to side looking for a way out, but it was in vain – me and Kumar had him well and truly stitched up. Backed into what had once been a storage room of the main maintenance depot of the old Mail Rail.

Back in the good old days of 1911, when London's streets were covered in horse manure and traffic congestion could give you a parasitic infection as well as a headache, the Post Office decided to utilise two new cutting edge technologies – electric rail and the Greathead Shield Tunnel Boring System – to create a mini railway for the post. It would run from Whitechapel to Paddington and allow the mail to glide from one side of the city to the other untroubled by traffic jams, inclement weather or, during the occasional world war, high explosives. It opened in 1924 and was only closed in 2003 because 'being awesome' no longer registered on the Royal Mail's balance sheet.

Even narrow gauge trains weigh several tons and, unlike its big brother, the Mail Rail didn't conveniently surface in the suburbs to allow maintenance under an open sky. So under Mount Pleasant sorting office an engineering depot was decreed, a great long artificial cavern currently filled with enough spiky cast iron, Bakelite and rheostat-using technology to cause the most jaded industrial archaeologist to swoon.

Running just beside the Engineering Depot is the River Fleet. So when the current owners, the British Postal Museum and Archive, decided that it would make a wonderful corporate entertaining spot stroke heritage train ride Fleet naturally took an interest. And where Fleet takes an interest her sister Lady Ty is rarely far behind. It's a Hampstead watershed thing. Which is why when the first planned event – a sort of proof of concept soiree with an obscure literary bent – was gatecrashed by a man in a rat suit, I got called in. Me being the Met's current expert on high maintenance river deities.

I'd dragged in Jaget because ever since we'd invented the triple sewer luge with a visiting FBI agent he'd been my go-to guy for all matters concerning the Underground.

'Is this going to take long?' called Fleet from behind us. She and her sister had found Melvin skulking in a half-flooded maintenance pit just to the left of where they were going to serve canapés.

It's a police rule of thumb that anything involving members of the public takes twice as long as you think it will, so I told Fleet to give us some room to work. No custody sergeant in the city would be happy with me dumping someone this smelly in their nice clean custody suite – not until I'd at least made an effort to palm them off on the mental health system. Plus he didn't look all that compos mentis to me, what with the sniffing and twitching.

'How long have you been a rat?' I asked.

Melvin twitched and rubbed his hand across his cheek.

'About a month,' he said.

'And before that?' I asked.

'Before that what?'

'Well you told us your name was Melvin,' I said. 'What's your surname?'

'Norvegicus,' he said.

'Rattus norvegicus,' said Jaget. 'Latin for rat.' And, it turned out, an LP by a band called The Stranglers – although Jaget admitted that he didn't think that last fact was relevant.

'Did you have a different name before you were a rat?' I asked, proving once more that politely asking the same bleeding question again and again is the backbone of modern policing.

'Starkey – my name was Starkey.'

'Melvin Starkey?'

Melvin nodded and Jaget wrote it down.

'What do you do for a living, Melvin?' asked Jaget.

'I scurry,' said Melvin. 'And hurry and fight the dogs and kill the cats.'

Jaget made another note – obviously thinking that we should check with Islington Environmental Health and the RSPCA.

'What about before you were a rat?' asked Jaget.

'I was an estate agent,' he said.

'And where did you live?'

He gave us an address in Primrose Hill.

Me and Jaget stepped back so we could talk amongst ourselves. Melvin stayed where he was, squatting on his haunches, nose twitching and his pathetic felt ears bobbing back and forth,

'I think we have enough for an ID,' I said.

'Can you handle him on your own?' asked Jaget.

I said I could and he trotted off to find a place where his Airwave would work.

Fleet and Lady Ty glided forward, champagne glasses in their hands and a determined look in their eyes.

'So is it to be a prisoner transport?' asked Fleet. 'Or an ambulance?'

'Or pest control?' said Lady Ty. 'I'm sure Fleet would be happy to whoosh him down to the Thames if you wanted a discreet disposal.'

'Really,' I said. 'Is that something you've done before?'

Fleet smiled at her sister, 'He's so suspicious these days.'

'We're just offering.' said Lady Ty. 'I'm sure you have better things to do.'

'You called me. Remember?'

'Fair point,' said Fleet. 'Do you think he's under the influence?'

He was under the influence, alright. I just couldn't tell what of: drugs, alcohol, misfiring brain cells – magic?

'Why don't you stand back and let me work,' I said.

Lady Ty looked at Fleet and they both giggled. I hoped that it was the alcohol because I didn't like the idea of the Goddess of the River Tyburn giggling – it was disturbing on so many levels.

I went back to Melvin the Rat and tried to narrow down the possibilities.

'So when did you decide to become a rat?' I asked.

'It's not a question of wanting to be a rat,' said Melvin. 'It just sort of happens to you. All of a sudden you realise that's what you want to be.'

'And this realisation came a month ago?'

'Yeah,' said Melvin. 'Have you got any cheese?'

'My colleague has gone to fetch some,' I said. 'Can you remember what you were doing?'

'I was asking about a house,' he said.

Specifically: making inquiries into whether a particular person might want to sell their four storey Georgian terrace on St. Mark's Terrace near Regent's Park. Melvin thought it was worth a go because the same person had owned the house since 1956 and in that period the value had risen from merely expensive to ludicrous.

'I was hoping it would be an old lady,' said Melvin, who explained that he was particularly skilled at talking the old dears into relinquishing their property. 'I play fair, though,' he said. 'I make sure they get a good price.'

Presumably the 'old dears' then headed for Hastings or Bournemouth with a nice capital nest egg and the streets of Camden were made safe for the super-rich.

'So did you persuade her to sell?'

'I don't remember,' said Melvin. 'And in any case, that's when I realised my true nature.'

'Do you remember going up to the front door?'

'Yes,' he said. 'I remember that.'

'Did you ring the doorbell?'

'Yes,' said Melvin and explained that he remembered the door opening and there being a smell, a strong animal smell, like something from a zoo.

And then his true nature as a rat became clear and off he scampered towards his office on Camden Parkway.

He couldn't remember anything about the woman who answered the door.

He'd acquired the rat suit at Escapade's costume shop in Chalk Farm and had naturally found himself drawn to the sewers. I asked him how he ended up underneath Mount Pleasant and he said it was an accident – he'd been searching for a bite of cheese and had just followed his nose.

'This is your lucky day,' I said. 'Not only am I going to introduce you to a nice Scottish doctor so you can be checked out, you're going to be provided with cheese and old rope and whatever else it is your little ratty heart desires.'

And stick your head in an MRÍ and give blood samples and throw the gauntlet of science into the face of the inexplicable. Although I expected Dr Walid might want to get him washed up first. The key thing being that it wouldn't be me trying to get him into a shower.

So when Jaget got back we arranged for Dr Walid to come and take Melvin to a place of safety under Section 136 of the Mental Health act. Jaget had confirmed Melvin's identity and that he had been reported missing a month earlier. Once we had him wrapped in a blanket and stuffed into the back of an ambulance I popped back inside.

I asked Fleet and Lady Ty whether they knew anything about the address on St Mark's Crescent.

'No, nothing,' said Lady Ty.

'I never go down that way,' said Fleet. 'I'm not really a Primrose Hill, Regents Park person. When I want to go for a walk I go up the heath. Although the view from the top of the hill is really good.'

Which just goes to show that Lady Ty is a much better liar than Fleet.

Still I knew better than to try the direct approach with these two. So off I went, with my constabulary duty still to be done.

St Mark's Crescent was Georgian semis down one side and a slightly later terrace on the other. According to Google Earth the semis all backed onto Regent's Canal which would have been enough to raise my suspicions even if Jaget's IIP check hadn't thrown up that the ground rent, mortgage, rates and then council tax had all been paid by London Zoo since the early 1960s.

So we swapped my Asbo for Jaget's even more inconspicuous Vauxhall Corsa and staked out the house. We were just getting bored enough to consider playing 'how much do you reckon that house is worth?' – a favourite game amongst Londoners – when a Forest Green Range Rover pulled up outside and Lady Ty and Fleet disembarked.

We let them get halfway up the front stops before making ourselves known in the time honoured police manner.

'Oi!,' I called. 'What do you think you're doing?'

'Oh, shit,' said Fleet.

'Told you,' said Lady Ty.

'We just want to have a quiet word,' said Fleet. 'No need for this to get all official.'

'A quite word with who?' I asked.

'Whom,' said Jaget.

'With whom?' I asked, taking Jaget's word for it.

'We think she's the spirit of Regent's Canal,' said Fleet.

'Like you are with the rivers?'

'No,' said Lady Ty firmly, 'not like us.'

'Definitely not,' said Fleet. 'Canals are tricky and, anyway, she may also have something to do with London Zoo.'

'Oh really,' said Jaget obviously remembering who was paying the council tax. 'What makes you think that?'

'She's an orang-utan,' said Fleet.

On that we all withdrew to a safe distance while Fleet and Lady Ty explained.

'We think she was brought over to be a mate of Charlie – the first orang-utan to be kept in the monkey house. But she escaped before she could be settled in.' Regent's Canal actually bisects the zoo and it was feared that she'd gone into it. Word of the escape was kept secret and, this being the 1950s, the secret was kept.

'We only found out about her when we went for a walk down the tow path,' said Fleet. 'We were minding our own business when this ape woman came out of nowhere and started haranguing us.'

Apparently she had some kind of aggro with Mama Thames, but the sisters had never found out how it started.

'You don't ask Mum about that kind of stuff,' said Fleet. 'Not unless you want to be on suicide duty for a year straight.'

'But this is the last straw,' said Lady Ty. 'Unless you

believe it was a coincidence that Melvin the Rat turned up at a party we were hosting.'

Actually I thought it probably was, but I found that when people are nursing a grievance it's a waste of time trying to explain the ubiquitous nature of coincidence in the universe. People always want things to happen for a reason.

'So, to recap,' said Jaget. 'A female orang-utan who may be the goddess . . .'

'Spirit,' said Lady Ty and Fleet together.

'. . . who may be the spirit of Regent's Canal and/or London, is the most likely suspect to have convinced Melvin that he is a rat?'

'Pretty much,' I said. 'Let's go and have a word with her.'

'You should leave this to us,' called Fleet after us as we headed towards the house. 'She'll have you for breakfast.'

'Tell you what,' I called back as Jaget rang the bell. 'If we're not out in half an hour, you can come and rescue us.'

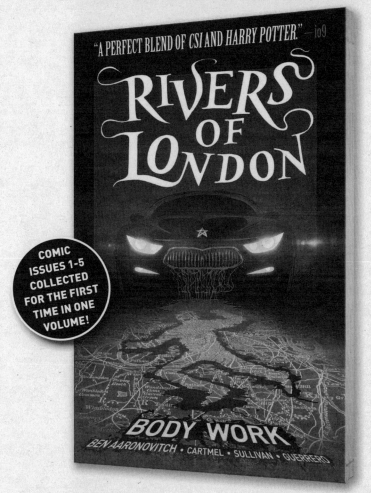

BRINGING NEWS FROM OUR WORLDS TO YOURS . . .

Want your news daily?

The Gollancz blog has instant updates on the hottest SF and Fantasy books.

Prefer your updates monthly?

Sign up for our in-depth newsletter.

www.gollancz.co.uk

Follow us 🐦 @gollancz

Find us 🅕 facebook.com/GollanczPublishing

Classic SF as you've never read it before.

Visit the SF Gateway to find out more!

www.sfgateway.com